To Stephen Lees

Susanna Gregory was a police officer in Leeds before taking up an academic career. She has served as an environmental consultant, doing fieldwork with whales, seals and walruses during seventeen field seasons in the polar regions, and has taught comparative anatomy and biological anthropology.

She is the creator of the Thomas Chaloner series of mysteries set in Restoration London as well as the Matthew Bartholomew books, and now lives in Wales with her husband, who is also a writer.

Also by Susanna Gregory

MURDER BY THE BOOK

The Eighteenth Chronicle of
Matthew Bartholomew

Susanna Gregory

SPHERE

First published in Great Britain in 2012 by Sphere
This paperback edition published by Sphere in 2013

Copyright © 2012 Susanna Gregory

The moral right of the author has been asserted.

*All characters and events in this publication, other
than those clearly in the public domain, are fictitious
and any resemblance to real persons,
living or dead, is purely coincidental.*

A CIP catalogue record for this book
is available from the British Library.

ISBN 978-0-7515-4257-8

Typeset in New Baskerville by Palimpsest Book Production Limited,
Falkirk, Stirlingshire

Printed and bound in Great Britain by Clays Ltd, St Ives plc

Papers used by Sphere are from well-managed forests
and other responsible sources.

MIX
Paper from
responsible sources
FSC® C104740

Sphere
An imprint of
Little, Brown Book Group
100 Victoria Embankment
London EC4Y 0DY

An Hachette UK Company
www.hachette.co.uk

www.littlebrown.co.uk

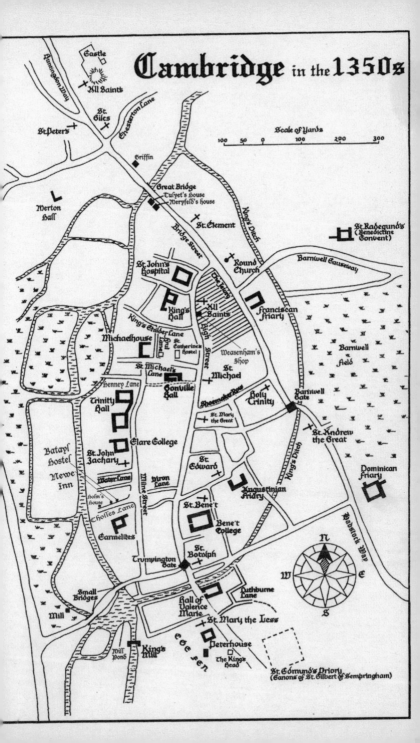

PROLOGUE

Poitiers, September 1356

On a warm autumn morning, two armies faced each other across a gently rolling plain. A pretty wood lay behind the English troops, its trees already turning from green to gold. There was a river nearby, too, where a heron stalked, hunting fish in the gurgling shallows. The sun shone, bees hummed and the air was full of birdsong. The scene was peaceful and idyllic.

Suddenly, trumpets brayed to announce a French attack, and the sounds of innocent morning were lost amid a thundering tattoo of charging hoofs and bloodcurdling war cries. Arrows hissed from Welsh and English longbows, quickly followed by the screams of the wounded. Eventually, there was another sound, too, one that startled the French warhorses, and made them buck and rear. It was the staccato bark of the Prince of Wales's newfangled artillery.

The Sire de Rougé watched from the French right flank, cursing as smoke billowed across the field, making it difficult for him to see what was happening. He had heard of the device known as the ribauldequin, which used exploding powder to discharge several missiles simultaneously, but he had never seen one in action. He had hoped he never would – he considered them an abomination beyond belief, and so did every other right-thinking warrior.

There was a bright flame in the wood, followed by a much louder boom. He narrowed his eyes, straining for a glimpse of the things, but they were too well concealed.

There was a fire, though, and he could see the English rushing to put it out. It burned only briefly, but that particular weapon did not speak again. Rougé assumed it had blown up – the cursed inventions might be terrifying to the opposition, but they were equally capable of killing their operators.

He itched to join in the affray. Unfortunately, the previous day, King Jean had informed him that he was unlikely to be needed – a French victory was a certainty, because they outnumbered the enemy three to one. They would, Jean had stated confidently, kill or rout them all, and the English would never set hostile feet in France again. Rougé and his small unit of horsemen were to remain in reserve, and not to deploy unless specifically ordered to do so.

The French army had three main divisions. The strongest and best was commanded by Jean himself, while his son the Dauphin and the Duke of Orléans led the others. When the smoke cleared, Rougé saw that the Dauphin had attacked first, but it had been a long dash towards the English position, especially wearing heavy armour and under a constant hail of arrows, and their bold charge had lost its impetus by the time they reached their goal. They had turned to retreat, but immediately became entangled with Orléans's troops, who were marching up behind. Panic and chaos ensued, and now both units were stumbling from the field in disarray.

Rougé gripped his reins so hard that his knuckles were white, and his heart thudded wildly as King Jean stood up in his stirrups and raised his arm to signal the advance of his own division. Immediately, the great mass of knights and men-at-arms began to trot forward. They were the cream of the French army, and a splendid sight with their streaming pennants and the sunlight glinting off

2

their polished helmets. Rougé began to relax. No grubby English rabble could withstand such a powerful force, and Jean had been right to brag of success that day.

To quell an almost overwhelming urge to race into the affray regardless of orders, Rougé pondered the English artillery again. First, there were the squat, malignant 'bombards', which sent stone balls careening into enemy lines. And second, there were the newer, lighter ribauld-equins. These were wildly inaccurate, and their spluttering fire was making no difference to the battle one way or the other, yet Rougé could see their potential. Not only were the flames, noise and smoke unnerving, especially to horses, but it would not take much to adapt them into something truly deadly.

His musings were interrupted by a flurry of activity along the English lines: the archers had run out of arrows, and were snatching up hammers and daggers instead. Rougé sneered his disdain. It was an act of desperation, as such paltry weapons were no match for the great broadswords wielded by the French knights – and there were a great many of those in the proud wave that was pounding magnificently forward. But he detected another move-ment, too, in the woods to his left, where the Prince of Wales had stationed his Gascon cavalry.

There was a tremendous clash as the two armies met, followed by an indescribable cacophony of screams and howls. The spiteful clap of the ribauldequin sounded again, and more smoke drifted across his line of vision. Rougé leaned forward in his saddle, straining his eyes against the billowing whiteness. Just when it thinned, the ribauldequin cracked out yet again and Rougé gave up trying to see what was happening. To distract himself, he thought about the circumstances that had brought the two countries to war in the first place.

It was all to do with who should be King of France. Edward III of England thought it should be him – his great-grandfather had held the title, and Edward was the only legitimate offspring of that particular bloodline. Unfortunately for him, no French noble wanted an Englishman as his monarch, and most of the country supported the House of Valois. The dispute had dragged on for almost three decades already, and although Edward now preferred the comfort of his palaces to a campaign tent, his son was full of fervour for his birthright. For months now, the Prince of Wales had been leading a ragtag army across France, leaving a trail of death and destruction wherever he went. It was, thought Rougé bitterly, high time that bellicose pup was sent packing with his tail between his legs.

Suddenly he became aware that battle cries had given way to cheers. He smiled: Jean had won, and France would soon be free of the brutal marauders. Then the smoke thinned, and his grin faded. The victory had been won at a terrible price – the ground was littered with French dead, their pennants trampled and filthy underfoot, and their bright armour foul with dirt and blood. Then he frowned, as more of the smoke blew away.

The tight, glorious mass of Jean's division was gone, and in its place was disorganised, shattered confusion. A few knights fought in isolated clumps, but the majority were running for their lives. With a shock that made him gasp his horror, Rougé saw that it was not the French who were cheering, but the English! Worse, he could see Jean battling for his life, virtually alone and beset on all sides by the enemy.

Appalled, Rougé called his men to order and galloped towards him. All around, English, Welsh and Gascon warriors were howling their triumph, but he thundered on, riding over anyone who tried to stop him. An arrow killed his horse from under him, but he rolled away from its body and continued on foot, sword in one hand and shield in the other. His men, he realised dully, were no longer with him; they had seen that the situation was hopeless, and had quit the field while they could.

He stumbled forward. Jean was not far away now, a sharp flash of silver armour amid a sea of rough brown leather jerkins. Then the unthinkable happened. Jean put up his sword, and handed his glove to some minor knight in a grimy surcoat. The King had surrendered! Stunned, Rougé staggered to a standstill, and was too shocked to resist as he was relieved of his weapons and bundled away to sit with the other prisoners.

That evening, there was a great deal of celebration in the English camp – songs, feasting, laughter and boasting. The mood was very different in the cramped corral to which the French prisoners had been herded, where disbelief was turning slowly to despair and shame. Rougé sat dejectedly with the Archbishop of Sens and the Count of Eu.

'This is a black day for France,' Sens was saying. He wore full armour under his religious habit, and his hawkish face was taut with anger and humiliation. 'There cannot be a noble family in the country that has not lost a son in today's slaughter.'

'No,' agreed Eu numbly. He had been wounded, and owed his survival to the English *medicus* who had been on hand to sew him up. He was not yet sure whether to be grateful. 'I still do not understand why we lost. We outnumbered them, for God's sake!'

'It was Orléans's fault,' said Sens bitterly. 'When he and the Dauphin fled, the Prince of Wales thought he had won, and ordered his troops to put the rest of us to rout.

Filled with triumph, even his archers surged forward to fight, and they slammed into us with such force that we could not hold them. And then there were the Gascons.'

'Why?' asked Eu tiredly. 'What did they do?'

'They sneaked through the woods and struck our left flank. Their timing was perfect, because it threw us into utter confusion. Many of our warriors ran to take refuge in Poitiers, but the townsfolk refused to open their gates, so the Gascons slaughtered them all outside the walls.'

'Worse will follow,' predicted Rougé, speaking for the first time since he had been taken. His voice was hoarse, and he did not think the terrible ache in his heart would ever ease. 'The Prince will march on Bordeaux next, killing and looting as he goes.'

Sens sighed gloomily. 'This disaster was our own fault. First, we underestimated them, which was foolish. Second, the lie of the land was in their favour, which we ignored. Third, there was a lack of cohesion among our leaders – the Dauphin should never have become entangled in Orléans's division, and neither one should have retreated. And last, we certainly should have predicted that Gascon trick.'

'They had ribauldequins, too,' added Eu, somewhat defensively. 'It conferred an unfair advantage on them, because using such evil devices is tantamount to cheating, not chivalrous at all. Look – they have left one standing over there. Have you ever seen a more diabolical creation?'

Rougé turned to stare at the weapon. It comprised a row of slender tubes, each with its own powder-pot at the opposite end to the muzzle. There was a ratcheted lever behind them, curving upwards like the tail of a scorpion, so that the barrels could be aimed higher or lower, and the whole thing was on wheels, allowing it to be trundled from place to place.

'I saw it spit out its deadly missiles,' Eu said with a shudder. 'It made a lot of noise and produced a hellish stench. It terrified the horses, and caused many of my men to take flight – they thought it was some manner of witchcraft.'

'That is no excuse,' said Rougé sourly. 'They should have stood firm. France needed us all today, and we failed her.'

'Perhaps we did,' sighed Sens. 'And it galls me to think that our capture will earn a pretty penny for King Edward – money that will be used to advance his claim on our throne, no doubt.'

'What?' asked Rougé, uneasily. 'How?'

'Ransoms,' explained the Archbishop. 'We shall all be taken to England, and I have already been told that my freedom alone will cost eight thousand pounds. Eu's will be six, and you will not fetch less than one and a half. God only knows what price will be put on King Jean.'

Rougé was silent. He knew about the practice of ransoming, of course, but he was suddenly stricken with the realisation that his desperate attempt to rescue his monarch would ruin his family – and ruin them it would, because years of war had taken their toll on his estates, and fifteen hundred pounds was an impossible sum. He closed his eyes in despair. The conflict had brought famine and poverty to France already, and the ransoms would exacerbate the problem beyond endurance. The common folk would refuse to buy their masters' freedom, and there would be rebellion and anarchy.

It was then that he knew he hated England with every fibre of his being, and would do anything humanly possible to avenge himself on the nation that had wreaked such havoc on his own. In the fading light, he could see the carnage of the battlefield, the once-proud banners fluttering forlornly in the evening breeze, and the undignified piles of corpses set ready for mass burial the following morning.

'I shall avenge our dead,' he vowed, his resolve strengthening by the moment. 'I shall ensure that France never suffers a rout like this again. Not ever.'

His companions regarded him askance. 'How?' asked Sens. 'You are a guest of the English now, and there is not much you can do from the Tower of London.'

'I have a plan,' replied Rougé. 'It entails me learning a secret.'

A gleam of hope flared in the Archbishop's eyes when he heard the conviction in the younger man's voice. 'What secret?'

Rougé's face became cold and hard. 'One that will change the world for ever.'

Cambridge, early May 1358

It was not often that the University at Cambridge called a Convocation of Regents – a gathering of all its masters – but one was certainly organised when Sir Eustace Dunning offered to finance a Common Library. It was a contentious matter, and while some scholars were delighted by the prospect of unlimited access to books, others thought the concept was fraught with dangerous precedents, and argued that the gift should be politely but firmly declined.

The Regents, who were the University's governing body and so responsible for deciding what was best for it, began to arrive at the church of St Mary the Great long before noon, when the meeting was scheduled to begin. As it was a formal occasion, they wore their ceremonial robes: scarlet gowns and hats for the seculars, and best habits for the monks and friars. Tensions were high, and spats had broken out long before Chancellor Tynkell called for silence, intoned some prayers, and declared the Convocation officially open.

There was an immediate clamour as virtually every man present strove to make his views known. Tynkell, a timid, ineffectual man wholly incapable of controlling hundreds of opinionated scholars, could only wave his hands in feeble entreaty, and it was left to his Senior Proctor, the plump, charismatic Brother Michael, to take charge. Once he had stilled the commotion, Michael indicated that Philip de London was to speak first.

'Books are expensive,' London began in a quiet, dignified voice. He and his brother were scribes, employed by the University's stationer. 'And only the wealthiest foundations can afford them. A Common Library will ensure that even our poorest scholars will see texts that—'

'There are more important issues at stake here than the education of paupers,' interrupted John Teversham, a Fellow of Bene't College, whose exquisite robes suggested that money would never come between him and the tomes *he* wanted to study. 'And I believe that such a foundation will endanger our University.'

'How?' asked London irritably. 'Oxford has had one for the past thirty years, and no harm has befallen it. Indeed, its scholars say it is an excellent addition to—'

'What that rabble does is not always sensible,' interrupted Teversham. 'Besides, where will this collection go? We do not have a suitable building for it.'

'Actually, we do,' interjected Tynkell. He smiled nervously, knowing that his news would receive a mixed reaction. 'Sir Eustace Dunning has given us Newe Inn in Cholles Lane.'

Half the scholars cheered their delight, while the others booed and hissed, and it was some time before Michael was able to restore calm again. Once the church was quiet, he let Principal Coslaye of Batayl Hostel speak first, because the man was scarlet with apoplectic rage, and Michael was afraid he might have a fatal seizure if he was not permitted to have his say soon.

'The University cannot have Newe Inn,' Coslaye bellowed furiously. 'Dunning promised that building to *us*. To Batayl!'

'I beg to differ,' countered Prior Etone of the Carmelites, startled. He was a serious, unsmiling man said to be better at administration than scholarship or religion. 'He promised it to *me*, and—'

'Lies!' screamed Coslaye. 'Dunning would never break his word to us.'

'Or to us,' retorted Etone coolly.

'Well, it seems he did both,' said Tynkell, when Coslaye was too angry to form coherent words and could only splutter with rage, hopping from foot to foot as he did so. He held up a document. 'Because I have the deed of ownership here. Dunning gave it to me this morning, and if the vote goes as he hopes, Newe Inn will become the Common Library with immediate effect. He would like an official opening at the Feast of Corpus Christi.'

'Well, he will not have it,' roared Teversham, beside himself with indignation. 'Because only fools will favour such a scheme, and my fellow Regents will have more sense than to—'

The rest of his statement was lost amid cheers from those who opposed the 'grace' to found a Common Library, and catcalls from those who supported it.

'I suggest we move directly to the vote,' said Michael, once he had quelled the uproar a third time. 'It is obvious that we have all made up our minds, so further discussion is pointless. All those who oppose the grace will move to the south aisle.'

There was an immediate stampede that included Teversham and Coslaye. They stood in a tight, belligerent huddle, hooting and jeering at those who remained, so that the ancient building rang with feisty voices.

'Come over here,' hollered Coslaye to the London brothers, his stentorian tones carrying through the din. 'You are members of Batayl, so I order you to stand with us. It——'

'And those who support the grace will move to the north,' boomed Michael.

The remaining Regents hurried to where he pointed, and when the shuffle was complete, it was clear that the result was going to be close. Tense and heated, they continued to harangue each other as Michael and Tynkell counted heads. And then counted them again.

'The grace is carried by three votes,' announced Tynkell at last.

There was a cheer from the north and a roar of disappointment from the south. The two sides converged in a fury of bawling voices and violently wagging fingers. And then something dark sailed through the air. It was a book with wooden covers, and its corner struck Coslaye hard on the side of his head. The Principal of Batayl Hostel dropped to the floor and lay still.

'Who threw that?' demanded Michael, in the shocked hush that followed.

There was silence. The University's medical men – from both sides of the debate – hurried to the stricken man's side, but their faces were grim as they inspected the wound.

'He is bleeding inside his skull,' said one. 'I doubt he will survive. He has been murdered!'

CHAPTER 1

Cambridge, June 1358

The corpse was on its back, eyes fixed sightlessly on the sky above, arms flung out to the sides and legs dangling in the river. It was a youth with fair curls, a shabby tunic that had once been stylish, and ink on his fingers. It was a wicked shame, thought Matthew Bartholomew, physician and Doctor of Medicine at the College of Michaelhouse, that his life had been cut so brutally short.

'You can see why I called you,' said Richard Tulyet. He was Cambridge's Sheriff, a slightly built man, whose wispy beard and boyish looks led criminals to underestimate him; they never made the same mistake twice. 'His clothes and the stains on his hands . . .'

'You think he is a scholar,' surmised Brother Michael, leaning on Bartholomew's shoulder to peer down at the body. As Senior Proctor, it was his duty to determine whether the dead boy was a member of the University, and if so, to investigate what had happened. 'I do not recognise him.'

'I do,' said Bartholomew. 'His name is Adam, and he has just started to work for the University stationer. I treated him for a summer ague a few days ago.'

'Did he mention any enemies?' Michael shuddered. 'His throat has been cut from ear to ear, so he clearly did something to annoy someone.'

'Not necessarily.' Tulyet's expression was sober. 'He is the third person to have been found with a slashed throat near the river over the last eight weeks or so.'

13

Bartholomew was horrified. 'There is a killer on the loose? Who are his other victims?'

'A beggar whose name no one knows, and one of my night-watchmen,' replied the Sheriff.

'I hope there is no trouble brewing between your town and our University,' said Michael uneasily. 'We have been living in comparative harmony for months now, and it occurred to me only yesterday that we are overdue for a spat.'

'Not on our part,' averred Tulyet. 'Now that summer is here at last, we are more interested in tending our crops than in quarrelling with you – none of us want another winter of crippling shortages, such as we had last year. However, your scholars have been rather warlike of late.'

'Over the Common Library,' said Bartholomew, nodding. 'The grace to establish it passed by a very slim margin, and the losers are still resentful. It has caused a bitter rift.'

'A rift that is likely to widen even further today,' predicted Michael gloomily. 'The Chancellor has called another Convocation of Regents because we need to elect a new Junior Proctor, but the occasion will be used to reignite the library trouble, I am sure.'

'*Another* Junior Proctor?' asked Tulyet. 'But that makes three this year alone, Brother! What happened to your last deputy?'

'He resigned,' replied the monk shortly. 'Just because I told him to put down a quarrel between Maud's Hostel and Bene't College. The spat was over that wretched library, of course.'

'It was a pitched battle, not a spat,' Bartholomew pointed out. 'And it involved weapons.'

'So what?' shrugged Michael. 'He had ten stalwart beadles at his back, and I fail to understand why he was so reluctant to do his duty. I had the matter resolved in a few moments.'

During his years in office, the portly Benedictine theologian had amassed considerable power in the University, and it was common knowledge that he, not the Chancellor, made all the important decisions. He was thus a force to be reckoned with, and had restored the peace with no more than a few sharp words. No Junior Proctor could expect to do likewise, however, and the last incumbent had been so appalled by the expectation that he was to wade into such a vicious mêlée of waving knives and flailing fists that he had quit on the spot.

Unfortunately, it would not be easy to replace him. The work was poorly paid, often dangerous and had few perks. Moreover, Michael could be something of a tartar, impatient with those less intelligent than himself and intolerant of failure. No volunteers were likely to come forward at the Convocation, and the post would almost certainly remain vacant until some unsuspecting newcomer was persuaded to take it.

'I heard about that fight,' Tulyet was saying. 'Several injuries and numerous arrests. However, Adam's death will have nothing to do with those troubles. I believe he was killed because he, like the beggar and my guard, witnessed something he should not have done.'

'Such as what?' asked Michael, bemused.

'Smuggling – a perennial problem for any town near the Fens. Unfortunately, as soon as we catch one crew, another takes its place. There is a lot of money in the business, so the perpetrators tend to be protective of their interests, and will certainly kill to defend them.'

'I hope Adam's death will not prove to be too time-consuming,' said Michael worriedly. 'The new library is due to open a week tomorrow – on the Feast of Corpus

15

Christi – and I have my hands full trying to keep the peace. Not to mention Coslaye.'

'Coslaye?' queried Tulyet.

'The Principal of Batayl Hostel, who was very nearly killed when someone lobbed a book during the last Convocation. Murder might not have been the culprit's intention, but it was a wicked thing to do regardless, and he needs to be caught.'

'I will find out what happened to Adam,' offered Tulyet. 'You have helped me often enough in the past, and I am already investigating two similar crimes. *I* shall bring his killer to justice.'

Michael smiled gratefully. He and the Sheriff had always enjoyed a good relationship, and there was rarely any squabbling over jurisdiction. 'But you must be busy, too, Dick. The town celebrates this particular festival in style, so you will have pageants to organise, miracle plays to commission . . .'

'The Guild of Corpus Christi is managing all that this year,' replied the Sheriff. 'The only pressing matter I have at the moment is the King's taxes – mostly collected and counted, but still requiring a mound of documentation before they can be sent to London. It is tedious work, and at the risk of sounding callous, hunting killers is a welcome diversion.'

'I hope you catch them,' said Bartholomew, folding the corpse's hands across its chest and closing its eyes. 'Because Adam was little more than a child – too young to die.'

'You say he was a scribe?' asked Tulyet.

Bartholomew nodded, recalling what the lad had told him when they had met. 'The University stationer, John Weasenham, hired him, because he can . . . he *could* write extremely fast.'

'Weasenham produces anthologies of set texts called

16

"exemplars",' elaborated Michael, when Tulyet's puzzled expression showed that he did not understand why this should be important. 'Which students then hire. They are in constant demand, so speedy scribes are essential.'

'The Carmelite Priory has a scriptorium,' said Tulyet. 'Perhaps the friars there will help to produce these exemplars until Adam can be replaced.'

'No – the Carmelites produce fine books and illustrated manuscripts,' explained Michael with a tolerant smile at such ignorance. 'They are wholly different undertakings. And if you want an analogy, compare that donkey over there with your best warhorse.'

'Adam wanted to join the Carmelites,' said Bartholomew, sorry the youngster had not lived to realise his ambitions. 'He told me that writing was his life.'

'Then I had better set about finding out who killed him,' said Tulyet quietly.

'And I had better break the news to Weasenham,' added Michael reluctantly. 'I shall do it the moment the Convocation is over.'

Although it was not long past dawn, the sun had already burned away the early morning mist, and it promised to be a fine day. The sky was a clear, unbroken blue for the first time in weeks, and Bartholomew breathed in deeply as he and Michael left the riverbank. The ever-present stench of animal dung and human waste was dominant, but the sweeter scent of flowers and grass lay beneath them. Summer had arrived at last.

The previous winter had been long and hard, and although they had seen little snow, a series of fierce frosts had claimed a number of Bartholomew's more vulnerable patients. There had been starvation, too, because the harvest had failed, and even the alms dispensed by the convents had not been enough to save some folk from an early grave. The town had celebrated with foolish abandon when the first blossoms had appeared on the trees, relieved beyond measure at this sign that the weather was finally beginning to relinquish its icy hold.

The quickest way to St Mary the Great from the river was via Cholles Lane, a narrow alley bounded on one side by the high wall that surrounded the Carmelite Priory, and a row of houses on the other. There were only three buildings of note. First was the shabby hostel run by Principal Coslaye, which he called Batayl; next was Newe Inn, the former tavern that was being converted into the Common Library; and the last was a pretty cottage occupied by Will Holm the surgeon, who had arrived two months before – on Easter Day – to set up practice in the town.

'I see work is proceeding apace on Newe Inn,' said Bartholomew conversationally, as they walked. The sawing, hammering and chiselling had started the day after the Convocation, and its sponsor, Sir Eustace Dunning, had promised the craftsmen a handsome bonus if they finished before the Feast of Corpus Christi. Needless to say, the artisans were eager to oblige.

Michael scowled. 'I still cannot believe that ridiculous grace was passed. And by only three votes, too! It will mean nothing but trouble.'

'No – it will mean that *all* our scholars will have access to texts they might otherwise never see,' countered Bartholomew. He had voted for the proposal, much to Michael's disgust, and while he knew he would never persuade the monk to his point of view – or vice versa – they still argued about it every time they passed Newe Inn in each other's company.

'But Newe Inn is wholly unsuitable for the purpose.'

Michael stopped to glare at it. 'It is the wrong size, the wrong shape, and most of its windows face north. It will be too dark to read most of the time, and too cold in winter. Moreover, Batayl Hostel *and* the Carmelites think it should be theirs.'

'It is Sir Eustace Dunning's property. He can give it to whoever he likes.'

'No good will come of it,' predicted Michael sourly. 'And I still cannot believe that *you* supported its foundation. I thought I had made it clear that I was against it, and that I expected all the Regents from my own College to vote accordingly.'

'A lot of good will come of it, Brother,' said Bartholomew, who had resented being ordered to act against his beliefs. 'I am tired of running all over the University every time I want to consult a text – and of hoping that its owner will deign to let me see it. A Common Library will mean they are all stored in one place, and will thus be available to everyone.'

'That is idealistic claptrap! First, this collection will be open to every member of our *studium generale*, which means the demand on its resources will be enormous. You may never see the books you want because others will get to them first.'

'But at least those in the poorer foundations will have a *chance* to—'

'And second, there is the issue of benefactions. Our College rarely buys books, because they are too expensive – most have been *bequeathed* to us. But a central repository will be more attractive to donors, and they will favour it in their wills. What will become of Michaelhouse?'

'We will use the Common Library.'

'You are missing the point!' cried Michael, exasperated. 'I do not refer to the academic value of books, but to their

19

actual value. We sold our spare copy of Holcot's *Postillae* earlier this year, and it raised enough money to keep us in bread for a month. *Ergo*, they are a vital asset, and your Common Library will deprive us of it. And we are not rich as it is.'

'Books are not a commodity, Brother, to be bought and sold like—'

'Of course they are a commodity! Even Deynman our Librarian, who is as fanatical about his charges as a mother hen with chicks, agreed that it was right to let the Holcot go.'

Bartholomew had no desire to debate the matter further. He changed the subject, and began to talk about the experiments he was conducting with his medical colleagues instead. They were trying to develop fuel for a lamp that would burn at a constant and steady rate, which they hoped would let them see what they were doing when patients summoned them at night.

'We added myrrh yesterday,' he said, blithely unaware that Michael was not very interested. The monk might have been, had the *medici* made progress occasionally, but they were no further towards their goal than they had been when the project had started some months earlier.

'Your colleagues are an unprepossessing crowd,' Michael said, brusque because the previous discussion had reminded him that he was still sulking over the fact that his closest friend had defied him at the Convocation. 'Gyseburne's obsession with urine is sinister; Rougham is arrogant; Meryfeld is stupid; and Vale is sly.'

'And our new surgeon – Holm?' asked Bartholomew, rather taken aback by the monk's vehemence. 'Do you dislike him, too?'

'Yes. Although, his arrival has meant that you no longer

perform those nasty techniques yourself, which is not a bad thing.'

Bartholomew said nothing. He had saved a number of patients with surgery, but it was the domain of barber-surgeons, and virtually everyone disapproved of his unconventional talent for it. He started to change the subject a second time, but they had arrived at St Mary the Great, where the Convocation was about to begin.

Bartholomew and Michael walked into the church to find it full. Chancellor Tynkell heaved a sigh of relief when he saw the monk. The election of a Junior Proctor was not a contentious piece of business, but most of those present were actually there to reiterate their opinions of the Common Library, and he knew he would be unable to keep the peace once the more rabid of the Regents began to hold forth.

'I bid you all welcome,' he said nervously to the assembly, after he had intoned a rambling and somewhat incoherent opening prayer that betrayed the depth of his unease. 'We are here to see about the election of another Junior—'

'*I* am here to express my displeasure about this wretched library,' cut in Teversham hotly. His Bene't colleagues were at his shoulder, nodding vehement agreement. 'Work is proceeding far too fast, and it is unseemly.'

'We are trying to finish by Corpus Christi,' explained William Walkelate, the erudite, amiable architect from King's Hall, who had been given the task of transforming Newe Inn from run-down tavern to functional library. The appointment had made him unpopular with his colleagues, however – King's Hall was one of the project's fiercest detractors. 'Dunning has set his heart on—'

'It is all wrong,' snapped Teversham. 'The wealthier

21

foundations, such as my own, already have repositories for books, and so do the convents. We do not need another.'

'But what about those scholars who are not members of rich Colleges or religious houses?' asked Walkelate with quiet reason. 'It is all but impossible for them to gain access to books, and a Common Library will transform their lives.'

'I do not care about them,' spat Teversham. 'I care about what will happen to my College now that this ridiculous grace has been passed – namely donors giving their collections to it, and Bene't being overlooked. Then *we* shall be impoverished!'

There was a rumble of agreement from the Colleges and convents, which tended to be well endowed with reading matter, and cries of 'shame!' from the hostels, which were not.

'If Bene't finds itself short of books, it can use the Common Library like everyone else,' said a philosopher named Sawtre, once the hubbub had died down. He was also from King's Hall, and disbelieving glances were exchanged between his colleagues at this disloyal remark. 'And quite rightly. As matters stand, the hostels are at a serious disadvantage, and it is hardly fair.'

'What does fairness have to do with anything?' asked Teversham, genuinely puzzled. 'It is the natural order of things that some of us have access to books, and some do not. We have managed without a general library for hundreds of years, so why foist one on us now?'

There was another growl of approval from the Colleges and convents, while the Regents from the hostels clamoured their objections.

'Has our University existed for hundreds of years?' asked Chancellor Tynkell, more to himself than to the assembly.

'I thought it was established during the tenth year of King John, which makes it roughly a hundred and fifty—'

'Treachery!' shrieked Teversham. 'It was founded by King Arthur, and to say otherwise means that Oxford is older than us and therefore superior. And none of us believe *that*!'

There was a chorus of unanimous appreciation: on this point, everyone was agreed.

'Quite so,' said Michael. 'Now let us return to the matter in hand. We must appoint a Junior Proctor as soon as possible, because I shall need help at Corpus Christi, and—'

'You only need help because of this vile library,' said Teversham bitterly. 'Allowing a townsman to come along and tell us that we should have one is a dangerous precedent, and I advise you to bring an end to the scheme while you can.'

'We voted, and the grace was passed,' said Michael sharply. 'I was not very pleased, either, but we are bound by the decision, and there is no more we can do.'

'That ballot was tainted,' stated Coslaye, his stentorian bellow cutting through the frenzy of objections and cheers. 'I was nearly murdered after it was taken, so I demand another.'

Everyone had assumed that Coslaye would die when he had been injured during the last Convocation, but Bartholomew had relieved the pressure on his brain by drilling holes in his skull. Now, six weeks later, the only visible evidence of his brush with death was the fact that the hair on one side of his head was shorter than the other, on account of it being shaved off. Unfortunately for Bartholomew, his success with what had been widely viewed as a hopeless case still did not alter the fact that physicians were not supposed to demean themselves with surgery, and his colleagues, medical and lay alike, roundly condemned him for what he had done.

'Oh,' said Tynkell, swallowing uncomfortably. 'I see your point. Well . . . I suppose . . .'

'No,' said Michael firmly, before the Chancellor could agree to something untenable. 'It is undemocratic to demand another poll because you do not like the result of the first. The losers must accept the will of the majority.'

'Three votes is not a majority,' argued Coslaye. 'It means we are split down the middle. *Ergo*, we should give the matter further consideration.'

'No,' said Michael again, struggling to make himself heard over the rising clamour of voices. 'The vote must stand. Our statutes are quite clear on this point.'

'But this horrible library will be a cuckoo in our midst,' wailed Teversham. 'A cuckoo that will steal books from the Colleges, and that will reside in a house that Dunning had already pledged to two other foundations.'

'It will not be a cuckoo,' argued Walkelate, offended. 'It will be a magnificent eagle, one that will allow our scholars – *all* our scholars – to soar into the lofty firmament of learning.'

'Eagles are evil predators that prey on the helpless,' flashed Teversham. 'And so is anyone who supports this wicked notion.'

'I agree,' bawled Coslaye. 'Dunning's offer should have been rejected.'

'But you run a hostel, Coslaye,' Sawtre pointed out reproachfully. 'You should support a scheme that will give your scholars the same access to books as College men.'

'My lads would rather be bookless than spend another winter in cramped misery,' snapped Coslaye. 'We *need* that building.'

'It was promised to us,' said Prior Etone of the Carmelites

24

sharply. 'No matter what Dunning claims now. And its loss is a bitter blow, because we had plans for it.'

'This nasty library has caused all manner of strife among us,' interjected Doctor Rougham of Gonville Hall sadly. He was a physician, unattractive of countenance and character. 'It is not just Colleges and hostels fighting each other – it is worse. There are divisions within foundations, too, and they are tearing us apart. I am ashamed to admit that even Gonville has a traitor.'

'One who has dared not show his face here today,' added another Gonville scholar sourly. 'Namely Roger Vale, our second Master of Medicine.'

'Vale is not a traitor,' said Sawtre firmly. 'He just likes the idea of a Common Library. As do I.'

'It is the Devil's work,' declared Thomas Riborowe, who ran the Carmelites' scriptorium. He was a skeletally thin specimen with a cadaverous pallor. 'We should all unite against Satan's evil designs, and vote to repeal the grace with immediate effect.'

'You cannot really believe that!' cried Sawtre over the resulting hubbub. 'The only reason you are able to read the tomes you love so dearly is because your priory owns them. Surely, others deserve that right, too?'

'And they can have it – *if* they take holy orders and become friars,' screeched Riborowe.

'Enough!' roared Michael, cutting through the furious squabble that followed. 'We did not come here to bicker about a grace that has already been passed. We came to discuss my new Junior Proctor. Are there any volunteers?'

Suddenly, the church went quiet, and Bartholomew noted with amusement that some Regents were holding their breath, afraid to move lest they attracted unwanted attention. Others stared fixedly at the floor or the ceiling, unwilling to risk catching Michael's eye. When Tynkell declared an end to the gathering a short while later, there was a concerted dash towards the door, still in total silence. Outside, however, the debate about the library continued in venomous brays.

'I was not expecting a plethora of offers,' said Michael ruefully, watching the last of the Regents jostling through the door. 'But it is disappointing when not one colleague is prepared to help me. And if there had been a willing candidate, his first duty would have been to visit Weasenham and break the news about Adam. I confess, it is not a task I relish.'

'No,' agreed Bartholomew, glad it was not his responsibility.

A crafty look came into Michael's eye. 'It will be a terrible shock, and Weasenham's scribes may need the services of a physician. You must come with me.'

The stationer's premises occupied a strategic spot on the High Street, and was where scholars and scribes went to purchase the supplies they needed for their work – pens, ink, glue, parchment and vellum, books and, of course, exemplars. It stood near All Saints-in-the-Jewry, conveniently close to King's Hall, where the University's wealthiest academics lived, and was a grand affair with a tiled roof and several spacious rooms. Weasenham and his household lived on the upper floor, while the lower one was dedicated to business.

Bartholomew had always liked the place, with its sharp, metallic aroma of ink and the rich scent of new parchment, although he was less keen on its owner. Weasenham, a thin, rodent-faced man with long, oily hair, was an unrepentant gossip, and could always be trusted to turn any innocent incident into scurrilous rumour.

The shop was busy, despite the early hour, which explained why he was one of the richest men in the town. Two Fellows from Bene't College were discussing whether to purchase a second copy of Gratian's *Decretum*, watched enviously by a gaggle of scholars from Batayl Hostel who could not afford their first. A group of friars was admiring a new shipment of psalters, and students clamoured at Weasenham's assistants for the exemplars they needed for the next stage of their studies.

The stationer himself was talking to William Walkelate, the King's Hall architect.

'We are doing very well,' Walkelate was saying happily. 'There is no reason why we should not be ready by next Thursday. Dunning will be delighted, because he has set his heart on a grand opening at Corpus Christi. I do not blame him – it is one of our greatest religious festivals, and will be an auspicious start for his foundation.'

Weasenham smiled, eyes bright with greed. 'I shall be busier than ever once our scholars sample the many tracts stored there, and commissions for exemplars will be so numerous that I do not know how we shall cope. Thank God for Adam and his lightning pen!'

Bartholomew and Michael exchanged an uncomfortable glance.

'We need to talk to you, Weasenham,' said Michael, once Walkelate had collected his supplies and left the shop, beaming affably at everyone he passed. The poorer scholars smiled back, appreciative of his labours. The wealthier ones glared, although Walkelate did not seem to notice; like many academics, he was not very sensitive to atmospheres.

'Have you heard the latest?' whispered Weasenham, glancing around furtively in the way he always did when he was about to impart something that he should probably have kept to himself. 'The Common Library is unlikely to open on time. Walkelate just told me.'

Bartholomew stared at him in confusion. 'But he just said it would. I heard him.'

'He did, but he has his doubts – I could see them in his face.' Weasenham winked conspiratorially. 'And have you heard about Dunning's youngest daughter? She is my wife's sister as you know. Well, it transpires that she is to marry Holm, the town's new surgeon.'

'Perhaps we could go somewhere private,' suggested Michael, while Bartholomew wondered how the stationer contrived to make even the most innocuous of events sound indecently salacious. 'We have news.'

'Certainly,' said Weasenham, delighted. 'I like news. Come. We shall talk in the back room.'

The 'back room' was a spacious chamber with large windows. There were ten desks for writing, although only seven were occupied. Two scriveners were copying theological tracts, while the remainder were preparing an exemplar comprising a selection of work by Aristotle.

'We are short-handed this morning,' said Weasenham, gesturing to the empty tables. 'The London brothers are late, and so is Adam. It is unlike Adam to be tardy, because he is very keen.'

'And the London brothers are not?' asked Michael, more to postpone his unpleasant duty than because he really wanted to know.

Weasenham leaned forward with a spiteful leer. 'They like to malinger.'

'That is unfair,' objected one of the scribes. He was a handsome man, perhaps thirty years old, with jet black hair that fell in curls around his face. 'The brothers do sometimes arrive late, but they always work long after the rest of us have gone home.'

'This is Bonabes, my Exemplarius,' said Weasenham to Bartholomew and Michael. As exemplars were studied very closely by the students who hired them, it was vital that they were error-free, and to ensure a consistently high standard, the work was checked by a senior scribe; Weasenham always referred to his as the Exemplarius. 'He is right to defend the people under his care. However—' Here he gave Bonabes a sharp glare '—he should not feel compelled to do it over the just criticism of his employer.'

'I speak the truth,' said Bonabes firmly. 'The Londons are loyal and conscientious workers. They are also a driving force in our experiments to produce paper.'

'Paper?' asked Michael curiously.

'It is a comparatively new material made from rags,' explained Bonabes. 'If we can perfect its manufacture, everyone will benefit, because it will be far cheaper than parchment.'

'I visited a paper mill in France once,' said Bartholomew. 'It stank, and polluted the local drinking water.'

'Perhaps so, but we cannot allow that to interfere with progress,' said Weasenham. He lowered his voice, eyes alight with malice. 'Did you know that the London brothers are members of Batayl Hostel? I cannot imagine what possessed them to choose *that* disreputable foundation and—'

'They enrolled because they are interested in alchemy and Batayl owns two books on the subject,' interrupted Bonabes irritably. The other scribes also looked annoyed by the stationer's disparaging remarks. 'There is nothing unsavoury about the association.'

'If you say so,' sniffed Weasenham, making it clear that he would think what he liked. He turned to Michael and Bartholomew. 'Now what did you want to tell me?'

'I am afraid we bring bad news.' Michael took a deep

29

breath to steel himself. 'Adam is dead. The Sheriff's men found him by the river this morning.'

There was a crash as Bonabes knocked over an inkwell, his face white with horror. Weasenham gripped a table for support, and the other scriveners clamoured their disbelief.

'No!' whispered Bonabes. 'You are mistaken. Adam cannot be dead!'

The noise brought Weasenham's wife running. He had recently remarried, and it was no surprise that he had opted for a lady who matched his wealth and social standing. Ruth Dunning, the elder of Sir Eustace's two daughters, was a pretty woman with dark hair and arresting eyes.

'What is the matter?' she cried, bending down to mop up the mess Bonabes had made. 'Help me, quickly, or this will stain.'

'Never mind the floor,' said Weasenham shakily. 'Brother Michael has news.'

Michael told what little he knew, then tried to answer the distraught questions that followed. Bonabes was the most distressed, because he and Adam had started to work for Weasenham at the same time, and the older man had harboured a fatherly affection for the eager youngster. Ruth put a compassionate hand on his arm while he wept.

'Bonabes is French,' whispered Weasenham, to explain the Exemplarius's unmanly display. 'But I still think I must be dreaming. Adam! How can this be true?'

'The Sheriff will visit you soon,' said Michael. 'When he comes, please tell him everything you can about Adam's last movements. It may help him catch the killer.'

'Adam said he would come in early today, to help finish the Aristotle,' sobbed Bonabes. 'I was surprised when he failed to appear, and I wish to God I had gone to look

30

for him. I might have been able to save . . .' He could not finish.

'It would have made no difference,' said Bartholomew kindly. 'His body was cold, and I suspect he died yesterday, not this morning.'

'The rest of us stayed here all last night, working,' said Ruth. 'The demand for exemplars is very high at the moment, you see. But Adam is still recovering from his summer ague, so we sent him home when it grew dark, although he objected to being singled out for favoured treatment.'

'Oh, no!' breathed Bonabes, ashen-faced. 'Please do not say that is why he died – because we sent him out at dusk, thinking to be kind.'

It was highly likely, but neither Michael nor Bartholomew wanted to add to their anguish by saying so. Michael shook his head reassuringly, while Bartholomew, never good at prevaricating, stared at his feet. When the scribes were calmer, the monk resumed his questioning.

'None of you left?' he asked, looking at each in turn. 'Not even for a moment?'

'No,' replied Weasenham. 'We were too busy. So, if your question aims to determine whether any of us killed him, you are barking up the wrong tree.'

'Who did this terrible thing?' demanded Bonabes, grief giving way to anger. 'Adam did not have an enemy in the world – he was a polite, quiet lad. And he was like a son to me . . .'

'Dick Tulyet believes smugglers might be to blame,' replied Michael.

'Smugglers,' spat Weasenham. 'I hate them! They flood the town with untaxed supplies that make mine seem expensive. And now Adam . . . How could they? He was just a child!'

Bartholomew and Michael left them to their mourning, and stepped into the High Street. The day was getting warmer as the sun climbed higher in the sky, and there was not a cloud in sight. Neither was cheered by the sight, though, after their grim work. Wordlessly, they started to walk to Michaelhouse, but stopped when they saw Bartholomew's book-bearer hurrying towards them.

'Here comes trouble,' predicted Michael grimly. 'I can see in his face that something awful has happened.'

Cynric had been with Bartholomew since his student days in Oxford, and the physician had lost count of the times they had saved each other's lives. The Welshman was an experienced warrior, and also the most superstitious man in Cambridge.

'There has been a death,' reported Cynric tersely. 'In Newe Inn's garden.'

'Newe Inn?' asked Michael. 'But we passed it not long ago. Are you sure?'

'Of course,' replied Cynric. 'The message comes from Principal Coslaye. He says the fellow is quite dead, so there is no need to hurry, but he would appreciate you arriving before this evening, because he and his scholars want to see a mystery play in the Market Square.'

'I see,' said Michael, eyebrows raised. 'Then we had better oblige.'

Besides teaching medicine and trying to serve a list of patients that was far too long for one man, Bartholomew was also the University's Corpse Examiner, which meant he was obliged to provide an official cause of death for any scholar who died, or for any person breathing his last on University property. Newe Inn fell firmly under his jurisdiction, whether the dead man transpired to be scholar or townsman, so he turned and followed Michael back to Cholles Lane.

When they arrived, he took a moment to view Newe Inn from the outside, to assess whether the monk was right to say it was unsuitable for a library. He supposed its round-headed windows were on the narrow side, while he could attest from personal experience that stone buildings were chilly in winter – he lived in one himself, and could not recall ever being as cold as he had been in February and March. Yet these seemed minor issues compared to the advantages the place would confer when it was finished.

He was about to enter, when voices farther up the lane made him glance around – Prior Etone was leading his friars home after a lengthy post-Convocation gripe with the Dominicans. The Carmelites were a powerful force in Cambridge, with about fifty brothers and an army of laymen and servants. Most were regarding Bartholomew rather coolly.

'You were wrong to vote for that library, Matthew,' called Etone. 'It is not a good idea to have one of those in our *studium generale*.'

'Especially as it is to be housed in Newe Inn,' added the skeletal Riborowe. 'That building was promised to us, and you had no right to support a scheme that saw us dispossessed.'

'I told him all that before the Convocation,' Michael called back before Bartholomew could reply. 'But he did not listen – thinking about urine and leeches, probably.'

At that moment, a bell chimed inside the convent to tell the friars that a light meal was available in the refectory, and most of them trooped off to enjoy it, but Prior Etone crossed the lane to continue berating Bartholomew.

He was accompanied by Riborowe and a tiny, sparrow-like man named Jorz, with a nose like a stubby beak.

'Wait, Matt,' ordered Michael, as Bartholomew edged towards Newe Inn's door, unwilling to be rebuked yet again for doing what he had felt was right. 'The Carmelites are still seriously piqued over the Common Library, and a few moments smoothing ruffled feathers will not go amiss.'

'Easy for you to say,' muttered Bartholomew. 'You are not the one about to be scolded like an errant schoolboy.'

'That stupid grace passed by three votes,' said Riborowe, his thin face flushed with irritation. 'Three! If you and one other Regent had shown a shred of decency, it would have been defeated.'

'Bartholomew is not the only one who betrayed us,' chirped Jorz. 'Others voted contrary to orders, too. They include Vale of Gonville Hall; the London brothers from the stationer's shop; Sawtre and Walkelate from King's Hall; and, I am ashamed to say, Northwood from our own Order. All are traitorous wretches who should be made to pay.'

'They should,' agreed Riborowe. 'But most will have realised the folly of their ways by now, so you must call another Convocation, Brother. I imagine the result will be very different next time. How about July? That is a lovely month for making decisions.'

Bartholomew regarded him coolly. 'Most hostels close during July. Scholars from the Colleges and the religious Orders will still be here, but the others will have gone home.'

'Will they really?' asked Riborowe, feigning surprise. 'What a pity that their voices will not be heard, then. Still, I suppose that is democracy for you.'

'All our members should have equal access to books,'

argued Bartholomew, becoming exasperated. 'And as a University, we have a moral obligation to see that they do.'

'These are dangerous principles, Matthew,' warned Etone. 'I cannot say I approve.'

'They are not dangerous principles,' came a voice from behind them. Sawtre, the gentle philosopher from King's Hall, had overheard the remark as he was passing, and had stopped to join the debate. He was a clever, likeable man with a shiny bald head. 'They are enlightened principles.'

'Enlightened is another word for heretical,' countered Riborowe. 'And your opinion counts for nothing anyway, because *you* are another dissenter.'

Sawtre smiled with kindly patience, unruffled by the friar's hostility. 'And how does having a mind of my own negate my opinion, exactly?'

Riborowe knew he was unlikely to win a battle of logic with a scholar of Sawtre's standing, so he continued to rail at Bartholomew instead. 'I thought you would have learned your lesson about unorthodoxy by now. It is said in the town that you are a warlock.'

Bartholomew winced. He did not need reminding that his medical successes had resulted in a tale that said a pact with the Devil was responsible. His patients – mostly the town's poor – did not care as long as he made them better, but he disliked the reputation he had acquired. It was especially galling as he had been to some trouble to avoid controversy over the last few years, keeping his ideas and theories to himself, and only practising surgery as a last resort.

'He is not a warlock,' said Michael impatiently. 'And as most of you White Friars are his patients, I am astonished to hear such remarks from your lips.'

'You are right,' said Prior Etone, after a brief moment

of contemplation. 'Matthew is the only *medicus* who brings relief to my chilblains. Where would I be if he took umbrage and declined to tend me? So I hereby retract my objection to his foolish opinions about libraries.'

'There are other *medici* in Cambridge,' said Riborowe sullenly. 'And our Order should not use one who communes with the Devil, anyway. No matter how good he is with chilblains.'

'Perhaps not, but I would not recommend employing Vale in his place,' said Jorz fervently. 'He is more interested in inventing a universal cure-all than in treating real patients. Did I tell you that I showed him my haemorrhoids, and he laughed?'

'Who first mooted the idea of having a Common Library?' asked Etone, in the uncomfortable silence that followed. 'I cannot imagine Dunning coming up with it on his own.'

'It was Chancellor Tynkell,' replied Michael bitterly. 'He said he wanted to do something "worthwhile" before he retires from office next year.'

'Then you must bear some responsibility for the situation, Brother,' said Riborowe nastily. 'Of course Tynkell will be keen to be remembered as something other than your puppet!'

'If he were my puppet, we would not be having this discussion,' growled Michael, 'because a grace to found a Common Library would never have been proposed in the first place. Tynkell arranged the whole thing slyly, without my knowledge. I was outraged when I found out that he had been making arrangements behind my back.'

'I am sure you did your best to thwart it,' said Etone kindly.

'Yes,' agreed Jorz. 'It is not *your* fault that you were betrayed by your closest friend and other vipers like him.

Speaking of vipers, there seems to be a profusion of them this year. We killed three in our grounds only yesterday.'

'Did you?' asked Bartholomew in distaste. 'Why? They are harmless if left alone.'

Jorz regarded him askance, while Riborowe crossed himself. 'You defend serpents? The beasts whose forked tongues caused our expulsion from the Garden of Eden? That is heresy!'

Sawtre smiled rather patronisingly. 'You have overlooked the concept of free will, Jorz. Shall we debate the matter? I happen to be free for the next five or six hours and—'

'We should go home, or there will be nothing left to eat,' snapped Jorz, turning abruptly and walking away before the philosopher, who was known to be wordy, could claim the rest of his day. Riborowe followed, although not before treating Bartholomew to a final glower.

'My apologies,' said Etone with a pained smile. 'They have been trying to invent a fast-drying ink, and it is weariness that renders them testy. They are usually perfectly amiable.'

'You see, Matt?' asked Michael, when Etone and Sawtre had gone. 'Your silly library is causing all manner of dissent among our members. But we had better visit this corpse before any more of the day is lost.'

Bartholomew had not been inside Newe Inn since it had ceased to be a tavern, and looked around with interest as he entered. It was cool, dark and smaller than might have been expected from the street, because, in typical Norman fashion, its walls were hugely thick. It was simple in design: the ground floor comprised a large, low-ceilinged basement that would be used for storage, while the upper floor had two chambers where the precious books would be kept.

As the storeroom was deserted, Michael aimed for the stairs, to look for someone who could tell them why they had been summoned. Cynric was at his heels, while Bartholomew lagged behind, reluctantly acknowledging to himself that perhaps Newe Inn was unsuitable for a library – it was gloomy, cool even on a warm summer day, and definitely damp.

'Personally, I suspect Dunning is glad to be rid of this place,' muttered Cynric disparagingly. 'Donating it to the University brings a princely number of masses for his soul when he is dead *and* a free tomb in St Mary the Great. He has done well out of the bargain.'

They arrived at the upper chambers to find them in a flurry of activity. Walkelate could have shoved up a few shelves and been done with it, but he had taken his assignment seriously, and the result was a masterpiece. The walls were panelled in light beech, and the bookcases were of different heights and depths to accommodate variation in the size of the tomes they would hold. They were all exquisitely carved with classical and biblical images.

When he saw he had visitors, the architect came to greet them.

'Welcome,' he cried jovially. 'I know we are all sawdust and muddle at the moment, but the chaos is superficial. The main work is finished, and it is just details now. We shall certainly be ready by Corpus Christi.'

'Oh, good,' said Michael without enthusiasm. 'It is a—'

'But you have not been here before,' interrupted Walkelate, looking at Bartholomew and beaming widely at the prospect of a new admirer. 'Allow me to show you around.'

'Not now,' said Michael quickly. 'We were told there is a corpse to inspect.'

'A corpse?' echoed Walkelate, startled. 'There is no cadaver here, I assure you!' He turned eagerly back to Bartholomew. 'Like all decent libraries, ours will be in two sections. The room in which we are standing holds the *libri distribuendi* – duplicates, cheaper volumes and exemplars. These may be lent to scholars, to take home.'

'And the *libri concatenati*?' asked Bartholomew.

Walkelate led the way to the adjoining chamber. It was larger than the first, and finer, with specially designed carrels and lecterns for reading. 'As you know, the *libri concatenati* are expensive or popular books. They will be chained to the walls or to lecterns, and will not be removed from the building.'

'Our library will be magnificent,' said Bartholomew warmly, his reservations about the building's suitability quite vanished. He pointed to a huge rough chest in the middle of the room, which stood in a sea of wood shavings. 'Although I assume that will not be staying?'

'That is a *cista exemplarium* – a box for storing spare exemplars – and will eventually live in the basement. However, for now, it provides a convenient work table.'

To prove his point, he sat next to it. On the *cista* was a hefty bust of Aristotle, meticulously carved in oak, which he picked up and began to buff lovingly.

'This will be mounted atop the first bookcase our scholars will see upon entering,' he explained. 'To welcome them to this sacred hall of learning.'

'I am surprised you accepted Dunning's invitation to design this place,' remarked Michael. 'Your College is violently opposed to the scheme, and King's Hall has always been rather keen on unity.'

'I know,' said Walkelate with a sigh. 'They remind me of my dissension at every meal.'

'Then why did you do it?' asked Bartholomew curiously.

His own colleagues were still peeved with him for the way he had voted, and he could not imagine what it would be like for Walkelate, who had not only supported the venture, but was its architect, too.

'Because I firmly believe that they will appreciate its benefits in time,' replied Walkelate. 'And that they will come to love it. Besides, this project represented a challenge, and I like my skills to be tested.'

'You have worked very hard,' acknowledged Michael. 'However, a grand opening during Corpus Christi will be a red rag to a bull. A discreet, quiet ceremony the week after would be far more suitable. I do not suppose you might consider . . .'

'I cannot delay the work to suit you, Brother,' said Walkelate reproachfully. 'Dunning has offered the craftsmen a substantial bonus if they finish on time, and it would be cruel to deprive them of such a prize after all their labours.'

He smiled as two men walked into the room, laden down with wood and buckets of nails. The first man, who was enormous, carried the bulk of the supplies. He looked like a wrestler, and his thick yellow hair was tied in a tail at the back of his head. The second was smaller, with sad eyes and a wart on the side of his nose. Both looked exhausted, and when they deposited their materials on the *cista*, they heaved weary sighs.

'This is Kente,' said Walkelate, indicating the smaller of the pair. 'He is responsible for all the carving, while Frevill here built the shelves.'

'Another week,' said Kente, bending slowly to pick up a hammer. 'Then we shall be finished, and I will sleep for a month. I cannot recall ever working so hard!'

'Nor I,' growled Frevill. 'But the bonus will be worth the pre-dawn starts and the late finishes. My father says it will eliminate all the debt our family has incurred this winter.'

Bartholomew sincerely hoped that Dunning would be able to pay what he had promised, because it was clear that the artisans had given everything they had to meet his deadline.

He was about to compliment Kente and Frevill on their achievement when there was another clatter of footsteps on the stairs. A man stood in the doorway, hands on hips, as he regarded Michael with considerable anger.

'What are you doing up here?' he demanded in a powerful West Country burr. He was short, although he carried himself as though he were taller, and had straight, grey-brown hair. His name was Robert Browne, and he was a teacher at Batayl Hostel. Bartholomew braced himself for some unpleasantness – Browne was not one of the University's more congenial members.

Michael regarded Browne in surprise. 'Why should I not be here?'

'Because your duties lie in Newe Inn's garden,' snarled Browne. 'Not in its damned library.'

'The corpse,' surmised Michael. 'So there is one after all. However, your Principal said there was no immediate hurry, and—'

'Coslaye is not the one obliged to loiter next to it until the Senior Proctor deigns to appear,' snapped Browne angrily. 'And he may not consider murder urgent, but *I* do.'

'Murder?' asked Michael uneasily. 'How do you—'

'If you can bear to bring an end to your sightseeing,' replied Browne waspishly, 'you may come and see for yourself.'

* * *

41

It had been several years since anyone had tended Newe Inn's grounds and they screamed of neglect and decay. Some weeds were taller than Bartholomew, who was not a short man, while nettles choked what had once been vegetable beds, and the grass was thigh-high. The tavern must have been leased to a long succession of negligent landlords, and he wondered whether Cynric was right to say that Dunning was glad to be rid of the responsibility it would pose.

'Will anything be done to tame this wilderness before the library opens?' he asked, trying to fight his way free of a bramble with thorns like talons. It retaliated by ripping his shirt. 'It is downright dangerous!'

'It is,' agreed Cynric, kicking viciously at a huge thistle.

'Dunning declined to renovate the house *and* clear the garden,' explained Michael, following Browne along a barely discernible path, which ran by the side of the teetering wall that divided Newe Inn from neighbouring Batayl. 'So Tynkell decided to leave the grounds until next year. Doubtless he will use them to instigate some other foolish plan to see himself immortalised.'

Eventually, they arrived at a large pond where past owners had bred carp and trout. It reeked, although the stench was partly masked by a fragrantly scented patch of lily of the valley to one side, a bright jewel of beauty in a place that was otherwise unsightly. Floating in the middle of the pond, face-down and with an arrow protruding from its back, was the body.

'Now can you see why I had the audacity to suggest murder?' asked Browne archly. He shot Bartholomew an unpleasant glance. He had never liked the physician, preferring staid traditionalists to those who favoured new ideas. 'You do not need a Corpse Examiner to tell you that he did not do that to himself.'

'Who is he?' asked Michael.

'His face is in the water and his clothes are black with mud,' replied Browne tartly. 'So how am I supposed to know that? However, I can tell you that he is not supposed to be here.'

'Obviously,' muttered Cynric. 'Cadavers bobbing about in fish ponds is hardly right.'

Browne's lips compressed into a thin line. 'I meant that no one is supposed to frequent these grounds. They are University property and therefore private.'

Michael regarded him through narrowed eyes. 'Yes, they are, which means you should not have been here, either, yet you were the one to raise the alarm. What were you doing?'

Browne looked decidedly furtive. 'I occasionally slip over the wall to ensure all is well. It is unwise to leave a place unattended too long, and I take my neighbourly responsibilities seriously.'

'I am sure you do,' said Michael coolly. 'However, it does not explain why you were *here*, at this pond. It is far beyond benefiting from philanthropic inspections.'

Browne was defiant. 'Times are hard, especially for a poor foundation like ours, and there are fish in this pool. You, from rich old Michaelhouse, will not know what it is like to be hungry.'

Michael, Bartholomew and Cynric said nothing, but the truth was that their College was not wealthy at all, and they understood all too well what it was like to exist on meagre rations. They possessed several fine buildings, along with land that kept them supplied with vegetables, but their roofs leaked, they were crippled with debt, and a fire had not burned in the hearth for weeks. Not even a windfall resulting from a recent journey to York had helped them for long.

43

'So you are a poacher,' surmised Michael, fixing Browne with an icy glare. 'How often do you raid University property, exactly?'

'Bagging the occasional carp hardly makes me a poacher,' objected Browne indignantly, although Bartholomew was sure the law would not agree.

'Was the corpse here yesterday?' snapped Michael impatiently.

'If so, I would have reported it then,' Browne shot back, then added defensively, 'Not that I visit every day, of course.'

'Of course.' Michael turned to Bartholomew. 'We need to tug him out. I am not sure how, though – he is some distance from the bank.'

Bartholomew fashioned a grappling hook by tying one of his surgical implements on to a piece of twine. Then he flung it towards the body, aiming to snag it and draw it across to him. Unfortunately, it was caught on something below the surface, and the makeshift device was not strong enough to let him pull it free.

'You had better wade in after him,' said Michael. 'Or we shall be here all day.'

'You do it,' objected Bartholomew. 'My remit is to tell you how he died, not go paddling about in dirty ponds while you stand by and make unhelpful suggestions.'

'*I* am not going,' said Cynric firmly, when the monk turned to him. He crossed himself with one hand, while the other gripped a couple of the talismans that hung around his neck. 'This pool is infested with an evil kind of faerie.'

'Surely, you have a charm to protect you?' asked Michael irritably. 'You seem to be wearing at least four, not to mention pilgrim tokens and a holy relic. No one in Cambridge is better protected from wicked spirits than you.'

44

'Almost certainly,' agreed Cynric comfortably. 'But I am still not going in that pond.'

'Nor am I, lest you think to ask,' said Browne. 'It is not my responsibility, either.'

'And I cannot swim,' added Michael. He grinned rather triumphantly at Bartholomew. 'So either you must do it, or we shall have to wait until a beadle deigns to arrive.'

As it was nearing the date when his students would take their final disputations, and he was keen to return to College to make sure they were hard at work, Bartholomew sat down and began to untie his boots. Michael was right: it might be some time before a beadle – one of the army of men he hired to keep unruly scholars under control – put in an appearance, because they were still busy ensuring that no trouble was bubbling after the Convocation.

'It will not take a moment,' said Michael consolingly. 'Then you can return to terrorising your pupils, and I can continue to soothe ragged tempers over this library. You know what happened the last time our Colleges and hostels took against each other.'

Bartholomew was unlikely to forget the events of the previous February, when a ruthless killer had fanned the flames of dissent between the University's warring factions. He stood and put one foot in the water, but it was bone-chillingly cold – far more so than he had expected – and he withdrew it hastily.

'Just jump,' advised Michael. 'It will be unpleasant for an instant, but then all you have to do is wade a few steps, grab the corpse and haul it back to us.'

'There is a platform just under the surface,' supplied Browne, rather more helpfully. 'Built to allow servants to walk out and catch the fish with nets. You can see it if you look carefully. Use that.'

Bartholomew saw there was indeed a structure beneath

the water. It was made from old planks, and was black with age and slime. He supposed it would normally be exposed, but recent rains meant the water level was higher than usual. He stepped on to it, wincing at the frigid temperature a second time, and was relieved to find it only reached mid-calf. Gingerly, he moved along it, wondering just how old the planks were, and whether they were stable. The thought had no sooner formed in his mind when he felt them move. He froze in alarm.

'Stop,' said Cynric urgently. 'Come back, and I will—'

The rest of his sentence was lost under a tearing groan. Bartholomew flailed his arms in a desperate effort to keep his balance, but the wood crumbled beneath his feet, and into the pond he went. It was so cold after the warmth of the day that he gasped involuntarily, inhaling water that made him choke. He struck out for the bank, but a piece of planking landed on him and forced him beneath the surface. There, looming in the darkness, was a dead face. Startled, he gulped a second time, swallowing yet more water.

'You did not bring the body,' said Browne, grinning his amusement as the physician scrambled up the bank, dripping and disgusted. 'You will have to go back for it.'

'I saw it under the water.' Bartholomew coughed, and Cynric pounded him on the back. 'Your beadles will have to trawl for it, Brother. I had no idea this pond was so deep.'

'It *is* deep,' agreed Browne. 'The fish would have died years ago, were it not. But the corpse is not under the water, Bartholomew. It has not moved.'

Bartholomew glanced behind him, and saw that Browne was right. 'But I saw a face,' he said, wondering whether he had imagined it; the pond was murky after all. 'It floated past me . . .'

'There are *two* corpses,' cried Cynric, the shrillness of his voice making everyone jump. 'I told you this place was evil!'

Bartholomew looked to where he was pointing, and saw the unmistakable shape of a second body, bobbing a short distance from the first.

'Actually, there are three,' breathed Michael, gesturing in entirely another direction. 'Lord save us! It is a veritable graveyard!'

CHAPTER 2

It was late afternoon by the time the beadles had completed an initial dredge of the pond. The first body had been snagged on the underwater structure, and it had taken three of them to haul it free; the other corpses had been recovered by dropping hooks into the water. The pond released a foul odour as it was disturbed, and several beadles claimed to feel faint, so Michael sent Cynric to fetch Bartholomew, who had gone home. The physician arrived to find the men sullen and fearful, but was unsympathetic when he learned why.

'The smell is *not* the Devil's breath,' he said firmly, glaring at his book-bearer as he did so – he knew exactly who had put that thought into their minds. 'It is just stagnant water.'

'We found four bodies in the end,' said Michael, pointing to a row of shrouded shapes. 'And a bucketful of bones that could represent yet more unfortunates.'

Bartholomew inspected them quickly. 'Chickens and geese, Brother, from the tavern's table. And one or two cats that must have tried to catch the fish and tumbled in. The sides of the pond are steep, and if the water was low, it might be difficult to climb out again.'

'No, the evil faeries had them,' countered Cynric matter-of-factly. 'Cats have excellent balance, and do not fall into pools while hunting. And even if they did, they can swim.'

'Normally, I would ask you to examine these bodies – the human ones, I mean – immediately,' said Michael,

48

ignoring him and addressing Bartholomew. 'But we are all tired, so it can wait. My beadles will take them to St Mary the Great, and you can look at them tomorrow, when inconsiderate book-bearers are not making unsettling remarks about demonic spirits and the like.'

'But it is true,' objected Cynric, stung. 'I told you this garden had a sinister aura, and the presence of corpses here proves it.'

'I had better do it now, Brother,' said Bartholomew. 'The tale is already out that bodies have been found, and people have gathered in the lane outside, clamouring to know names. Apparently, several people have gone missing over the last few weeks, and their loved ones are eager for answers. Perhaps, like Browne, these four had a penchant for Newe Inn's fish.'

'That is unlikely,' said Michael. 'One careless poacher might have fallen in, or even two, but not more.'

Bartholomew lifted the blanket that covered the first. The body was fresh, and he doubted it had been immersed for more than a day. He inspected it quickly.

'There is no sign of a slit throat. Or any other wound for that matter, although I will look more carefully tomorrow.'

Michael frowned. 'A slit throat?'

'Like the beggar, Tulyet's night-watchman and Adam,' explained Bartholomew. He shrugged at the monk's bemused expression. 'You are right in that four people are unlikely to have died of natural causes here, so unless we have two killers on the loose . . .'

'But Dick said the others were probably executed because they saw smugglers. Smugglers will not be operating in the grounds of Newe Inn, so the two cases cannot possibly be connected.'

Bartholomew was not sure what to think. He stared at the corpse's unfamiliar features. Its clothes indicated a man of some substance, because they were of excellent quality and almost new. The same was true of the next victim, who bore an uncanny likeness to the first. Both had deeply ink-stained fingers.

'Have any brothers been reported missing?' he asked. 'Clerks, perhaps, or scribes?'

'Yes – and you were there when it happened.' Michael sounded shocked. 'Philip and John London, who work in the stationer's shop. Weasenham mentioned they were late for work today.'

'He also said they were members of Batayl,' said Bartholomew, glancing in its direction. 'Which lies next door, and whose scholars raised the alarm about a corpse here.'

'Not *these* corpses, though. They were underwater, and invisible until you stirred them up.'

'Are these the London brothers?' asked Bartholomew. 'I never met them.'

Michael peered at them. 'Yes, more is the pity. They have helped Weasenham quietly and efficiently ever since the Death.'

The plague that had scoured the civilised world, killing entire communities in a matter of days, had been such a terrible experience that people nearly always used it to refer to events in the past – everything was either before the Death or after it. Bartholomew covered the brothers, and removed the blanket that had been placed over the next victim.

'Northwood!' he exclaimed in horror. He looked up at Michael with a stricken expression. 'He is the Carmelite who voted in favour of the Common Library – against the wishes of his colleagues. I liked him, Brother. He gave my fellow *medici* and me some helpful advice about developing our clean-burning lamp fuel.'

'I knew him only by reputation – for his lively mind and interest in alchemy. Who is the last?'

Bartholomew pulled the cover from the fourth body, and pushed the sodden hair away from its face. It was the one with the arrow in its back. He recoiled with shock a second time.

'It is Vale,' he said in a voice that was not quite steady. 'The Gonville Hall physician. No wonder he was not at the Convocation earlier! His colleagues mentioned his absence, if you recall.'

'Vale?' echoed Michael. 'But this makes no sense! What do a friar, two scriveners and a *medicus* have in common?'

Bartholomew did not know, but the day seemed suddenly colder and darker.

Dismayed and saddened by what he had seen, Bartholomew was tempted to ignore Michael's recommendation to leave the examinations until the following morning, and do it straight away. But he had been up most of the previous night with a patient and knew better than to undertake such an important task when his wits were sluggish from lack of sleep. He followed Michael and Cynric through the garden to the small gate that led into Cholles Lane.

'Walkelate and his craftsmen were no help,' said Michael, once he had reported what little he knew about the victims to the anxious crowd outside, and was walking away. 'The pond cannot be seen from the house, and neither can the gate. None of them saw or heard anything amiss, despite the fact that they work on that accursed building all the hours God gives.'

'I will ask around,' offered Cynric. 'Someone will have noticed something peculiar, because four men do not die with no witnesses.'

'I hope you are right,' said the monk fervently. 'Do you mind starting now?'

Because it was a pretty evening, the streets were busy, and Michael and Bartholomew met a number of people they knew as they walked to Michaelhouse, some enjoying a relaxing stroll and others going home after work. The physician's sister and her husband were among the former. They were deep in conversation, and Edith's worried frown deepened when she saw her brother.

'We were just talking about your grisly discovery at Newe Inn, Matt,' she said sympathetically. 'The tale is already all over the town. It must have been horrible for you.'

'Do you know the names of the victims yet?' Oswald Stanmore was a wealthy cloth merchant, a handsome, grey-haired man with a neat beard and fine clothes.

Bartholomew nodded. 'Vale, Northwood and the London brothers.'

Edith's hands flew to her mouth in dismay. 'Not Northwood! He was a lovely man, and often came to our house to talk about cloth-dyeing. He was interested in such things.'

'He was,' agreed Stanmore, shaken. 'He liked anything to do with mixing different ingredients together, and recommended several improvements that saved me a lot of money. He was interested in your efforts to create a clean-burning lamp, Matt, and wanted to be part of it.'

Bartholomew nodded again. 'Unfortunately, Rougham and Holm will only experiment with other *medici*, and refused his offer. It was a pity, because I think he would have been useful.'

'He would,' whispered Cynric to Michael. 'And they should have accepted his help, because they are making scant progress on their own. Personally, I suspect they will never succeed.'

'I wish you would hurry up with it, Matt,' said Stanmore. 'I should like to be able to work winter nights without straining my eyes. So would many other folk, and I predict your non-flickering lamp will make you very rich, although I know money is not what drives you.'

Bartholomew did not reply. He was feeling despondent, partly because he hated to admit that several months of experiments had produced nothing worthwhile, but mostly because of what had happened to Vale and Northwood.

'It seems to me that half of Cambridge is busy trying to invent something at the moment,' said Edith. 'The *medici* with clean-burning fuel, Northwood with dyes, the Carmelites with ink, Weasenham with paper-making, to name but a few.'

'Yes,' said Michael. 'It all began in January, when a deputation of scholars from Oxford came and bragged about some experiments they were conducting. As you can imagine, our Regents hated the prospect of being outshone by the Other Place, so quite a number of them turned inventor.'

'Is that what has prompted this recent spirit of enquiry?' asked Edith, amused. 'A desire not to be bested by academic rivals?'

'Partly,' agreed Michael. 'But it is also about being more attractive to benefactors and patrons. And about drawing the best students. Applications to study here have increased tenfold since some of our Regents have become alchemists.'

'I imagine they have,' said Stanmore dryly. 'These pupils all hope to be part of these discoveries, so they can claim a slice of the profits when they are sold. But to return to the bodies at Newe Inn, Weasenham told us that one had an arrow in its back, and—'

'Weasenham!' spat Michael in disgust. 'Must he gossip

53

about *everything*? Of course, he probably did not know then that two of his scribes are among the victims.'

'That will make three of his scriveners dead in a single day,' said Edith. 'Poor Ruth! She was distressed about Adam, but she will be heartbroken over the London brothers. She was fond of them, because her husband tended to curtail his rumour-mongering when they were to hand.'

'So once again our town is plagued by killers,' said Stanmore bleakly, placing a protective arm around his wife's shoulders. 'I cannot imagine what it is about Cambridge that attracts them.'

'Matt has not inspected the bodies yet,' warned Michael. 'And until he does, we cannot say that murder—'

'Of course they were murdered,' interrupted Stanmore scornfully. 'A man cannot shoot himself in the back with an arrow. Nor do four men choose the same spot in which to dispatch themselves, while if it was an accident, you would have seen it straight away. They were unlawfully slain all right. Poor Northwood! And poor John and Philip London, too!'

'What about poor Vale?' asked Michael.

It was Edith who answered. 'I shall pray for his soul, but I disliked him. He pestered my seamstresses relentlessly, and I had to order him to stay away from them in the end.'

'He was sly, as well as a lecher,' added Stanmore. 'He tried to cheat me when I sold him some cloth, and I was incensed that he should consider me a fool.'

'Perhaps it was a misunderstanding,' said Bartholomew, troubled by the remarks. 'I am sure he would not have—'

'Dear Matt,' said Edith fondly, reaching out to touch his cheek. 'Always thinking well of even the most brazen of villains.'

54

'Incidentally, I am pleased to hear that the Common Library is almost ready,' said Stanmore. 'I have it in mind to donate my collection of breviaries to the venture.'

'But you have always said those would come to Michaelhouse,' cried Michael in dismay.

'I have changed my mind. Chancellor Tynkell has promised twice as many masses for my soul if I give them to him instead. It—'

'Who is that?' asked Bartholomew suddenly, pointing to where a man and a woman were walking together. He had seen them before, and there was something about the lady that reminded him of Matilde, the love of his life who had disappeared from Cambridge before he could ask her to marry him. That had been three years ago, almost to the day, and he had spent many months searching for her, but had finally resigned himself to the fact that he would never see her again. That did not mean he never thought about her, though, and the woman who walked along Milne Street bore an uncanny resemblance.

'Sir Eustace Dunning and his younger daughter Julitta,' replied Stanmore. 'He is an influential member of the Guild of Corpus Christi, and thus a powerful voice in town affairs. You should know him, Matt – he was the one who gave Newe Inn to your University.'

'Julitta,' repeated Bartholomew, a little dreamily.

'Sister to Weasenham's wife Ruth,' Stanmore went on. 'You can see the likeness, with their fair skin and pretty eyes. And in their intelligence, too.'

'Julitta is betrothed to Surgeon Holm,' added Edith. 'Although I cannot say *I* would like to marry a surgeon. They probably bring home some shocking stains.'

Dunning was a handsome man in his fifties, whose thick grey hair and matching beard made him appear venerable, like a modern-day Plato. He had fought in the Scottish wars, where his courage had earned him his spurs, and he had inherited a sizeable fortune from his father.

'I am sorry my benefaction continues to cause strife, Brother,' he said, as Michael and Bartholomew approached. 'It was intended to please the University, not be a source of discord.'

Julitta laughed, a pleasant sound that reminded Bartholomew even more acutely of Matilde. His stomach lurched, and he could not stop staring at her. She had long, silky brown hair that she wore in a plait, and her slender figure was accentuated by the elegant cut of her kirtle. But it was her face that was her most striking feature. It was clear and sweet, and with the exception of Matilde, he could not ever recall seeing anyone so lovely.

'What did you expect?' she asked, eyes dancing. 'Cambridge's academics are clever men with strong opinions. I imagine any proposal will meet with opposition, no matter how kindly meant.'

'True,' admitted Michael grudgingly. 'Of course, it is a pity the Carmelites *and* Batayl feel they have a right to Newe Inn. It would have been better had you donated a different building to the venture, and I understand you have plenty. Perhaps you will give us another.'

It was Dunning's turn to laugh. 'You scholars are never satisfied!'

'On the contrary, we are very grateful,' said Michael, although he failed to sound sincere. 'But my point was that you had already promised—'

'I promised nothing,' interrupted Dunning wearily. 'The White Friars and Batayl have been clamouring at me for months to give them Newe Inn, and in an effort to shut them up, I said I would consider their applications. *Consider*, not agree to them. And that is all.'

56

'I suspect Principal Coslaye and Prior Etone embellished the tale because they want my father to withdraw his offer to establish a library,' explained Julitta. 'They are not naturally sly, but the issue seems to have made them extraordinarily excitable.'

'We have just visited it,' said Dunning with a sudden smile. 'I go there as often as possible, to monitor progress. Walkelate is an impressive fellow; he vowed it would be ready by Corpus Christi, and I am beginning to think he will succeed.'

'Yes,' said Michael. He did not add 'more is the pity', but it was evident in his tone.

'Our scheme is a good one, Brother,' insisted Dunning, hearing the censure. 'And Chancellor Tynkell assures me that it will benefit all concerned, even those who object now. A lack of books prevents many scholars from achieving all they might. A library will help them, and earn your *studium generale* the respect and fame it deserves.'

'I suppose it might,' conceded Michael reluctantly. 'But Tynkell's motives for encouraging this scheme are not altruistic. He wants to be remembered after he retires next year.'

'Is that so terrible?' asked Julitta. 'I understand he has done very little else during his tenure.'

'The library will be a credit to you, Sir Eustace,' said Bartholomew, finding his voice at last. 'In fact, Kente has already made you immortal by carving your face on one of the lecterns.'

'You noticed, did you?' Dunning was pleased. 'There is one of Julitta, too, and of Ruth, my other daughter.'

'Kente has immortalised Tynkell, too,' said Michael sullenly. 'As Eden's serpent.'

'Nonsense, Brother!' exclaimed Julitta, laughing again. 'What an imagination you have!'

Dunning changed the subject by turning to Bartholomew and asking conversationally, 'Surgeon Holm, who is soon to be my son-in-law, told me last night that you drilled a large hole in Coslaye's skull after it was crushed by a flying book at the Convocation. Is it true?'

Bartholomew found himself strangely reluctant to have Julitta think badly of him by admitting that he regularly trespassed on barber-surgeon territory, especially as she was betrothed to one of them. 'Well,' he hedged awkwardly. 'It was . . .'

'He also said that Coslaye would have died had you not done so,' added Julitta. 'I think you were extremely brave to have undertaken such a difficult procedure. Brave and noble.'

'You do?' asked Bartholomew, taken off guard. He was unused to praise for his surgical skills.

Julitta nodded. 'He said that he would not have dared do it, and was astonished that you did.'

Bartholomew made no reply, but was dismayed to hear that a tried and tested technique like trephining was beyond the talents of the town's new surgeon. In fact, he recalled being unimpressed with Holm's 'help' during the entire procedure, and it added to his growing suspicion that the man was not as proficient as he would have everyone believe.

'Perhaps you should not have bothered,' said Dunning tartly, 'given that Coslaye recovered to spread lies about the promises I am alleged to have made.'

'Really, Father!' admonished Julitta. 'That is not a nice thing to say, and Coslaye has his virtues. He is said to be an excellent teacher.'

'You are quite right, my dear,' said Dunning with a sigh. 'It has been a long day and I am tired. We had better go home before weariness leads me to say something else I do not mean.'

58

They moved away. Bartholomew watched them go, and might have stared at Julitta until she was out of sight, had Michael not prodded him, bringing him to his senses.

The two scholars resumed their journey, but had not gone far before their attention was caught by an altercation between four men. Browne was one of them, and Principal Coslaye another. Coslaye was a large man with rough, soldierly features and a notoriously hot temper, and he was shouting at the top of his voice. The objects of his ire were Riborowe and Jorz from the Carmelite Priory, and there was a lot of finger-wagging involved.

Bartholomew skirted to one side, loath to become involved in any debate that involved the waving of digits; in his experience men who employed such gestures were invariably bigots and closed to reason. However, the Senior Proctor could not walk past a quarrel that looked set to become violent, and when Coslaye jabbed Riborowe hard enough to make the skinny friar stagger, Michael stepped forward to intervene.

'What seems to be the problem?' he asked, interposing his considerable bulk between them.

'There is a rumour that the University is going to sell Newe Inn's garden to the Carmelites,' explained Browne when his Principal was too enraged to speak. 'But Chancellor Tynkell said *we* could have first refusal on any sale of land.'

Riborowe sneered at him. 'If you took Tynkell's word for anything, you are a fool. He will say anything for a quiet life, and is always reneging on agreements.'

'Tynkell would have pledged no such thing,' said Michael firmly. 'He knows better than to annoy me further with anything concerning the Common Library.'

That was certainly true, thought Bartholomew: Tynkell

had been wholly unprepared for the extent of Michael's wrath when the monk had learned that the Chancellor had been negotiating with wealthy benefactors behind his back. Some very harsh words had been aimed in his direction, and Tynkell had been desperate to make amends ever since.

'You do not need more land,' snarled Coslaye, ignoring him and addressing the Carmelites. 'You have lots already. But we do not, and if you were good Christians, you would let us have it.'

'Please, gentlemen,' began Michael. 'This is hardly the—'

'How will you pay for it?' sneered Jorz. 'You are paupers. However, we White Friars have the money to buy any land we choose.'

'We can find funds,' shouted Coslaye, incensed. 'We have generous friends who will—'

'Enough!' roared Michael. He lowered his voice when both the Carmelites and the Batayl men regarded him in astonishment. 'People are staring at you, laughing at your unedifying behaviour.'

'I do not care.' Coslaye's face was mottled, and Bartholomew hoped rage would not induce a seizure. 'Besides, the White Friars started it.'

Michael scowled at each of the four in turn. 'Bring your grievances to me at St Mary the Great tomorrow, and we shall attempt to resolve the matter amicably.' He raised a plump hand when all four began to object. 'Not another word, or I shall fine all for breaching the peace.'

'Who told you that the University was going to sell Newe Inn's garden to the Carmelites?' asked Bartholomew of the Batayl men in the resentful silence that followed. 'Because Michael is right: Tynkell would never have made such an offer.'

'What business is it of yours?' demanded Browne, regarding him with dislike. 'No one invited you to join this discussion.'

'There is no need to be rude,' snapped Coslaye. 'I owe Bartholomew my life, in case you do not recall. He even waived his fee for the help he gave me, on account of our poverty.'

'Yes, but the Devil probably paid him in kind,' said Riborowe slyly. 'I have heard that Satan is partial to poring over exposed brains. It amuses him.'

'And how do *you* come to be party to Satan's preferences, pray?' asked Michael archly. He turned to Browne while the Carmelite was still floundering about for a suitable reply. 'Matt posed a good question. Who told you this tale?'

'The stationer,' replied Browne. 'Not that it is—'

'Weasenham!' spat Michael in disgust. 'His lying tongue will see our town in flames yet. But we shall discuss this tomorrow. Good evening, gentlemen.'

Riborowe opened his mouth to object to the curt dismissal, but Jorz grabbed his arm and pulled him away, sensing it was unwise to irritate the Senior Proctor further.

'The experiment we are running with the ink should be finished by now, Riborowe,' he muttered. 'Let us return to the scriptorium and see the results.'

'I am complaining to the Bishop about you, Brother,' called Riborowe threateningly over his shoulder, struggling to free himself from Jorz's grip. 'You run the University like a tyrant.'

'Try it,' shouted Coslaye challengingly. 'It will do you no good. He is the Bishop's spy, and he has accrued his power with de Lisle's approval and connivance.'

Bartholomew suspected that was true: Michael could not have reached such dizzying heights without the backing of some extremely influential supporters. 'How are you feeling, Coslaye?' he asked, eager to change the subject to one that was less contentious; Michael was looking angry. 'Any headaches?'

Coslaye sniffed. 'Yes, a great big one. It is called the Carmelites!'

'We should have asked whether they have noticed any suspicious behaviour around Newe Inn's pond recently,' said Bartholomew, once he and Michael were alone again. 'The Carmelites and Batayl Hostel are among its nearest neighbours, after all.'

'I considered it, but tempers were running too high – both sides might have invented stories just to see the other discredited. I shall quiz them tomorrow, when they are calmer. But we had better speak to Weasenham about gossip that disturbs the peace. Will you come with me?'

'What, now?' groaned Bartholomew. 'It is getting late and I am tired.'

'Yes, now,' replied Michael firmly. 'Who knows what damage the man might do if we delay?'

On warm summer evenings, the University stationer could usually be found sitting on the bench outside his shop, enjoying the fading daylight and devising salacious and invariably fictitious tales about passers-by. He was there that night, Ruth on one side, and Bonabes on the other. He was uncharacteristically subdued, though, while Bonabes was pale and Ruth had been crying.

'Is it true?' asked the Exemplarius, coming quickly to his feet as Michael and Bartholomew approached. 'You found Philip and John London in Newe Inn's pond?'

Michael nodded. 'News travels fast, it seems.'

'We heard it from one of your beadles,' explained Weasenham. 'It is a wretched shame, especially after poor

Adam. I know scribes are ten a penny in Cambridge, where every other man you meet can write, and I shall have no trouble finding replacements. But I liked Adam and the London brothers.'

'We shall all miss them,' added Ruth in a small voice. 'Philip and John were so . . .' She trailed off, unable to speak.

'Calm,' supplied Bonabes. 'When business was frantic, with everyone screaming at us for completed exemplars, they soothed hot tempers with quiet words.' He shot Weasenham a pointed glance. 'And they were always quick to point out the undesirability of gossip.'

'They were sanctimonious in that respect,' nodded Weasenham. 'And I am not a gossip. I just like to share what I know with other people.'

'You gossiped to Browne about the Carmelites buying land from the University,' said Michael.

'I never did,' declared Weasenham, although his eyes were furtive, while Ruth and Bonabes exchanged a pained glance that made it clear the stationer was lying.

'What is wrong with you?' Michael was exasperated and angry. 'You know how irate our scholars get over anything to do with the Common Library.'

'That is hardly my fault,' said Weasenham defensively. 'And I had the tale on good authority, anyway – Tynkell came to my shop this morning, and I heard him tell Sawtre that Newe Inn's garden will be worth a lot of money one day, because it is strategically sited near the town centre.'

Bartholomew regarded him askance. 'That is hardly the same as Tynkell saying he will sell it to the Carmelites.'

'Of course he will sell it to the Carmelites,' said Weasenham irritably. 'They want it, and will pay above the odds to get it. Of course the University will trade with them. It is a matter of logic.'

'It is an erroneous assumption that caused a quarrel,' said Michael sternly.

Weasenham's eyes brightened. 'Really? Was there any violence? But of course there was, and I am not surprised. The Batayl men are fierce and aggressive, while that Browne is a nasty—'

'There was no violence,' interrupted Bartholomew hastily, appalled by the way Michael's words were being twisted.

Ruth took Weasenham's hand. 'Please, husband. The Carmelites are good men. They do not deserve to be set at odds with Batayl.'

'They are good men,' admitted Weasenham. 'Although I cannot say I like Riborowe and Jorz. Whenever they come to my shop, I am always under the impression that they are spying.'

'Spying?' asked Michael warily. 'On what?'

'On our paper-making experiments,' explained Bonabes. 'They run a scriptorium, so any advances in the manufacture of writing materials is of interest to them.'

'Of course, spying will do them no good now the London brothers have gone,' said Weasenham gloomily. 'They were the ones who enjoyed meddling with dangerous substances, and the rest of us do not really know what we are doing. Perhaps we had better give up now that they are no longer here to guide us.'

'No,' said Bonabes. There was a catch in his voice. 'They worked hard on this, and succeeding meant a lot to them. So I shall continue their endeavours, in my own time, if necessary. And when I learn how to do it, I shall name the paper-making process after them.'

Weasenham's sly features softened. 'There is no need to use your own time,' he said, his voice uncharacteristically gruff. 'You are right: they did work hard to succeed, and it would be a pity to let their labours go to waste. We shall all help you finish what they started.'

Bonabes turned away at his master's unexpected and uncharacteristic kindness, and Ruth began to cry again. Bartholomew and Michael left Weasenham trying ineptly to comfort them.

They had not taken many steps towards Michaelhouse when they were intercepted by Meadowman, Michael's favourite beadle, who had come to say that a quarrel had broken out between Bene't College and Essex Hostel, and the Senior Proctor's presence was needed to soothe the situation.

'They are arguing over the library,' Meadowman explained, rolling his eyes. 'Again. Apparently, Master Heltisle made some remark about the grace being passed by ignorant ruffians, and Essex took exception. I wish the Chancellor had never had the stupid idea in the first place.'

'You are not alone,' muttered Michael, as they hurried away together.

When they had gone, Bartholomew found himself reluctant to go home, despite his weariness. He was unsettled by the events of the day, and suspected he would not sleep if he went to bed anyway. Besides, he felt a certain obligation to tell his medical colleagues in person that Vale was dead, so he began to walk towards Bridge Street, to the home of John Meryfeld, which had become the meeting place of the Cambridge *medici* in their quest for steady-burning lamp fuel. They had planned to resume their experiments that evening, and Bartholomew had been sorry that his duties as Corpse Examiner had prevented him from joining them.

He made his way past the jumble of alleys known as

the Old Jewry, where Matilde had lived, and entered Bridge Street. A breeze was blowing from the east, carrying with it the scent of the Fens – stagnant water, rotting vegetation and wet earth. It was a smell he had known since childhood, and one he found curiously comforting and familiar. Then there was a breath of sweetness from some honeysuckle, followed by a rather unpleasant waft from a latrine that needed emptying.

He arrived at Meryfeld's house and knocked on the door, hoping it was not too late and his colleagues would still be there. Since beginning their quest the previous winter, the physicians had met at least once a week, and he had come to enjoy the sessions, despite their lack of progress. They were opinionated and dogmatic, and Bartholomew would never share his more novel theories with them, but he had come to accept their idiosyncrasies – and they his – and they had all gradually adopted attitudes of comradely tolerance.

Meryfeld's plump face broke into a happy grin of welcome when he opened his door. He was always smiling, and had a habit of rubbing his hands together when he spoke. He was not the cleanest of men, and his affable, pleasant manner concealed an intensely acquisitive core, but Bartholomew liked him anyway.

'Hah!' Meryfeld exclaimed. 'We thought you were not coming. Vale did not arrive, either, so we assumed that you must have received summonses from patients. Come in, come in.'

His home was airy and comfortable, and smelled of the home-made remedies he liked to dispense. Most were ineffectual, and comprised such innocuous ingredients as honey, mint and angelica, but he still charged a fortune for them. Bartholomew was always amazed when one worked, and could only suppose that it was the patient's faith in what he was swallowing that had effected the cure; there was a tendency amongst laymen to believe that the more expensive the remedy, the more likely it was to do what it promised.

William Rougham, portly, smug and arrogant, was reclining in Meryfeld's best chair. He deplored the fact that Bartholomew had trained with an Arab physician, and regarded his methods as controversial and dangerous. In turn, Bartholomew despised Rougham's traditionalism and resistance to change. But they had reached a truce over the years, and although they would never be friends, there was no longer open hostility in their relationship.

John Gyseburne was by the hearth. He was an austere, long-haired, unsmiling man in his fifties, who was of the firm belief that the only reliable diagnostic weapon was the inspection of urine. He always had a flask to hand, and rarely conducted consultations without requesting a sample; Bartholomew had even heard him demand one from a patient with a grazed knee. Despite this, Bartholomew had come to respect his opinions, and felt there was much to be learned from him.

The last of the gathering was Will Holm. Bartholomew had been delighted when the surgeon had first arrived, because Cambridge's last sawbones had retired, and there had been no one, other than Bartholomew himself, to suture wounds, draw teeth or amputate damaged limbs. Unfortunately, it had not taken him long to learn that Holm was alarmingly hesitant, and while caution was admirable in one sense – his predecessor had forged ahead when it would have been kinder to let well alone – it was frustrating in another. Patients had died whom Bartholomew felt could have been saved. It was unusual for a mere surgeon to be included in a gathering of physicians, but Holm was a lofty sort of man who had taken his acceptance as an equal for granted. He was cleaner, better dressed and infintely more refined than most of his fellows, and Bartholomew was always under the impression that he considered himself a cut above not just other barber-surgeons but above physicians, too.

'You are late,' Holm said brusquely, draining the contents of his goblet and setting it on a table. He was a tall, astonishingly handsome man with a luxurious mane of bright gold hair. 'We were just about to leave.'

'We were discussing Coslaye again,' said Gyseburne, his tone rather more friendly than Holm's. 'We are still stunned by his recovery.'

'I would not have opened his cranium,' said Rougham. 'Brains are easily damaged, and you might have hastened his end by drilling that hole in his head. I am surprised you dared do it.'

'There was no choice,' explained Bartholomew, wondering how much longer they would continue to debate this particular case. Trephining was an ancient, well-tested technique, and he failed to understand why they insisted on making so much of it. 'Coslaye was bleeding inside his skull, and he would have died had we not relieved the pressure.'

'He allowed me to examine his scar yesterday,' said Gyseburne. 'It has healed beautifully.'

'Pity,' murmured Holm. 'He is one of those who opposes the Common Library. Still, the project proceeds apace regardless, and I am looking forward to seeing it opened next week. Dunning, my future father-in-law, has promised me a prominent role in the ceremony, and it is always good to be seen and admired by people who might be patients one day.'

'A central repository for texts is a foolish notion,' declared Rougham uncompromisingly. 'Chancellor Tynkell should be ashamed of himself for coming up with it, and I have told him so.'

'I do not know what all the fuss is about,' said Meryfeld. 'I learned everything I know from my father, and I have never felt the desire to expand on it by consulting dusty old tomes.'

'Yes, and it shows,' muttered Rougham snidely. He glanced at Bartholomew. 'Why did you come tonight? It is too late to begin an experiment now.'

'It is,' agreed Gyseburne with a yawn. 'I wonder what happened to Vale. He did not mention previous appointments when I saw him earlier, and he told me he would be here.'

'When was that?' asked Bartholomew.

Gyseburne rubbed his chin. 'I suppose it was last night. Like me, he had been busy with a tertian fever, and we met on our respective ways home. I heard you were similarly inconvenienced, Matthew. Weasenham saw you walking home after tending some hapless soul *all night*.'

'Tertian fevers do seem to be more virulent this year,' mused Rougham. 'It must be something to do with the weather. But Vale must have been summoned again after you saw him, Gyseburne, because he missed College breakfast. I went to look for him, but his bed had not been slept in.'

'He is dead,' said Bartholomew, sorry when he saw the shock on his colleagues' faces, especially Rougham's – the two Gonville men had been friends. 'That is why I did not join you this evening. I was inspecting his body after it was pulled from the pond in Newe Inn's garden.'

'He was perfectly healthy when I saw him last,' said Rougham unsteadily. 'Was he murdered?'

'Probably,' replied Bartholomew. 'There was an arrow

69

in his back, and Northwood and the London brothers were in the pool with him—'

'Northwood?' demanded Rougham. 'What was Vale doing in company with that old rogue?'

'He was not a rogue,' countered Meryfeld sharply. 'He was a very clever man.'

'Let us not quarrel,' said Gyseburne softly. 'This is terrible news, and we should all go home quietly, and pray for the souls of these hapless men.'

The streets were quiet as the *medici* said their farewells, and it would not be long before the curfew bell sounded. The last of the Market Square traders were wending their way home, some on carts and others on foot. Friars and monks had completed vespers, and were already ensconced in their convents, Colleges or hostels. A few students roamed, obviously intent on breaking University rules and sampling the town's taverns, but Michael's beadles also prowled, ready to arrest and fine any lad caught out without a plausible excuse.

Gyseburne lived near the castle, so went north when the five *medici* parted company. Rougham went with him, saying he had a patient who had summoned him earlier, although Bartholomew was unimpressed that he had kept the person waiting while he drank wine and chatted with his friends. It left him walking south with Holm.

'I thought I saw lamps in Newe Inn's grounds last night,' said Holm thoughtfully. 'I live next door, as you know. But I assumed I was mistaken – Walkelate and his craftsmen are labouring frantically to finish the library by next week, and they often work late. However, they rarely venture into the garden, and I put the lights down to my imagination. It seems I should not have done.'

'Have you seen them before?'

Holm nodded. 'But Cholles Lane is not a salubrious part of town. The riverfolk and Isnard the bargeman live nearby, for a start, and they are desperate criminals. I shall move somewhere nicer when I am married to Dunning's daughter.'

'The riverfolk and Isnard are not criminals,' objected Bartholomew. They had been his patients for years, and he was fond of them.

'Oh, yes, they are. Isnard is almost certainly a smuggler, while the rest of that rabble poach and steal as the whim takes them. Then there are the murders that the Sheriff is investigating. If Isnard and the riverfolk are innocent of those, I will drink my own piss.'

'You had better work up a thirst, then,' said Bartholomew coolly, 'because the riverfolk would never kill. Or smuggle.'

Holm sneered. 'Shall we have a bet on it? Five marks?'

It was a colossal sum, and one Bartholomew did not have, but he found himself shaking hands to seal the wager anyway. He sincerely hoped his faith was not misplaced, especially in Isnard, who was hardly a model citizen.

'I shall not need your money when I marry Julitta, because she comes with a big dowry,' said Holm smugly. 'But I am not averse to having more. Did I tell you how I met her? I was visiting my friend Walkelate in Newe Inn, admiring the progress he had made on his library, when Julitta and her father arrived. She fell in love the moment she saw me, being a woman of impeccable taste.'

'I see.' Bartholomew was not sure what else to say in the face of such unabashed conceit. 'Have you been betrothed long?'

'Ever since I realised how wealthy her father is,' replied Holm with a smirk. 'I rejected her at first, because I wanted to snare someone more worthy of me. But I made enquiries

71

about Dunning's assets, and decided she would do. The family is not particularly venerable, but it suits my purposes.'

'And what about *your* family?' Bartholomew was the last man to denigrate surgeons, but it was a lowly profession, and Julitta would certainly be his social superior.

'I am related to the Holms of Norfolk,' replied Holm haughtily. 'We are a highly respected clan already, but I still intend to make the name known throughout the civilised world.'

'How?' asked Bartholomew, forbearing to say that he had never heard of the Holms of Norfolk.

'I have not decided yet, although it will be easier when I have a wealthy wife. I shall be able to leave the cautery to you and concentrate on more interesting matters. Perhaps I shall invent a special paste for whitening teeth or develop a pill for gout.'

Bartholomew felt his spirits sink. He should have known that having a surgeon in Cambridge was too good to be true, even if it was one with mediocre skills.

'The lamp fuel represents my best chance of fame, though,' Holm went on. 'And fortune, because whoever discovers it will be fabulously rich – everyone will want to buy some. I shall conduct my own experiments when I am married and can afford to buy the ingredients myself. Then there will be no need to share the profits with the rest of you.'

Bartholomew laughed. 'I imagine our colleagues will have something to say about that.'

'They can say what they like: I shall not give them a penny.' Holm was silent for a while, and so was Bartholomew, stunned by the bald promise of future betrayal. Eventually, the surgeon spoke again. 'It is a pity about Vale. He was the best of all the physicians, and I wish it had been Gyseburne, Rougham or Meryfeld who had died. Or you, for that matter.'

Once again, Bartholomew could think of no reply to such a remark. He found himself beginning to dislike the man.

Suddenly, Holm smiled. 'I love the tales of when you and the others first started experimenting with lamp fuel – when you almost blew yourselves up.'

Bartholomew winced. 'We produced a substance that was explosive, very sticky and impossible to extinguish once it was alight. In the end, we had to bury it, to deprive it of air.'

'Interesting,' mused Holm. 'Tell me more.'

'None of us can remember what went in it – we had been to a wake, and had imbibed too liberally of our host's claret. But thank God our minds are blank, because the stuff was akin to the "wildfire" mentioned in the battle accounts of the ancients, and—'

'Wildfire is not used these days,' interrupted Holm. 'I was at the Battle of Poitiers, and while I heard plenty of bombards and ribauldequins being deployed, there was no wildfire.'

Bartholomew had been at Poitiers, too, because bad timing had put him there during his quest to find Matilde. It had been a dreadful experience, and still haunted his dreams. Thus he disliked discussing it, and was disinclined even to address the curious coincidence that Holm should have been on the field, too.

'That is because wildfire is banned,' he explained instead. 'The Second Lateran Council declared it "too murderous" a weapon for war.'

Holm guffawed his disbelief. 'But war is murderous! And I would have used it, had I had some in my arsenal at Poitiers. I did not enjoy being on the losing side.'

Bartholomew blinked, not sure he had understood correctly. 'You fought for the *French*?'

Holm nodded blithely. 'I thought a military campaign would be a good way to gain experience of wounds. Of course, most of the injuries were too severe to bother with, but I was pleased with an ear I managed to sew back on. I would have preferred to stay with the English army, of course, but the French offered me a lot more money.'

'Oh,' said Bartholomew, feeling that a larger salary should have been immaterial at such a time.

'I understand you were there, too. Did you see the ribauldequins at work? Unfortunately, they produced so much smoke that I could not really tell how effective they were.'

'I do not believe any of their missiles found a target. However, there were injuries galore when one exploded – all to its own crew.' Bartholomew spoke quietly. The wounds had been horrific, even to a man inured to such sights, and he did not want to dwell on them so late at night. 'They are evil devices, and I cannot imagine what was in the mind of whoever invented them.'

'On the contrary,' argued Holm, 'their presence on the battlefield may mean an early capitulation by an enemy, thus *saving* lives. If the French had owned a few, loaded with some of that unquenchable substance you created, there would never have been a battle at Poitiers, because the Prince of Wales would have surrendered.'

'I do not want to discuss this,' said Bartholomew, the very notion of a ribauldequin that hurled wildfire bringing him out in a cold sweat. 'It will give me nightmares.'

'I wish you could recall how you made it,' said Holm wistfully. 'The formula would be worth a fortune to a military commander.'

74

'No doubt,' said Bartholomew. 'But even if we could remember, we are physicians. We save lives: we do not invent ways to cut them short.'

'You were not drunk that night,' pressed Holm. 'I wager you know what went in that pot.'

'It was dark,' said Bartholomew curtly. 'And Rougham, Gyseburne and Meryfeld were hurling ingredients around without bothering to read the labels. Even if I could recall *what* was added, I would have no idea *how much* was used. The experiment is unrepeatable – and I thank God for it.'

Bartholomew parted from Holm near All-Saints-in-the-Jewry. He bade the surgeon goodnight, then paused for a moment outside the house in which Matilde had lived, hoping that thoughts of her would dispel the bad memories his conversation with Holm had awakened. They did, yet failed to make him any happier. He still loved her with a passion that was painful, and he wondered whether he was destined to feel the pangs of loss for the rest of his life.

To take his mind off it, he pondered the bodies that had been found in Newe Inn's pond. Their discovery meant that there had been seven suspicious deaths in Cambridge, counting the three that Tulyet was investigating. Were they connected? He was inclined to believe not, partly because of what Michael had said – that Vale and the others were unlikely to have stumbled across smugglers in Newe Inn's garden – but mostly because they had not had their throats cut.

So had the four scholars been together when they had died, or had someone brought their corpses to the pond to hide them? And if the former, what had they been doing? They had all liked experimenting – the brothers with paper,

Vale with his universal cure-all, and Northwood with any kind of alchemy – but how could that be relevant? With a sigh, Bartholomew supposed that some of his questions might be answered when he examined them properly the following day.

He let his thoughts return to Holm, and was surprised by the intensity of the dislike he was beginning to feel for the man. He did not take against many people, but there was something deeply distasteful about the surgeon, something that went beyond his dubious medical skills, his repugnant attitude towards his fiancée, and the fact that he had sided against his countrymen in what had been a bitter and terrible battle. Then it occurred to him that he had known Holm for a good two months, but he had never found his faults objectionable before. Meeting Julitta had certainly had an impact!

He was still pondering the surgeon and his bride-to-be when he reached St Michael's Lane, and it was then that the attack happened. Figures shot from the graveyard opposite and darted towards him. He stopped walking when he saw the unmistakable glint of steel, and peered into the darkness, trying to ascertain whether his assailants were men he knew, but all were cloaked and hooded. There were three of them, and they moved quickly to back him against a wall. Two held cudgels, while the shortest had a dagger.

'Who are you?' he demanded, sounding a lot braver than he felt. 'And what do you want?'

'Tell us the formula, and we will give you a clean death,' said the knifeman, the leader.

'I cannot – we have not discovered it yet,' replied Bartholomew shortly. 'Lamp fuel is—'

'We do not mean lamp fuel,' snapped the leader. 'We mean the other substance.'

'What other substance?' Bartholomew rummaged in the medical bag he always wore over his shoulder, and hauled out some childbirth forceps that Matilde had given him. He was rarely called on to help pregnant women, because that was the domain of midwives, but the forceps had served as a weapon more times than he cared to remember. He hated to imagine what Matilde would think if she ever discovered the use to which he usually put them.

'The one that burns and cannot be doused.'

'Holm?' asked Bartholomew, wishing the night was not so dark and he could see his assailants' faces. 'I have already told you that I do not know. Now stop this ridiculous charade and—'

'Oh, I think you do,' hissed the leader. 'And it is a valuable secret, so you will appreciate why we do not want you blathering to anyone else. It would not do for our enemies to have it.'

'Enemies?' asked Bartholomew, simultaneously alarmed and bemused. 'What enemies?'

'Tell us the recipe, or we shall force it from you,' ordered the leader, adding in a voice that was distinctly menacing, 'And you will not enjoy that, I promise.'

He nodded to his companions, who stepped forward eagerly. Bartholomew did not wait to find out what they had in mind. He lashed out with the forceps, and caught the leader a blow that made him reel away with a howl of agony. The other two dropped into defensive stances, and Bartholomew could tell from the way they moved that he was in the presence of professionals.

He struck out again, but the biggest ducked and the third man took advantage of his momentary imbalance to knock the forceps from his hand. Then one arm was twisted savagely behind his back, and he was forced to his knees. A blade flashed in the gloom.

'I will teach you to challenge us,' snarled the leader. 'You will regret your lack of cooperation.'

As the weapon began to descend there was a sudden thump and the fellow reeled away with a muted cry, a dagger lodged in his thigh. Then there was a second thud, and the tallest howled and began to dance around on one foot.

'Run!' the leader screeched. 'Quick! He must have beadles watching out for him.'

They fled, two hobbling painfully. Bartholomew waited, but no beadles appeared. The leader was wrong – Michael's men would have come to accept his thanks if they had been responsible for the rout. So who had saved him? He called out in an unsteady voice, but there was no reply.

After a few moments, he retrieved his forceps and took several steps down St Michael's Lane, expecting at any moment to feel a searing pain as a knife landed. But none did, and it was with considerable relief that he pounded on the College gates and shouted for the porter to let him in.

He aimed directly for the kitchens, feeling an overpowering need for a drop of medicinal wine, and was just pouring his second cup when a sound behind him made him jump.

'I am starving,' said Michael plaintively, although his substantial girth suggested that was unlikely. 'That thin pottage we had for supper did nothing to quell my hunger, and I shall expire if I do not have something else before morning. You are very pale. What is wrong?'

'I have just been waylaid by three men eager to know the formula for wildfire,' explained Bartholomew, taking another large gulp of claret.

Michael regarded him sharply. 'I thought you said your fellow physicians were drunk when they stumbled across

78

that particular mixture, and no one can remember exactly what went in it. Of course, *you* were sober. Do you recall what they did?'

Bartholomew looked away. 'Not precisely.'

'But you know enough to be able to make some more?'

'Yes, I believe so,' admitted Bartholomew. 'But please do not tell anyone else.'

Michael watched him finish the wine and pour some more. 'You do not usually guzzle claret with such gay abandon at this time of night, so I surmise these three men did rather more than "waylay" you. Tell me what happened, Matt.'

In a voice that was still unsteady, Bartholomew obliged. 'I have no idea who they were,' he finished. 'They had disguised themselves with hooded cloaks, and it was dark. They may have been strangers, but they may equally well have been men we know – scholars or townsfolk. Of course, they will be exposed if they walk around town tomorrow, because two of them will be limping.'

'You fought three villains and emerged victorious?' asked Michael, startled. 'Lord, Matt! Ever since Poitiers, you have become something of a lion. Perhaps you should abandon medicine and take up the sword instead. Of course, you will have to learn to ride properly first.'

'Someone drove them off by throwing knives.' Bartholomew was not in the mood for levity. 'I could not see who, but he saved my life. Those men meant business . . .'

'Then we had better find them,' said Michael. 'We do not want you "waylaid" again.'

CHAPTER 3

Bartholomew slept poorly that night, unsettled by his encounter with the three men. He was also plagued by stomach pains, and supposed he must have swallowed tainted water when he had fallen in Newe Inn's pool. He certainly recalled gulping a good deal of it, and pond water was dangerous at the best of times; when corpses had been soaking in it, he imagined it was deadly.

Afraid his restlessness would disturb the students who shared his room, he rose and left, stepping carefully over the slumbering forms. Although more spacious than most hostels, Michaelhouse was cramped at night, when mattresses were unrolled and laid on the Fellows' floors for their pupils. The current crush was because the Master had recently enrolled more scholars than they had places for, in order to claim their tuition fees. Some were due to graduate that summer, which was at least partly why Bartholomew was determined that his lads should pass – the College could not house them for another year, should they need to try again.

He stepped into the yard, and breathed in deeply of the pre-dawn air. There was a slight lightening of the sky in the east, indicating that dawn was not far off, but it was still dark, and he could only just make out the buildings that had comprised his home for the last fifteen years.

The core of Michaelhouse was an airy, spacious hall, with kitchens, larders and pantries below. At right angles to it were two accommodation wings, and Bartholomew lived in the older, more decrepit, northern one. The square was completed by a thick wall, against which leaned the stables and the porters' lodge. A heavy gate led to St Michael's Lane, making the College as secure a foundation as any in the town.

One hand on his rebellious stomach, Bartholomew walked across the yard, thinking he would pass the hour or so before dawn with some quiet reading. The College 'library' comprised a corner of the hall that had been provided with shelves and two lockable chests. The books were either chained to the wall or stored in the boxes, depending on their value and popularity.

Although it did not possess many tomes, Michaelhouse had a Librarian. The post had actually been created to prevent its current holder from qualifying as a physician and venturing out among an unsuspecting public: Robert Deynman had been accepted as a student because his father was rich, not for any academic talent, and everyone had heaved a sigh of relief when he had been persuaded to abandon medicine for librarianship. As the position was funded by his proud family, the College was even spared the need to pay him – a blessing when money was so tight.

Bartholomew climbed the spiral staircase, then stopped in surprise when he saw a lamp burning. Deynman was there, and although it was not unusual for Fellows to study at night – it was often the only time they had to themselves – the Librarian was not in the habit of depriving himself of sleep to perform his duties.

'Rob?' Bartholomew called softly. 'Why are you here? Are you unwell?'

Deynman jumped. 'What are you doing up so early?'

'I could not sleep.' Bartholomew frowned when he saw Deynman's red-rimmed eyes and wet cheeks. 'What is the matter? Is your father ill? Or your brother?'

'They are well,' sniffed Deynman. 'It is something else that is destroying my happiness.'

Bartholomew sat next to him, supposing he was about to be regaled with some tale of unrequited love. 'Perhaps I can help,' he said kindly. 'Tell me what—'

'You can do nothing,' said Deynman bitterly. '*You* were one of the villains who voted for it.'

'The Common Library?' Bartholomew was bemused, but then understood what was bothering the lad. 'You are afraid it will render your post obsolete! Well, you need not worry. Master Langelee told me only yesterday that there was no one he trusted more with our books.'

Deynman was unconvinced. 'But if the likes of you have their way, we shall have no books.' He ran a loving finger across the one that lay in front of him; its leather cover had been buffed to within an inch of its life, and shone rather artificially. 'They will all be in this Common Library, where undergraduates will be able to get at them.'

'But that is a good thing,' said Bartholomew, struggling not to smile at the disapproval Deynman had managed to inject into the word 'undergraduates'. 'They are here to learn, and access to the works they are required to study is—'

'But they do not need to *handle* them!' cried Deynman, distraught. 'They can listen to a master reading. Or, if they must see the words themselves, they can hire an exemplar. They do not need to see the original texts. To *touch* them.' He shuddered at such a terrible notion.

'But books are meant to be read,' argued Bartholomew. 'And—'

'They are meant to be cherished, not mauled by grubby students. You should have voted properly at the Convocation – you were Michaelhouse's only dissenter. And you should be careful, because I heard what happened to Northwood, Vale and the Londons.'

Bartholomew was puzzled. 'What do you mean?'

Deynman pursed his lips. 'Vale voted against the wishes of his Gonville colleagues; the London brothers voted against their friends at Batayl; and Northwood voted against his Carmelites. All supported that evil Common Library. And now they have been murdered for their perfidy.'

Bartholomew supposed that all four had backed the grace to found the Common Library, but that had been six weeks ago, and he was inclined to believe it was coincidence.

'We do not know for certain that they have been murdered,' he said, although without much conviction. 'I have not examined them yet.'

'Well, when you do, you will find that they are dead by the hand of someone who deplores traitors,' said Deynman firmly. Then his expression changed from angry to concerned. 'Are you unwell, sir? You are very pale, and you keep gripping your stomach. Perhaps I had better fetch you some milksops from the kitchens. Do not look alarmed. I shall not poison them.'

'I did not think you would,' said Bartholomew, startled by the notion. 'And I do not need anything to—'

But Deynman had gone, leaving Bartholomew wondering whether he should have voted against the Common Library after all. It would have meant going against his principles, but he compromised those all the time – when he failed to tell people that his more successful medical techniques had been learned from his Arab teacher; when he opted not to share innovative theories with his fellow physicians because he did not want to be accused of heterodoxy; and when he concealed his reliance on certain 'heretical' texts.

And opposing the library would certainly have made for a more peaceful life.

He was not feeling much better when dawn came and the bell rang to tell Michaelhouse's scholars that it was time to attend their morning devotions. He trudged wearily into the yard.

'What is the matter?' asked Father William, a grimy Franciscan whose habit was generally considered to be the filthiest garment in Christendom. He also possessed some deeply repellent beliefs, and although Bartholomew had grown used to his ways and had learned to ignore them, the newer Fellows found him difficult to take. 'You look terrible.'

'You do,' agreed Thelnetham, one of the more recent arrivals. 'Very wan.'

He was a Gilbertine canon and a celebrated scholar of law. He was also brazenly effeminate, and was known for livening up the plain habit of his Order with flamboyant accessories. That morning, there was a purple bow tied around his waist in place of a simple rope cingulum. He and William could not have been more different, and had become bitter and implacable enemies the moment they had set eyes on each other.

'Shall I fetch you some wine, Matt?' offered Ayera, a tall, intelligent geometrician who liked horses, dogs and outdoor pursuits. Other than a deep and – to Bartholomew's mind, at least – irrational aversion to anatomy, he was easy and congenial company, and the physician liked his ready wit, wry humour and dedication to his students.

'Will your indisposition prevent you from teaching today?' asked Suttone, the College's only Carmelite, when Bartholomew shook his head to the offer of strong drink so early in the day. He was a plump man in a creamy white

84

habit. 'If so, I decline to mind your class in your absence. The last time I obliged you, they rioted.'

'Only because you told them the plague would return within the year,' objected Bartholomew defensively. 'They tend to believe what senior scholars say, and were worried. When I came back, I was hard pressed to prevent them from leaving Cambridge to warn their loved ones immediately.'

'But it *will* return within the year,' declared Suttone. 'I know I have been saying that for a decade, but this time I am right. I feel it in my bones.'

'Then let us hope your bones are wrong,' said Michael fervently. 'I remember spending the entire time being extremely frightened.'

'You were right to be,' declared William loftily. 'It was God's judgement on the wicked. I shall survive if it returns, naturally, because I am saintly. However, the same cannot be said for the rest of you miserable sinners.'

He shot a disparaging glance at Thelnetham's purple bow, then treated every other Fellow to a similarly haughty glare. Except Bartholomew. He had publicly accused the physician of being a warlock the previous summer, and had later been sorry. Guilt and a determination to make amends meant the physician could do no wrong. It would not last, but Bartholomew was finding it pleasant while it did.

'I am sorry about the men who died yesterday,' said Clippesby, the last of Michaelhouse's seven Fellows currently in residence; the eighth was spending the summer at Waltham Abbey. Clippesby was a Dominican, whose penchant for talking to animals, and claiming they talked back, led most people to assume he was mad. That morning, he was cuddling what looked suspiciously like a rat. 'Vale, Northwood and the London brothers were kind and good.'

'They were not,' argued Thelnetham immediately. 'They were scoundrels.'

'You disliked Northwood?' asked Bartholomew in surprise. 'But he was a talented scholar.'

'Being a talented scholar did not make him a decent person,' retorted Thelnetham. 'Moreover, I heard he was not always honest when dealing with tradesmen. And he was obliged to treat with lots, because his duties included buying supplies for the Carmelites' scriptorium.'

'Did you hear that from Weasenham?' asked Bartholomew. His feelings towards Thelnetham were ambivalent: the mincing canon had a sharp tongue that he often used to wound, yet he was also intelligent and insightful.

'Yes,' replied Thelnetham rather stiffly. 'Not all his tales are fiction, and he furnishes me with some extremely interesting information. Such as that a certain Dominican spent hours last week conversing with bats, and a certain Franciscan was given a book for our College that has not yet been passed to Deynman.'

'The bats have been very vocal of late,' said Clippesby, smiling serenely. He rarely took umbrage at his colleagues' gibes. 'It must be the weather.'

'What book?' demanded William at the same time, although his furtive expression suggested he knew exactly what Thelnetham was talking about.

'Did Weasenham regale you with any tales about Northwood, Vale and the London brothers?' asked Michael, always interested in rumours about those whose deaths he was obliged to explore.

'No,' replied Thelnetham. 'However, I am sure I do not need to remind you that all four voted for the Common Library. Damned villains! Of course, Vale only did it because Gonville does not have many medical books. Like

86

Bartholomew, he was motivated by selfishness, despite the fact that approving such a venture might damage Michaelhouse.'

'Now wait a moment,' said William dangerously. 'Matthew has already explained why he voted contrary to the rest of us: he followed his conscience.'

'Then his conscience is wrong,' spat Thelnetham. 'But that is to be expected from a heretic.'

Bristling angrily, William began to defend Bartholomew, but was cut short by the arrival of Ralph de Langelee, the College's Master. Langelee was a large, barrel-chested man, who did not look like a scholar, even in his academic robes, and whose previous career had involved acting as a henchman for the Archbishop of York. He knew little of the philosophy he was supposed to teach, and Thelnetham was firmly of the opinion that he should return where he came from, although the other Fellows were satisfied with his careful, even-handed rule.

Langelee indicated that Cynric was to ring the bell again, then led his scholars up St Michael's Lane towards the Collegiate church. Ayera hurried to walk next to him, muttering something that made him laugh, almost certainly an amusingly worded account of their colleagues' latest squabble. Langelee and Ayera were friends, partly because – like Bartholomew – neither had taken major religious orders and both retained a healthy interest in women; and partly because they hailed from York and had known each other there.

'I wish we had not elected Thelnetham as a Fellow,' murmured Michael in Bartholomew's ear, as they took their place in the procession. Michaelhouse's scholars were not supposed to talk as they went to church, but it was a rule the Fellows generally ignored.

'Because he has an acid tongue?' asked Bartholomew,

rather offended that the Gilbertine should think he had supported the Common Library for selfish reasons, when he had actually been motivated by altruistic sympathy with his poorer colleagues.

'Yes. Our conclave used to be a pleasant place, with no bickering or nastiness. But he has taken against William – and against you when he forgets that you mix an excellent tonic for biliousness – and the rest of us are caught in the middle.'

'Michaelhouse is not the haven of peace it was,' acknowledged Bartholomew. He jumped when a gate was slammed in nearby Ovyng Hostel, causing a crack like one of the Prince of Wales's ribauldequins. Michael patted his shoulder sympathetically.

'Do not worry, Matt. I will start looking for the three men who attacked you as soon as church is over. It will not be easy with no Junior Proctor, but I shall do my best.'

'I doubt you will find them, not when I cannot furnish you with even the most basic of descriptions, and you have too much else to occupy your time. Forget them, Brother. I cannot see them trying again, not now they know I cannot give them what they want.'

'Perhaps,' said Michael, unconvinced. He changed the subject. 'I had a letter from my Bishop today, commenting on the ransoms that were demanded by our King for the French prisoners who were taken at Poitiers. Some have still not been paid.'

'That is because they were so high,' explained Bartholomew. 'The one put on King Jean was at least twice France's gross annual income. Moreover, the peasants resent being obliged to pay for the release of nobles who fail to protect them from English marauders, and the whole country is on the verge of a serious uprising.'

'And all over a crown,' sighed Michael. 'I have no great

88

love for the French, but I would not have wished this on them.'

Attendance at meals in Michaelhouse was obligatory, so after the morning mass – over in record time because William was officiating and he took pride in the speed at which he could gabble the sacred words – Langelee led the procession home. The scholars milled around in the yard, enjoying the early morning sunshine, until the bell sounded to announce that breakfast was ready. Then there was a concerted dash for the door. Michael was one of the first to thunder up the staircase to where the victuals were waiting, with Suttone and William not far behind: all three had healthy appetites.

'I do not know why they are always so keen to be first,' remarked Bartholomew to Clippesby. His stomach was still unsettled, and the thought of food was unappealing. 'No one can start before the Master has said grace, and he does not do that until we are all standing in our places.'

Clippesby smiled. 'But there is nothing to stop them from grabbing bread from the baskets while the rest of us are still climbing the stairs. Have you never noticed the crumbs?'

It had been so long since Bartholomew had arrived at a meal before the others that he had forgotten his more voracious colleagues' penchant for the common victuals.

'I hope that is not a rat,' he said, looking at the whiskery nose that poked from the Dominican's habit. 'I will overlook frogs, snakes, rabbits, birds, pigs and even slugs. But not rats.'

'What is wrong with rats?' asked Clippesby, offended. 'They mean us no harm.'

'On the contrary – they invade granaries and were

responsible for some of last winter's starvation. Please do not bring it into the College again. It is hardly hygienic.'

'But this one has something to report,' objected Clippesby. 'She knows a little about the four scholars who died in Newe Inn.'

The Dominican liked to roam the town after dark, communing with his furred and feathered friends. It meant he often witnessed dubious human behaviour, and had helped Michael's enquiries several times in the past. Unfortunately, his unique way of reporting what he had learned made it difficult to separate fact from fiction.

'She says they often met in Cholles Lane after dark,' he went on. 'Then they all slipped inside Newe Inn's grounds together. But there were usually others with them.'

'Who?'

'She could not tell, because they were all cloaked and hooded. She cannot even say if they were men or women. She knows they took care to be quiet, though, and never let anyone see them.'

Cloaked and hooded, thought Bartholomew. Could they have included the three men who had attacked him the previous night? But virtually everyone in Cambridge possessed a cloak with a hood, and drawing conclusions from such attire was foolish and likely to be misleading.

'I do not suppose she knows what these people did in Newe Inn, did she?' he asked, although not with much hope. While Clippesby witnessed all manner of bizarre and inexplicable happenings, he was rarely moved to investigate them further. On the whole, Bartholomew was glad, because it might have been dangerous, and he was protective of the eccentric Dominican.

'No. But it took them some time – they were gone for at least an hour. Sometimes longer.'

'Were they in Newe Inn's garden or in the house – the Common Library?'

Clippesby shrugged. 'The rat cannot answer that, Matthew. All she saw was people entering the property via that little gate in the wall. She watched them gather on Tuesday night, in fact – Northwood, the Londons, Vale and one or two others. Incidentally, she has been watching Surgeon Holm, too. He has a lover, who visits him most evenings.'

'Yes – Julitta Dunning. They are betrothed.'

'They are betrothed,' agreed Clippesby. 'But Julitta's father would never allow his daughter to entertain him before they are married. Holm's fancy is someone else.'

'I do not want to know,' said Bartholomew, holding up his hand. He had never liked gossip.

'As you wish. But the rat will tell you, should you change your mind. She would like someone to warn Julitta, you see – to tell her that Holm will bring her pain if the marriage goes ahead. And I agree. As a priest, I could never sanction a union that will lead to such inevitable misery.'

As soon as breakfast was over, Bartholomew set his students an exercise to keep them busy while he went to St Mary the Great. He did not feel like examining bodies, and was developing a headache to go with his roiling stomach, so he only half listened to Michael talking about how he intended to solve the mystery surrounding the four deaths. However, he snapped into alertness when he became aware that the monk was making plans on his behalf.

'I cannot help you, Brother,' he objected. 'My students are taking their final disputations soon, and they are not yet ready for—'

'They are better prepared than any class in the

91

University,' countered Michael. 'And if they are lacking in some vital area, it is too late to correct it now. You are not needed as they re-read the texts they have already studied, and your presence will only make them nervous. It would be kinder if you let them be.'

'What do you mean?' demanded Bartholomew, a little indignantly.

'I mean that you have unreasonably high expectations, and the pressure may have an adverse effect. Let them revise without interference, and help me instead. It will be better for everyone.'

'But—'

'No buts, Matt. You have become a tyrant in the lecture hall, and it is time to stop. You cannot push them as hard as you push yourself.'

Bartholomew was about to deny the charge when he recalled that his students *had* accused him of intimidating them on occasion. Moreover, Michael was right in that there was no point in trying to teach them anything new now, and his senior students were more than capable of reading exemplars to the others. He supposed, reluctantly, that he could afford to let them relax a little.

'If there was foul play, then I would like to see the killer brought to justice,' he conceded grudgingly. 'I liked Northwood, and Vale was a colleague.'

'You did not like Vale, too?' pounced Michael, too astute not to notice the careful wording of his friend's capitulation.

Bartholomew hesitated, but supposed Michael had a right to know his opinion of the man whose death he was going to explore. 'I thought him unsuited to our profession. He lacked tact, and he behaved inappropriately with female patients.'

'Did he?' Michael was intrigued. 'I know Edith said he

made a nuisance of himself with her seamstresses, while Jorz claimed he laughed at an embarrassing ailment.'

'He was more interested in devising a cure-all than in his patients,' Bartholomew went on. 'It meant he did not take the time to listen to their symptoms before prescribing a solution, and he sometimes made mistakes. He was not a very good physician.'

'Well, we shall bear his failings in mind as we investigate. Of course, I still have Coslaye to consider, too. I promised to catch the villain who nearly killed him.'

'I imagine that was an accident – the tome was thrown more in frustration than a serious attempt to wound. Besides, it was weeks ago. Any trail will be cold by now.'

'It was cold before I started, or the villain would have been arrested already. However, a crime is a crime, and I am unwilling to forget that one. I do not want scholars thinking that St Mary the Great is a good venue for lobbing missiles at colleagues who make contentious remarks.'

'It is fortunate that Coslaye has an unusually thick skull, or the blow would have killed him outright. Even so, I was afraid that he would not survive the surgery. He was very lucky.'

'The collision damaged the book, too,' recalled Michael. 'Acton's *Questio Disputata*. Not a great treatise, but respectable enough. I gave it to him once he was up and walking again, as compensation for all his suffering.'

'Did you?' asked Bartholomew, thinking this a little insensitive.

'I thought he could sell it for— Oh, Lord! Here comes Cynric, and he wears the expression that tells me something terrible has happened. Again.'

'You are both needed at King's Hall,' announced Cynric. 'Master Sawtre has had an accident.'

'What sort of accident?' asked Michael warily.

'Apparently,' replied Cynric, 'he has been crushed under a bookcase.'

It was not far along the High Street to King's Hall, Cambridge's largest, richest and most prestigious College. It enjoyed the patronage of the King himself, and the sons of nobles were sent to it for their education. It was an impressive foundation, with a great gatehouse and powerful walls that would protect it from all but the most determined attacks – and as its ostentatious affluence was infuriating to many townsfolk, defence was a necessity. Behind the gate were several handsome accommodation blocks, an assortment of houses and a large hall for teaching.

A porter conducted Bartholomew and Michael to the building that housed the College's collection of books. Somewhat unusually, King's Hall had elected to store them in purpose-built, ceiling-high racks – most University foundations preferred their shelving to be nearer the ground for ease of access. The racks were heavy, especially when filled, and one had toppled forward, shooting its contents across the floor. All that could be seen of the man underneath was a hand. Bartholomew knelt quickly and felt for a life-beat, but the wrist was cold and dead.

At least twenty King's Hall Fellows had gathered around the corpse in a mute semicircle. In the middle was their Warden, a timid, retiring gentleman, who struggled to control the large number of arrogant, wealthy young men under his supervision. Walkelate was there, too, tearful and frightened, and Bartholomew recalled that the architect and Sawtre were the only two members of King's Hall who had voted in favour of the Common Library. He felt a twinge of unease, recalling what Deynman had said about dissenters being eliminated.

'We could see that there was no need to pull Sawtre out quickly,' said Warden Shropham, breaking into his troubled thoughts. 'So we left everything as we found it, for you to . . .'

He trailed off, clearly distressed, and a brash scholar named Geoffrey Dodenho, whose academic prowess was nowhere near as great as he thought it was, came to rest a kindly hand on his shoulder.

'Sawtre was dusting the shelves,' Dodenho explained. 'Which was his particular responsibility. We heard a crash, and rushed in to see the bookcase had torn away from its moorings.'

He pointed, and Bartholomew and Michael both looked upwards. There were six sizeable holes in the wall, and when they glanced back to the bookcase, it was to see six corresponding nails jutting out from the back of it.

'He must have tugged on it, reaching for the top shelf,' said Walkelate, pale and shaking. 'The floor is not very level, you see, and there was always a danger that this particular unit might topple.'

'Then why did you not do something about it?' asked Michael, prodding the floorboards with his toe. They were indeed uneven.

'We were going to,' said Shropham wretchedly. 'At the end of term, when our students have finished their disputations. Mending it will be noisy, and we wanted to avoid needless disturbance at such a stressful time.'

A number of Fellows stepped forward to lift the rack, eager to play their part for a fallen comrade. It was extremely weighty, and required every one of them. Once it was upright, Bartholomew began removing the books that covered Sawtre's body, picking them up carefully and handing them to Dodenho, who piled them neatly and lovingly to one side.

Despite the fact that his mind should have been on the duties for which he was being paid, the physician noticed that King's Hall had some unusual and beautiful volumes, including several on medicine that he had never read. He wondered if Shropham would grant him access to them, but then thought that he might not have to ask if the Common Library lived up to expectations.

'I wonder if it is divine justice,' mused Dodenho, brushing dust from Dante's *Inferno*. 'Sawtre voted inappropriately at the Convocation, and now he is dead in the very library he wronged.'

'He did not wrong this library,' objected Walkelate. He sounded dispirited: like Bartholomew, he was tired of repeating himself to colleagues who were so vehemently and immovably opposed to his point of view. 'He supported the founding of a central repository because he felt poor scholars deserve access to books, too.'

'You would say that,' muttered Dodenho. 'You voted with him – against our Warden's orders.'

'Actually, I told everyone to act as his conscience dictated,' said Shropham quietly.

'Quite,' said Dodenho. '*My* conscience would never let me do anything to harm King's Hall.'

Other Fellows joined the discussion, but Bartholomew was not listening – he had finally moved enough books to allow him to examine the body. He was vaguely aware of the debate growing acrimonious, and of Michael standing silently to one side, drawing his own conclusions from who said what, but his own attention was on Sawtre.

'He was crushed,' he said, eventually finishing his examination and standing up. Immediately, the squabbling stopped and the men of King's Hall eased closer to hear his verdict. 'The bookcase landed squarely on his chest, and its weight snapped the ribs beneath. These pierced his lungs. I imagine death came very quickly.'

'Thank God for small mercies,' said Shropham, crossing himself.

Walkelate began to sob, so Dodenho put an arm around his shoulders and led him away, leaving the remaining Fellows to discuss what had happened in shocked whispers.

'Was it a mishap, Matt?' asked Michael in a low voice. 'Or did one of Sawtre's "grieving" colleagues arrange an accident in order to punish him for dissenting?'

'They seem genuinely distressed to me,' replied Bartholomew. 'And there is nothing on the body to suggest foul play – no sign that Sawtre was forced to stand under the case while it was toppled, or that he was incapacitated while the deed was done.'

'Very well,' said Michael with a sigh. 'But he makes five Regents dead who voted in favour of the Common Library. If we held a second ballot now, the grace would be repealed.'

'Then it is just as well a second ballot is not in the offing,' said Bartholomew shortly. 'Newe Inn is almost ready, and there would be a riot if you abandoned the project at this late hour.'

'I have a bad feeling we shall have one of those anyway. Its more rabid detractors will not let the opening ceremonies pass off without incident.'

There was no more to be done at King's Hall, so Bartholomew wrapped Sawtre's body, ready to be carried to the church, and followed Michael towards the gate. Shropham accompanied them.

'I know how this looks,' he said, when there was no one to overhear. 'Sawtre went against his colleagues, and now he is dead. However, it was an accident.'

'Probably,' agreed Michael. 'Yet you cannot deny that there was ill feeling among the Fellowship towards him. And despite what you said in the library, I am sure you must have made it perfectly clear how you wanted them all to vote.'

'I did nothing of the kind,' said Shropham tiredly. 'I am not a despot. I instructed every man to act as he thought appropriate. I imagine you did the same at Michaelhouse.'

'Actually, I told my colleagues to oppose the grace with every fibre of their being,' replied Michael. He glanced coolly at Bartholomew. 'But not all of them obeyed.'

'It must be awkward for Walkelate here,' said Bartholomew, pitying the kindly architect for the uncomfortable position he occupied, especially now he had lost Sawtre's support. 'He not only voted for the library, but he is the one fitting it out.'

Shropham sighed. 'Well, if we must have the wretched place, it is only right that the University's best architect should design it. Walkelate produced a book-depository for the King, you know, in Westminster.'

'Did he?' Bartholomew was impressed. 'Are there many books in the royal collections?'

Shropham gave one of his sad smiles. 'None that will interest you, Matthew. They nearly all pertain to law and property.'

'Oh,' said Bartholomew. 'So how did Walkelate come to be chosen for such a task?'

'Because his father is the King's sergeant-at-arms,' explained Shropham. 'So Walkelate is known at Court, and the Lord Chancellor is a great admirer of his work.'

'You mean his father is a soldier?' asked Bartholomew.

Michael shot him a patronising look. 'It is an honorific post, Matt. They see to ceremonials and the like. It has nothing to do with warfare.'

'Although Walkelate did receive knightly training in his youth,' added Shropham. 'But like most of us, that was rather a long time ago.'

Once out of King's Hall, Bartholomew and Michael resumed their walk to St Mary the Great, and it was not long before they reached its bright splendour. Sunlight filtered through its stained-glass windows, casting bright flecks of colour on the stone floor, and there was a pleasant aroma of incense and from the greenery that bedecked its windowsills.

The four bodies had been placed in the Lady Chapel, where they lay in a line on the floor, each covered with a blanket. Water had seeped from them during the night, leaving puddles. Michael watched Bartholomew remove the cover from the first victim, but promptly disappeared on business of his own when the physician began his examination by prising open the corpse's mouth. As Senior Proctor, he had an office in one of the aisles – larger and better furnished than the one occupied by the Chancellor, as befitted his status as the University's most powerful scholar – and it was a far nicer place to be than watching his Corpse Examiner at work.

Bartholomew had started with Vale, because he happened to be the nearest. Deftly, he removed his colleague's clothes, so he could look for injuries or suspicious marks, but there was only one: the puncture wound between his shoulder blades. The arrow's shaft had been snipped off to facilitate transport the previous day, but its head was still in place, and he was surprised by how easy it was to remove. Puzzled, he took a probe and inserted it into the hole. The laceration was shallow, and unlikely to have been fatal.

He turned Vale on to his back, and pushed on his chest

– if froth bubbled from the nose and mouth, it meant water had mixed with air in the lungs. In other words, the victim had drowned. But what seeped from Vale was clear, and there was not a bubble in sight. He began a more systematic examination, looking for evidence of disease or other injuries. There was an ancient scar on Vale's knee, but nothing else was apparent.

Trying not to let his bafflement influence him, he moved to the next corpse, which was the older of the two London brothers. Again, there was no evidence of drowning. The younger sibling yielded an equally curious lack of symptoms, and so did Northwood.

When he had done all he could, Bartholomew replaced their clothes, then sat back on his heels and stared at the corpses in confusion. How had they died? Could they have swallowed poison? But then how had they all ended up in Newe Inn's pond?

Absently, he took a knife from his bag, wondering whether anyone would notice if he made a small incision to inspect the inside of one of the victims' stomachs. He had never done such a thing before, but he had witnessed a dissection in Salerno where a case of poisoning had been discovered by a mass of ulcers in the innards. There had been no external symptoms, and the killer might have escaped justice had it not been for the skill of the anatomist.

But defiling the dead was frowned upon in England, although Bartholomew considered it a foolish restriction, because much could be learned from cadavers. Without conscious thought, the knife in his hand descended towards Vale's middle.

'What are you doing?' came an incredulous voice behind him.

Bartholomew leapt to his feet and spun around to find

100

himself facing Dunning and Julitta. Dunning's aristocratic face was pale with horror, although Julitta seemed composed.

'Examining these bodies,' he replied, aware that his voice was far from steady. It was partly because Dunning's loud question had made him jump, but mostly because he had been a hair's breadth from doing something recklessly grisly. He was horrified with himself, not for almost giving in to the urge to delve into the forbidden art of anatomy, but for coming so close to doing it in St Mary the Great.

'With a knife?' demanded Dunning sceptically.

'If he is to conduct a thorough examination, he must remove their clothes, Father,' said Julitta reasonably. 'Obviously, the blade is to deal with stubborn laces.'

'What is wrong with untying them?' asked Dunning, still unconvinced.

'They have been immersed in water,' explained Julitta patiently. 'And water causes knots to tighten. You know this.'

Bartholomew stared at her, noting the way her fine kirtle hugged the slim lines of her body and her hair caught the sunlight from the windows. When she smiled at him, he found himself thinking that Surgeon Holm was a very lucky man.

'Well, it looked to me as though he was going to take a lump out of Vale,' Dunning was saying, disgust vying for precedence with horror in his voice. 'There are tales that say he is in league with the Devil, and I know such men need bits of corpses for their diabolical spells.'

'Doctor Bartholomew is not a sorcerer,' said Julitta firmly, while Bartholomew continued to gaze gratefully at her. 'That is a silly story put about by the likes of my brother-in-law. I am fond of Weasenham, but he really is the most dreadful gossip.'

'He is,' conceded Dunning. 'But he was a good match for Ruth, so I am not complaining.' He turned back to Bartholomew. 'So have you learned anything from these hapless corpses yet? They died in the property I have donated to your University, so I have a right to ask.'

'Yes, you do,' said Michael, who had heard voices and had come to investigate. 'And you shall have a full account as soon as my Corpse Examiner has written his official report. Would you like me to bring it to your house later? Perhaps close to the time your dinner is served?'

Julitta's eyes widened at the brazen hint, and she smothered a smile. 'You are welcome to dine with us, Brother,' she said graciously. 'And Doctor Bartholomew must come, too, lest we have any technical questions.'

'But I want to know what he has surmised now,' objected her father.

'Of course you do, but he has not finished yet,' said Julitta. 'And we must visit the Market Square, to ask the baker to increase the amount of bread we dispense to the poor. Summer might be here at last, but the crops are still far from ripe, and they need our charity more than ever now their winter supplies are exhausted.'

'You are lucky Julitta has a quick brain and an eye for a pretty face,' said Michael, once she and Dunning had gone. His green eyes were wide with shock. 'I saw exactly what you were going to do with that knife. No, do not deny it, Matt! It was obvious. What in God's name were you thinking?'

Bartholomew rubbed a hand over his eyes. 'I was not thinking, Brother. I do not feel well, and my wits are like mud this morning.'

'Why?' demanded Michael. 'Did those men hurt you when they attacked last night?'

'No – I swallowed too much of Newe Inn's pond. It is not healthy to drink water that contains corpses. In fact, it is not healthy to drink water at all, unless it has been thoroughly boiled and—'

'None of your wild theories today, please,' interrupted Michael, still angry. 'However, I would like to know what you have learned about our victims.'

Bartholomew shrugged. 'There are no injuries – the arrow wound in Vale is superficial – and they were not suffering from any obvious diseases or ailments.'

'They drowned, then. They fell or were pushed into the pond.'

'They did not drown. The only other thing I can think of is poison, which was why I . . .' Bartholomew waved the hand that still held the knife.

Michael looked away quickly. 'Surely, there is a better way to find out than dissection?'

'Not that I am aware: there is nothing in their mouths to suggest they swallowed a toxin, and no marks on their hands. However, they may have ingested something that damaged their stomachs or lungs, but that will only be determined by an internal examination.'

'No,' said Michael firmly. 'There will be no anatomising in my jurisdiction.'

'Then I can tell you no more, Brother. Externally, there is nothing to suggest anything other than natural deaths.'

'All four of them? At the same time? I do not think so!'

'And they did all die at roughly the same time.' Bartholomew turned to stare at the bodies again. 'Clippesby saw them entering Newe Inn's grounds together on Tuesday night, and Browne found them dead on Wednesday morning.'

Michael rubbed his chin, fingers rasping on the bristles. 'What about communal suicide?'

'Four men agreeing to take their own lives simultaneously would have had a very strong reason for doing so, and that reason is likely to have been explained in a note or a message left with friends. There was no such missive, or you would have mentioned it. Moreover, your theory does not explain why Vale was shot.'

'The arrow,' pounced Michael. 'Perhaps they were forced to jump into the pond.'

'Then they would have drowned, which they did not. However, you are right in that it means someone else was there when they died – someone who put their corpses in the water. And Clippesby saw them enter the garden with one or two other people . . .'

'And other people, at least one of whom was armed with a bow, means murder.'

Bartholomew nodded. 'But I am afraid you will have to ask the culprits how they dispatched their victims, because your Corpse Examiner cannot do it.'

'I shall,' determined Michael. 'Your point about a message left with friends is an interesting concept, though. We shall spend the rest of the morning questioning those who knew them best.'

'You did not do that last night after leaving Weasenham?'

'No – I was busy quelling a fight between Bene't College and Essex Hostel over the Common Library. So first we shall visit Weasenham's shop, to ask about the London brothers. Then Gonville Hall to enquire after Vale. And finally the Carmelite Friary regarding Northwood.'

Bartholomew fell into step at his side, and they walked along the High Street to the stationer's premises. It was full of activity as usual, crammed with scholars and clerks, some trying to read the exemplars without paying for them, some passing the time of day with friends, and others queuing up to be served. Weasenham was with a customer, so Bartholomew and Michael were obliged to wait. While they did so, the monk took a leaf out of Weasenham's book, and began to gossip.

'Our stationer did well when he married Ruth Dunning.'

'Did he?' Bartholomew was more interested in Weasenham's wares, wishing he had funds to spare. He needed more parchment for the treatise on fevers he was writing, and he was running low on ink, too. Unfortunately, any money he earned was needed to buy medicine for those of his patients who could not afford it themselves, and luxuries like writing equipment were currently beyond his means.

'Oh, yes. Dunning will invest handsomely in the business now, which will allow Weasenham to expand. In fact, I think he already has, because look at the number of books that are on sale today. He never had that many in the past. He even has Augustine's *De Trinitate*!'

'And Dioscorides's *De Materia Medica*.' Bartholomew was impressed. 'I have not seen that in its entirety for years. Perhaps this copy is destined for the Common Library, and I shall be able to read it. Or maybe Holm will give me five marks, so I can buy it for myself.'

'Five marks? Why would he give you such an enormous sum?'

'When he learns that Isnard and the riverfolk are not killers and smugglers,' replied Bartholomew. He shrugged when he saw Michael's mystified expression. 'He irritated me into agreeing a wager.'

'But you do not have five marks!' cried Michael. 'And you will certainly need it, because Isnard is a scoundrel, and you are a fool if you think him untarnished. And as for the riverfolk . . .'

'Yes, but they do not kill,' insisted Bartholomew. 'And

I do not believe they are connected with the smugglers Dick Tulyet is hunting, either.'

'We had better speak to Weasenham,' said Michael, declining to argue. 'He is still busy, but I cannot wait here all day. Who knows what else you may do or say to shock me in the interim?'

Weasenham was at the front of his shop, standing behind a table as he demonstrated to a group of fascinated scribes why quills made from swan feathers were better than those from geese. His audience comprised mostly friars who worked in the Carmelites' scriptorium, and included Riborowe and Jorz. He was being assisted by his wife and his Exemplarius.

'Two birds with one stone,' whispered Bartholomew to Michael. 'You can quiz the White Friars about Northwood at the same time.'

'No – it is better to tackle them separately. Look at Jorz's hands! Are they stained with blood? We had better loiter behind these shelves for a while. We could learn a lot by eavesdropping.'

'. . . did not succeed,' Jorz was twittering to Weasenham. 'I tried adding red lead, to see if that would help, but the ink took just as long to dry. How goes your paper-making?'

'We have done nothing since we heard that John and Philip London . . .' Bonabes swallowed hard. 'We shall start experimenting again after their funerals.'

The birdlike Jorz crossed himself. 'Perhaps we should suspend our work until after our brother Northwood is buried, as a mark of respect. What do you think, Riborowe?'

'Why?' asked Riborowe. 'He voted against our Prior's orders in the matter of the Common Library, and I have still not forgiven him for it.'

'Have you heard the news?' asked Weasenham in a conspiratorial voice, while the other Carmelites gaped their shock at Riborowe's unfeeling remark. 'About the murder of Sawtre in King's Hall? Someone pushed a heavy bookcase on top of him, and—'

'Warden Shropham said it was an accident,' interrupted Bonabes. 'He stated quite firmly that Sawtre tugged on a piece of furniture that was notoriously unstable.'

'Well, he would,' said Weasenham maliciously. 'But I know better. Sawtre was killed because he voted against his College. King's Hall does not take kindly to treachery.'

'That is untrue!' cried Ruth. 'Sawtre was—'

'Tell me what you know about the Newe Inn murders,' said Weasenham, cutting across her to address the Carmelites, all of whom were regarding him with contempt. They exchanged pained glances at the mention of the place where one of their brethren had died.

'We know nothing at all,' replied Jorz. 'A beadle came last night to report Northwood's death, but he was unable to tell us how or why it had happened. And since then, Prior Etone has kept us too busy saying masses for Northwood's soul to ask questions.'

'And busy making ink, apparently,' muttered Bartholomew. Michael jabbed him with his elbow, warning him to be quiet.

'Does Northwood's soul need prayers, then?' fished Weasenham. 'I imagine it does – I have heard tales about him.'

Michael grabbed Bartholomew's arm as the physician began to step forward, unwilling to stand by while a man he had liked was maligned.

'Northwood was a hard taskmaster to the novices under his care,' Jorz was saying icily, while behind his back several of the younger friars exchanged glances that indicated this was an understatement. 'But he was honest and fair. There will be no "tales" about him.'

'Oh, yes, there will,' said Weasenham smugly. 'Because he was a thief.'

Michael's grip intensified when Bartholomew started forward a second time. 'Wait!' he hissed. 'Thelnetham said much the same, and I want to hear what Weasenham has to say.'

'Husband, please,' begged Ruth. 'Northwood is dead, and it is not nice to speak ill of him.'

'I speak as I find,' snapped Weasenham, displeased by the admonition. 'There is a ridiculous tendency in this town to think that anyone who dies before his time was a saint. Well, Northwood did some very devious things, and the fact that he suffered a premature end does not change that.'

'And what did he do, exactly?' asked Jorz, frost in his voice.

Well,' began Weasenham, delighted to be asked, 'it involves the exemplars your novices prepare in the scriptorium.'

'The Carmelites do not produce exemplars,' whispered Michael to Bartholomew, bemused. 'They create beautiful works of art – bibles, prayer books and psalters.'

'Exercise pieces.' Riborowe's expression was as puzzled as Michael's. 'To allow them to hone their skills. It was my idea: I remember from my own noviciate how disheartening it was to produce texts that no one ever looked at, so I decided that they should copy parts of great theological works instead. Then we can sell them to you, and the money covers the cost of the materials they use, with a little left over for the poor. But why do you—'

'They produced two last week,' interrupted Weasenham. 'And I paid for both. However, when I mentioned the matter to Prior Etone, it became clear that Northwood had only handed him the cash for one of them. He had kept the rest for himself.'

'No,' said Jorz firmly. 'You are mistaken. Northwood would not have done that.'

'He told us that the work on one of the exemplars was substandard,' said Riborowe, 'and thus unfit to be sold. He only brought the better copy here . . .'

'No, he brought two, and the work on both was excellent,' gloated Weasenham. 'I can show you if you like. Fetch them, Bonabes.'

'No,' said Jorz stiffly. 'We do not want to see. Come, brothers. We are finished here.'

The door closed after them with a resounding crack.

'There will be an explanation for what Northwood is accused of doing,' said Bartholomew to Michael, refusing to believe ill of the man. 'Weasenham has a nasty way of twisting even the most innocuous of incidents. He is a malign force, and I wish the University would oust him.'

'Unfortunately, we need more than a penchant for intrigue to deprive him of his livelihood. Rumour-mongering is despicable, but not illegal, no matter what you think of it.'

Weasenham's sly face became eager when he saw Michael and Bartholomew, anticipating that they would supply him with more information to fuel his scurrilous tongue. Next to him, Ruth hung her head, while Bonabes grimaced.

'I suppose you are here to provide details about the London brothers,' Weasenham said. 'Good. I am distressed by their demise, and demand to know what happened to them.'

'I am sure you do,' said Michael flatly. 'But I need information before I can furnish you with answers. What can you tell me about them?'

Weasenham looked disappointed, but began to oblige, always ready to talk about someone else. 'They worked with me for years, and we rubbed along nicely together. I shall miss them, although not nearly as much as Adam. He was cheap, whereas I was obliged to pay them a decent wage.'

'Is there anything else?' asked Michael, unimpressed. 'Or is that it?'

'Well, they were sanctimonious,' Weasenham went on. 'They told me I was a gossip, which was unfair. All I do is share information with friends. Where lies the harm in that?'

'They had no family, other than each other, and they lived in the house next door,' supplied Bonabes, rather more practically. 'They were polite and kind, but tended to keep to themselves.'

'Did they know Northwood or Vale?' asked Bartholomew.

It was Ruth who answered. 'Yes, they often met Northwood when he came to purchase supplies for the Carmelite Priory, and they occasionally enjoyed a drink together in the Brazen George. Northwood liked to tell them his alchemical theories, and they liked to listen.'

'Did they understand them?' asked Michael doubtfully. 'Northwood devised some very lofty hypotheses, most of which left me bemused. And I am as razor-witted as any man.'

'Because they were interested, he took the time to explain,' replied Ruth. 'Besides, they were scholars themselves – members of Batayl Hostel, albeit non-residential ones.'

'Philosophers by training,' elaborated Bonabes. 'They stepped in to teach the trivium when Coslaye was injured. Master Browne said they were invaluable during that difficult time.'

'And they died in the property that adjoins that

110

particular foundation,' mused Michael. 'I must make time to visit Batayl and ask a few questions.'

'The brothers and Northwood were often in each other's company,' added Weasenham eager not to be left out of the discussion. 'In fact, I would say he was their only friend. As Bonabes said, they kept to themselves.'

'What about Vale?' asked Bartholomew. 'Did they know him?'

Ruth looked away, and her eyes filled with tears. 'Yes. They were his patients, as were we.'

'We asked him to be our *medicus* the moment he arrived,' elaborated Weasenham. 'We had been with Doctor Rougham, but he is expensive these days. Not to mention arrogant.'

'Why Vale?' asked Michael. 'Why not Gyseburne or Meryfeld?'

'Because Gyseburne's interest in urine is unsavoury, and Meryfeld is never clean,' replied Weasenham. He shot Bartholomew an arch glance. 'And we would never agree to be treated by him, because he is a warlock. The whole town knows it, and while he might well save more lives than the other physicians, I do not like the notion of him summoning the Devil on my behalf.'

'The story about Doctor Bartholomew's pact with Satan is a stupid rumour concocted by the ignorant,' said Ruth spiritedly. Bartholomew regarded her with surprise, unused to people coming to his defence. He wondered whether she had been conferring with her sister about him.

'Were Philip and John London in low spirits?' asked Michael, changing the subject before Weasenham could argue. 'Or did they ever discuss taking their own lives?'

'No,' said Ruth, shocked. 'They were perfectly content.'

'And excited about making paper,' added Weasenham. 'You do not commit self-murder if you have an enthralling project to hand. You are wrong if you think they were suicidal, Brother.'

'Everyone is experimenting these days,' mused Ruth. 'The Londons with paper, the White Friars with ink, Vale with his cure-all, the medical men with lamp fuel . . .'

Absently, Bartholomew imagined what her list might sound like to outside ears. People would assume that Cambridge was full of mad intellectuals, all busily hurling ingredients into cauldrons as they pursued their lunatic theories.

'Yes – that deputation of scholars from Oxford back in January has a lot to answer for,' muttered Weasenham unpleasantly. 'We were more interested in reading books than in conducting experiments before they came along with the smug implication that they were better than us because of their scientific discoveries.'

Michael asked several more questions, but neither Bonabes nor Ruth could add anything more of interest, and Weasenham's opinions were unreliable, so he and Bartholomew took their leave.

'As we are here, we should look in the London brothers' home,' said Michael. 'They have no next-of-kin to object to a search, and my beadle obtained the key last night.'

They walked to the cottage next door. It had been given an attractive wash of pale yellow, and was well maintained. Michael unlocked the door, and stepped inside. He gave a squawk of alarm when a shadow flitted across the room, and Bartholomew fumbled for his childbirth forceps. But then the figure stepped into the light, and both recognised it instantly. Bartholomew's heart sank.

It was Michael's formidable grandmother, Dame Pelagia. And if she was in Cambridge, then there was trouble afoot for certain.

CHAPTER 4

'Grandmother!' exclaimed Michael, shoving past Bartholomew and going to take the old lady's hands in his own. There was genuine delight in his voice.

Dame Pelagia was tiny, with a wrinkled face and white hair that was tucked decorously under a matronly wimple. She had unfathomable eyes that twinkled like shiny buttons, and an enigmatic smile. At a glance, she was an elderly gentlewoman, but appearances could be deceptive, and Bartholomew knew for a fact that she had spent the greater part of her life spying for the various monarchs through whose reigns she had lived. She was also ruthlessly skilled with knives.

'It was you who saved me last night,' he said in sudden understanding. 'When those men cornered me.'

Pelagia inclined her head. 'I thought you might appreciate a little help.'

'Did you know them?' asked Michael, surprised.

'Unfortunately not, but dead men keep their secrets, so I took care only to maim them. They will be easy to identify from their limps, and then they can be arrested and questioned properly.'

'Why are you here?' asked Michael. 'I am pleased to see you, of course, but I thought you had gone to southern France, to live in quiet retirement in a place where the sun shines every day.'

'Paradise can be tedious,' replied Pelagia. Bartholomew had no idea whether she was making a joke. 'Besides,

113

France is not very friendly to the English at the moment. Not after Poitiers.'

Bartholomew regarded her sharply. 'Do not tell me you were there? At the battle?'

Pelagia favoured him with one of her impenetrable smiles. 'I may have been in the vicinity.'

'Lord!' muttered Bartholomew, staggered but not entirely surprised.

'You have not answered my question,' said Michael. 'Why are you *here*?'

Pelagia reached up to pat his plump cheek with a wizened hand. 'Can I not visit my favourite grandson without an inquisition? Besides, I am to celebrate living three score years and ten next week, and there is no one in the world with whom I would rather mark the occasion.'

'I see,' said Michael. 'However, that still does not explain what you are doing in the home of two men who died in mysterious circumstances. How did you get in?'

'The door was open.' Bartholomew and Michael both knew it had been locked, but neither liked to contradict her. 'And I heard that this cottage might be sold soon, given that its owners are dead. I have a mind to settle in this little town of yours, so I decided to inspect it.'

'But it is dark in here,' said Michael. 'Why not open the window shutters? Or light a lamp?'

'Because I have only just arrived,' explained Pelagia evenly. 'But you may kindle one now, and we shall explore the place together. Then you can decide whether you think it is suitable for me.'

She gestured imperiously that Bartholomew was to oblige with the lantern, then held out her arm for Michael to escort her to a bench. She leaned heavily on him, although Bartholomew could tell by the way she moved

114

that it was a pretence of frailty, and that she was probably as fit as her grandson, and almost certainly a good deal more agile.

The lamp illuminated a pleasantly furnished chamber with a sizeable hearth at its far end, and while Michael and Pelagia discussed family affairs, Bartholomew prowled, looking for something that might tell him why two respectable scribes should have died in an abandoned pond. Several books on alchemy lay on a table, and when he opened one he saw it had been heavily annotated. Some of the scribbles were in Northwood's distinctively untidy hand, but others were neat, and he suspected they were the work of either Philip or John.

He conducted as thorough a search as he could, tapping floorboards, peering up the chimney and running his fingers along the backs of shelves, but found nothing of relevance. However, as he finished, it occurred to him that Pelagia had not offered to help – and he was sure it was not because she trusted his investigative skills. He could only suppose that she had already ascertained that there was nothing to find. Unless there had been something, and she had removed it, of course.

He shook his head in response to Michael's questioning gaze, but Dame Pelagia said nothing, and he glanced warily at her. Could *she* have been responsible for the Newe Inn deaths? He knew she had taken lives before, and that she had done so without leaving a shred of evidence, but why would she want to dispatch two scribes, a Carmelite and a physician? He decided to ask her some questions, although he suspected he would be wasting his breath; Pelagia was not a woman who willingly shared information, or who incriminated herself with such replies as she did choose to give.

'The men who attacked me last night wanted to know

the formula for a certain substance,' he began, staring hard in an effort to read her. It was futile, of course. 'Do you think the same villains might have killed Northwood, the London brothers and Vale?'

'That is a wild leap of logic!' exclaimed Michael, startled. 'Why would—'

'Hooded cloaks,' explained Bartholomew tersely. 'I know that virtually everyone in Cambridge owns one, but it is summer, and most people have packed them away. However, Clippesby told me that Northwood and the others wore them when they met. So did the men who ambushed me last night.'

'It is a slender connection,' said Pelagia, rather contemptuously. 'I doubt that line of enquiry will take you very far. But what formula did they want from you? A recipe for a new medicine?'

'It was meant to be lamp fuel,' explained Bartholomew. 'But instead, my medical colleagues and I discovered something that is highly flammable and difficult to douse once it is alight.'

'Wildfire,' mused Pelagia. 'It has been around for centuries in various forms. But it is a nasty form of warfare, and you should have been more careful in your experiments, Matthew.'

'Yes,' agreed Bartholomew, chagrined. 'Unfortunately, the incident was witnessed by Sheriff Tulyet's talkative young son, and the other physicians have also spread the tale. *Ergo*, a lot of people know what we did, so I cannot be sure whether my attackers were local or strangers . . .'

'They all should have kept their mouths shut,' said Pelagia, and Bartholomew flinched at the sharp censure in her voice. 'It is not something that should have been bandied about. We are at war, you know, and we cannot have that sort of secret falling into the hands of the French.'

116

'Luckily, the *medici* were too drunk to recall what they did, so the recipe is lost,' said Michael quickly. 'Last night's villains will never learn anything deadly from them.'

'Is that so?' Pelagia regarded Bartholomew icily, causing him to understand exactly why she had been feared by so many enemies of the English crown. 'You had better take care the next time you are out after dark, because a secret of that magnitude will certainly warrant these rogues trying to get it again. It will be worth a lot of money.'

She stood and made for the door, moving with a sprightliness that belied her years. Once outside, she nodded a farewell to her grandson and turned towards Bridge Street. A cart blocked her from sight momentarily, and when it had passed, she was nowhere to be seen. Bartholomew realised that he had been holding his breath, uncomfortable as always in such a ruthlessly formidable presence.

'Do you think the next attack on me will come from her?' he asked, following Michael out of the house and watching him secure the door behind them. 'She is not very pleased.'

'No, she is not,' agreed Michael. 'And I do not blame her. What you did with your colleagues last winter was recklessly dangerous.'

'Did she tell you why she is really here?' asked Bartholomew, declining to dwell on it. 'Because it will not be to celebrate her birthday with you.'

'Not her seventieth, anyway,' said Michael. 'She passed that some years ago. All I can say is that if it is serious enough to warrant leaving her comfortable retirement, then it must be serious indeed. And it will involve some very powerful adversaries.'

*　*　*

There was more than enough time to visit Gonville Hall and the Carmelite Priory before they joined Dunning for dinner, so they retraced their steps along the High Street. Gonville was another wealthy foundation, and was in the process of building itself a chapel. Progress was slow, and although it had walls and a roof, it was still a long way from completion. Rougham chafed at the delay, because he had designed some stained-glass windows that he was eager to see installed, one of which depicted him in his physician's robes.

They were conducted across a yard to the hall, where the Fellows were teaching. Bartholomew listened for a moment, unimpressed by the standard of the arguments in the mock-disputation that was under way. He sincerely hoped Rougham's students would put on a better show when they took their final examinations, because otherwise they would fail.

After a while, Rougham became aware of the visitors, and came to greet them. The other Fellows started to follow, but Rougham, as Acting Master, waved them away.

'I shall deal with this,' he announced. 'The rest of you can continue teaching. My students have just set the standard for which you must aim, and if yours are not as good as mine in a week, there will be trouble.'

Bartholomew felt his jaw drop, but snapped it closed when Michael elbowed him. The monk was right: Rougham was easily offended, and would not cooperate with their investigation if they fell out with him.

'You look terrible, Bartholomew,' Rougham said, peering at his colleague in concern. 'Have you come to me for a remedy? Shall I whip you up a syrup of snail juice and frogs' blood?'

'No, thank you,' said Bartholomew hastily.

'He toppled into Newe Inn's pond yesterday, trying to retrieve Vale and the others,' explained Michael. 'And inhaling corpse water is evidently not recommended for good health.'

'Try drinking a quart of strong claret mixed with half a pound of salt, six raw eggs and a couple of bulbs of garlic,' advised Rougham. 'That should purge any cadaver-poisons from your system.'

Bartholomew felt sick just thinking about it.

'I am deeply sorry about Vale,' began Michael, after Rougham had escorted them out of the hall and into a comfortable solar, where they could speak without being disturbed.

'So am I,' said Rougham. 'It was pleasant, having a fellow *medicus* with whom to converse. We did not always see eye to eye, but he was a stimulating companion, and I shall miss him.'

'Do you know why he was in Newe Inn with the Londons and Northwood?' Michael asked.

'I do not,' replied Rougham. 'However, he was too superior a man to have dabbled in low company freely, so I can only assume that they seduced him there under false pretences.'

'Northwood was not low company,' objected Bartholomew. 'He was an excellent scholar.'

'Perhaps so, but he bullied the novice scribes in his scriptorium, and he was unpleasantly fanatical about his alchemy,' replied Rougham. 'He was not the genial philosopher-friar he liked everyone to see. He was ambitious and ruthless, and I think he led Vale astray.'

'How?' asked Michael, before Bartholomew could take issue with the remark.

Rougham scowled. 'I strongly suspect he was working on lamp fuel.'

'Lamp fuel?' asked Bartholomew. 'You mean he was in competition with us?'

'Yes!' growled Rougham. 'And whoever discovers a compound that emits clear, bright, steady light will be wealthy beyond his wildest dreams. When Northwood had wind of our experiments, he asked to join us, but Holm and I refused. He was livid, so I suspect he decided to conduct tests of his own, enlisting the London brothers to help.'

'And Vale?' asked Michael. 'Did he enlist Vale, too?'

Rougham pursed his lips. 'Vale would not have joined forces with him willingly.'

'What are you saying?' asked Michael. 'That the other three coerced him?'

For a moment, it seemed Rougham would not reply, but then he said, 'Vale had a lady friend, and liked to frolic with her on occasion. Northwood saw him once, and threatened to tell.'

'Northwood was blackmailing him?' asked Bartholomew doubtfully. 'I do not believe it!'

'That is your prerogative,' said Rougham pompously. 'However, Vale told me himself.'

'Why would he do that?' asked Bartholomew sceptically, thinking that Vale had not been a man to confess to shortcomings, especially to someone like Rougham, who would be judgemental.

'It happened after the Convocation of Regents where we voted on the Common Library. You see, I specifically told all my Fellows to oppose the grace, and was outraged when Vale disobeyed. I demanded an explanation, and that was the one he gave – that Northwood had forced him to support it. It is not such great leap of logic to assume that Northwood bullied him into other things, too.'

'Blackmail is a serious allegation to make against a senior member of the Carmelite Order,' said Michael warningly.

Rougham nodded. 'Yes, but it is true, nonetheless.'

'Was Vale sufficiently distressed about the situation to harm himself?' asked Michael.

Rougham released a sharp bark of laughter. 'Vale? Do not be ridiculous! He considered himself far too indispensable to consider anything of that nature.'

It was not a pleasant remark to make about a colleague, but Bartholomew was inclined to concur. Vale had held a highly inflated opinion of himself.

'What is the name of Vale's lady?' asked Michael. 'And why did you not advise him to give her up if the relationship was going to lead to him being forced into acting against his will?'

'I did suggest he transfer his affections elsewhere,' replied Rougham. 'But he declared himself to be in love. And the lady's name is Ruth Weasenham.'

'Really?' asked Michael, astonished. 'I would have thought her too respectable for extra-marital dalliances.'

'So would I, but can you blame her? Weasenham is hardly a man to satisfy a woman's dreams, and his last spouse wandered from the wedding bed, too, as I recall. I imagine the poor lasses do it to retain their sanity, because he cannot make for pleasing company.'

'Ruth was distressed by the news of Vale's death,' said Michael to Bartholomew. 'I saw her eyes fill with tears when we mentioned him.'

'Yes,' agreed Bartholomew cautiously. 'But she was upset by Adam's death, too, and the London brothers'. She is just a gentle lady with a kind heart, and I am not sure I believe this tale.'

'Perhaps we should start a rumour about it,' said

Rougham speculatively. 'Weasenham is a gossip, and it would be poetic justice for him to be the subject of an embarrassing story.'

'But that would hurt Ruth,' said Bartholomew, recalling how she had rallied to his defence when Weasenham had accused him of being a warlock. 'Please do not.'

Rougham sniffed. 'Very well, although only as a personal favour to you – Weasenham does deserve to be taught a lesson. Of course, you are wasting your time investigating these deaths.'

'We are?' asked Michael coolly. 'And why is that?'

'Because it is clear what happened: God did not like what Northwood and his helpmeets were doing, so He took measures to stop them. It was divine punishment on four men who were aiming to steal the secret of lamp fuel from its rightful discoverers – us.'

It was warm when Bartholomew and Michael left Gonville Hall and began to walk to the Carmelite Priory. Many people had snatched a few hours from work, and were using the time to smarten their houses for the Corpus Christi festivities the following week. The wealthier residents were having their homes painted, while the poorer ones contented themselves with a scrubbing brush and a bucket of water. Bartholomew had rarely seen the town looking so spruce. The work did not, however, extend to removing the piles of rubbish that festered on every street corner.

Edith was supervising the beautification of her husband's business premises, which involved a wash of pale gold, and hanging baskets of flowering plants from the eaves. Stanmore's apprentices were thoroughly enjoying themselves, horsing around on ladders and making a good deal of high-spirited noise. Edith fussed about beneath them like a mother hen, exhorting them to take care and not to lean out so far with their brushes.

'They will not listen to me,' she cried, agitated. 'Can they not see that fooling around on steps is dangerous? What shall I do if one of them falls?'

'Hire me to stick their smashed pates back together,' came a smooth voice behind her. It was Surgeon Holm, elegant in a scarlet tunic and matching hose. Meryfeld was with him, short, grubby and unsavoury by comparison, although he was smiling as usual.

'I thought you disliked cranial surgery,' Meryfeld said, rubbing his hands together. 'I, however, have several potions that can knit cracked skulls without resorting to knives and spillages of blood.'

'You do?' asked Bartholomew doubtfully. 'Such as what?'

Meryfeld tapped the side of his nose. 'That is a secret, and I am not in the habit of sharing my miraculous cures with rivals, as you know perfectly well.'

'He is not a rival,' said Edith, standing with her hands on her hips. She regarded Meryfeld with dislike. 'He is a colleague. Tell him this cure, so he may use it to help others.'

'I most certainly shall not,' said Meryfeld, the smile slipping. 'He may purchase a pot of my remedy, but I am not giving the recipe to anyone.'

'Perhaps he will be able to buy some when he wins five marks,' said Holm silkily. 'He and I have a little wager, you see. I believe that Isnard and the riverfolk are inveterate criminals, but he maintains they are angels. Who do you think is right, Mistress Stanmore?'

Edith regarded her brother incredulously. 'You staked five marks on Isnard and his friends being law-abiding? Were you drunk? Or ill? You do not look well today.'

'Neither,' said Bartholomew shortly, aware of Michael chuckling next to him. 'But people are always maligning

123

the riverfolk, just because they are poor, and I am tired of it. They are no more corrupt than the next man, and a good deal more honest than many.'

'You have been spending too much time with your book-bearer,' drawled Holm. 'Because these are the kind of sentiments Cynric likes to expound in the King's Head, to like-minded malcontents who itch to overturn the proper order of things.'

'Matt was simply defending his patients,' said Michael. 'His remarks have nothing to do with the seditious banter that is bandied about in that particular tavern.'

'If you say so,' smirked Holm. 'And while we are on the subject, will you tell Cynric to desist his nasty prattle about peasants and uprisings? We should leave that sort of thing to the French, because I do not want my country turned upside-down by some silly revolution.'

'I would not mind,' said Meryfeld. 'Disorder is lucrative – all those injuries to tend.'

'Have you learned any more about the unfortunate demise of Vale, Brother?' asked Holm. 'It is a most peculiar case, and I do not envy you your investigation.'

'Neither do I,' agreed Meryfeld, before Michael could answer. 'However, I doubt you will solve it. Riborowe has just informed me that those four scholars died by the hand of God, and we all know that He works in mysterious ways. I recommend you abandon the enquiry, lest you annoy Him. But I have patients waiting and remedies to concoct, so I must be on my way. Goodbye.'

'I dislike them,' said Edith, when the pair had gone. 'Meryfeld is all smiles and cheery manners, but he is greedy and selfish. And Holm is greasy.'

'Greasy?' queried Michael, amused.

'Oily,' elaborated Edith. 'Smug. Self-satisfied. Slippery. Untrustworthy. Full of—'

'We have your meaning,' interrupted Michael, laughing. 'And I am inclined to concur.'

'Not about Meryfeld,' objected Bartholomew. 'He is—'

'He is unwilling to share his cures with you, despite the fact that you always answer *his* questions,' interrupted Edith crossly. 'It is hardly fair. However, even though Holm is greasy, no one can deny that he is extraordinarily handsome. Perhaps more so than anyone I have ever seen.'

'Holm is?' asked Bartholomew, incredulously.

Edith laughed. 'You will not understand, Matt. You are not a woman.'

They turned as footsteps approached from behind. It was Sheriff Tulyet, with Bonabes at his side. Tulyet's hands were splashed with ink, and he was full of the taut restlessness he always exuded when administrative duties had kept him indoors for too long. The Exemplarius, meanwhile, was distinctly sheepish, and the front of his tunic was soaking wet. He was carrying a soggy bundle.

'There was an incident,' Bonabes said in response to Michael's questioning glance. 'Weasenham and I were stirring the rags in our paper-making vat when he lost his balance and fell in. It took some time to fish him out.'

'Is he hurt?' asked Bartholomew solicitously.

Bonabes grinned as he shook his head, although he struggled for a sober expression when Tulyet shot him a warning glare. 'Only his pride. I could not rescue him alone, so Ruth summoned reinforcements. Sheriff Tulyet came, and so did Walkelate of King's Hall, Rolee and Teversham of Bene't College, Riborowe and Jorz of the Carmelites, Coslaye and Browne from Batayl, Gyseburne—'

'In other words, half of Cambridge witnessed his predicament,' interrupted Tulyet, regarding Bonabes balefully.

'And there was a good deal of merriment before the poor man was extricated.'

Bartholomew smiled, while amusement gleamed in Michael's green eyes and Edith laughed openly. Bonabes studied his feet, to prevent himself from joining in.

'So why the disapproval, Dick?' asked Michael. 'It is not every day that a gossip receives his comeuppance. Surely, you do not feel sorry for him?'

'No, but during the rescue, pails were overturned, and one contained lye. It splashed on the ceremonial cope that belongs to the Frevill family who live next door, which had just been washed ready for the Corpus Christi pageant next Thursday.' Tulyet indicated Bonabes's bundle.

'It was not our fault that they left it on the wall to dry,' objected Bonabes. 'It is a—'

Tulyet silenced him with a look. 'Needless to say, the Frevills are vexed, and harsh words were exchanged between scholars and townsmen. In the interests of peace, Weasenham has agreed to pay for its repair. Can your seamstresses manage it in time, Edith?'

'Do you mean the Frevill who is helping to build the Common Library?' said Bartholomew irrelevantly, watching Edith inspect the ravaged garment. 'He is a carpenter.'

'No, I mean the powerful and wealthy Frevill who heads the Guild of Corpus Christi – the carpenter is a lowly second cousin,' replied Tulyet tersely. He turned to Edith. 'Frevill will play an important role in the festivities, and the cope is an essential part of it. It is imperative that he is suitably adorned.'

'I am sure we can do something,' replied Edith soothingly.

'Good.' Tulyet treated Bonabes to another glower. 'And

126

no complaints about the price they charge, if you please. You should have been more careful.'

Michael sniggered as he and Bartholomew resumed their walk to the Carmelite Priory, gratified that Weasenham had not only suffered considerable embarrassment in front of a large number of people, but that it was likely to cost him a good deal of money, too.

'He has inflicted all manner of heartache on others with his wagging tongue, and it is satisfying to see him in trouble with the Sheriff. Perhaps some of his victims will gossip about it, and he will know what it feels like to be on the wrong end of scurrilous chatter.'

'I do not believe Ruth was Vale's lover,' said Bartholomew, thinking more of the stationer's wife than the stationer. 'I simply cannot see what would attract her to such a man.'

'Can you not? Vale was young, reasonably handsome and he could be witty. Compared to Weasenham, he was a veritable Adonis.'

'Dunning seems to like marrying his daughters to disagreeable men,' said Bartholomew. 'He is going to foist Surgeon Holm on Julitta soon. You would think he would want better for them.'

'Nonsense, Matt. You heard what Edith just said about Holm's beauty, and other women have told me much the same. I imagine Julitta is delighted to have won such a fine specimen.'

'She is not stupid, Brother. She will be able to see beyond his looks.'

'Will she? There is no suggestion that she is averse to the match. Indeed, I would say that she is rather pleased by it. And what do you know of women, anyway?'

Bartholomew supposed the monk had a point, given that he had failed to keep the one lady who had meant more to him than any other. Although scholars were not permitted to fraternise with women, he was currently seeing a widow who lived near the Great Bridge. However, while he liked her greatly, and enjoyed all she had to offer, he could not imagine giving up his University teaching for her, as he would have done for Matilde. No woman would ever compare to Matilde, he thought unhappily, a familiar pang of loss spearing through him.

He and Michael had almost reached the Carmelite Priory when they saw Langelee and Ayera, walking slowly with their heads close together. Ayera was talking in an urgent whisper, and Langelee's face was a mask of worry. As the Master rarely allowed much to dent his natural ebullience, the expression was cause for concern. His smile was strained when he saw his Fellows.

'It is a pleasant time for a stroll,' he said, all false bonhomie. 'Neither too hot nor too cold.'

Bartholomew's disquiet intensified; the bluff, soldierly Langelee was not a man to chat about the weather, either. 'What is wrong?' he asked in alarm.

'Just the usual,' replied Ayera, when Langelee hesitated. 'College finances. As you know, my uncle died recently, after promising a substantial benefaction to Michaelhouse. Unfortunately, I have just learned that he had nothing to leave. Once his debts were paid, he was penniless.'

'I am sorry,' said Bartholomew. 'You planned to spend your share on a horse . . .'

Ayera shrugged. 'I shall manage without it. I am just sorry to disappoint my College.'

He gave a small, courtly bow and went on his way, his abrupt departure leaving Bartholomew with the impression that he was more disturbed by the news than he wanted them to know.

'It is a damned shame,' said Langelee, watching him go. 'That money would have kept us afloat for more than a year, and the horse would have been a welcome addition to our stables. We could have made a tidy profit from putting him to stud, too.'

'Ayera worked on his uncle for weeks to include us in his will,' said Bartholomew, recalling his colleague's jubilation when the old man had capitulated. He glanced at Langelee. 'And you travelled to Huntingdon with him last month, to witness the new document.'

'And to see my youngest daughter,' said Langelee, fondness suffusing his blunt features.

It was not the first time the Master had mentioned offspring, and Bartholomew was keen to learn more about them, but Michael overrode the question he started to ask.

'A wasted journey,' the monk said in disgust. 'One that cost us money, too.'

Langelee sighed ruefully. 'Well, at least I enjoyed myself. Ayera is excellent company, and he impressed me with his martial skills. He was a soldier once, you know.'

'We had gathered that from the tales you and he exchange of an evening,' said Michael dryly. He regarded the Master pointedly. 'Although *he* at least has the decency to regret the violence he has inflicted on others.'

'Yes,' agreed Langelee with a rueful sigh. 'It is a pity, because he is otherwise a fine man. And he is a considerable improvement on Bartholomew, who manages to make the great victory at Poitiers sound dull.'

Bartholomew rarely discussed the battle, and wondered what he could have said to give the Master that impression. There were many words he might have used to describe it, but 'dull' certainly would not have been one of them. 'Do I?'

'Oh, yes.' Langelee folded his hands and gave a disconcertingly accurate impression of the physician's voice. '"The Prince of Wales sounded the charge, we ran forward and the French surrendered." An extremely vibrant account, to be sure.'

Bartholomew shrugged, suspecting Langelee would not understand if he confided that the battle was a blur in his mind – of wildly flailing weapons, screams and blood. He vividly recalled the injuries he had tended afterwards, but no one was very interested in those.

'Have you discovered what happened to those four scholars in Newe Inn yet?' the Master asked, changing the subject abruptly. 'The whole town is abuzz with rumours.'

'No,' replied Michael. 'But my beadles have been busy with questions today.'

'Good,' said Langelee. 'However, I strongly advise you to hurry, because our University seethes with bile and bitterness at the moment, and the sooner you can present us with a culprit, the sooner wounds and rifts will begin to heal.'

Michael did not need to be told.

At the Carmelite Friary, a lay-brother conducted Bartholomew and Michael to the pleasant cottage that served as the Prior's House, where Etone sat at a large table surrounded by documents and a sizeable ledger.

'We are here to ask about Northwood,' explained the monk. 'Will you answer some questions?'

'Of course,' replied Etone. 'But this interview should take place in the scriptorium, where he worked. His colleagues knew him better than I did.'

The scriptorium was a grand name for the room above the refectory, which boasted large windows to admit the light. There were about a dozen desks, and a scribe stood at each; among them were Riborowe and Jorz. Another four were novices, labouring over some basic writing exercises.

'Riborowe has set them a series of theological tracts to copy,' explained Etone, when Michael paused to look. 'They will eventually be sold to Weasenham as exemplars. It is a good idea – it allows them to practise before we set them loose on vellum and expensive coloured inks.'

'How many did Northwood sell last week?' asked Michael innocently.

'One,' replied Etone. 'There were two, but he said the other was of insufficient quality.'

'Weasenham!' exclaimed Jorz, overhearing and exchanging an angry glance with Riborowe. 'That man delights in causing mischief. We should have let him drown in his paper vat today!'

'Now, now,' admonished Etone. 'Those are unworthy sentiments for a friar.'

'Well, he is going around telling everyone that Northwood did sell him the second exemplar, but that he kept the money for himself,' said Jorz sulkily.

'Then he deserves your compassion, not your ire, because the tale is clearly a lie,' said Etone mildly. 'He must be a deeply unhappy man to invent such tales about the dead.'

Jorz did not look convinced, and neither was Bartholomew. Weasenham had always seemed perfectly content to him, and had good reason to be, with his flourishing business, succession of pretty wives, and robust health.

'What else do you do here?' he asked. 'Besides providing exemplars for the stationer?'

'We produce bibles mostly, along with prayer books and psalters.' Etone smiled, proud of his scriveners' talents. 'Obviously, we do not expect our illustrators to be able to draw everything, so we encourage them to specialise in particular letters or specific animals. For example, Willelmus here excels at Js and As.'

Willelmus was a man of middle years, small and hunched, with the milky eyes of incipient blindness. Poor vision was an occupational hazard among illustrators, and Bartholomew wondered what he would do when he could no longer see well enough to work. Etone read his thoughts.

'I shall make him parish priest at Girton soon,' he whispered. 'He objects, of course, as he loves being here. But he will need what remains of his eyesight to settle into his new life.'

'I draw chickens, too,' Willelmus was saying shyly, smiling up at Michael.

'Chickens?' asked the monk, amused. 'Is there much call for fowl in sacred manuscripts, then?'

Willelmus nodded fervently. 'You would be surprised at how often they can be inserted, Brother. They are lovable beasts, and it amuses me to immortalise them.'

'Right,' said Michael, regarding him as though he were short of a few wits.

'Meanwhile, Jorz here does climbing foliage,' boasted Etone. 'And devils.'

Jorz smiled rather diabolically. 'It is good to remind people that not everything is pretty flowers and happy hens. The occasional demon lurking in the greenery is a warning that Satan is never far away. People should remember this, even when reading their scriptures.'

'There are rather more imps here than angels,' remarked Michael, squinting over Jorz's work. Willelmus was not the only one whose eyesight was not all it had been. 'Is that appropriate?'

'Prior Etone says I must not draw cherubs and devils

with the same hand,' explained Jorz. 'So I paint fiends with my left, which is comfortable, but I am clumsy with my right, so angels take longer and are not so fine when I have finished. That is why there are more demons.'

Etone shrugged when Michael regarded him questioningly. 'I was afraid there might be an urge to make them overly similar, otherwise. And then where would we be, theologically speaking?'

'I specialise in depicting weapons,' declared Riborowe, cutting into the bemused silence that followed. 'And my bows, bombards, swords and ribauldequins have dispatched many a chicken and sprite. I get the manuscripts last, you see, to add the finishing touches.'

Michael's eyebrows almost disappeared under his hair. 'You amaze me! I would have thought there was even less demand for weapons in sacred texts than for poultry and denizens of Hell.'

'The Bible is a very violent book,' said Riborowe approvingly. 'It is full of wars, battles, fights and murders, and people are always smiting enemies. So is God. Look at the ribauldequin I have drawn here. It is a perfect copy of the ones used at Poitiers.'

'How do you know?' asked Michael doubtfully.

'Because I was there,' declared Riborowe proudly. 'I was a chaplain with the English army.'

'Lord!' exclaimed Michael. 'How many more of our scholars are going to confess to taking part in that vicious occasion? We have three so far, with you, Holm and Matt.'

'So I have heard,' said Riborowe, shooting Bartholomew an unpleasant glance before going to fetch more ink from a little antechamber at the far end of the room. He called back over his shoulder, as he went, 'However, *I* did not wield a weapon and nor did I side with the French, like Holm.'

'You are limping,' observed Bartholomew. He might not

have remarked on it, but Dame Pelagia's words about men with leg wounds clamoured at him, and Riborowe's look had irritated him.

'I tripped running away from a batch of ink that exploded,' said the friar, rather coolly. He held up red-stained hands. 'See the mess it made?'

'When did—' began Bartholomew.

'Look at this manuscript,' interrupted Jorz, brandishing a sheaf of pages that were a blaze of colour. 'It is a gift for Sir Eustace Dunning – a Book of Hours.'

'If we give it to him,' said Etone grimly. 'I have not forgiven him for depriving us of Newe Inn yet. Or for facilitating the establishment of a Common Library.'

'Speaking of Newe Inn, do any of you know what Northwood was doing in its grounds?' asked Michael. 'Or why he should have been there with Vale and the London brothers?'

'I have no idea at all,' replied Riborowe. 'We have a lovely garden here, in the friary.'

'When did you last see him?' asked Bartholomew.

'Tuesday evening,' supplied Riborowe. 'He said he was going to find somewhere quiet to read. The next day, we noticed that his bed had not been slept in.'

'Was that unusual?' asked Bartholomew.

It was Etone who answered. 'No. He was an avid reader, even at night when he was obliged to use a lamp. He told me he was looking forward to your success with good fuel, Matthew, because Willelmus's plight had shown him what happens to those who strain their eyes.'

'I understand he liked alchemy,' said Michael. 'Do you think he might have decided to investigate that particular matter himself, in competition with the *medici*?'

'He might have done,' said Etone, silencing Jorz's immediate denial with a raised hand. 'But I think he would have told them. He had his failings, but deceit was not one of them.'

'What failings?' pounced Michael.

'Voting in favour of the Common Library,' said Riborowe immediately. 'He was the only White Friar to flout our Prior's instructions. None of the rest of us want such a vile place in our midst.'

'No,' agreed Etone. We considered the scheme inadvisable before Dunning provided Newe Inn for the purpose, but we are even more opposed to it now.'

'That was Northwood's only fault?' probed Michael.

Etone sighed. 'No. If you must know, he was vain about his intellect and impatient with those he deemed inferior.'

'I never found that,' said Bartholomew, feeling the judgement uncharitable.

'That is because he admired you, and went to some trouble to cultivate your friendship,' said Etone with a pained smile. 'He thought your mind was worthy of his notice. However, he was considerably less amiable with those who had not won his approbation.'

'And he was a bully,' Willelmus muttered, while the novices nodded fervently. 'He worked the boys very hard, then dismissed their efforts as inadequate.'

'He often made us stay late,' added one. 'And we were afraid that we would grow as blind as Willelmus, because he kept us here long after sunset, when we could barely see.'

'For the money, it would seem,' said Michael, 'which he kept for himself.'

Etone pursed his lips. 'He was not a thief, Brother. And if you do not believe me, then inspect his cell. You will find no ill-gotten gains there.'

'Very well,' said Michael agreeably. 'Lead on.'

* * *

135

Etone was piqued that Michael was unwilling to take his word about Northwood's probity, but ordered Riborowe to take the monk and his Corpse Examiner to the dormitory anyway. Sniffing, to indicate his disapproval, the thin priest led the way out of the scriptorium, across the yard, and up a flight of stairs. The dormitory was a large, airy room with flies buzzing around the rafters, and an enormous hearth at each end, to keep the friars warm during inclement weather.

The cubicle that had been occupied by Northwood was about halfway down. There was nothing in it except a bed, a box containing some writings on alchemy, and a spare habit.

'You see?' said Riborowe triumphantly. 'These tales about his greed are lies.'

'Unless someone guessed that we might inspect his possessions, and made sure all was in order,' said Michael sombrely. Bartholomew had been thinking the same thing.

'That is a dreadful charge to lay at our door!' declared Riborowe indignantly. 'How dare you!'

Michael was silent for a moment. 'I have a legal and an ethical obligation to find out what happened to Northwood, and if that means poking into matters that are awkward, distressing or embarrassing, then that is what I must do. I take no pleasure from it, and nor will I gossip about what I learn, but it must be done if the truth is to come out.'

Riborowe softened when he sensed the monk's sincerity. 'Very well. Northwood *was* vain about his intellect, and he *was* strict with the novices. However, he did *not* sell exemplars to profit himself – he was not that kind of man. He was your friend, Bartholomew: you know I am right.'

'It is true, Brother,' said Bartholomew. 'Northwood was not interested in material wealth, only in expanding his mind and learning more about alchemy.'

'His fondness for flinging potions together was not a virtue,' said Riborowe stiffly. 'It led him into dubious company – such as yours, Bartholomew, and that of the Londons and Vale. I cannot imagine why he sought *them* out. The brothers were stupid, while Vale was plain nasty. Jorz and I are decent alchemists – look at our experiments with ink – so why could he not have been satisfied with us?'

'Where did he meet them?' demanded Michael. 'And when?'

'In Weasenham's shop, in St Mary the Great, talking in Cholles Lane.' Riborowe shrugged. 'They were always chatting. The last time I saw all four together was perhaps five days ago. They were laughing, although Northwood declined to share the joke when I asked what was so amusing.'

'In other words, their society was friendly?' asked Michael. He exchanged a brief glance with Bartholomew: Vale would not have been guffawing with Northwood if the Carmelite had been blackmailing him.

'Yes, of course,' said Riborowe, puzzled. 'Why would it not be?'

'There is some suggestion that Northwood discovered Vale had a lover,' said Michael bluntly. 'Do you know anything about that?'

'He never mentioned it to me,' said Riborowe, startled. 'He was not a gossip.'

Michael indicated that he had finished his search, and Riborowe led them back down the stairs and across the yard to the gate.

'I am not sure what to think, Matt,' said Michael, once they were outside. 'To you, Northwood was a kindly philosopher; to his novices and Willelmus, he was a tyrant; to Weasenham, he was dishonest; to Etone and his fellow friars, he was an eccentric academic; to Rougham, he was a competitor in the race to produce fuel; and to Vale, he was a blackmailer. Which is the real man?'

Bartholomew had no reply, uncomfortable with what they had learned about a person he thought he had known. To avoid addressing the issue, he changed the direction of the discussion.

'Perhaps Vale concocted this tale about a lover, so that Rougham would not berate him over voting for the Common Library. Rougham keeps a lady himself, so would certainly be sympathetic to the notion of being black-mailed over one.'

'Yes, but why did Vale vote against his College's wishes in the first place?'

Bartholomew shrugged. 'Gonville's medical books are all very traditional. Perhaps he hoped there would be a wider choice in a Common Library.'

Michael was thoughtful. 'Yet Northwood was determined that our University should have a central repository for books. He was passionate about it, in fact. And it would not be the first time a scholar did something underhand to get his own way, believing himself to be in the right.'

Again, Bartholomew had no answer.

Once away from the Carmelite Priory, Michael aimed for Newe Inn, to re-examine the place where the four scholars had died. Bartholomew trailed after him, feeling they were wasting their time.

'Do you have any theories about what happened yet?' he asked, watching the monk poke the edge of the pond with a stick. 'Or suspects?'

'Not really. However, on reflection, I think you are right about Vale: he did lie about having a lover to avoid Rougham's censure for taking for the wrong side at the

138

Convocation. Of course, the only way to be sure is to ask Ruth.'

'I doubt she will tell you.' Bartholomew began to pick some late-flowering lily of the valley. It was useful in remedies for dropsy, and there was so much growing by the pond that he did not think anyone would mind him harvesting a bit. It was past its full glory, but would still do what he wanted. 'She has nothing to gain by confessing to adultery.'

Michael grimaced. 'True, but we shall have to make the attempt, anyway. So what have you deduced? And please do not tell me that you believe God is responsible. Or the Devil.'

'I am fairly sure Northwood, Vale and the Londons were poisoned.' Bartholomew spread his hands, both full of flowers. 'I can think of no other reason why they should have died at the same time – and we know they *did* die at the same time, because Clippesby saw them all alive together on Tuesday night. He told me himself.'

'Very well,' conceded Michael. 'Then who did it? And why?'

'Not my medical colleagues,' said Bartholomew immediately, stuffing the flowers into his bag. 'Perhaps Northwood did recruit friends to help him experiment with lamp fuel after Rougham rejected his offer of help, but none of us would have felt strongly enough about it to kill them.'

Michael gave a sharp bark of laughter. 'Not you, perhaps, but the others would! Moreover, if anyone knows how to poison people without leaving evidence, it is a *medicus*. And just look at the choices: Meryfeld is greedy and ruthless; Rougham is arrogant and vengeful; Gyseburne is enigmatic and inscrutable; and Edith says Holm is greasy.'

'But none of them are killers,' said Bartholomew firmly.

139

'However, the notion that all four victims voted for the Common Library disturbs me. Do you think that is why they were killed?'

'I am inclined to say no, because several hundred scholars from the hostels also supported the scheme, and none of them are dead. Of course, none came from foundations that had ordered them to vote the other way.'

'Do you think I am in danger, then?'

'It is possible, so you had better take Cynric with you when you go out at night from now on. He can protect you from men who demand formulae for wildfire, too.' Michael stopped poking at the pond. 'Do you think Sawtre was murdered as well – that his "accident" was anything but?'

'King's Hall seems happy to blame an unstable piece of furniture, and there is nothing to suggest they are wrong. Of course, there is nothing to say they are right, either.'

Michael tapped his leg with the stick, thinking. 'What do you think of Browne as a culprit? I know he has friends at King's Hall, so getting into the place would be easy for him. He found the four bodies, too. Experience tells me to look closely at the fellow who raises the alarm.'

'Well, he certainly disapproves of the Common Library. Do you think Coslaye helped him?'

'Possibly. I shall have to interrogate them soon, although it will not be easy when there are no facts to encourage them to confess.'

Bartholomew followed him along the path, back towards the library building. 'You are due to make your report to Dunning soon. What will you tell him?'

Michael shrugged. 'The truth: that the four men who died here were almost certainly killed unlawfully, but that we have no idea by whom or why. I hope he does not

140

decide that the information is not worth a meal, because I am hungry.'

They passed the library as they aimed for the gate, which rang with the sounds of industry as usual. Someone was whistling as he worked, a tune that marked time with the rap of a hammer, and apprentices were sweeping sawdust into bags, ready to be sold to farmers.

'It has just started, Doctor,' called one lad. He was Alfred de Blaston, a youth whose family had been Bartholomew's patients for years. 'If you hurry, you will not have missed much.'

'What has started?' asked Bartholomew, bemused.

'The tour of the library for future benefactors,' explained Alfred impatiently. 'I am sure you will be a donor, because you are very rich.'

'I am?' Bartholomew was astonished to hear so.

Alfred nodded. 'Of course, or you would not have been able to provide my little brother with milksops and free medicine all winter.'

Michael grinned. 'Now I shall know whom to approach when I need to borrow some money. But I would not mind participating in this tour, and we have enough time before dinner.'

They arrived to find Walkelate standing on the stairs, addressing a group of men and women. There were perhaps thirty of them, and they included Chancellor Tynkell, burgesses from the Guild of Corpus Christi and a number of senior scholars. Tynkell was alarmed when he saw Michael, and sidled through the assembly towards him. The Chancellor rarely looked healthy, mostly because of his unfortunate aversion to hygiene, but he seemed especially pallid that day.

'Please do not make any remarks that will put them off,

Brother,' he begged. 'It will not be much of a library without books, and that is the purpose of this gathering – to secure donations.'

'Is it, indeed?' asked Michael coolly. 'And why was I not told about it?'

'Because I was afraid you would cause trouble,' explained Tynkell bluntly. 'A few well-chosen words from you will see these would-be benefactors turn tail and run.'

'Do you really consider me so petty?' Michael was indignant.

The Chancellor did not deign to answer.

'And now, if you will follow me upstairs, I shall show you the library proper,' announced Walkelate, beaming at the throng and clearly delighted to be showing off his work.

The visitors began to shuffle up the steps, cooing at the carved handrail and the decorative corbels. The hammering and sawing that had been echoing around the garden promptly stopped. Bartholomew, Tynkell and Michael joined the end of the party.

'It is a remarkable achievement,' Bartholomew said, looking around appreciatively and noting in particular the lifelike features of Aristotle. 'The craftsmen have worked wonders.'

'It is beautiful,' conceded Michael grudgingly. 'The hostel men will enjoy coming here, although such splendour is wasted on them. Is that Dunning over there, talking to Weasenham?'

The Chancellor nodded. 'He is often here, checking on progress, while Weasenham has promised us several very expensive books and a large number of exemplars. They are both vital to the success of this scheme, so please be nice to them, Brother.'

'I shall be my usual charming self,' promised Michael, surging forward.

'That is what I was afraid of,' said Tynkell worriedly to Bartholomew. 'So I had better ingratiate myself with the Frevill clan. Several are wealthy, and their kinsman works here, so perhaps they will provide us with books, should Michael's "charming self" do any damage.'

Bartholomew watched him approach several tall, well-built gentlemen, one of whom was the carpenter he had met before. Frevill saw Bartholomew looking at him, and came to talk.

'We cannot really afford to stop work and deal with visitors,' he said in an undertone. 'Not if we are to finish in the allotted time. But Walkelate says securing well-wishers is important, so . . .'

'You look tired,' said Bartholomew, seeing lines of weariness etched deep into the man's face.

'So do you,' countered Frevill, smiling. 'But I am well, although I worry about Kente. He suffers from dizzy spells, and I am sure it is the long hours he keeps. Will you speak to him?'

As he followed Frevill into the adjoining room, Bartholomew heard Michael ask Weasenham – loudly – whether he had recovered from his mishap in the paper vat. The question brought a gale of laughter from those who heard it, and Tynkell winced at Weasenham's furious glare.

The room containing the *libri concatenati* stank of the oil that had been used to stain the wood. It was not unpleasant, but it was strong, and Bartholomew was not surprised that Kente was light-headed. The craftsman was sitting atop the *cista*, treating an exquisitely carved lectern to a liberal smothering of brown grease.

'This will make it shine like burnished gold,' Kente said, glancing up when Frevill and Bartholomew approached. He was pale, but there was genuine pleasure in his face. 'I am looking forward to the opening next week.'

'Your paste reeks,' said Bartholomew. 'And Frevill says you have not been feeling well.'

'Nothing that a few days' rest will not cure,' said Kente, waving his concerns away. 'And I shall have those next week, once this place is finished. We are very close now.'

'Try to go outside occasionally,' advised Bartholomew. 'For fresh air.'

'I do not need fresh air,' stated Kente scornfully. 'I have been inhaling this lovely oil all my life, and I like its scent.' He grinned suddenly. 'Tomorrow, or the day after, we shall close this room to keep it pristine while we add the finishing touches to the *libri distribuendi* next door. That chamber is slightly behind schedule, but nothing we cannot rectify with a bit of hard work.'

There was little that Bartholomew could do if Kente declined to listen to him. He shrugged to Frevill, and began to wander, smiling when he saw Michael's chubby features in a carving depicting the feeding of the five thousand. He half listened to the discussions of the benefactors around him, pleased when he heard several begin to compete with each other's generosity.

'My entire collection of breviaries,' declared Stanmore to the head of the Frevill clan.

'The complete works of Bradwardine,' countered Frevill. 'Religious and philosophical.'

'And I shall donate my bestiary,' said a quietly spoken scholar from Bene't College named Rolee.

'You will?' blurted Bartholomew in astonishment. 'Does your College not have an opinion about that? Bene't is one of this place's most fervent opponents.'

Rolee nodded. 'I know, and I voted against it myself, as I was ordered. But now I see it, I wish I had given it my support. It is a grand venture, and one that is a credit to our *studium generale*. When my colleagues see it for themselves, they will think the same.'

'I hope you are right,' said Bartholomew fervently. 'And that they are won around soon. Michael said it caused a fight between your College and Essex Hostel last night.'

'Yes,' agreed Rolee ruefully. 'But even if they do remain antagonistic, they will not mourn the loss of my bestiary. They consider it a waste of space, and say our shelves would be better graced with tomes on theology or law.'

Bartholomew browsed a little longer, and was about to leave when he spotted his sister talking to Ruth and Julitta. As he went to pay his respects, a shaft of sunlight pierced the room and bathed Julitta in its golden rays. It turned her eyes to sapphire and her skin to the purest alabaster. When she turned to smile a greeting at him, he found himself gazing at the face of an angel.

'Ruth asked whether you had heard what happened to her husband, Matt,' said Edith loudly, pinching his arm to gain his attention. He blushed when he realised they had been speaking to him for several moments, but he had not heard a word of it.

'No,' he stammered. 'I mean yes.'

Julitta laughed. 'Your brother seems discomfited by the presence of so many ladies. University men are not used to us, so perhaps we had better leave him in peace.'

They had gone before Bartholomew could say he was perfectly happy to be discomfited by her, then was glad she had not given him the chance when he saw Holm nearby. The surgeon was regarding him coolly, and Bartholomew felt his face grow red a second time.

'My sister likes to tease,' said Ruth. 'Take no notice of her. Unless you want to, of course.'

145

To cover his confusion at the enigmatic remark, Bartholomew blurted the first thing that came into his head. 'Did you know Vale the physician?'

'You know I did,' said Ruth, bemused. 'I told you when you came to our shop earlier today that I was his patient.'

'Someone mentioned . . . there is a rumour . . .' Bartholomew trailed off, heartily wishing he had never started the conversation. It was hardly his responsibility to ask embarrassing questions for Michael's investigation.

'There was a nasty report, some weeks ago, that he was my lover,' said Ruth frostily. 'Is that the subject you have chosen to discuss with me? I assure you, it is quite untrue. There was never any shred of impropriety between Vale and me. I credit myself with more taste.'

'The tale was malicious, then?' Bartholomew wondered who would do such a thing. Was it someone who had fallen prey to Weasenham's tattle, and who had decided to strike back?

Ruth grimaced, then said in a less hostile tone, 'Or wishful thinking.'

Bartholomew stared at her. 'You think Vale might have . . .'

'Imagined it, yes,' finished Ruth. 'He liked to think of himself as an Adonis, and once told Bonabes that he could seduce any woman he pleased. However, he certainly did not try to seduce me. He was never anything but polite and proper.'

Bartholomew began to apologise for raising the matter, loath for her to think badly of him. As he did so, he became aware that he was doing it because he did not want her to tell Julitta about his boorish behaviour, and that it was her younger sister's good opinion that he really wanted to keep. He started to stumble over his words, disconcerted by what he was learning about himself, and was relieved when Walkelate interrupted by bustling up to them.

'I have just told Brother Michael – again – that I saw and heard nothing unusual on the night that those four men died,' the architect blurted out, troubled. 'But he seems reluctant to believe me.'

'Why?' asked Bartholomew.

'Because he says the pond is a mere stone's throw from here, and we must have noticed something. But we did not! We were oiling the shelves, which was tedious work, so Holm hired a couple of singers to entertain us while we laboured.'

'Holm did? Why?'

'It was an act of kindness – we are friends,' replied Walkelate. 'He is our nearest neighbour, too, and likes to stay on our good side. My artisans and I all joined in the songs – loudly and cheerfully – so we heard nothing amiss.'

'But you must have gone into the garden at some point,' pressed Bartholomew. 'I imagine you store some of your materials there.'

'We used to, but there is no need now that all the shelves, floors and panels are in place.'

Bartholomew was frustrated on Michael's behalf. 'But four people died here! Surely, you noticed something unusual – the gate ajar, an odd noise, torches in the undergrowth? Holm certainly did, from next door.'

'I wish we had,' cried Walkelate, distressed. 'But we rarely look out of the windows when we are working – our attention is on our hands. And it would not have helped the victims if we had – you cannot see the pond from here. You cannot see the gate, either, so an elephant could have marched into the garden, and we would have known nothing about it.'

'It is true,' said Ruth, who had been listening to the

147

exchange. 'The craftsmen are always intent on their work, because they aim to have the bonus my father promised for finishing by next week.'

'What about the apprentices?' persisted Bartholomew. 'Boys will not be so absorbed.'

'No,' agreed Walkelate. 'But they have school lessons in the evenings, so they are never here. But ask them anyway. Perhaps they noticed something unusual during the day.'

Bartholomew did, but his efforts went unrewarded. They worked as hard as their masters, and had no time for fighting their way through the weeds to the fish pond. And as it had a reputation for housing evil sprites, none of them had been inclined to do so anyway.

'I went up there once,' confided Alfred. 'When we first started working here, as a dare. I did not see any faeries, but I could feel them watching me, flexing their claws ready to leap out and drag me down into their evil pond. I ran away as fast as I could.'

'You had better get a charm from Cynric if you intend to spend much more time there, Doctor,' advised another boy, his young face solemn. 'He will make sure you are properly protected.'

Bartholomew was sure he would.

CHAPTER 5

'Lord! I am hungry,' said Michael, as he and Bartholomew walked to the handsome house owned by Dunning a short while later. 'I could eat a horse, although I hope they do not give me one.'

'We have made scant progress today,' said Bartholomew, more concerned with their investigation than Michael's culinary preferences. 'Over Northwood and the others.'

'True,' agreed Michael, reluctantly dragging his mind away from food and back to the murders. 'And there is the fact that my grandmother is in Cambridge.'

Bartholomew nodded slowly. 'True. Do you have any idea what brought her here?'

Michael was thoughtful. 'Well, our university boasts a lot of clever minds, ones that have taken to invention enthusiastically since that deputation from Oxford virtually challenged us to compete with them. Perhaps the King sent her here to keep an eye on us.'

'I sincerely doubt we warrant that sort of attention, Brother!'

'Do not be so sure. Some of these discoveries will be worth a fortune, and His Majesty is interested in money. Moreover, there is the attack on you to consider.'

'What does that have to do with anything?'

'It occurred because someone believes you know how to make wildfire – another invention.'

Bartholomew shook his head. 'I do not think an agent of Dame Pelagia's standing would have been dragged from retirement to spy on a few academics who like to experiment, not even ones who have stumbled across a formula for wildfire. She is here for another reason, although it is entirely possible that we may never learn what it is. She is not exactly forthcoming.'

'No,' agreed Michael wryly. 'However, I think you are wrong. She was in the London brothers' house when we found her, which makes me suspect that they were dabbling in something rather more sly than making paper, probably in company with Northwood and Vale.'

'Competing with us over lamp fuel,' said Bartholomew. 'Although we have nothing to prove it. Rougham made the accusation, but he disliked Northwood.'

'Prior Etone said it was possible, too, and I shall certainly bear it in mind as I make my enquiries. *Ergo*, I am loath to cross your medical colleagues off my list of suspects for the deaths of those four men. As I said earlier, physicians know how to poison people without leaving evidence, so one of them might well have dispatched the competition.'

'No,' said Bartholomew firmly. 'They would not—'

'Rougham, Gyseburne, Meryfeld and Holm,' mused Michael, overriding him. 'None are what I could call pleasant characters. But here we are at Dunning's house, so we had better discuss this later. I would not like anyone else to know the route our suspicions have taken.'

He had knocked on Dunning's door before Bartholomew could inform him that *his* suspicions had taken him nowhere near the *medici*. It was opened by Julitta. She was wearing a blue kirtle that matched her eyes, and a gold net, called a fret, covered her glossy hair. When she smiled a welcome, Bartholomew found himself at a loss for words. He was unsettled by the emotions that surged inside him, having experienced nothing like them since he had lost Matilde. Uneasily, he acknowledged that he could very easily become smitten with Julitta.

'I hear you are betrothed, mistress,' Michael was saying conversationally as he followed her inside, bringing Bartholomew back to Earth with a considerable bump. 'To Holm the surgeon.'

Julitta nodded. 'Yes. We shall be wed within the month.'

'Is that what you want?' blurted Bartholomew, recalling Clippesby's contention that the union would not be a happy one, along with Holm's open admission that he was only interested in her father's money. Julitta regarded him in surprise, and so did Michael.

'Of course,' she replied, bemused. 'Do you think I do not know my own mind?'

'No . . . well, yes,' said Bartholomew, flustered. 'But Holm . . . A surgeon is . . .'

'He is talented, charming, handsome and he loves me,' said Julitta quietly. 'And the match pleases my father. I am more than content with the arrangement.'

Bartholomew was tempted to inform her of what Holm had said, but he had the distinct feeling that she would not believe him, and it was not in his nature to tell tales anyway. He followed her along a narrow corridor to a room overlooking a pleasant garden. The window shutters had been thrown open, and the air that wafted inside was rich with the scent of flowers and herbs.

Michael need not have worried about going hungry, because the food was good and plentiful. There were roasted chickens, salted pork, wheaten bread, vegetables braised in butter, pea pottage and a raisin tart. Bartholomew's stomach had not recovered from its bout with sickness the previous night, so he ate and drank sparingly. Michael, by contrast, ate and drank everything that was set near him

151

as he summarised Bartholomew's findings about the four dead scholars, and so did Dunning, who became garrulous as the evening wore on.

'I am a member of the Guild of Corpus Christi, so it is only right that the Common Library I enabled should open on our Feast Day,' he declared. 'It is a fitting tribute to my generosity.'

'Really, Father,' murmured Julitta. 'A little humility would—'

'And I *have* been generous,' Dunning brayed on. 'Everyone else donates scrolls, altar cloths or relics, but my gift will go down in the annals of history as unique. I shall make sure you are remembered in perpetuity, too, Julitta, given that you were the one who encouraged me to do it.'

Bartholomew smiled at her, surprised and impressed that she should have done something so munificent. Julitta merely stared at the table, apparently mortified by her father's bragging conceit.

'Tell us about the arrangements for the Corpus Christi pageant,' suggested Michael, reaching for the wine jug and tactfully changing the subject. 'Will it be as spectacular as last year?'

Dunning beamed delightedly. 'I think it will, because it will culminate in the opening of my library. The procession will be led by Frevill, who will wear a fancy cloak. The rest of the Guild will follow, along with the town's priests, various University dignitaries – including that peculiar Chancellor Tynkell – and the burgesses.'

'Why do you say Tynkell is peculiar?' asked Michael curiously.

Dunning lowered his voice. 'Well, there was a rumour not long ago that he was pregnant.'

'That was a silly story put about by one of my students,

152

as a joke,' explained Bartholomew. It had actually been started by Deynman, who had believed it.

'Yet there is something odd about the fellow,' said Dunning. 'Do you know what it is, Doctor?'

'He does, but he refuses to tell,' said Michael. 'It is very annoying, because I work closely with Tynkell, and would dearly like to know what makes him . . . different.'

'It is a pity that those four scholars died in Newe Inn's garden,' said Dunning, leaping to another subject with the convoluted logic of the drunk. 'It was remiss of them, so close to the opening.'

'It is an odd case,' mused Michael, while Bartholomew regarded Dunning in distaste, feeling the remark was extraordinarily insensitive. 'As I said during my summary just now, Matt can find no apparent cause of death.'

'They were not men I would have imagined enjoying each other's company,' confided Dunning. 'I liked Northwood and the London brothers, who praised me effusively for founding a Common Library, but I did not take to Vale. He was arrogant.'

'*Confident* might be a kinder word,' said Julitta. 'He—'

'I dislike medical men, on the whole,' declared Dunning. He winced and bent down to rub his ankle – Julitta had kicked him under the table – then regarded Bartholomew sheepishly. 'Present company excepted, of course.'

'Yet you will allow your daughter to marry one,' observed Michael.

'Holm is a surgeon, which makes it all right,' explained Dunning. 'You can see what surgeons are doing, even if it is all rather bloody, whereas physicians only inspect urine or pretend to work out what is wrong by devising horoscopes. I know physicians are generally regarded as superior, but I prefer surgeons, because they cut hair, which is actually useful.'

'Will Holm be giving you a trim for Corpus Christi?' said Michael, struggling not to smile.

'Me and the entire Guild,' boasted Dunning. 'We shall all look very well groomed.'

When servants came to clear the table, Dunning invited his guests to an elegant solar on the upper floor, to inspect his books. They could not help but be impressed, because his collection included theological and philosophical works, as well as tomes on law, astronomy and music.

'Have you read all these?' Bartholomew asked, running an appreciative finger along the bindings.

Dunning regarded him askance. 'Why would I? They contain nothing I want to know.'

'Then why do you have them?' asked Bartholomew, taken aback in his turn.

'They look nice on the shelves,' explained Dunning. 'And Julitta likes them. I wish now that I had let her learn to read, because her fascination with literature means that we have to pay students to do it for her. Still, I shall save money once she is wed, because Holm will read to her.'

Julitta smiled in happy anticipation of romantic evenings to come, and Bartholomew felt a surge of dismay, sure Holm would do nothing of the kind. As if on cue, there was a clatter on the stairs, and a maid announced that the surgeon would be joining them for a cup of wine. Bartholomew watched Julitta's face light up when Holm swaggered into the room. The newcomer made a courtly bow to her and Dunning, then saw they had company.

'Bartholomew,' he said, not altogether pleasantly. 'And Michael. What brings you here?'

'They came to dine,' explained Dunning, nodding to Julitta to fetch more claret from the kitchen. 'We have

154

been discussing the celebrations for Corpus Christi. And books.'

'Dunning arranged for me to be elected to his Guild,' said Holm with careless pride. 'So I shall be part of the pageant, too. I think I shall buy myself a new gown, perhaps with the five marks I am about to win.'

'I hope you have not been gambling,' admonished Dunning. 'I do not approve of it.'

'A simple wager that I cannot lose,' explained Holm smoothly. 'It was hardly sporting of me to accept it, to tell you the truth, but I could not help myself. Who am I to overlook free money?'

Dunning was unconvinced. 'In my experience, there is no such thing as free money, but you know best, I suppose. You come very late tonight. Have you been with a patient?'

'Yes – I have just saved a child's life. He was screaming with the pain of an earache, so I gave him a good dose of mandrake and poppy juice. Now he is sleeping like a . . . well, like a baby.'

Bartholomew was horrified: those were very powerful substances for an infant. 'Have you tried dropping a little oil of camomile or mullein into the infected ear?' he asked, struggling to be tactful. 'It usually serves to reduce—'

'I cannot be bothered with feeble remedies,' said Holm dismissively. 'I usually treat earache by inserting a probe into the patient's ear, and waggling it about. It loosens any wax, you see.'

'Christ!' blurted Bartholomew. 'Do any of your patients go deaf after your ministrations?'

'No one has complained yet,' replied Holm shortly. 'And I have poked around in the ears of dozens of small children.'

Children who might not appreciate the fact that they had been deprived of one of their senses, thought

155

Bartholomew, deeply unimpressed. Dunning spoke before he could pursue the matter.

'How about a little music, Holm? You say you have a fine voice, but we have yet to hear it, and I am in the mood to be entertained.'

Holm had hummed when he had 'assisted' Bartholomew with the surgery on Coslaye's skull, and the physician recalled flinching several times at the sour notes that had emerged – and being obliged to ask him to desist in the end, lest it distressed their semi-conscious patient.

'Another time,' said Holm, but not before Bartholomew caught the flash of alarm in his eyes: he had lied about his accomplishments. 'When you have a lutenist to accompany me.'

'I can play the lute,' said Bartholomew wickedly. He was not very good at it, but he suspected it would not be his lack of talent that would be evident.

'And I sing,' said Michael, who did indeed have a fine voice. 'We shall perform a duet.'

'A duet?' cried Julitta, entering the room with a jug. 'How delightful!'

Holm stepped forward, took her hand and raised it to his lips. For the first time, Bartholomew studied him closely, to see why so many women considered him attractive. Reluctantly, for he found himself loath to think anything good about the man, he conceded that Holm was unusually handsome: he had arresting dark blue eyes to go with his golden mane, and his tight-fitting gipon, or tunic, had been cut to show off his slender figure to its best advantage. When he smiled at Julitta, even Bartholomew, who was not usually very observant about such matters, could see her heart melting with adoration for him.

'Not tonight, dearest. I am hoarse from advising patients

all day, and when you hear me sing, I want my voice to be at its best. I should hate to disappoint you.'

Julitta held his hand and gazed fondly at him until Dunning broke the moment by beginning to describe the ceremony at which Holm had been installed as a member of the Guild of Corpus Christi. The surgeon preened when Dunning remarked that he had never heard the oath of allegiance taken with such gravitas and dignity.

'Vale said the same,' he confided smugly. 'Before he died, of course.'

'Did you know Vale well?' asked Michael, pouring himself more claret.

'Not really,' Holm replied. 'We both arrived in Cambridge on Easter Day, so as newly established practitioners, we were naturally drawn to each other. But we were not friends.'

'You told me you liked him,' pounced Bartholomew, recalling Holm's wish, expressed as they had walked home together the previous evening, that it had been another physician who had died.

'No, I said I preferred him to the other *medici*,' corrected Holm pedantically. 'That is not the same as liking him.'

'So what did you think of him?' Michael sounded a little exasperated.

'That he was a scoundrel, particularly where women were concerned. No lady was safe from his pawing advances, not even married ones.'

'Vale once boasted to Bonabes that he was going to seduce Ruth,' said Dunning, scowling his indignation. 'Bonabes said he would run him through if he tried.'

'But please do not tell her,' begged Julitta uncomfortably. 'She does not know that part of the story, and it would embarrass her if she thought she had been the subject of such a discussion.' She glanced pointedly at her

157

father. 'In fact, I thought we had agreed to keep it between ourselves.'

'So we did,' slurred Dunning, chagrined. 'I forgot. Anyway, suffice to say that, out of spite, Vale put about a tale that Ruth was his secret lover. I imagine some folk believed it.'

'I doubt it,' said Holm chivalrously. 'No one could believe ill of Sir Eustace Dunning's daughters. They are paragons of virtue, as well as beauty.'

Greasy, thought Bartholomew sourly, recalling what Edith had said about the surgeon.

The discussion ranged off on to other matters then, and Bartholomew listened with half an ear, feeling his dislike of Holm mount by the moment. Was it because the man was an appalling sycophant, and his toadying was nauseating? Or because he was a dismal surgeon, too timid to perform procedures that should have been second nature, yet unafraid to dose children with unsuitable medicines or jab probes into their ears? Or because he was so flagrantly wrong for Julitta? Bartholomew studied her covertly. He longed to know her better, but in less than a month her marital status would mean that even the most innocent of friendships would be inappropriate.

'Will some of these books wend their way to the Common Library?' Michael asked when the conversation returned to Dunning's collection. 'Or will you spread your largesse more widely? Michaelhouse is always looking for new tomes.'

Bartholomew choked into his wine, startled by the brazen rapacity of the remark.

'Michaelhouse cannot have these,' replied Dunning. 'They will be Julitta's when I die.'

'What if she would rather have them sooner?' asked Holm. He smiled at his fiancée. 'Perhaps you should consider making them part of her dowry. Then I shall be able to read them to her as we spend romantic evenings together by the fire.'

Julitta flushed with pleasure at the notion, although Bartholomew was inclined to suspect that the surgeon was simply trying to negotiate himself a more profitable arrangement. Or was jealousy making him ungracious? But when Dunning shook his head at the suggestion, and he saw the flash of avaricious disappointment in Holm's eyes, he knew he was right to be suspicious.

'She cannot have them yet,' slurred Dunning. 'I may not peruse the things myself, but I like to see them on my shelves. They look pretty in their neat rows. Do you not agree?'

Unwilling to listen to Holm's gushing agreement, Bartholomew took down a psalter. He suspected, from the profusion of chickens, devils and ribauldequins, that it had come from the Carmelites, and was impressed by their collective talent. The weapon in particular was uncannily accurate, right down to the specks of rust on its metal barrels. He found himself thinking about Poitiers, and the fact that Dame Pelagia had admitted to being there, which led him to consider anew her reasons for descending on the town.

Had she dispatched Vale and the others, perhaps because they were experimenting on the sly, and she disapproved? But if she had, then surely she would not have lingered in Cambridge afterwards? Or had the quartet encountered the hooded men who had demanded the formula for wildfire, been mistaken for *medici* and killed when they had been unable to provide what was wanted? Bartholomew shuddered. It was not a comfortable thought.

The sun was setting, a great orange ball in a cloudless sky. A blackbird trilled from the top of the oak tree in

Dunning's garden, and there was a pleasing scent of warm earth and summer flowers. Michael settled more comfortably on a bench and refilled his goblet, but Bartholomew stood to leave. He still did not feel completely well, and knew it would be sensible to go home and secure a decent night's sleep.

'You ate virtually nothing this evening,' said Julitta, escorting him down the stairs. He was acutely aware of Holm's proprietary gaze on her as they went. 'Are you ill?'

'My stomach is unsettled from swallowing bad water. It is nothing serious.'

'I see.' Julitta looked thoughtful. 'What would you prescribe for a patient who came to you with the symptoms you are experiencing?'

'Nothing too strong. Perhaps a tonic of lovage root and mint. Why?'

'I shall make you one.' Julitta raised her hand when he began to object. 'Come with me to the kitchen. I have those ingredients, and it will not take a moment to boil some water.'

'You boil water for tonics?' asked Bartholomew, impressed. He did the same himself, although it was a practice his medical colleagues deemed deeply unorthodox.

'Of course! *Un*boiled water causes fluxes. I strain it, too, through a cloth, to eliminate further impurities.'

Bartholomew was very interested. Here was a woman after his own heart! 'Have you evidence to suggest that strained water is more effective?' he asked keenly.

Julitta smiled. 'I am afraid not. You see, so much sinister-looking sludge adheres to the cloth after filtering that I would never dream of not doing it now. I strain and boil all our water, even the stuff we use to wash our hands.'

Bartholomew gazed at her. The benefits of hand-washing was another practice his fellow *medici* scoffed at, yet here

160

was Julitta speaking as though hygiene was routine in her household. He found himself warming to her even more.

They reached the kitchen, which was spacious and spotlessly clean. Julitta indicated he was to sit at the table while she worked, and began chatting about mutual acquaintances – especially Edith, for whom she held a particular affection. At that point her conquest of Bartholomew was complete, for he was always willing to think well of people who praised his beloved sister. He listened to her with mounting affection, quite forgetting her fiancé sitting upstairs.

Eventually, she presented him with a cup. He sipped the contents warily, not sure how he felt about a woman preparing medicines he usually made himself. Its flavour was more pleasant than his own brews, and he realised that she had added honey. He resolved to do likewise in future – assuming his bet with Holm did not plunge him deep into debt, of course, and prevent him from purchasing ingredients for remedies ever again.

'Thank you for reasoning with your father in St Mary the Great this morning,' he said, watching her place the used pan in a bucket, ready to be washed the following day. 'I think he might have decried me as a warlock had you not intervened.'

'Oh, he would,' she agreed. 'And you do have a reputation for necromancy.'

'Yes, but it is undeserved,' he said defensively.

Julitta regarded him with raised eyebrows. 'Is it? Despite my defence of you, I know you *were* planning to slice into Vale. I could tell by the angle of your blade.'

Bartholomew was horrified – he did not want her to think him a ghoul. Or a sorcerer, for that matter. 'Then why did you tell your father I was cutting knotted laces?'

'Well, it was only Vale, and I have never liked him.'

Bartholomew glanced sharply at her, and saw her eyes were twinkling: she was teasing him. Then her expression became sombre. 'I defended you because I want you to find out what happened to Northwood, which you cannot do if you are in gaol for desecrating corpses. He was a dear, kind man, who often came to read to me, and I shall miss him terribly. He was teaching me philosophy.'

'Was he?' Here was yet another aspect of Northwood's complex character: the patient tutor. 'Why?'

'Because the subject fascinates me. If he was feloniously killed, I want the culprit brought to justice, and if that means misleading my father about the Corpse Examiner who is helping to investigate his death, then so be it. Besides, I know you wielded the knife only because you wanted answers. There was no wickedness in it.'

Bartholomew hesitated, but then forged on, feeling her remarks entitled her to an explanation. 'I think Northwood and the others were poisoned, but an external examination will never prove it. The only way to know for certain is to look inside them, to see whether damage to entrails . . .' He trailed off, not sure how much detail to provide.

Julitta winced. 'I can see how such a procedure might be useful, but it is horrible nonetheless. Perhaps you had better not embark on it, especially in St Mary the Great, where the chances of being caught are rather high.'

'It will not happen again,' he said fervently. 'I have learned my lesson.'

Julitta smiled. 'Good. Then let us say no more about it.' She cleared her throat apprehensively. 'At the risk of sounding selfish, one of the reasons I was distressed by Northwood's demise was because he had offered to teach me to read. I do not suppose you would oblige, would you?'

Bartholomew blinked, wondering whether he had

misheard, but could tell from the hope in her eyes that he had not. His heart clamoured at him to say yes, to earn time in her company, but the rational part of his mind reminded him that he was too busy and she was betrothed.

'If you like,' he heard himself say. 'But why ask me? I imagine Holm would enjoy—'

'It will be my wedding gift to him,' said Julitta, eyes sparkling. 'A literate woman to manage his household, and to provide him with intelligent conversation during long winter evenings.'

'Holm is a very lucky man,' said Bartholomew quietly.

Julitta laughed happily. 'And I am a very lucky woman.'

It was dark by the time Bartholomew left Dunning's house. The High Street was full of apprentices and labourers who had spent the evening beautifying their masters' property in preparation for the upcoming festival, and who had then gone to slake their thirst in alehouses. Now they were spilling out in drunken gaggles. Although there had been no serious trouble between the University and the town for months, a lone scholar still presented an attractive target for drink-fuelled townsmen, so Bartholomew cut down the alley that led to Milne Street to avoid unnecessary confrontations. He recalled that Cynric was supposed to be accompanying him out at night, as per Michael's recommendation following the attack by the hooded men who had wanted the formula for wildfire, but it had not occurred to him to ask the book-bearer to oblige.

Unfortunately, Milne Street contained its own collection of rowdy gangs, so with a weary sigh, he aimed for Cholles Lane instead. He strode past Batayl Hostel, Newe Inn and Holm's house, and turned right when he reached the river. There were no taverns on or by the towpath, and he would be able to enter Michaelhouse by its back gate.

As he walked, the clouds drifted away from the moon to reveal shadowy figures on the path ahead. He slowed, assuming some of the boisterous rabble had decided to cool themselves with a refreshing dip. They were everywhere that night, it seemed.

But there was nothing in the swift, confident way the figures moved to suggest they had been at the ale, and as he watched, he had the distinct impression that they were engaged in something felonious. He turned away, not so foolish as to challenge them on his own, and supposed that he would have to find yet another route home. But he had taken no more than a few steps back the way he had come before he stopped again.

Two men stood in front of him. It was too dark to see anything of them, other than the fact that their clothes appeared to be black and they wore some form of armour – he could hear leather creak and the clink of metal as they moved.

'Cut his throat,' said one to his companion. 'We have no time for nuisances.'

The other stepped forward, so Bartholomew whipped around and fled, acutely aware of footsteps pounding behind him. His route took him towards the shadowy figures farther on, but they had not ordered his death and he thought their presence would serve to foil the killers on his heels. He soon realised his mistake. Heads jerked up at the sound of running feet, and he heard the distinctive hiss of swords being drawn. Too late, he saw they were wearing the same kind of armour as the pair who were chasing him.

He skidded to a standstill, and one of his pursuers barrelled into him, sending him sprawling. He tried to stagger to his feet, but they forced him to the ground again. Someone grabbed his hair and yanked his head back.

Visions of Adam's slit throat flooded his mind, and he fought as hard as he could. Then he was released abruptly, and all he could hear was retreating footsteps. He struggled to his knees, spinning around in alarm when he sensed a presence behind him.

'Easy, Doctor. It is only us.'

The voice was familiar, but Bartholomew could not place it. He shot to his feet, and began to back away. His heart was pounding hard enough to hurt, and his stomach was churning. Where was Dame Pelagia when he needed her?

'It is Torvin,' came the voice again. 'The riverman.'

Bartholomew peered at him. Torvin was one of his patients, a member of the silent, insular community who lived in the ramshackle hovels that lined this part of the river. They eked a meagre existence from fishing and scraps scavenged from the Market Square, and their womenfolk weaved baskets and mats from rushes, which were exchanged for bread.

'I am here, too,' came another voice, this one instantly recognisable. It was Isnard the bargeman, swinging along on his crutches – Bartholomew had amputated his leg after an accident some years before. 'But you should not be. This is no place for a scholar after dark.'

'Nowhere is, tonight,' muttered Bartholomew. He looked around for his assailants, but all he could see were riverfolk, distinctive in their ill-assorted rags and reed hats. 'Who were those men?'

'I have no idea,' replied Isnard. 'However, this is the rivermen's domain, and they do not take kindly to strangers coming at night. They drove the trespassers off with a few well-placed arrows.'

'We just frightened them,' Torvin clarified hastily. 'We are not killers, despite what is being brayed about us in the town.'

'I know.' Bartholomew smiled briefly at the silent throng. 'But I suspect the rogues you just drove off are; I think they are the men who murdered Adam, the beggar and the night-watchman. Sheriff Tulyet has been trying to find them.'

'Unfortunately, he will not succeed,' said Torvin. 'They are too clever for him.'

'I thought you said they were strangers.' Bartholomew's voice was unsteady now the danger was over, and so were his legs. 'So how do you know they are too clever?'

'Because I have eyes,' replied Torvin softly. 'And I have watched them several times now. They move like water rats – silent, fast and deadly. The Sheriff is no match for them.'

'Are they smugglers?' asked Bartholomew.

'Maybe,' said Isnard. 'They certainly like to loiter around the town's quieter waterways. Moreover, they are well-armed and ruthless, and you are right – it probably *was* them who killed Adam, the night-watchman and . . .' He trailed off, and shot the rivermen an awkward glance.

'And my nephew,' finished Torvin. 'But the Sheriff thinks he was a beggar.'

'Do not tell Tulyet, though,' said Isnard to Bartholomew in an undertone. 'They cannot afford a priest or a gravedigger, but the Sheriff can, and he will see things decently done. The lad will gain more from being thought a vagrant, than from being named as one of them.'

'Very well,' said Bartholomew. 'But I will have to report what happened. Tulyet needs to know that armed men are haunting his town.'

'I will tell him, too,' said Isnard. 'First thing tomorrow. Thank you for betting five marks on our integrity, by the way. Holm is always saying vile things about me and the riverfolk, and we were touched by your faith.'

166

Wryly, Bartholomew supposed that if the five-mark wager had induced them to come to his rescue, then it was money very well spent.

The next day was cloudy, but still warm, and the breeze was from the south. It carried the scent of ripening crops, and Bartholomew inhaled deeply as he stood in Michaelhouse's yard, waiting to walk to church. He stifled a sigh when William and Thelnetham began sniping over who was to preach that day. Suttone joined in, but the debate came to an abrupt end when Clippesby's rat made an appearance. It shot towards Thelnetham, who shrieked girlishly, and pandemonium erupted, with the Gilbertine cowering, William guffawing and Suttone yelling at Clippesby to catch it.

'Our Dominican is not as lunatic as he would have us believe,' said Ayera, as he watched. 'He released that thing deliberately, to quell the spat. And it worked, after a fashion.'

Langelee arrived, scowling when he saw his Fellows in such noisy disarray. Crossly, he whipped open the gate, and strode towards St Michael's, leaving them to scramble to catch up with him. Ayera ran to his side, and a reluctant smile stole over the Master's face when he heard what Clippesby had done. Bartholomew was next, with Michael slouching beside him; William, Suttone and Clippesby were on their heels; and Thelnetham was last, because it had taken him longer to regain his composure. He was still furious, although Bartholomew suspected it would be William, not Clippesby, who would bear the brunt of his ire.

'What time did you come home last night?' Bartholomew asked Michael, noting that the monk looked decidedly fragile.

167

'I cannot recall, and I should not have stayed so late, because Holm is hardly congenial company. But I kept hoping that Dunning would let something slip about the men who died in the garden of the house he donated to the University.'

Bartholomew regarded him askance. 'Dunning is a suspect now?'

Michael put a hand to his head. 'I cannot recall why I thought so now, although it made sense at the time. But it was a waste of effort – I learned nothing to help us. Other than that Dunning has a theory to explain why Coslaye was almost killed by Acton's *Questio Disputata*.'

'What is it?' asked Bartholomew, when the monk paused.

'That some scholar decided its binding was inferior, so elected to hurl it as far away from him as possible.' Michael smiled. 'I only wish it were true, because a bibliophile with those sorts of standards would be easy to identify.'

'You still have not given up on that case? Everyone else has forgotten about it.'

'Coslaye has not, and neither have his Batayl colleagues. Besides, as I have explained before, we cannot have scholars resorting to violence when ballots do not go the way they hope.'

'I suppose not. What will you do today?'

'Loiter in Cholles Lane and waylay passers-by to see whether anyone noticed anything odd on Tuesday night or early Wednesday. I shall question the Carmelites and the Batayl men again, too.'

'Do you want me to help?'

'I can manage, thank you. Terrorise your students into cramming more knowledge into their already overloaded minds today, and we shall resume our enquiries together tomorrow.'

Bartholomew took him at his word, and after church

168

he staged a series of mock-disputations designed to hone his pupils' debating skills. He drove them hard, but felt it was worthwhile, despite the fact that they reeled from the hall at the end of the morning complaining that their heads were spinning. He left them to their grumbles, and went to tell Tulyet what had happened the previous night.

Although Cambridge was mostly flat, it did have a hill, and it was on top of this that the Normans had raised a castle some three hundred years earlier. It had originally comprised a wooden structure atop a motte, but a lot of money had been spent on it since, and it was now a sizeable fortress. There was a spacious bailey, enclosed by curtain walls and ditches; at each corner was a sturdy drum tower, while the south-eastern wall boasted the huge, cylindrical Great Tower, the strongest and most formidable part of the complex.

Access to the bailey was gained by crossing a rickety drawbridge and ducking under a portcullis that was rumoured to be hanging by a thread. It was not that Tulyet was careless about maintenance, but that he preferred to divert funds to more urgent causes than the upkeep of a castle with no serious enemies. Beyond them was the Gatehouse, an impressive structure bristling with arrow slits and machicolations. Bartholomew was waved through it with smiles and cheerful greetings from the guards, most of whom he had treated for the occasional bout of fever or minor injury sustained during training.

The Sheriff was in his office in the Great Tower. Clerks, not warriors, surrounded him, and he was sitting in his shirtsleeves, almost invisible behind the piles of documents that awaited his attention. He beamed when he saw Bartholomew, and rose to his feet with obvious relief.

'You cannot leave!' objected one of the clerks, as Tulyet

made for the door. Bartholomew was surprised to note it was Willelmus from the Carmelite Priory – the man who liked to draw chickens. 'We have not finished the tax returns for—'

'They can wait,' said Tulyet crisply. 'We have been labouring all morning, and I need a rest.'

'I thought you were a White Friar,' said Bartholomew to the scribe.

'He is,' replied Tulyet, as Willelmus squinted, trying to identify the physician from his voice. 'And he would much rather be painting hens. But my own clerks are overwhelmed by the additional work the taxes represent, so Prior Etone lent him to me.'

Willelmus did look as though he would rather be in his scriptorium, especially when the man he was supposed to be helping abandoned his duties to pass the time of day with friends, leaving him to twiddle his thumbs. He sighed his exasperation as the Sheriff escaped, standing in such a way that one hand rested pointedly on a pile of documents. Clearly, there was still a lot to do.

'He is so keen to get back to his real work that he is something of a slave-driver,' confided Tulyet, clattering down the spiral staircase. 'I am eager to finish, too, because the King hates his money to be delivered late. But I have my limits.'

When they reached the bailey, Tulyet stretched until his shoulders cracked. Then he turned his face to the sun and closed his eyes, breathing the fresh air with obvious relief. He had always hated sitting indoors, being a naturally energetic, active man.

'If you are working on these levies, who is investigating Adam's death?' asked Bartholomew.

Tulyet opened his eyes. 'I am, with every free moment I have. But the taxes are almost ready now. We have great crates of coins locked in the Great Tower, waiting to be taken to London.'

'Perhaps you should post extra guards on the Gatehouse,' suggested Bartholomew. 'I imagine every robber in the county will be interested in "great crates of coins".'

Tulyet laughed. 'It would have to be a very bold thief who attempted to raid a royal castle. But what can I do for you today? Are you here to tell me what happened last night? Isnard said you would come.'

Bartholomew described the events of the previous evening in as much detail as he could, yet although Tulyet listened attentively, the physician was acutely aware that he had little of substance to relate. He could not describe the men, other than to say that they had worn armour, and he was unable to guess what they had been doing. His only real contribution was that the riverfolk considered them strangers, so they were probably not townsmen or scholars.

'I sent one of my soldiers to inspect that strip of river-bank, but there was nothing to see,' said Tulyet when he had finished. 'Isnard had garnered a few more details from the riverfolk – for which I am grateful, because they would never have confided in me – but it all adds up to very little.'

'I think they are the men who killed Adam,' said Bartholomew. 'One of them ordered his crony to cut my throat.'

'You are almost certainly right. Moreover, I suspect they have claimed more than three victims. Several other folk have gone missing of late, and I cannot help but wonder whether they have had their throats cut, too, and their bodies hidden or tossed in the river. It is a bad state of affairs, and I would be hunting these villains now, were it not for these damned revenues.'

'Can you not delegate those to someone else?' asked Bartholomew, thinking that catching killers was a lot more important than money, although he suspected the King would disagree.

'I wish I could, but I have no wish to lose my post because a minion is careless with his arithmetic. The King takes his taxes seriously – it is expensive to keep the Prince of Wales campaigning in France. Did I tell you that we are ordered to provide a ribauldequin this year, too, as part of our payment? Still, it could have been worse – York had to make five hundred hauberks.'

Bartholomew, gazed at him, disgusted that the taxes his College was forced to pay – which always necessitated draconian economies and sacrifice – were being spent on such a wicked contraption. He was not stupid enough to say so to one of His Majesty's most loyal officers, though, and floundered around for an innocuous response. 'Are ribauldequins difficult to manufacture?'

'Very. They require precision casting of high-quality metal. It is finished now, thank God. It took a while, because I had never seen one, and I had to find out what they entail.'

'The King's clerks did not provide specifications?'

'They did, but we needed more detail. I would have asked you to help – you saw them in action at Poitiers – but I had a feeling you would refuse, like Northwood did.'

'Northwood?' asked Bartholomew, startled. 'Why would you ask him?'

'Because he was also at Poitiers, as chaplain to one of the Prince's generals. But he said that while he would be happy to destroy a ribauldequin, he would never assist in the making of one.'

'I did not know he was at the battle,' said Bartholomew. 'He never mentioned it.'

'He claimed it was the nastiest experience he had ever had, and disliked talking about it. He confided in me only because we were friends.'

'Holm was at Poitiers, too.' Bartholomew felt like adding that the surgeon had sided with the French, but was not entirely sure how Tulyet would react, and although he disliked Holm, he did not want to be responsible for his arrest.

'I doubt he did any fighting,' said Tulyet disparagingly. 'The man looks lean and fit, but there is no real strength in him. Women fall at his feet – and even my wife claims he has the body of a Greek god – but he is a feeble specimen in my view.'

'It is a pity we spend money on fighting the French,' said Bartholomew. He fully agreed with Tulyet, but was afraid that once *he* began to list the surgeon's faults, he might not be able to stop. 'There are much better causes.'

Tulyet nodded ruefully. 'Like dredging the King's Ditch, which is so full of silt that anyone can paddle across it after a dry spell, and it provides no kind of defence for the town at all.'

'Or feeding the town's poor,' added Bartholomew.

Tulyet was not listening. 'I had hoped the French would sue for peace after Poitiers. Their country is in a terrible state: their army is in disarray, their peasants are on the verge of rebellion; and their King is our prisoner but they cannot afford the ransom. Neither can a number of their nobles, including the Archbishop of Sens, the Count of Eu and the Sire de Rougé.'

'It was in a terrible state before the battle,' said Bartholomew, recalling the devastation wrought by the Prince of Wales's troops. 'Crops and villages burnt, live-stock slaughtered. I do not blame the peasants for declining to pay these ransoms. Why should they, when

173

these nobles taxed them in order to raise troops for defence, but then failed to protect them?'

'That is a recklessly seditious remark, Matt,' said Tulyet mildly. 'Although Northwood said much the same. Incidentally, have you heard the rumour that his death is connected to Sawtre's – that all five dead scholars were struck down because they went against the wishes of their College, hostel or convent by supporting the University's new library?'

'Yes, but there is no evidence to say it is true.'

'There is also a tale that says God is the culprit,' Tulyet went on, 'although I do not believe it myself. However, it is a notion that is gaining credence in many quarters.'

'I have heard that the Devil might be responsible, too.' Bartholomew smiled. 'There cannot be many instances where God and Satan are credited with the same deed. But how did you build your ribauldequin if you have never seen one and people refused to advise you? No, do not tell me! Riborowe! He has an unhealthy fascination with the infernal things.'

'Yes, he does, thankfully, or I would have been floundering. Langelee and Chancellor Tynkell were helpful, too, and so was Walkelate.'

'Walkelate?' said Bartholomew doubtfully. 'But he is an architect.'

'Precisely. And architects build things. He was able to take the others' sketches and convert them into working plans. Would you like to see the finished article? It is quite impressive.'

'No, thank you!' Bartholomew shuddered. 'If I never set eyes on one of those vile creations again, it will be too soon.'

Bartholomew was called to Batayl Hostel before he could return to Michaelhouse, but was not sorry that the summons meant he would miss the midday meal. His innards were still tender, despite Julitta's tonic, and nothing at College was likely to tempt him – the recent tax demand meant that Michaelhouse was in an especially lean phase, so Langelee had ordered the cooks to make meals as unappetising as possible in the hope that his scholars would eat less, and thus save him money.

Batayl was a small, shabby building, comprising a single room in which Coslaye, Browne and their eight students ate, slept, taught and relaxed. There was a tiny yard at the back that contained a reeking latrine, and any cooking was either done at the hearth, or taken to the communal ovens in the Market Square.

'Sorry, Matt,' said Michael, who was waiting outside for him. 'I came to ask my questions, but when I saw the state of its residents . . . well, suffice to say that I sent for you, and will leave my investigation until they are feeling better.'

When Bartholomew entered Batayl, he was immediately assailed by the reek of cheap candles, burnt fat and unwashed feet, an odour he had come to associate with the poorer kind of hostel. He was taken aback to see that one wall had been given a garish mural, sure it had not been there the last time he had visited.

'It is the Battle of Poitiers,' explained Coslaye, hands on his stomach as he lay on a pallet. Several lads were curled in groaning misery around him, while the rest were outside, vying for a place in the latrines. 'Most of the action took place near a wood, which you can see at the bottom. The English warriors are the ones with haloes, and the French have horns, tails and forked tongues.'

'Lord!' breathed Bartholomew, staggered by the amount of blood that had been depicted.

'It is Principal Coslaye's handiwork,' said Browne, his

voice dripping disapproval. 'He did it when he was recovering from the surgery you performed on his head.'

'It is very . . . colourful,' said Bartholomew, aware that Coslaye was waiting for a compliment, although the truth was that the whole thing was ridiculously gruesome. In one section, headless French knights were still busily doing battle with the angelic English, their limbs operated by the demons that sat on their shoulders.

'It was either this, or a picture of Satan being welcomed at the Carmelite Priory,' elaborated Coslaye. 'I opted for Poitiers when I learned that red paint is cheaper than all the white I would have needed for their habits.'

'I see.' Bartholomew changed the subject, unwilling to be drawn into a dispute that was none of his concern. 'What happened here? Did you drink bad water? Or eat tainted food?'

'No, we have been poisoned,' declared Coslaye. 'By the Carmelites. They slipped a toxin into the stew we all ate. Well, Browne did not have any, because he does not like French food.' He indicated a handsome student who was older than the others. 'Pepin did the cooking today, you see, and he is French.'

'Is he?' Bartholomew was unable to stop himself from glancing at the mural.

'Yes, but he is not the same as his countrymen,' whispered Coslaye confidentially. 'He is a decent soul, whereas the rest of them are villains. We do not think of him as foreign.'

'Right,' said Bartholomew, wondering how Pepin could endure such bigotry. He turned his thoughts back to medicine, and looked at Browne. 'What did you eat?'

'A bit of bread and cheese,' replied Browne. 'But I am poisoned, too, because I feel sick.'

'That is because you are in a stuffy room with a lot of

176

vomiting men,' surmised Bartholomew. 'Go outside, and you will feel better.'

'You want me out of the way so you can chant spells without me hearing,' said Browne accusingly, although he went to stand by the open door. 'You know how I deplore your association with Lucifer.'

'Bartholomew has no association with Lucifer,' snapped Coslaye irritably. 'You talk nonsense, man – and in front of our students, too. You should be ashamed of yourself.'

'What was in this meal you shared?' asked Bartholomew quickly, eager to identify the cause of the problem so he could escape. The smelly hostel was no place to linger, and he had no wish to spend time with the antagonistic Browne, either.

'It was a recipe from my home in Angoulême,' supplied Pepin in such perfectly unaccented French that it could only be his mother tongue. 'It contained—'

'Angoulême?' blurted Bartholomew before he could stop himself. 'That is near Poitiers.'

'Actually, it is some distance away,' countered Pepin, shooting an uneasy glance at Coslaye. 'And the roads are poor, so it is impossible to ride from one to the other in less than three days.'

Bartholomew knew he was lying: he had done it in half a day, on foot. But he said nothing, already regretting having made the observation in the first place.

Coslaye regarded Pepin suspiciously. 'If you were in the area, did you see the battle fought?'

'No, of course not,' replied Pepin, swallowing hard. 'I am a scholar, not a warrior.'

'So is Bartholomew, but he still joined in,' jibed Browne. 'And it is not something to be proud of, either. Civilised men should know better than to slaughter each other like savages.'

'Nonsense,' countered Coslaye. 'It was a great day for England, and I wish I had been there. I am envious of you, Bartholomew. I am envious of Riborowe of the Carmelites, too, and Holm the surgeon, although *he* contradicts himself when he describes the action, and his account does not tally with others I have heard. *Ergo*, I am disinclined to believe he took part.'

'You should not be listening to battle stories at all,' muttered Browne. He did not speak loudly enough for Coslaye to hear, although Pepin nodded heartfelt agreement. 'It is unseemly.'

'Are you sure you were not at the battle, Pepin?' Coslaye asked, turning his fierce gaze on the student again. 'We shall not expel you, if you were. I only want to know out of interest.'

'No, I was not there,' said Pepin levelly. 'I rarely visit Poitiers. It is dirty and smells of onions.'

'What was in the stew?' asked Bartholomew, leading the discussion back to medicine. He hoped his incautious remark would not bring trouble to Pepin in the future.

'It is called *tout marron*,' replied Pepin, patently grateful to be talking about something else. 'And it contained all manner of things – meat left over from Sunday, a bit of fish, some winter vegetables. And a lot of garlic. Garlic works wonders on food past its best.'

'It might disguise the flavour, but not the impact,' said Bartholomew. 'And Sunday was five days ago. That is a long time for meat to be stored, especially now the weather is warm.'

'Times are hard,' said Browne. 'We cannot afford to throw food away, no matter what its state of decomposition. We are not rich, like cosseted Fellows in Colleges.'

'It is cheaper than buying medicines for the consequences,' retorted Bartholomew tartly, writing out a tonic

178

for the apothecary to prepare. He carried enough to soothe one or two roiling stomachs, but nowhere enough to remedy an entire hostel. Batayl would have to purchase its own.

He returned to Michaelhouse just in time to intercept his students, who were on their way out. All had combed their hair and donned their finery in anticipation of an afternoon in the town.

'We worked hard this morning, sir,' explained Valence, his senior pupil, defensively. 'So we thought we would . . . sit in the garden and continue our studies in a more relaxed atmosphere.'

'Very relaxed,' remarked Bartholomew dryly. 'You do not have a single scroll among you.'

Valence flushed, caught out. 'But the other Fellows are letting their lads study alone for the rest of the day! You are the only one who insists on holding classes.'

'Perhaps they are satisfied with their pupils' progress,' said Bartholomew. 'But you still have much to learn. Can you tell me how to make an infusion of lily of the valley?'

'I imagine you boil it up,' replied Valence sullenly. 'Or pound it into a pulp.'

'For which ailments can it be used?' asked Bartholomew, unimpressed.

'Spots,' suggested another lad. 'Colic, fevers and consumption. And warts and broken limbs.'

Bartholomew raised his eyebrows. 'If all that were true, medical herbaria would never need grow anything else. But these are basic questions, and you should know the answers.'

'All right,' said Valence, throwing up his hands in defeat. 'You win, sir. Shall I read about lily of the valley to the others, or will you do it?'

Supposing he could concede to their desire to be outside,

Bartholomew took them to the orchard. It was pleasant, sitting under the fresh green leaves, with bees buzzing in the long grass and birds twittering above their heads. He read until the bell rang to announce the end of the day's teaching, and was wholly mystified when his students made an immediate and unanimous bid for freedom.

While he had been busy, patients had sent word that they needed to see him, so he spent the rest of the afternoon and most of the evening visiting. His customers included Isnard, who had been punched during a brawl at the King's Head; Prior Etone, whose chilblains were paining him; and finally Chancellor Tynkell, who had worked himself into a state.

'I am agitated to the point of nausea,' Tynkell announced, when Bartholomew reached the Chancellor's office in St Mary the Great. 'I wish I had never started this library business. The strain is too great.'

'Why should it distress you now?' asked Bartholomew, reaching into his bag for a remedy to soothe ragged nerves. 'By this time next week, the building will be open. You are past the worst.'

'Walkelate has been splendid,' agreed Tynkell miserably. 'I did not think he would succeed in time, but he has worked extremely hard. But it is the inaugural ceremony I am worried about now. Opinionated men from Batayl, King's Hall, Gonville and the Carmelite Priory will make a fuss and spoil it. I asked Brother Michael if we could ban them from the festivities, but he said no.'

'Did he explain why?'

'Because barring the Colleges and convents would leave the hostels, and the scholars enrolled in those cannot always be guaranteed to behave, either.'

'Why do you need a ceremony? Why not just unlock the door and let people in?'

'Because Dunning wants one. Besides, I am hoping it will encourage donations of books.'

Bartholomew had no answers for him. 'Are you really retiring next year?' he asked instead.

Tynkell nodded. 'Yes. I am tired of being Michael's lackey. Everyone knows he runs the University anyway, so he can have himself elected properly. He is not very pleased, but it is time I put my foot down.'

'What will you do?'

'I shall pursue my private studies. Why do you think I want a Common Library? I am not a member of a wealthy College, and it was the only way I could get access to all the books I shall want to read.'

'I see,' said Bartholomew, surprised by the selfish admission.

'And I want to be remembered for something other than being Michael's puppet, too,' Tynkell went on. He swallowed the draught Bartholomew handed him, then released a gusty sigh. 'Thank you. And thank you for having the courage to vote for my library. It cannot have been easy to stand against Michael. I know I would not have done it, had I been in your shoes.'

Bartholomew laughed. 'He is not such a dragon when you come to know him.'

'But I do know him. And he is a dragon – a great big fat one with heavy bones.'

It was late evening by the time Bartholomew returned to the College. The students were in the hall, some revising for their examinations but most enjoying the opportunity to relax with their friends. He made for the conclave, the pleasant chamber at the far end of the hall that was the undisputed domain of the Fellows; students and servants were not permitted inside.

'Where are Langelee and Ayera?' he asked, taking a

181

seat at the table and pouring himself a cup of wine that had been watered to a pale pink. All the other Fellows were there.

'Who knows,' replied Thelnetham, patting a bright yellow scarf in place around his neck. He primped and fluffed even more when he realised that William was watching, clearly intending to antagonise the incendiary Franciscan. 'They said they were going out, but declined to mention where.'

'Langelee would never confide in you,' scoffed William. 'He thinks you are a peacock.'

'That is a compliment compared to what he said about you,' Thelnetham flashed back. 'But I shall not repeat it in public. Obscenities offend my delicate sensibilities.'

And then a quarrel was in progress. Suttone took William's side, not because he liked the friar, but because he disliked the Gilbertine. Clippesby sat in a corner, and gave his entire concentration to the animal he was cradling. Bartholomew frowned when he saw it was the rat.

'I had a wasted day, just as I predicted,' said Michael, speaking loudly to make himself heard over the acrimonious babble. 'Although I did successfully quell a spat between Ovyng Hostel and Peterhouse over the Common Library. Of course, arguments over that place are so common these days that it is hardly worth mentioning them.'

'You learned nothing to help us with our enquiries?' asked Bartholomew.

'Not a thing. Let us hope we have better luck tomorrow.'

182

CHAPTER 6

Bartholomew slept unusually well, and woke, wholly refreshed, just before dawn. He rose, washed in the bowl of water that Cynric had left for him, and rummaged in his chest for a clean shirt. Then he spent a few moments in the library, preparing the texts he wanted his students to read that day. It was a Saturday, so lessons would end early, but there was still a good deal that could be accomplished in the few hours available.

By the time he had finished, his colleagues were gathering in the yard, ready to walk to church. He joined them, chatting to Suttone about the plague and trying to make Clippesby understand that rats in the College were unacceptable, even when they came to inform Michaelhouse that strange men had prowled the town the night before, and that one had sworn at a barking dog.

'Ayera was out all last night,' said Thelnetham snidely. 'Perhaps he did the swearing.'

'He likes dogs,' said Clippesby, his eyes wide and without guile. 'He would never offend one with vulgar language.'

'Christ's blood!' muttered Thelnetham, regarding him askance. 'Sometimes I wonder why I joined this College, for none of its Fellows are normal. You are a lunatic; Suttone is obsessed with the plague; Bartholomew is a warlock; Langelee and Ayera are womanising hedonists; Michael is the Bishop's spy; and William is . . . well, William is William.'

'And what do you mean by that, pray?' demanded William, narrowing his eyes.

Fortunately, Thelnetham was prevented from providing an answer because the gate opened to admit one of Tulyet's soldiers. He was breathless and white faced, and had clearly run as hard as he could. His name was Helbye, and he was one of Tulyet's most trusted sergeants.

'You are needed at the castle, Doctor,' he gasped urgently. 'Now.'

Bartholomew looped his medical bag over his shoulder, and followed him out. Helbye immediately started running, so Bartholomew did likewise. He was growing alarmed. He was often summoned to tend Tulyet's men, but was rarely expected to sprint there.

'We have been attacked,' gasped Helbye, by means of explanation. 'There are casualties . . .'

Bartholomew gaped at him. 'Attacked? But the place is a fortress!'

Helbye flapped his hand to tell Bartholomew to go on without him. 'I should ring the bell in All Saints . . . warn folk to be on their guard.'

The bell began to clang shortly afterwards, its panicky jangle distinctly different from the gentle chimes that announced dawn prayers. People poured from their homes, and word soon spread that the castle had suffered a raid by armed men. Meryfeld, emerging from his house wearing a long nightgown, tried to waylay Bartholomew and ask questions, but the physician only yelled at him to dress and run to the fortress as quickly as possible. If the situation was as serious as he was coming to suspect, then he would need all the help he could get.

Tulyet was waiting when the guards – vigilant and heavily armed – ushered Bartholomew through the Gatehouse. The Sheriff was pale, and there was blood on his shirt.

'Not mine,' he said, waving away Bartholomew's concern. 'And not the enemy's either, more is the pity. I was trying to help the injured – until Holm and Rougham ordered me away.'

He led Bartholomew across the bailey to where a number of soldiers lay in a row. The faces of some were already covered, and Holm and Rougham were nearby, deep in discussion.

'It all happened so fast,' said Tulyet tightly. 'They took us completely by surprise.'

'Who did?' asked Bartholomew, kneeling next to the first casualty. The man was groaning, clutching an arm that poured blood, and the physician wondered why Holm had not stemmed the flow. He bound it quickly, then moved to the next patient; he would suture the wound later, once he was sure he was not needed more urgently elsewhere first. It was a practice he had learned at Poitiers, when he had been all but overwhelmed with men screaming for his help.

'I wish I knew. Christ, Matt! You and I joked only yesterday about the place being raided, and I declared so flippantly that it would never happen!'

Bartholomew became aware that Tulyet was not the only person hovering behind him. He glanced around, expecting it to be Holm or Rougham, but it was Cynric. The book-bearer was breathless, having dashed to the castle the moment the bells had announced that trouble was afoot. Without a word, he pulled a handful of bandages from the physician's bag, ready to pass to him as and when they were needed.

'We had no inkling it was going to happen,' Tulyet continued. His voice was unsteady with shock. 'Obviously, we knew armed men had been prowling at night – you and Isnard told us about them – but we did not anticipate this! I had arrived at dawn to begin work on the taxes, and suddenly, without any warning, my bailey was full of howling intruders.'

'French?' asked Cynric, watching Bartholomew remove his cloak and tuck it around a man who had only moments to live. 'They howl. I heard them at Poitiers.'

'Their army is still in disarray and in no position to invade,' replied Tulyet tersely. 'And would not pick on Cambridge if it were – there are far more lucrative and easily accessible targets than us. I have no idea who these men are, but they came on us like furies.'

'What did they want?' asked Bartholomew, moving to a man with a chest injury that was well beyond his skills. He looked around, saw Michael hurrying towards him, and indicated that he was to give last rites. As a monk, Michael should not have been qualified, but he had been granted dispensation to hear confessions during the plague, and had continued the practice since.

'The tax money, of course,' replied Tulyet impatiently. 'They aimed straight for the Great Tower, where we keep it. Fortunately, my archers reacted with commendable speed, and we were able to fend them off.'

'Did you take prisoners?' asked Cynric. 'They will give you the location of their comrades' lair in exchange for their lives. Then we can raid *them*.'

'Just one.' Tulyet nodded to where a man was being bundled towards the castle gaol, guarded by three tense soldiers. 'But he declines to talk.'

'Will you track them, then?' asked Cynric eagerly. 'I will help.'

Tulyet gripped his shoulder gratefully. 'Thank you. If anyone can catch them, it is you.'

Bartholomew regarded them uneasily. 'It might be a trap, to lure you out and capture you. We talked

186

about ransoms only yesterday, and a Sheriff's will cost a fortune.'

'We will be careful,' promised Tulyet. 'And I am not waiting here for them to do it again.'

Bartholomew moved to the next victim, who had been shot in the neck. Fortunately, the arrow had missed the main blood vessels, although it would not be easy to remove the barb without compounding the damage, and he wondered whether Holm would be up to the task. The surgeon was still talking to Rougham, and now Meryfeld had joined them.

'We shall need a table, a good lamp, plenty of hot water and strips of clean cloth,' Bartholomew said to Tulyet. He glanced at the row of injured. 'Holm has enough work to keep him busy all day.'

'I want you to tend them, not him,' said Tulyet, snapping his fingers at a passing servant to organise what was required. 'They must have the best.'

There was a clatter of hoofs as saddled horses were backed out of stables. Strapping on a broadsword, Tulyet ran towards them, beckoning to Cynric as he went. He mounted up and galloped out of the bailey without another word, his men and the book-bearer trailing behind him. Michael sketched a blessing after them, but Bartholomew kept his attention on the injured. The next soldier he inspected was dead, and the one after that had lost part of his hand.

'Holm!' he shouted, wondering what the surgeon thought he was doing. 'Help me!'

'I am in conference,' Holm snapped irritably. 'A scribe has had a seizure, and we are discussing how best to treat him.'

Bartholomew saw a friar sitting on the ground at their feet, but did not think he deserved three *medici* while the rest of the injured were left with one.

'This soldier has just bled to death,' he yelled angrily.

187

'He need not have done, had someone thought to bind his wound. He died while you were chatting!'

'How dare you imply that I am to blame!' Holm took several angry steps towards him.

'What needs to be done?' It was Gyseburne, breathing hard as he raced across the bailey. 'We are all here now. Organise us, Matthew. You are the one with battlefield experience.'

'I have battlefield experience,' declared Holm indignantly. 'I have saved many a life with—'

'Then save some today,' interrupted Bartholomew curtly. 'See to this man. Gyseburne, tend the neck injury. Rougham, check my bandages are holding. Meryfeld, help me here.'

Once given specific tasks to perform, the *medici* worked well together. There were two arrows to be removed, five broken limbs to set, seven serious wounds to suture, a head injury to monitor, and a host of lacerations and bruises to treat. It promised to be a very busy day.

Although the castle was a hive of activity, with a lot of hectic coming and going, security had never been tighter, with every soldier armed to the teeth and archers stationed all along the walls. Tulyet's office was hastily converted into a makeshift hospital, and it was there that Bartholomew sawed, stitched, severed and sliced. Holm assisted to start with, but was more hindrance than help, and the physician soon relegated him to the less serious cases. Holm complied with obvious relief, and it was clear that he had been well out of his depth.

'No,' said Rougham firmly, when Bartholomew asked him to take Holm's place. 'I do not consort with blood. You must assign me to those patients who have already stopped leaking.'

'And I must leave you, I am afraid,' said Meryfeld, rubbing his filthy hands together. 'I have important business elsewhere.'

Bartholomew watched him bustle away in dismay, wondering what sort of man abandoned his colleagues in a crisis.

'It is the money,' explained Gyseburne. 'He knows that Tulyet will spend all available funds on catching these invaders, and so will not have enough to pay us for our work here today.'

'You are right!' cried Rougham in dismay. 'I had not thought of that. Damn!'

Gyseburne nodded to where Holm was struggling to wrap a sprained wrist, and lowered his voice. 'I am unimpressed with our surgeon. I distrusted him the moment I met him – my mother always says you cannot trust a man with an overly pretty face – and his ineptitude today does nothing to make me revise my opinion. If he was at Poitiers, then I am the Pope!'

'Never mind him! What about our fees?' asked Rougham. Then an acquisitive expression crossed his face. 'But Willelmus is a Carmelite, and they are a wealthy Order. Do you think they will pay for a horoscope? He has recovered from his seizure now, but an analysis of his stars might prevent it from happening again.'

Bartholomew glanced up from his work, and saw that the man who had commanded the attention of the three *medici* earlier was the White Friar who liked drawing chickens. He was sitting disconsolately on a bench, sipping wine. Once it had been established that Prior Etone would indeed pay for any course of treatment deemed necessary, Rougham volunteered to take him off Bartholomew's hands by escorting him home and tendering some personal care. Overhearing, Holm abandoned his bandaging and hared after them, declaring that such a serious case would require surgical expertise as well as whatever Rougham had to offer.

That left Gyseburne, whose contribution was to examine the urine of every patient. Surprisingly, some of his diagnoses were helpful, and when he saw his efforts were appreciated, he even agreed to hold the head of the man with the arrow in his neck while Bartholomew removed the missile, although he was careful to keep his eyes averted.

It was dark before Bartholomew had done all he could. He sank wearily on to a stool, wiping his face with his sleeve. His clothes were soaked in blood, right down to his shoes, and he was exhausted. But he had the satisfaction of knowing that six men now had a fighting chance of survival, while another four might live if they did not develop fevers. Three more had died.

Tulyet arrived shortly after nightfall, empty handed and dispirited. He immediately came to ask after his men, listening with a bowed head to the depressing tally.

'They have been with me for years,' he said in a hoarse voice. 'When I find the villains who did this, I will hang every last one of them. No one kills my troops and lives to tell the tale.'

'You caught one,' said Gyseburne. 'Will you hang him?'

'Not yet. But I had better speak to him, to see whether a day in my dungeons has loosened his tongue. Come with me, Matt. I am less likely to run the bastard through if you are there.'

Bartholomew stood to follow him to the Gatehouse, the basement of which served as a gaol, but Tulyet looked him up and down, and then grabbed a cloak that was lying on a bench.

'Wear this. I do not want you sauntering around

bespattered with gore; it will frighten the men. Of course, I may ask you to remove it when we reach our prisoner – you look like a torturer.'

Bartholomew glanced down at himself, and saw the Sheriff's point. He took the garment, and Tulyet led the way across the bailey and down some damp steps, nodding to a guard to unlock the door. It swung open to reveal a dismal little cell with damp walls and a filthy floor. The captive, who had the look of an old soldier about him, wore a boiled-leather jerkin, and his grey-brown hair was long and greasy. There was a dull, flat expression in his eyes, a combination of resignation and defiance.

'Your name?' asked Tulyet coldly.

'Why? It will mean nothing to you.'

'Almost certainly,' agreed Tulyet. 'But I would like it for my records nonetheless.'

'Very well. Then I am Robert Ayce of Girton.'

'Ayce,' mused Tulyet. 'I once knew a *John* Ayce. He provided the castle with eggs. He was murdered, if I recall correctly, some years ago.'

The prisoner's composure slipped a little. 'Your memory commends you, My Lord. I thought you would have forgotten. John was my son.'

'He was unlawfully killed by a fellow named William Hildersham,' Tulyet went on, frowning as details returned to him. 'He was tried by a secular jury, but claimed benefit of clergy.'

'Yes, Hildersham was a clerk,' said Ayce bitterly. 'He should have been hanged for murdering John, but just because he could read and write, he was passed to the Bishop for more lenient sentencing. But the Bishop lost him.'

'Lost him?' echoed Bartholomew, bemused.

'He escaped from the priests who were taking him to

191

Ely,' explained Tulyet. 'We searched, but a man can disappear into the Fens as if he had never been born. As I have learned today.'

'You did not look very hard for Hildersham,' said Ayce accusingly. 'You should have found him.'

'Yes, we should,' acknowledged Tulyet. Then his face turned hard and icy. 'But there are more pressing matters to discuss this evening. Why did you attack the castle?'

Ayce shrugged. 'I was not paid to ask questions, only to fight.'

'Paid?' pounced Tulyet. 'You are a mercenary? Who hired you?'

'They did not say, and I did not ask,' replied Ayce insolently.

'You are in a dire predicament,' said Tulyet, after a pause during which it was clear he was struggling to control his temper. 'Yet I am willing to concede certain favours – a visit from a loved one, perhaps. But only if you answer my questions. Why did you join these raiders?'

'Why should I not?' asked Ayce, shrugging again. 'I have never liked Cambridge. But it is late and I am tired. If you are going to hang me tomorrow, I want my last night to myself.'

'You will not hang tomorrow,' said Tulyet softly.

Ayce's composure slipped a second time. 'What? But I am a rebel. Of course I will hang!'

Bartholomew stared at him, weighing the weary hopelessness in the man's eyes and the injudiciously taunting remarks. 'You want to die,' he said in understanding. 'You will not risk Hell by committing suicide, so you are hoping that someone else will take your life—'

'Lies!' snarled Ayce, although Bartholomew could see that he was right. 'You know nothing about me!'

'I shall keep you alive for as long as it suits me,' said

Tulyet, turning on his heel and stalking out. 'Perhaps for years. Sleep on that, Robert Ayce.'

At that point, Ayce's equanimity broke, and he began to howl curses and threats.

'It seems I managed to capture the one man in that nasty little army who cannot be bribed with his life,' said Tulyet bitterly, as he walked up the steps. 'Luck was not with me today.'

It was impossible for Bartholomew to leave so many vulnerable patients that night, so he stayed at the castle. He slept for an hour around midnight, when Gyseburne relieved him, but then there was a crisis with the man who had been shot in the neck, and it was dawn before matters quietened again.

He had just ensured that everyone was resting comfortably when he heard footsteps. It was Holm, and he had brought visitors: Dunning and Julitta were at his side, while Weasenham, Ruth and Bonabes brought up the rear. Dunning and Bonabes wore swords, although the Exemplarius's was ancient, and looked as if it had been dragged out of some long-forgotten store.

'Dunning and his daughters insisted on viewing my handiwork,' said Holm in response to Bartholomew's questioning glance, waving a casual hand towards the more serious cases with a proprietary air, even though he had been nowhere near them the previous day. 'And Bonabes is here to protect us all, should the invaders strike again.'

'My father taught me how to wield a blade,' explained Bonabes. Then he regarded the weapon anxiously. 'However, it has been many years since—'

'So you have said, to the point of tedium,' interrupted Holm rudely. He turned to Bartholomew. 'How are my patients? I hope they all survived the night?'

'God's teeth!' exclaimed Dunning, leaping backwards when he saw Bartholomew's clothes. 'What in God's name have you been doing?'

'I imagine blood is inevitable when dealing with battle wounds, Father,' said Ruth dryly.

'I never make a mess when *I* perform,' declared Holm. He smiled engagingly at Julitta. 'I have always found it is better to leave a patient's blood *inside* his body, where it belongs.'

'If you really think that, then why do you practise phlebotomy?' asked Bartholomew, tired enough to be confrontational.

'Every respectable medical authority says that bloodletting is beneficial to health,' replied Holm shortly. 'And only maverick eccentrics claim otherwise. Besides, it is carefully controlled, and bowls are to hand. There is no wild splattering, such as I saw yesterday.'

'Will they all live?' asked Julitta, looking around with gentle compassion.

'They have a good chance now,' replied Holm, before Bartholomew could speak. 'It is a good thing I was here, because Cambridge could not have managed this crisis without a surgeon.'

'Oh, yes,' said Bonabes, humour flashing in his dark eyes. 'I imagine your arrival in the town will be celebrated on Easter Day for many years to come. Just as they will celebrate having a dependable old warrior like me to protect them.'

Holm either did not hear or chose to ignore him, and sailed away to inspect the injured, resting his hand on their foreheads to test for fevers, and poking at their dressings. They seemed reassured by the presence of another *medicus*, and as their well-being was his prime concern, Bartholomew resisted the urge to send him

194

packing. Dunning went with him, and did even more to aid their recovery by pressing coins into their hands.

'I hope you were not making sport of my fiancé, Bonabes,' said Julitta quietly. 'He has every right to be proud of his achievements.'

'Well, someone needs to be,' said Weasenham nastily. 'Because his colleagues are not: Rougham told me that he was more menace than help yesterday.'

'That is because Rougham is jealous of him,' said Julitta stiffly. 'So he told lies.'

'You may be right,' said Bonabes soothingly. 'Holm is a lot nicer than Rougham, after all.'

'Do you think so?' Bartholomew was surprised enough to voice the thought aloud.

Julitta's eyes narrowed, and Bartholomew wished he had managed to hold his tongue: the last thing he wanted was to annoy her. She inclined her head rather coolly, and went to where Holm was talking to a man with a broken leg.

'She adores him,' said Ruth, watching her go. 'And he knows exactly how to charm her, of course. I am glad she is happy, but I wish she saw him more clearly. She will be disappointed when she learns he is only human, like the rest of us.'

'I will make her see it,' offered Weasenham eagerly. 'I have soured more than one happy union in the past, and will be more than pleased to do it again. Just give the word, and I shall begin.'

'No!' said Ruth sharply. Then she softened. 'I appreciate your offer, husband, but your interference is likely to raise him even further in her estimation. I must think of another way.'

'Then do not leave it too long,' advised Weasenham. 'The nuptials are in less than three weeks.'

* * *

Bartholomew left the sickroom after a while, to escape Holm's self-important drone. He stood in the bailey, watching the castle's occupants rise and go about their duties. It was still not fully light, although at least a dozen cockerels were crowing, and two cows lowed impatiently, to say they were ready for milking. The atmosphere was tense among the human occupants: they spoke in whispers, and even the smallest stable boy carried a dagger. After a while, Dunning came to stand next to him.

'That sickroom reeks,' he said in distaste. 'Blood, vomit, urine and strong medicine. Horrible!'

Bartholomew nodded, although it was a smell he barely noticed any more.

'Julitta has decided to nurse these fellows, because some of them said that a woman about the place made them feel better,' Dunning went on. Bartholomew regarded him in surprise. 'I begged her to reconsider, but she is a lass who knows her own mind. Ruth has offered to help, too.'

Weasenham and Holm joined them, both bristling with indignation. 'Who will assist me in my shop if Ruth stays here?' demanded the stationer angrily. 'I have already lost Adam and the London brothers. Now I am to lose Ruth, too. Well, thank God for Bonabes. He will not desert me.'

'I say we leave them to it,' suggested Holm sulkily. 'They will soon learn not to waste their time on dying men.'

'Dying men?' asked Dunning. 'But you just told them all that they were going to get better.'

'Of course I did,' explained Holm silkily. 'All *medici* say that – it is the only way people will let us get anywhere near them. My dear old father always said that to be a surgeon, you need not a sharp knife and a steady hand, but a silver tongue.'

Bartholomew, disgusted and irritated in equal measure, watched Holm and Weasenham walk away. Dunning lingered, chatting about the Feast of Corpus Christi, and how it was even more important to make it a day to remember now, as morale in the town would be low.

'I spent the entire night rethinking the pageant, making changes in the light of yesterday's raid,' he confided. 'Julitta, Ruth and Weasenham helped – none of us went to bed. And Holm longed to join us, of course, but he was here all night, tending the wounded. Just as he did at Poitiers.'

Bartholomew said nothing, but Holm had disappeared long before sunset the previous evening, and had not shown his face again until he had accompanied his entourage shortly before. He could only suppose that the surgeon had lied to secure himself a good night's sleep. He itched to say so to Dunning – along with the fact that if Holm had indeed tended the injured at Poitiers, they would have been Frenchmen, and almost certainly only after he had fled to a safe distance – but it would have sounded like sour grapes, so he held his tongue.

'I am not very impressed with Tulyet,' said Dunning idly. 'He virtually invited those villains to attack, with his lax security and his cavalier attitude to essential repairs.'

'That is untrue,' objected Bartholomew, dragging his thoughts from Holm's penchant for fabrication to defend his friend. 'No one could have predicted what happened.'

'No? There have been numerous reports of armed men sneaking around after dark, while several people have vanished or been murdered. How could Tulyet not see that all this pointed to something sinister? Is that your colleague Ayera striding towards us? What does he want?'

'Michael said you would be here, tending the injured,' said Ayera to Bartholomew as he approached. 'So I came to see whether I could help.'

Bartholomew shook his head, although he was touched

that his colleague should have made the effort to ask. No one else had bothered, except Michael. 'But thank you.'

Ayera sighed. 'What a dreadful business! Langelee posted student-guards all around Michaelhouse's walls last night, and he and I were up all night supervising them. How is Tulyet's hunt proceeding? Is there any news?'

'No, but he rode out again this morning, while it was still dark.'

'Rather him than me. Tracking men who do not want to be found is nigh on impossible in the Fens. I see he has tightened his defences here, though. It was not easy to get in this morning.'

'But too late,' said Dunning acidly. 'It is like bolting a door after the horse has fled.'

'It is not too late for next time,' Bartholomew pointed out shortly.

Dunning stared at him. 'There will not be a next time! The raiders were repelled, and they will not come again. I doubt such cunning fellows are stupid.'

'No,' agreed Ayera. 'But Tulyet did well yesterday, given the unexpectedness of the assault. A number of his men were killed or wounded, but soldiers are expendable and it is the castle that is important. And Tulyet still holds it.'

Bartholomew supposed it was true from a military perspective, but was uncomfortable with the remark even so. 'Tulyet would not agree,' he said. 'He is protective towards his people.'

'An unwise trait in a commander,' said Ayera. 'He must learn indifference. Incidentally, do you know how many of the enemy were dispatched by his warriors?'

'I heard five,' replied Dunning. 'Four outright, and one by his own comrades when they saw they were going to have to leave him. These men are extremely ruthless.'

198

Bartholomew thought about Tulyet and Cynric in the marshes, and hoped they were safe.

The sun was only just beginning to show its face when he and Ayera left the castle and began to walk down the hill together. Bells were ringing everywhere, because it was Trinity Sunday, and an important day in the Church's calendar. St Clement's was full of white flowers for the occasion, and their sweet scent wafted out as they passed it. Ayera inhaled deeply.

'I have always liked flowers. They are one of life's great pleasures.'

Bartholomew regarded him in astonishment. It was not the sort of sentiment he would have expected from the manly geometrician, especially after his comment about the expendability of soldiers.

'Many are poisonous,' Ayera went on gleefully, indicating that he did not have a sensitive side after all. 'Although they present a pretty face to the world. There is much to admire in flowers.'

'Yes,' said Bartholomew, not sure how else to respond to such a declaration.

'Were there any by Newe Inn's pond? It might explain what happened to those four dead scholars. Michael said there was no obvious cause of death, you see, so I have been mulling over possible explanations for him.'

'I did not notice. Besides, toxic plants are unlikely to kill four men simultaneously.'

'Why not? It has happened before – when Langelee was living in York, several guests died at his dinner table. The culprit was found to be lily of the valley, which the cook had mistaken for wild garlic and had made into a soup.'

'His guests died, but he did not?' Bartholomew vaguely

recalled Langelee telling him the same tale when they had travelled to York together a few weeks before, but the details eluded him.

Ayera nodded. 'He had decided to forgo the broth, to save himself for the meat that was to follow. So he survived, but all his visitors perished horribly.'

Bartholomew stared at him, a sudden vivid recollection of the garden flashing into his mind. 'Actually, there *were* lilies of the valley by the pond. I picked some.'

'Well, there you are then,' said Ayera with a shrug. 'I have solved the case.'

'But there is nothing to say that Northwood and the others ate them. And even if they did, they would not have been overcome at the same time.'

Ayera shrugged a second time. 'Oh, well, it was just an idea. Let us talk of happier matters, then. What do you think these raiders wanted from the castle?'

'The tax money,' replied Bartholomew, not convinced that this constituted a 'happier matter'.

Ayera considered his reply. 'Yet it is going to be transported to London in a week. If I were a thief, I would have waited until it was on the road, not attempted to snatch it from a fortress.'

It was a valid point.

When Langelee saw the dried blood that stained Bartholomew's skin, hair and clothes, he ordered him to the lavatorium, a shed-like structure built for those who cared about personal hygiene. Bartholomew usually had it to himself. Gratefully, he scoured away the gore, donned fresh shirt, leggings and tabard, and went to hand the soiled ones to Agatha the laundress.

Women were not usually permitted inside Colleges, although laundresses were exempted if they were old and

200

ugly, and thus unlikely to tempt scholars into an amour. Agatha fitted the bill perfectly, because not even the most desperate of men was likely to mount an assault on her – her ferocious temper was legendary, and she had a powerful physique to go with it. She regarded the stained clothes Bartholomew handed her with a dangerous expression.

'Have you been committing surgery again? You know you are not supposed to do that.'

'Yes,' said Bartholomew tiredly. There was no point arguing, because Agatha was not a lady to lose confrontations.

'I shall overlook it this time,' she went on. 'But only because one of my nephews was among the casualties, and he said he would have died had you not been to hand.'

Bartholomew supposed he should not be surprised to learn that Agatha had kin at the castle. She was related to at least half of Cambridge. 'Which one is he?'

'Robin, who had an arrow through his neck. It is a pity that Holm is so useless, because people will say you are a warlock as long as you flout tradition and perform the procedures that *he* should be doing. And one day it will see you banished from here. Or worse. I should not like that, and neither would your patients.'

'The Senior Proctor will never let that happen,' said Michael, hearing her last words as he came to join them. 'Of course, Matt will lose my protection when I am appointed to an abbacy or a bishopric and I move to another town. And it is only a matter of time before important people recognise my worth, so I do not antici- pate being here much longer.'

'Modestly put, Brother,' said Bartholomew dryly. 'Perhaps that is why your grandmother is here: to size you up for promotion.'

'No, she would have told me,' said Michael, quite seriously. 'She is here for something much more grave, and I cannot help but wonder whether it is to do with the raid on the castle.'

'You think she led an armed invasion?' asked Bartholomew. He would not put it past her.

'Do not be ridiculous! I meant she might be here because she heard some rumour of trouble in the offing, and came to prevent it.'

'Then she did not do a very good job,' said Agatha. 'Incidentally, Robin thought he recognised one of those brigands last night. He said it was Principal Coslaye of Batayl Hostel.'

'Then he is mistaken,' said Michael firmly. 'Coslaye is still mending from the head injury he suffered at the Convocation, and would not be strong enough to fight.'

'I beg to differ,' said Agatha, while Bartholomew nodded in agreement: Coslaye had made a complete recovery. 'And he is a rough-tempered brute, obsessed with battles.'

'Well, yes, he is, but he still would not have joined a raid on the castle,' argued Michael. 'However, if Robin goes around telling folk that he did, the town will fight the University for certain. Order him to desist, Agatha. He will listen to you. Go now, before the tale seeps out.'

Agatha inclined her head, and sailed majestically towards the gate.

'As soon as we have completed our duties at church, we had better visit Coslaye,' said Michael, walking across the yard to where their colleagues were gathering. The service would be later than usual because it was Sunday.

Bartholomew blinked. 'You think there might be truth in Robin's claim?'

'Of course not, but Robin will need to be convinced

202

that he is wrong before we can trust him to stop gossiping, and the best way to do that will be to tell him Coslaye's alibi.'

'If he has one,' warned Bartholomew. 'The raid was before dawn, when most people were asleep. His students may not be able to prove that he did not wake up and slip out.'

'We shall cross that bridge when we come to it.' Michael fell into step at Bartholomew's side as Langelee led the procession out of the College and up the lane. 'Meadowman and I spent much of last night in Newe Inn's garden, monitoring the pond. Just when I was beginning to think we were wasting our time, the gate opened, and we had a visitor.'

'And?' prompted Bartholomew, when the monk paused.

'And he began poking about its rim with a stick. I charged forward to grab him, but Meadowman and I fell over each other in the dark, and the fellow escaped. However, the incident tells me that the pool definitely warrants further investigation.'

'What will you do?' asked Bartholomew. 'Dredge it again?'

Michael nodded. 'More thoroughly this time. Hopefully, when we find what that fellow came for, we will understand what caused four of our scholars to die.'

'Do you have any idea who this visitor was?'

'None. He was cloaked and hooded – obviously a disguise, because the weather is mild.'

'Was there anything distinctive about his cloak? Or his gait?'

'I thought he was limping, but could not be sure.'

Bartholomew frowned. 'Do you think he was one of the men who attacked me?'

'Why would he be? They wanted your formula for

wildfire, so why would one go to Newe Inn's garden? It is not likely to be there!'

Bartholomew fiddled with a frayed seam on his sleeve as he thought. 'We believe Northwood, Vale and the London brothers were competing with my medical colleagues to develop a clean-burning lamp. We are always being told that this invention will be worth a lot of money, so perhaps these mysterious men are interested in *any* new discoveries.'

'It is possible, I suppose,' acknowledged Michael. 'And then, when Northwood and the others declined to share the fruits of their labours, these men killed them. Or perhaps they did talk – for a price – and as they drank a victory toast with their new partners, they were poisoned.'

'The men who accosted me did not offer to pay for information,' said Bartholomew doubtfully. 'They made it perfectly clear that they were going to take what they wanted by force. But perhaps you should discuss this with your grandmother. I doubt it was coincidence that she was to hand when those men tackled me, and I have a feeling that she knows exactly who they are.'

But Michael shook his head. 'You are wrong, Matt – it *was* coincidence. I dined with her yesterday, and she confided that she is here to hunt down a dangerous French spy.'

'So she did lie about being here to see you,' said Bartholomew, not surprised.

Michael smiled suddenly. 'She is an incredible woman, though, do you not think? I wish I had known her in her prime, when she won knife-throwing competitions against the King's best warriors, and was the most feared spy the French had ever known.'

She was more than impressive enough for Bartholomew in her dotage, and the thought of her young, strong and lithe was deeply unsettling. He changed the subject to the attack on the castle.

'Mercenaries were hired, but the one who was captured refuses to talk. His son, John Ayce, was murdered, apparently, and he still grieves. He does not care what happens to him.'

'I remember that case,' mused Michael. 'Young Ayce sold eggs to the castle, but he was a brute, and his father was the only one who mourned him. His killer – one William Hildersham – escaped while being transported to the Bishop's prison in Ely. I recall being pleased when I heard.'

'Why?' It was unlike the monk to condone murderers evading justice.

'Ayce was a bullying brawler who had terrorised and even injured other scholars. Hildersham claimed self-defence, and the University believed him. We all thought Ayce had been given his just deserts.'

'Yet the secular jury found Hildersham guilty. There must have been some reason why—'

'Secular juries always find against us, you know that. Their verdict meant nothing.'

'Ayce's father does not think so,' said Bartholomew. 'He is bitter and angry.'

'No parent likes to see his offspring stabbed, no matter what the circumstances. But it happened years ago, and cannot matter now.'

'On the contrary, Brother. It led Ayce to join the force that tackled the castle.'

Michael sighed. 'Cambridge was like a town under siege last night, its streets thick with soldiers. I rousted out all my beadles, too. I do not want these villains attacking the University.'

'You think they might?' asked Bartholomew, alarmed.

Michael shrugged. 'I have no idea, but precautions never go amiss.'

It was peaceful in St Michael's Church that morning. Sunlight filtered through the east window, and its thick walls muted the rattle of hoofs and iron-shod wheels on the cobbled streets outside. A dove cooed in the rafters, and the only other sound was Suttone chanting mass. Someone, probably William, had swept the church the previous day, and had put flowers on the windowsills, so their sweet scent mingled with the more pungent aroma of incense.

Afterwards, Michael requested that he and Bartholomew be excused from breakfast, slyly not mentioning that there might not be any if Agatha was still at the castle with her nephew.

'Why?' asked Langelee. 'Have you learned who tried to dash out Coslaye's brains at the Convocation at last?'

'No,' replied Michael with a grimace. 'Not yet.'

'Then I suppose it must be your investigation into the four dead scholars,' surmised the Master. 'The only one I knew was Northwood. He often stopped for a chat when our paths crossed, especially during the last two months or so. In fact, he was a bit of a nuisance, because I did not always have time for him.'

'Really?' asked Michael in surprise. Bartholomew agreed: Northwood's intolerance of slow minds made Langelee an unlikely associate.

'He was interested in my work for the Archbishop,' elaborated Langelee. 'I told him a good many tales that I have never dared share with anyone else here. In fact, I probably would not have shared them with him, either, had he not plied me with claret.'

'What sort of tales?' asked Michael in alarm. He did

not want his College's reputation sullied by the Master's drunken ramblings.

Langelee laughed, and waved a stubby finger. 'Now Northwood is dead, my secrets are my own again, and I shall not make the mistake of another indiscretion. Suffice to say that they entailed my experiences in battle, my knowledge of poisons and my skills as a burglar.'

'Lord!' exclaimed Michael, as Langelee went to lead his scholars back to Michaelhouse. 'When he makes remarks like that, it makes me wonder whether he is the right man to be Head of House.'

'He confessed a lot worse when we were in York a few weeks ago,' said Bartholomew. 'But I am content with his rule. He is better at it than the rest of us would be.'

'You only think so because he gives you licence to practise medicine however you see fit, and rarely condemns you for indulging in surgery. But it is too early to go to Batayl Hostel – they will still be at their devotions. We shall have breakfast in the Brazen George first.'

Although scholars were forbidden from frequenting taverns, which tended to be full of ale-swilling townsmen spoiling for a fight, Michael had always maintained that this particular stricture did not apply to the Senior Proctor, and he visited the Brazen George – a pleasant establishment on the High Street – so often that there was a chamber at the rear of the premises set aside for his exclusive use. It was a pretty room, overlooking a courtyard where the morning sunshine slanted across the herb beds, and where contented chickens scratched around a picturesque well. He ordered a substantial repast, which included cold meat, new bread and a dish of coddled eggs.

'But no cabbage,' he called after the departing taverner. 'I cannot abide anything green. It upsets my stomach, and keeps me in the latrines.'

'Only if you eat too much of it,' said Bartholomew. 'Every *medicus* who has ever written about food says that a balanced diet, with moderate amounts of meat, bread and vegetables is—'

'They were writing for the benefit of the general populace,' interrupted Michael haughtily. 'They cannot know about *my* innards. And these so-called balanced diets are a nonsense, anyway. How can they be balanced, when they include vegetables? Greenery is for slugs and caterpillars, not men with healthy appetites.'

Bartholomew knew better than to argue, and his attention was soon distracted from the discussion anyway – by the number of dishes that Landlord Lister brought to the table.

'God's blood, Brother!' he exclaimed. 'You and whose army will be eating this?'

'It is only a mouthful,' said Michael comfortably, tying a piece of linen around his neck to protect his habit from splattered grease. 'Barely enough to keep a sparrow alive.'

'It was a bad business at the castle yesterday,' said Landlord Lister conversationally, as he brought a large platter of roasted beef. 'I heard the raiders were after the taxes. Thank God they did not get them, or we would all have had to pay again.'

'It was a close thing, though,' said Michael. 'The villains had reached the foot of the Great Tower before Dick Tulyet's archers were able to drive them off.'

'Do you really think they wanted the taxes?' Bartholomew asked, when Lister had gone.

Michael stared at him. 'Of course! Why else would they tackle a castle? It is not as if they were part of an invading army, and needed to secure a fortress in order to control a region.'

'The place contains a lot more than money. There are

horses, weapons, all manner of documents and deeds. There are also prisoners in the gaol, and—'

'Then I am glad the mystery is not mine to unravel. My hands are full enough already.'

After mopping up the last of the grease with a piece of bread, Michael led the way out of the Brazen George. Bartholomew looked around appreciatively as they walked, again admiring the work that had been done to make the town pretty for Corpus Christi. The High Street looked especially picturesque, with its brightly painted houses and neat shops. The churchyards had been tidied, too – brambles and nettles trimmed back, and grass scythed.

Michael insisted on stopping at St Mary the Great as they passed, to see whether Beadle Meadowman had left him a progress report about dredging Newe Inn's pond. The Trinity Sunday service was still in progress, and Bartholomew smiled when he heard the sweet, pure notes of the choir. The church was full of fragrant white flowers, which would be kept until Wednesday evening, when a lot of red ones would be added for Corpus Christi.

They had not been in Michael's expensively furnished office for long – Bartholomew admiring Walkelate's sketches of the finished library, and the monk rummaging through mounds of documents in search of a message from his beadle – when there was a cough. It was the Chancellor.

'Come in, Tynkell,' said Michael, without looking up. 'How may I help you?'

'Have you solved the Newe Inn deaths yet?' asked Tynkell. He seemed bolder than usual, and Bartholomew wondered whether it was because he was wearing his robes of office, which conferred on him a confidence he did not normally possess. 'The Common Library will open its doors to readers in four days, and I do not want unexplained demises hanging over the occasion.'

'I am working as fast as I can,' replied Michael coolly. 'Unfortunately, I have been busy quelling spats among our scholars over your damned project – the most recent being last night, when Berwicke Hostel squabbled with King's Hall. Moreover, there has not been much in the way of clues about what happened to those four men.'

'Then you must find some, Brother.' Tynkell seemed unsteady on his feet. 'I want the opening ceremony to pass off without a hitch, and I shall hold you responsible if something spoils it.'

'What?' exploded Michael incredulously. 'How dare you—'

'You have a duty to prevent trouble,' Tynkell went on, wagging his finger. 'And there will be trouble, unless whoever killed those scholars is caught. So, who are your suspects?'

'I shall tell you when I am good and ready,' declared Michael angrily. 'And I am doing my best, so do not order me to work harder. I told you a Common Library was a bad idea, and I was right. You did not listen, because you are desperate to be recorded as the Chancellor who gave Cambridge what Oxford has had for years. But the whole business is a terrible mistake.'

'Rubbish,' said Tynkell. 'Besides, how else will I get to study Apollodorus's *Poliorcetica*?'

Bartholomew blinked. 'Why would you want to read that? It is about warfare.'

'I happen to be very interested in siege engines and artillery,' replied Tynkell, staggering when he tried to lean on the door frame and missed. 'Even Northwood, Langelee and Riborowe were amazed at the depth of my knowledge, and none of them is easily impressed.'

210

'Tulyet said you helped him to design a ribauldequin,' said Bartholomew, rather accusingly. 'Are you sure it is appropriate for scholars to meddle in such matters?'

'Of course, it is. Who else is going to do it? We are the ones with the clever minds.'

'Have you been drinking?' asked Michael suspiciously.

'I may have had a cup or two,' replied Tynkell airily. 'It is not a habit I usually indulge first thing in the morning, but today is Trinity Sunday, so I made an exception. Perhaps I should do it more often, because I feel like a new man. Indeed, I might even exercise my authority as Chancellor and make a decision about something.'

'The last time you did that, we ended up having to call a Convocation of Regents,' said Michael with considerable irritation. 'And our *studium generale* has not rested easy since. There are even rumours that Northwood, the London brothers, Vale and even Sawtre may have been killed because of the way they voted. So leave the decisions to those of us who know what we are doing, if you would be so kind.'

'Then you had better make an arrest fast,' slurred Tynkell. 'Because catching this villain may be the only way to prevent more trouble.'

'I know it, believe me,' said Michael tightly.

Tynkell grinned. 'I must be drunk, because I do not usually order you about. However, it feels very satisfying. I shall almost certainly do it again.'

'I would not recommend it,' said Michael, rather dangerously. 'So please ensure you are sober when we next meet.'

'He is right, though,' said Bartholomew, after Tynkell had lurched away. 'Solving the Newe Inn deaths might well prevent trouble, and you should try to have a culprit before Corpus Christi. That gives you four days.'

'Gives *us* four days,' corrected Michael. He scowled.

211

'Perhaps it is as well that Tynkell is retiring next year. He has no right to tell me what to do. Who does he think he is?'

'The University's Chancellor, I suppose,' said Bartholomew mildly.

When Bartholomew and Michael arrived at Batayl Hostel, Coslaye was sitting by the hearth with a book open on his knees, Browne was leaning against the wall behind him, and the students were crowded on to benches. All seemed to have recovered from their bout of illness, although several remained pale.

'We are reading Acton's *Questio Disputata*,' said Coslaye, lifting it so Bartholomew and Michael could see. 'So far, it is a lot of twaddle.'

'It is the book that almost deprived us of our Principal,' elaborated Pepin in his perfect French.

'I think we should have sold it, personally,' said Browne. 'Because times are hard, and—'

'Never! This particular tome serves to remind everyone that God saw fit to spare me,' interrupted Coslaye. He tossed it on to the table next to him, where it made a substantial thud. Its wooden covers rendered it weighty, and explained why it had done so much damage to his head. One corner had snapped off, indicating that it had also suffered from the encounter with bone. 'No, do not lean against that wall, Brother! It may damage my mural. Come to the front.'

Conditions were very cramped for teaching, and Bartholomew was not surprised that the Batayl men had entertained high hopes of moving to Newe Inn – it was not easy to pick his way through the students without treading on any. Michael took no such care, though, and Pepin was one of several who staggered as the monk's bulk travelled past them.

'Have you come to tell us who tried to kill me?' asked Coslaye. 'I know you have been busy of late, but I should not like to think the attempt on my life has been forgotten.'

'It has not,' Michael assured him. 'I promised you I would find the culprit, and I shall.'

'Thank you.' Coslaye turned to Bartholomew. 'Weasenham tells me that when you fought at Poitiers, you killed fifty Frenchmen with a spell that blasted them clean out of their armour. What a fabulous achievement! Will you tell us more?'

Bartholomew was horrified. 'No! I have never—'

'It seems that Poitiers was full of Cambridge scholars that day,' interrupted Browne with rank disapproval. 'Bartholomew, Holm, the villainous Riborowe – who says it is what precipitated his interest in ribauldequins. And now Weasenham tells me that Northwood was there, too.'

'I wish *I* had been,' said Coslaye wistfully. 'You really must tell us your experiences on the field, Bartholomew. I guarantee you will find us an enraptured audience.'

'No,' said Bartholomew shortly. 'Men died horribly there, and—'

'But most of them were French,' stated Coslaye. 'So who cares? Poitiers was a great day for our country, and I named this hostel after it. Batayl refers to the Battle of Poitiers.'

Pepin flushed with anger, and it was clear that he held his tongue with difficulty; Bartholomew wondered why he did not transfer to another hostel. Browne rested a sympathetic hand on his shoulder, although Coslaye did not seem to notice the effect his words were having.

'We *were* called St Remegius's Hostel,' Browne said. The bitter tone of his voice indicated that this was a matter that still rankled with him. 'But St Remegius was French,

213

and Coslaye said that was unpatriotic, so he changed it. I did not approve, personally, and—'

'Well, Bartholomew?' demanded Coslaye, rudely overriding him. 'Will you talk to us?'

'Ask Cynric instead,' suggested Michael tactfully. 'He is an excellent storyteller, and more willing to glorify slaughter and bloody death than Matt.'

'Tell him to come around tonight, then,' said Coslaye keenly.

'No,' said Browne, while Pepin looked appalled. 'I do not want to hear—'

'Too bad,' said Coslaye. 'Because I do, and I am Principal here. Incidentally, did you hear what happened on Friday night? A Carmelite novice burst in here and threw soot at my painting. I was so incensed that I rose before dawn the following day, and tackled Prior Etone about it.'

'You were in the Carmelite Friary when the raid took place?' asked Michael, exchanging a quick glance with Bartholomew. 'You were nowhere near the castle?'

'Why would I be at the castle?' asked Coslaye, frowning his puzzlement. 'The Sheriff will not want scholars in his domain, I am sure.'

'We came to discuss the bodies in Newe Inn's pond again,' said Bartholomew quickly. Coslaye was not the kind of man to take Robin's accusation with equanimity, so it was better he did not hear about it. 'As Batayl lies so close, we wondered whether any of you heard or saw anything odd.'

'No, as we have told you countless times already,' said Browne irritably. 'However, we understand that those four men died on Tuesday night, and we were all out then.'

'Out where?' asked Michael.

'At King's Hall,' replied Coslaye. 'Where there was a gathering of people opposed to the Common Library.'

'Everyone here went?' pressed Michael.

Browne nodded. 'Yes. We are all eager to see the grace overturned.'

'Unfortunately, it will not be,' said Michael sourly. 'I do not approve of it, either, but a vote has been taken and we are stuck with the result. It is a pity, but that is democracy for you.'

'Then democracy is a stupid system,' averred Coslaye. He scowled at Bartholomew. 'It is a good thing that you saved my life, because we all know which way you voted and I would have punched you for it by now, if I did not owe you some consideration.'

'The four men who died in the pond voted in favour of the library, too,' fished Michael.

'So did Sawtre,' said Browne. 'It strikes me that libraries are dangerous places, and that we should all stay well away from them. Especially from that evil abomination next door.'

'I understand Northwood supporting a Common Library,' mused Coslaye. 'He was a Carmelite, and therefore naturally sly. And Vale was not overly endowed with wits, so he probably voted the wrong way by mistake. But the London brothers should have known better.'

'They were members of Batayl,' Pepin reminded the visitors. 'So they should have opposed the scheme that saw us deprived of the house Dunning promised we should have.'

'And he *did* promise,' added Browne. 'No matter what he says now.'

'They lived in a lovely cottage on the High Street,' said Coslaye bitterly. 'Because Weasenham paid them a decent wage, and they could afford it. But the rest of us were not so fortunate.'

'Let us return to this meeting you attended on Tuesday,' said Michael. 'What time did it end?'

'Dusk,' replied Coslaye. 'Then we came home and went to bed. Yet I did hear one odd thing during the night . . .'

'Did you?' asked Browne. 'That surprises me. You have slept like a baby ever since Bartholomew sawed open your head.'

'I woke,' snapped Coslaye crossly. 'And I heard a bell.'

'A bell?' echoed Michael. 'You mean from a church? For vespers or compline?'

'No, it was too late for either, and it was too high-pitched to have been a bell from a church, anyway. It was a *small* bell. And it definitely came from Newe Inn's garden.'

Michael asked a few more questions, but the scholars of Batayl were an incurious, unobservant crowd, and had nothing else to add. Browne opened the door for them when they left, then stepped outside, lowering his voice so he would not be heard by his Principal.

'Do not put too much faith in this bell, Brother,' he whispered. 'Bartholomew should never have performed his evil surgery, because Coslaye has not been right since, and often claims to hear things the rest of us do not. Do not let his "testimony" lead you astray.'

CHAPTER 7

When they left Batayl, Michael insisted on visiting Newe Inn, to ask whether anyone there had heard a bell on the night Northwood and his friends had died. As usual, it was alive with the sounds of sawing and hammering, and apprentices tore up and down the stairs, yelling urgently to each other. The reek of wood oil was stronger than it had been the last time they had visited – the bust of Aristotle had been drenched in it and had been left outside to dry in the sun.

They walked up to the *libri distribuendi*, where Bartholomew admired the room's understated opulence yet again. It felt like a place of learning – venerable, solid and sober. Kente came to greet them, his face grey and lined with exhaustion.

'You should rest,' advised Bartholomew, regarding him with concern. 'You will make yourself ill if you drive yourself so hard.'

Kente managed to smile. 'It is only for another four days, and the bonus for finishing on time will more than compensate me for any discomfort. I am not the only one who is tired, anyway – Walkelate and Frevill have worked just as hard, if not harder.'

'They have,' agreed Michael, looking around. 'Although I still fail to understand why Walkelate accepted this project in the first place, given his College's antipathy towards it.'

'Antipathy!' snorted Kente. 'Downright hostile opposition would be a more accurate description. And he accepted because it is *right*. He is an ethical man – a little eccentric perhaps, and given to funny ideas, but so are all scholars, so we should not hold it against him.'

'What sort of funny ideas?' asked Bartholomew.

Kente sniffed. 'None as strange as yours, Doctor, with your hand-washing and affection for boiled water. His include things like making metal brackets for the book-shelves. We were skidding about on iron filings for days before I managed to convince him that wooden ones are better.'

'I know we have asked before, but do you have any theories about the four scholars who died not a stone's throw from here?' enquired Michael hopefully.

'Of course. It has come to light that they were using the garden for sly experiments – trying to make lamp fuel before the men who had the idea in the first place – and the Devil likes those kind of sinners. *He* came and took them.'

'Other people say it was God,' remarked Michael.

Kente shrugged. 'Well, neither will appreciate you probing their business, so I should let the matter drop if I were you. But you are not here to chat to me. Come, I will take you to Walkelate.'

Bartholomew and Michael followed him into the room containing the *libri concatenati*, where Walkelate was in conference with Frevill and Dunning. The King's Hall architect looked tired, and so did Frevill, although neither seemed to be teetering on the edge of collapse like Kente.

'I am alarmed by the amount of work still to be done,' Dunning was saying. 'Are you sure all will be ready?'

'Yes,' the architect replied firmly. 'Just one more polish, and we shall seal the door to this room until the grand opening on Thursday.'

'And we have almost finished the shelves for the *libri*

distribuendi, too,' added Frevill. 'We may have to labour frantically to see them absolutely perfect. But perfect they will be.'

'They will,' agreed Walkelate. He rested his hand on Frevill's shoulder, and beamed at Kente. 'I could not have hoped for better craftsmen. Working with you has been a privilege.'

The sincerity of his words seemed to give Kente new energy and he drew himself up to his full height. 'Come, Frevill. Let us see whether Aristotle is dry.'

The craftsmen left, and Dunning went with them, muttering about some aspect of the bust that was not to his liking.

'How may I help you, Brother?' asked Walkelate, beginning to make notes on a scrap of parchment using the *cista* as a table. 'Ah! Good day, Holm. How are you?'

Bartholomew turned to see the surgeon behind him, holding a large packet. Walkelate leapt to his feet and seized it eagerly.

'Is this it?' he demanded, eyes full of keen anticipation.

'It is, and I made it myself,' replied Holm, oozing smug confidence. 'Out of rose petals and lily of the valley. And I added cinnamon and nutmeg, too, for good measure.'

'It is to mask the stench of Kente's wood oil,' Walkelate explained excitedly to Bartholomew and Michael. 'Holm assures me that it will have eliminated all unwanted odours by Thursday.'

'I use it when wounds turn bad, and it always works,' smiled the surgeon. 'You are a friend, Walkelate, so I shall not charge you for my labour. A shilling will cover the cost of the ingredients.'

'Thank you,' said Walkelate gratefully, handing over the coins, although Bartholomew thought the price rather high. 'I shall fetch a bowl.'

Holm raised his hands in a shrug when the architect had gone, as if he felt the need to explain his friendship. 'He was kind to me when I first arrived, so I decided to continue the association. He ranks quite highly at King's Hall, and I am always happy to maintain good relations with those who might be useful to me one day. But what are *you* doing here?'

'Looking into the death of your colleague Vale and his friends,' replied Michael coolly. 'I do not suppose you noticed anything amiss, did you, from your home next door?'

'Only the lights, which I have already mentioned to Bartholomew,' replied Holm. 'And I *would* tell you if I had seen anything else, because I shall play a prominent role in this library's opening, and I have no intention of being deprived of an opportunity to shine.'

'Walkelate tells us that you hired singers that night,' said Michael. 'To entertain the craftsmen.'

Holm nodded. 'They were oiling shelves, which is painstakingly dull, so I took pity on them. However, I wished I had not – they joined in the songs and the caterwauling was dreadful. I could hear them from my house, and was obliged to close the windows in the end.'

Bartholomew regarded him thoughtfully. Why had the surgeon so suddenly decided to treat Walkelate's exhausted workforce? Did he have another reason for his uncharacteristic kindness – such as drowning out anything that might have been happening in the garden?

'Do you ever visit the pond?' he asked, watching Holm intently.

But he was wasting his time; he could read nothing in the bland features except a mild surprise at the question. 'No, of course not. I understand it is full of evil sprites.'

'Then did you ever see Vale, Northwood or the London brothers there?' asked Michael.

'I have better things to do than gaze into overgrown gardens. I only noticed those lights because I happened to leave a book on my windowsill, and I saw them when I went to move it.' Holm's expression turned salacious. 'Have you heard the rumour that Vale and Ruth were once lovers?'

Bartholomew struggled to mask his dislike of the man, and wondered how Julitta, who seemed sensible, could be deceived by the oily charm he oozed when he was with her. 'Yes,' he said curtly. 'But I do not believe it can be true. Ruth is a decent lady.'

'You are half right,' said Holm, with a nasty smile. 'It is not true. And the reason is because Ruth's heart belongs to Bonabes, and Bonabes's to her. Which explains why a man of the Exemplarius's abilities and intelligence continues to labour for the ghastly Weasenham.'

'I thought as much,' said Michael, although the claim came as a surprise to Bartholomew, who was not very observant about such matters. 'Bonabes is never far from Ruth, and I have seen the secret looks they exchange. They should take more care, because Weasenham is vindictive.'

'And he has poisonous substances to hand,' added Holm darkly. 'Ones for making paper.'

'Here,' said Walkelate, returning with a basin. He tipped Holm's concoction into it, and set it on a shelf. Bartholomew inspected it and saw that the mixture comprised mostly bits of stem, which would do little to combat noxious smells. Holm had cheated the man he claimed was a friend.

'We were lucky not to have been slaughtered in our beds yesterday, because Tulyet proved woefully inadequate

221

at defending us,' said Holm conversationally. 'I am going to complain to the King about him. Now I live in this town, it must be properly guarded.'

'I doubt you were in danger,' said Walkelate kindly. 'I suspect the raiders were local men who wanted the tax money, and they will know better than to harm the town's only surgeon.'

'That cannot be true,' said Bartholomew. 'Tulyet would have noticed any Cambridge resident assembling a private army—'

'I beg to differ,' interrupted Walkelate. 'The raiders headed straight for the Great Tower. In other words, they knew exactly where to go, which outsiders would not have done. Tulyet is scouring the marshes for the culprits, but he should be looking in the town.'

'You mean scholars?' asked Michael uncomfortably. 'It was not Principal Coslaye, if that is the rumour you have heard. He has an alibi for the time of the attack.'

'Coslaye?' asked Walkelate, taken aback. 'He is not the kind of man to take part in armed scuffles!'

'Oh, yes, he is,' countered Holm, all malice. 'He is a hot-tempered warmonger, who—'

'He was with the Carmelites during the invasion,' said Michael firmly. 'I assure you, no scholars were involved in that terrible business.'

'If you say so,' said Holm blandly, making no effort to look convinced.

There was no evidence of bells in Newe Inn or its garden, and when they had finished searching, Bartholomew said he needed to visit the castle, to check on his patients. Michael accompanied him, as he wanted to speak to Agatha's nephew about Coslaye.

'It is the sort of task I should have been able to delegate

to a Junior Proctor,' he grumbled, as they walked. 'But none of our lazy colleagues sees fit to help me.'

'Holm lives very close to the place where Vale and the others died,' Bartholomew remarked, declining to address the fact that no sane scholar would want to be Michael's minion. 'And as you have pointed out, all *medici* have a working knowledge of poisons.'

'You want him accused because you do not like him,' said Michael astutely. He shrugged at Bartholomew's sheepish smile. 'I do not blame you: he is a vile individual. So is Coslaye, come to that, yet here I am, racing to prove his innocence. Perhaps we should let the tale run its course, because I do not want bigots like Coslaye in my University.'

'We are not "racing" to save him, we are doing it to prevent the town from accusing scholars of assaulting the castle – a rumour that may end in a riot.'

'True,' conceded Michael with a sigh. 'I am not sure what to make of his claim of hearing a bell, though. Perhaps Browne is right: Coslaye just hears things these days.'

Bartholomew was thoughtful. 'The hooded man you chased out of Newe Inn's garden last night was looking for something. Why not a bell?'

Michael regarded him doubtfully. 'What would anyone want with a bell?'

'Perhaps Meadowman will be able to tell you if he finds one during his dredging. Look! There is Dunning again, with Ruth and Bonabes. Julitta is not with them, so I wonder if she is still at the castle.' He hoped so. It would be pleasant to see her again.

Michael glanced sideways at him. 'You seem rather taken with her. Does Holm have a rival for her affections? Is that why you are so eager for him to be our murderous villain?'

To his horror, Bartholomew felt himself blushing. 'No,

of course not! Besides, love is not for me, not after Matilde. In fact, I am giving serious consideration to joining a religious Order.'

'I would not recommend that,' said Michael, somewhat unexpectedly, for he was usually keen to snare his friend for the Benedictines. 'You might be used to poverty, but the obedience would be a problem. So would the chastity. Besides, you could do a lot worse than Julitta. She is made of much finer stuff than that pitiful widow you have been visiting.'

'You know about that?' asked Bartholomew, both surprised and chagrined.

'Nothing escapes the Senior Proctor,' said Michael smugly. 'And you should pursue Julitta, because Holm will not make her happy. Even Clippesby says so, and he is hardly an astute observer of human nature.'

Confused and more than a little embarrassed, Bartholomew changed the subject. 'So you think Holm is right when he says that Ruth has given her heart to Bonabes?'

He glanced to where Weasenham's wife and Exemplarius were walking side by side. Bonabes was carrying a heavy parcel, and it slipped at that moment. Ruth darted forward to help him, after which they exchanged a glance of such smouldering passion that Bartholomew was dumbfounded.

'I think we can assume he is,' remarked Michael dryly.

'Edith's seamstresses worked all night to repair Frevill's lye-burned cope,' said Dunning, indicating the package as their paths converged. 'We are just taking it back to him.'

'It is better now than it was before,' said Bonabes, setting the burden down and wiping his face with his sleeve. 'Although Master Weasenham will face a hefty bill, I fear.'

'It will not kill him,' said Ruth. She exchanged an unfathomable glance with Bonabes, then smiled at Bartholomew. 'Julitta is still nursing the wounded men. She refuses to leave them.'

'I told her there are more pleasant ways to spend the day,' added Dunning. 'But she said she must inure herself to such sights for when she is married to Holm.'

'Holm!' muttered Ruth in disgust. 'I wish she was betrothed to someone nicer.'

'She assures me that he is everything she has ever wanted,' said Dunning. 'Not that she has much choice in the matter, of course. I want my family affiliated with his, because he is related to the Holms of Norfolk. But never mind that. Weasenham told me today that someone is going around dispatching scholars who voted for my library. Is it true?'

'No,' said Michael firmly. 'Sawtre's death was an accident, and it is coincidence that the four men who died in Newe Inn's garden happened to support the scheme.'

'I hope you are right,' said Dunning worriedly. 'Because I did not donate a house so that people could be murdered over it.'

The sun was shining brightly by the time Michael and Bartholomew reached the castle, the mist and cloud having burned away. Bartholomew could hear sheep bleating in the fields outside the town gates, and the scent of recently milked cows was in the air. It was yet another pretty day.

The castle was still in a state of high alert. Bowmen stood at every arrow slit, and two mounted knights were stationed by the Gatehouse, ready to charge at the slightest threat. Meanwhile, the soldiers who loitered in the bailey were tense, wary and wore full armour.

All the casualties in the 'infirmary' were doing better than Bartholomew had dared hope, and he suspected it was because of Julitta, who moved among them with cups of water – which she assured him had been boiled – and encouraging words. He said so, and she smiled in a way that made his heart lurch. Flustered, he joined Michael at Robin's bedside.

'Yes, my Aunt Agatha came to see me,' Robin was saying. 'She told me not to tell anyone that it was Coslaye of Batayl Hostel who was among the invaders.'

'It was not Coslaye,' stated Michael. 'He was at the Carmelite Priory when the attack took place, squabbling with the friars about soot being thrown over his mural of Poitiers.'

Robin looked doubtful. 'But I saw him, Brother. He was wearing armour and a helmet, admittedly, so he looked different, but I am sure it was him.'

'You were mistaken,' said Michael firmly. 'It was someone who looked like him.'

'It is possible, I suppose.' Robin sighed. 'But Aunt Agatha has ordered me to keep it quiet, and I value my life too much to cross her. I shall not discuss it with anyone else, do not worry.'

His eyes began to close, so they left him to rest. Bartholomew tended the other patients, rather disappointed to learn that none of his colleagues had been to visit. Unimpressed, he saw they had abrogated the entire responsibility to him, almost certainly because there would be no payment.

He set about changing dressings and checking wounds for signs of infection, pleased when Julitta offered to help. She had deft, gentle hands, and learned quickly what needed to be done. It was late afternoon by the time they had finished, and he lingered over Robin for no other reason than that he was enjoying Julitta's company and was reluctant for it to end.

'My reading lessons with you will have to be postponed,' she said softly, nodding towards the patients. 'It seems we both have more important things to do now.'

'I could find the time,' said Bartholomew quickly.

She touched his arm and his stomach did somersaults. 'You are kind, but the wounded must come first. And now I must leave, because I promised to help my father with the finery he is to wear to the Corpus Christi celebrations on Thursday.'

Bartholomew watched her go, noting the way the sun caught her hair as she passed a window.

'It is a pity she is promised to Holm,' said Robin, also watching. 'She is wasted on him.'

Bartholomew was grateful when Gyseburne arrived, relieved to be thinking about medicine and not the complex gamut of emotions that seethed within him. His colleague did not want to listen to a detailed report of each patient's progress, however, and interrupted with an observation.

'Boiling the dressings we applied to these open wounds does seem to have reduced infection, although I cannot imagine why. However, as my dear old mother always says, heat and Hell go together, so I can only assume that Satan is somehow involved.'

'No!' exclaimed Bartholomew, shocked.

'You think God likes cooked bandages, then?' asked Gyseburne keenly. 'And prefers to lay His holy hands on them, rather than ones torn straight from old clothes or bedding?'

'I do not know.' Bartholomew was never happy when theology entered medicine.

'Well, there must be some explanation for why your

technique works,' insisted Gyseburne. 'There is a reason for everything – even for yesterday's attack.'

'Yes, and Tulyet will find it,' said Bartholomew, thankful to be on less contentious ground.

'Possibly, but you should ask Ayera first.' Gyseburne lowered his voice. 'I am going to tell you something because I trust you, but you can never reveal to Ayera that it came from me. Do I have your word?'

Bartholomew nodded warily, sensing he was about to be told something he would not like.

Gyseburne took a deep breath. 'He was among the raiders yesterday. There! It is out, and now it is *your* responsibility to make sure the relevant authorities hear about it. I am absolved.'

Bartholomew stared at him. 'He was not! He is a geometrician!'

'He was a soldier before he came to Cambridge. A very fine one. I know, because I practised medicine in York before I came here, and that is his home city, where he was involved in several questionable incidents. Indeed, there was one that touched your Master Langelee – he had been entertaining, and summoned me when all his guests fell ill. They had been poisoned.'

'I know,' said Bartholomew. 'Langelee told me the tale when we went to York a few weeks ago, and Ayera mentioned it, too.'

'Did Ayera also tell you that the cook who provided the soup was in his family's employ? Of course, he claimed it was a mistake anyone might make, but I have my suspicions.'

'Then they are wrong,' said Bartholomew firmly. 'Ayera would have had no reason to harm Langelee's visitors.'

'On the contrary, the stricken men were enemies of his powerful uncle – the one who died recently but who

228

transpired to be penniless. There was no evidence to prove anything, of course, but the entire episode stank. But regardless of this, I know what I saw yesterday.'

'And what was that?' asked Bartholomew, both bewildered and unsettled by the claims.

'Not long after dawn, I was returning home from seeing a patient in Girton – which is why I was late arriving to help you with the wounded – when I saw armed men racing away from the town at a tremendous speed. Ayera was among them. I hid, so he did not see me.'

'Then it is your duty to tell the Sheriff. He will find there is an innocent explanation for—'

'Yes, there might be,' interrupted Gyseburne. 'Although I cannot imagine what. However, I am not telling Tulyet anything. Ayera may seem courteous and refined, but there is murder in that man. I shall not cross him, and if you ever tell anyone that you heard this tale from me, I shall deny it. He is your colleague, so the matter is in *your* hands now.'

'Very well,' said Bartholomew, wishing Gyseburne had not burdened him with his unpleasant observations. He liked Ayera, and did not want to hear nasty tales about him.

'And there is something else,' Gyseburne went on. 'I met Rougham on my way here, and he has spent a lot of time with the Carmelite scribe who had the seizure. Apparently, Willelmus fainted from fright, because of what he saw.'

'What did he see?' asked Bartholomew warily.

'He would not say. However, I cannot help but wonder whether what terrified Willelmus was seeing a prominent scholar – namely Ayera – among the villains who attacked our town.'

Bartholomew said nothing, but suddenly the day did not seem quite so bright and pretty.

He was about to leave the castle when the rest of his medical colleagues arrived – not to visit the wounded, but to debate the lucrative business of being on-call for the Corpus Christi pageant. As they approached, he heard Meryfeld confiding to Holm and Rougham, with a mind-boggling lack of remorse, how he often misled patients about the contents of the cures he sold.

'Poppy juice is expensive,' he was saying. 'So why use it, when most folk are incapable of telling the difference? The tincture I call Poppy Water contains nothing but nettles and mint.'

'And your clients never suspect?' asked Holm, keenly interested.

'Of course not,' replied Meryfeld scornfully. 'They trust me, and believe anything I say.'

'I would never dare do anything like that,' said Rougham. Bartholomew was not sure whether Rougham was favourably impressed by Meryfeld's dishonesty and itched to emulate it, or whether he was disapproving. 'Most of my customers are scholars, and they tend not to be stupid.'

'Some of them are,' averred Meryfeld with a grin. 'Especially the rich ones at King's Hall.'

The conversation came to an abrupt end when they became aware that Bartholomew and Gyseburne were listening, and they hastened to present their plan for the pageant instead. They had decided that the town was to be divided into sectors, and each *medicus* was to have one, except Bartholomew who, it was anticipated, would still be too busy with his battle-wounded.

'You have your hands full already,' Rougham explained

unctuously. 'And we do not want to load you with even more work. How are they today, by the way?'

'They are doing extremely well, thanks to me,' said Holm, before Bartholomew could respond. 'Of course, I shall not be paid for my hard work, but money is not everything.'

'Is it not?' asked Meryfeld, bemused.

Holm looked smug. 'I earned far more than riches with my surgical skills yesterday – I earned the respect and adulation of the entire town. And that may be useful in the future.'

Bartholomew could not bear to listen to him, and changed the subject rather abruptly. 'I have been meaning to warn you all of some danger. Hooded men waylaid me the other night, and demanded the formula for that burning substance we created. The wildfire.'

'Why would anyone want to know that?' asked Rougham uncomfortably.

'I am not sure, but they threatened violence when I told them I could not recall it, so I recommend that you be on your guard.'

'But we do not remember it, either,' objected Meryfeld, alarmed. 'Indeed, I can barely recall that night at all, let alone provide anyone with a detailed list of the ingredients we used.'

'I recollect adding a lot of rubbish,' mused Gyseburne. 'Indeed, I think I tossed in a dash of slug juice at one point. But as to the specific formula, I have no clear memory . . .'

'Well, I was not there,' said Holm smugly. 'So I need not be concerned.'

'You should be – these villains might think we shared the secret with you,' said Rougham.

'But you never did!' cried Holm, horrified by the notion.

'I have asked for it on numerous occasions, but none of you are ever willing to discuss the matter.'

'I wish we had not done it,' said Bartholomew unhappily. 'We devised a terrible thing.'

'We did,' agreed Gyseburne soberly. 'Indeed, I wish I *could* remember the recipe, so we would know never to bring those particular ingredients together again.'

'Well, I wish I could remember so we could sell it,' stated Meryfeld baldly. 'Someone will recreate the stuff at some point, so why should we not be the ones to reap the reward? Do not look so shocked, Bartholomew. Just think of all the good you could do with a large sum of money.'

'The men who ambushed me were not interested in paying,' retorted Bartholomew. 'Indeed, I was under the impression that they were going to kill me once they had what they wanted.'

'Oh,' said Meryfeld uncomfortably. 'Well, that puts an entirely different complexion on it.'

'Your antics had better not result in my murder,' said Holm warningly, glaring at each of them in turn. 'I am about to marry a woman who will make me very rich, and I have no intention of being dispatched before I have had the chance to enjoy my good fortune.'

'It is true love, then, is it?' asked Rougham acidly.

'True love for her father's money,' confided Holm, treating his colleagues to a man-of-the-world wink. Bartholomew looked away.

'*Our* best chance of earning a fortune lies in perfecting the recipe for lamp fuel,' said Rougham, ignoring the surgeon and addressing the others. 'I pondered the matter at length yesterday, and I believe our last brew would have worked better with a teaspoon of honey.'

'Why would you think that?' asked Bartholomew tiredly. While he enjoyed the sessions with his colleagues, he sometimes found their capacity for peculiarly random statements wearisome.

'Because it is sticky,' explained Rougham. 'So it will bind the ingredients together in a more productive manner.'

'It is worth a try,' said Meryfeld, although Bartholomew rolled his eyes. 'And if that does not work, then I have been thinking, too. The addition of red lead will be beneficial.'

'Why?' asked Bartholomew, exasperated. 'Red lead has no known property that will—'

'Open your mind,' interrupted Rougham, gesturing expansively. 'I do not understand why you are so unwilling to experiment, especially as you do it on your patients all the time.'

'What do you mean by that?' Bartholomew was not in the mood for Rougham's insults.

Rougham took a step away, unused to the physician taking issue with him. 'I mean that you try new and unorthodox treatments on your clients, so why not do the same with the lamp fuel?'

'I do nothing of the kind,' retorted Bartholomew. 'All my treatments have either been effective in the past, or there are sound, logical reasons why they will work now. I would never—'

'Urine,' announced Gyseburne grandly. Thrown off his stride by the unexpected declaration, Bartholomew faltered into silence.

'What about urine?' asked Rougham warily.

'It contains flammable properties,' replied Gyseburne. 'My mother told me so, and she is right, I am sure. She usually is.'

'It can be combustible, under certain conditions,' acknowledged Bartholomew, wondering how Gyseburne's dam should have come by such information. Was she a witch? 'But—'

'Well, I like to live on the edge,' said Holm drolly. 'So red lead, honey and urine it is for next time, then. We shall reconvene tomorrow.'

'God's teeth!' muttered Bartholomew, as Meryfeld, Holm and Rougham marched away together, haughty and confident. 'I am beginning to think we are wasting our time with them.'

'All manner of great inventions have been discovered by chance,' countered Gyseburne. 'We may well stumble on something important by random testing.'

'Not with the compounds they have recommended.' Bartholomew was disgusted.

Gyseburne raised an eyebrow. 'Do you *know* how urine will react when heated with pitch? No? Then do you *know* that red lead will remain inert when mixed with brimstone? No again! Do not dismiss us out of hand, Matthew. It is unbecoming in a man who expects tolerance for his own eccentricities.'

A clatter of hoofs in the bailey heralded the arrival of Tulyet and his men, back from the Fens. There was mud on their armour, and the Sheriff looked tired and out of sorts. He stamped over to Bartholomew and Gyseburne.

'Give me a report,' he ordered curtly.

'A report about what?' asked Bartholomew, trying to keep the alarm from his voice. He was not ready to discuss Ayera with Tulyet – he wanted to tackle the geometrician alone first, and hear the explanation that he was sure would exonerate him.

'About the health of my men, of course,' snapped Tulyet. 'What else would I want from you?'

Bartholomew supposed it should have been obvious,

234

and hastened to oblige. Tulyet listened intently, and was relieved when he heard the prognosis was generally good.

'Thank you,' he said quietly. 'Although I shall never forgive myself for this debacle. How could it have happened? This is a castle, for God's sake, and if we cannot defend ourselves, how can we expect people to believe that we are able to protect their town?'

'They know you have learned from your complacency,' said Gyseburne soothingly.

Tulyet winced. 'Now perhaps you would do something else for me. The soldiers who died . . .'

'Bringing them back is beyond our abilities,' said Gyseburne sternly. 'We are not necromancers.'

'I do not expect you to raise the dead,' snarled Tulyet. He put his hands over his face, and scrubbed hard. 'Forgive me. I do not mean to keep barking at you. I am very tired . . .'

'Then rest,' advised Bartholomew. 'You will be no good to anyone if your wits are addled from exhaustion. Go home and sleep. Helbye will summon you if there is trouble.'

Tulyet nodded, although it was clear that he had no intention of complying. 'Today was a waste of effort. Those villains outwitted me with sheep.'

Bartholomew exchanged a bemused glance with Gyseburne.

'They drove a lot of ewes into the area through which they escaped,' the Sheriff went on, 'and not even Cynric could find their tracks among all the hoof-marks. We spent the whole day trying, but it was hopeless.'

'The Fens are a wilderness,' agreed Gyseburne. 'Men disappear there, never to be seen again.'

Tulyet scowled. 'I know, and it is frustrating when they happen to be men I want to catch. But enough of my troubles. Will you examine my dead soldiers, and tell me exactly what happened to them? I would like to furnish their families with an accurate account of their final moments.'

'Of course,' said Gyseburne, although Tulyet had been looking at Bartholomew. He set off towards the chapel, a wooden building set against the curtain wall, at a business-like clip.

'I am not sure what to think about him,' whispered Tulyet, following. 'He seems obliging and competent, but I sense something deeply unpleasant beneath that amiable veneer.'

'Do you?' asked Bartholomew, surprised. 'I have always liked him.'

'You like everyone, and it is a failing you should strive to overcome.' Tulyet sighed dispiritedly. 'I did not want to admit it in front of him, but I still have no idea who was responsible for that damned raid – and even less idea how to go about finding out.'

'Robin thought Coslaye of Batayl Hostel was among the invaders,' said Bartholomew. 'But Coslaye was at the Carmelite Priory when the attack took place, so Robin was mistaken.'

'Pity.' Tulyet saw Bartholomew's startled expression and hastened to explain. 'It would have given me a place to start.'

'I will listen for rumours,' promised Bartholomew. 'And will tell you if I hear anything.'

'Thank you, but you will not,' said Tulyet morosely. 'The attack was by strangers, not folk from the town. There will be no useful rumours, because the culprits do not live here.'

'Walkelate disagrees. He thinks they are locals, as they knew where you keep your money.'

'Then his reasoning is flawed: the Great Tower is the

236

most secure part of the castle, so of course we will lock our valuables there. You do not need local knowledge to guess that.'

They followed Gyseburne in silence for a moment, then Bartholomew began speaking again.

'I was waylaid by cloaked and hooded men on Wednesday. They wanted to know the formula for the wildfire my colleagues and I made last winter – the substance that could not be doused.'

Tulyet shot him a pained glance. 'I forbade my son to talk about what he had witnessed that night, but he rarely obeys me. In other words, I suspect it is fairly common knowledge that you are the one most likely to recollect which ingredients were used. Did you recognise these villains?'

'They were heavily disguised. Michael's grandmother drove them off with knives.'

'Dame Pelagia is back?' asked Tulyet, alarmed. 'Why?'

'To hunt down a French spy, apparently.'

'Then I hope she does not need my help,' said Tulyet grimly. 'Because I cannot oblige her as long as there is a hostile band of mercenaries lurking in the Fens.'

Inspecting the dead soldiers was a bleak business. Some were men Bartholomew had known for years, and he was acutely aware that they had kin relying on the wage they earned. Tulyet would not let their families starve, but it would not be easy for them, even so. He inspected each man with considerable sadness, calling out specific causes of death to Willelmus, the Carmelites' scribe, who stood with pen and parchment at the ready. Gyseburne left the chapel when they had finished, eager to be back among the living, but Tulyet had yet another favour to ask of Bartholomew.

'I need you to tend Ayce again. He is refusing to eat, and I do not want him to die just yet. He may decide to talk to me in a day or two, so it is important to keep him alive.'

It was hardly a pleasant mission, but Bartholomew agreed to do it. He was following Tulyet out of the chapel when he saw a peculiar collection of tubes, ratchets and wheels. He stopped dead in his tracks.

'That is the ribauldequin I was telling you about,' explained the Sheriff. 'The one we made for the King as part-payment of our yearly taxes.'

Bartholomew shuddered, recalling all too clearly the ones at Poitiers. Tulyet's creation had the same unholy malevolence, and the holes at the end of its muzzles looked for all the world like spiteful eyes.

'Does it work?' he asked.

'I hope so, but we cannot test it because we have no ammunition. However, if it fails, it will not be our fault – we should have been sent more detailed instructions. Indeed, were it not for Langelee, Walkelate, Riborowe and Chancellor Tynkell, we would not have got this far.'

'I wish they had refused. The device is immoral – they should have had nothing to do with it.'

Tulyet eyed him balefully. 'Fortunately for me, they do not concur. Indeed, they all told me that University-trained minds will be an essential ingredient for developing better artillery in the future – that warfare will remain primitive without their input.'

Bartholomew was disgusted, but supposed he should not be surprised. Academics were always intrigued by the kind of problem that only intelligence could solve. He looked at the ribauldequin with distaste. 'It is hardly the sort of thing that should be kept in a chapel, Dick.'

'It was in the Great Tower, but we had to move it when we reorganised everything to accommodate your infirmary.

I shall be glad when it has gone from here, though – my chaplains will insist on draping their wet laundry over it, and it is beginning to rust.'

A sudden, alarming thought occurred to Bartholomew. 'Do you think this is why the robbers came? They wanted your weapon to use in their next attack?'

Tulyet regarded him rather patronisingly. 'You cannot stage lightning strikes if you are loaded down with heavy pieces of artillery. It was the tax money they wanted, Matt, not this.'

Bartholomew did not know enough of military tactics to know whether Tulyet was right or wrong.

He insisted on going alone to Ayce's cell, suspecting that Tulyet's angry presence would be counterproductive. Ayce was sitting on the floor, rejecting the bed and stool that had been provided for his use. Bread and a greasy stew stood untouched by the door.

'I will not talk to you,' growled Ayce. 'So do not waste your time with questions.'

'It is the Sheriff who has questions, not me,' said Bartholomew. 'I am just a physician.'

Ayce hesitated for a moment. 'I was injured in the fighting, and it throbs horribly. Perhaps I shall accept your services, because I cannot think clearly through the pain.'

Bartholomew set about cleaning and binding the cut. When he had finished, he gave Ayce a potion to ease his discomfort, then indicated the food. 'You might feel better if you eat, too.'

Ayce picked up the bread and took a tentative bite. 'I should never have let myself be taken alive,' he said, more to himself than Bartholomew. 'But I was stunned by a blow to the head . . .'

'You are fortunate your comrades did not make an end

of you,' said Bartholomew, packing away his pots and potions. 'I understand they dispatched one of their number who was too badly wounded to run away.'

'It was what we had agreed before we began our mission. It is better that way.'

'Better for the men who hired you, perhaps.'

Ayce shrugged. 'We were well paid for it. Besides, I have not cared what happens to me since John was stabbed, and this seemed as good a way as any to make an exit from the world. I was more than happy to volunteer when they came hunting for recruits. And if we had been successful, I would have had enough money to drink myself to death.'

'Who are these men?' asked Bartholomew curiously.

'They did not say, and I did not ask. Not that they would have told me if I had.'

Bartholomew regarded him sceptically. 'You expect me to believe that strangers came along, and you joined them without knowing who they were or what they intended?'

'Oh, I knew what they intended. They said from the start that their aim was to attack the town.'

'For the taxes?' asked Bartholomew. 'Or the ribauldequin?'

Ayce regarded him blankly. 'What is a ribauldequin?' Then he held up his hand. 'No, do not tell me – I do not care. However, I am glad our raid caused such consternation. Cambridge is where John was murdered, and I hate everything about it.'

'People have been telling me about your son's death. It is said that he often bullied scholars.'

Ayce regarded him with dislike. 'And that gave a clerk the right to slaughter him?'

'No, of course not, but it explains how it came about. It was self-defence.'

240

'You *would* take Hildersham's side – you are a scholar. The town found him guilty, though, and steps should have been taken to catch him after he escaped. Now go away and leave me alone. I do not wish to talk any longer.'

The interview had depressed Bartholomew, and he was in a gloomy frame of mind as he left the castle. Outside, one of his students was waiting to tell him that he had been summoned by Prior Etone. It was dusk and he was tired, but he began to trudge towards the Carmelite Friary anyway. When he arrived, it was to find Jorz sitting with his hand in a bucket of cold water.

'It was Browne's fault,' the scribe twittered tearfully. 'He came up behind me, and deliberately startled me out of my wits.'

'He did,' agreed Riborowe. 'I saw it happen. Poor Jorz was boiling up a new recipe for red ink, when Browne came creeping in. He clapped his hand hard on Jorz's shoulder, and made him spill it all over himself.'

Bartholomew inspected Jorz's arm, but the cold water had already worked its magic, and although the scribe would be uncomfortable for a few days, he did not think there would be any lasting damage. He set about applying a soothing salve.

'Browne laughed when he saw I was hurt,' Jorz went on. 'He is a vile fellow – cruel and sly.'

'What was he doing in our domain in the first place?' asked Etone. 'I thought we had agreed that members of Batayl were barred, lest they stage some sort of revenge over the soot incident.'

'He claimed he wanted to buy some ink,' explained Riborowe. 'But I know for a fact that he does not have any money – he is always saying that times are hard. So I imagine he was here to spy, to look around and see what might be done to repay us for our novice's high spirits.'

'Almost certainly,' agreed Etone worriedly. 'We shall have to ask Michael's beadles to keep a protective eye on us for the next few days.'

'Or you could apologise for the soot, and offer a truce,' suggested Bartholomew.

'Apologise?' spluttered Riborowe. 'Never!'

'Actually, that is a good idea,' countered Etone, somewhat unexpectedly. 'I am weary of this dispute, and see no point in continuing it. I shall apologise, and Matthew will go with me, as a witness.'

'Now?' asked Bartholomew unenthusiastically.

'Yes, now,' said Etone. 'Before I decide it is too great a burden for my pride to bear.'

Unhappily, Bartholomew trailed after him, but when they reached Batayl it was to discover everyone out except Pepin, who had been left on guard. The Frenchman said that the students had gone to hear a sermon in St Mary the Great, while Coslaye and Browne were in Newe Inn.

'Why there?' asked Bartholomew suspiciously. 'I thought they disapproved of the library.'

'They do,' replied Pepin. 'But Walkelate thinks he can win them over by showing them his finished lecterns. The man is a fool. His nasty library has deprived Batayl of better living conditions, and no amount of fine carving will ever make us overlook that fact.'

'Well, I intend to overlook the wrong that has been inflicted on me,' said Etone loftily. 'I do not have the energy to hold grudges – not against Dunning for breaking his promise, and not against Batayl for challenging us about it.'

Once again, Bartholomew found himself in Etone's wake, as the Prior strode towards Newe Inn. The door was open, so they entered.

'Good God, it reeks in here!' exclaimed Etone, waving his hand in front of his face. He grinned a little spitefully. 'The guests at its grand opening are going to be asphyxiated.'

Bartholomew followed him up the stairs, where they could hear voices. They entered the room containing the *libri distribuendi*, and found Walkelate proudly displaying some finished mouldings to an unlikely audience that included Coslaye, Browne, Dunning and Bonabes. Meanwhile, Kente and Frevill, exhausted after yet another day of gruellingly hard work, were packing up their tools.

'They are all right, I suppose,' Coslaye was saying grudgingly. 'But battle scenes would have been preferable to all this Paradise nonsense. And you should have made Aristotle more manly.'

'We should not linger here, Coslaye,' said Browne, also regarding the bust with contempt. 'Libraries are dangerous. Five men have died in and around them already.'

'I hardly think—' began Walkelate indignantly.

'Etone! What are you doing here?' Browne's instantly furtive expression suggested that he probably had intended to harm Jorz by slinking up behind him, and was now worried that the Prior intended to demand reparation.

'I came to offer a truce,' replied Etone. 'We are even now: our novice should not have put soot on your mural, but you should not have startled Jorz when he was working with hot liquids. I should like to bring an end to our dispute. What do you say?'

'I shall think about it,' said Coslaye coldly. 'And I will send you my decision later. Or perhaps I shall reject your slithering advances. You will just have to wait and see.'

Head held high, he sailed away. With a churlish smirk, Browne followed.

'You see, Matthew?' said Etone in exasperation. 'It is hopeless! I offer them an olive branch, and they spit on it. Well, they can have a feud, if that is what they want.'

'No!' cried Walkelate, distressed. 'You are right to end this silly spat. It would be a pity for ill feelings to sour our opening ceremony on Thursday, and—'

But Etone was already striding away, so Walkelate was obliged to scurry after him to finish what he wanted to say. Kente and Frevill were hot on his heels, tool-bags slung over their shoulders, eager to wash the wood dust from their throats with cool ale. Bonabes, Dunning and Bartholomew followed more sedately.

'You are wasting your time if you think you can help forge a truce between Batayl and the Carmelites, Bartholomew,' said Bonabes. 'Neither side seems wholly rational to me.'

'Nor to me,' agreed Dunning. 'And I object to them saying that the source of their discord is my so-called promise to give each of them Newe Inn. I did nothing of the kind.'

'What were you doing here?' Bartholomew asked. 'Surely it is a little late for guided tours?'

Bonabes winced. 'We happened to be passing, and Walkelate raced out and hauled us inside to inspect Aristotle's newly buffed bust. It is not the first time he has ambushed me to admire his works of art, so I think I must avoid Cholles Lane in future.'

Dunning chuckled good-naturedly. 'He is something of a menace in that respect.'

They walked down the stairs, and when they reached the bottom, Etone used the opportunity afforded by their arrival to escape from Walkelate. Bonabes and Dunning followed him, and they could be heard laughing in the lane together, amused by the architect's eccentric enthusiasm. Oblivious of the reason for their mirth, Walkelate began talking to Bartholomew.

'I am glad you came, because I have something to tell you. Alfred, our youngest apprentice, informed me today that he heard a bell in the garden last week – he spent a night here, you see, sanding a cornice. He only remembered it today, but he wanted me to inform you or Michael. However, I imagine he fell asleep and dreamt it, because bells do not ring at that hour.'

'I am not so sure. Coslaye heard one chiming when Northwood and the others died.'

'Really?' Walkelate shook his head, baffled. Then a happy grin stole across his face. 'Kente put the finishing touches to the lecterns for the *libri distribuendi* an hour ago. Come and see them.'

'Another time.' Bartholomew saw the disappointment in Walkelate's face, and hastened to make amends. 'It is too dark to appreciate them properly now.'

'We made excellent progress today,' said Walkelate, his excitement bubbling up again. The *libri concatenati* are ready, and we shall keep their room closed now, until our grand opening. Well, we shall have to oust the bale of hay, but that will not take a moment.'

'The bale of hay?' asked Bartholomew, nonplussed.

Walkelate smiled. 'Holm's concoction was not working, so Dunning suggested an old country remedy instead – the theory is that dry grass absorbs strong odours from the air. He assures me that by Thursday, the room will smell as sweet as a meadow.'

Bartholomew started to walk home to Michaelhouse, aware that the daylight was fading fast. Recalling what had happened the last two times he had wandered about the town after dark on his own, he broke into a trot, eager for the sanctuary of the conclave, where wine and perhaps some cake would be waiting. He jumped in alarm when Cynric materialised in front of him.

'You should not be out at this time of night without me,' the Welshman said admonishingly. 'It is not safe.'

'No,' agreed Bartholomew. 'But we are almost home.'

'You cannot go home,' said Cynic. His expression became sympathetic when he saw Bartholomew's tiredness. 'You are needed at Bene't College.'

'Are you sure?' asked Bartholomew doubtfully. 'They are Meryfeld's patients.'

'There was a dispute about overcharging, apparently, and Meryfeld declines to answer their summonses until they acknowledge that he is in the right.'

'But Master Heltisle does not like me,' said Bartholomew, too weary for a confrontation with the prickly Master of Bene't. 'It would be better if you fetched Gyseburne or Rougham.'

'Neither is home. I am on my way to Batayl, by the way, to tell them about Poitiers, but I will walk with you to Bene't first.'

Bartholomew had forgotten about Cynric's invitation to lecture, and hoped the talk would not induce a lot of patriotic fervour that would be uncomfortable for Pepin.

'Do not mention me in your account,' he begged. 'Half the town believes I am a warlock, and I do not want the other half thinking I am a warrior. Tell them about your own exploits.'

'Very well,' promised Cynric. 'But here we are at Bene't. Knock on the door to make sure they are willing to let you in. If not, I shall escort you back to Michaelhouse.'

Bartholomew was disappointed when the porter stepped aside and indicated he was to enter, because Cynric's offer of company home was appealing. The book-bearer nodded a farewell and disappeared into the gathering shadows, as silent-footed as a cat.

'Damn!' muttered Thomas Heltisle, a tall, aloof man with neat silver hair, when he saw which physician had answered his summons. 'I had hoped one of the others would be available.'

'I am happy to leave, and you can wait for—'

'No,' said Heltisle hastily. 'I do not want the Devil's crony in my College, but John Rolee has knocked himself senseless, so it is an emergency and I have no choice. Come.'

He began hauling Bartholomew across the yard before the physician could take issue with him. As they went, it occurred to Bartholomew that he had never been in Bene't's library before. The heads of the other Colleges were happy to let him use their books, but Heltisle had always refused.

When they arrived, he was impressed. The room – a chamber above one of the teaching halls – was crammed with texts of all shapes and sizes. Unlike King's Hall with its mighty bookcases, Bene't had opted for a low mezzanine gallery that ran around all four walls to provide additional storage; access to it was via an elegantly crafted but rather unstable set of wheeled steps.

Heltisle's six Fellows stood in a huddle near the window. They nodded wary greetings to him, and one or two crossed themselves, as if they expected Satan to be close at hand now he was there.

'Over here,' called a small, feisty scholar named Teversham. He was crouching next to someone on the floor. 'We have tried shouting and tapping his face, but we cannot wake him up.'

Bartholomew's heart sank as he approached. Rolee's head lay at a peculiar angle, and it was obvious that his neck had been broken.

247

'I am afraid it is too late,' he said, kneeling and performing a perfunctory examination to confirm what he already knew. 'He is dead.'

'He cannot be!' cried Heltisle, shocked. 'He was talking with us not half an hour ago. We were discussing elephants, and he came to fetch his bestiary, to show us what they look like.'

'And he fell?' asked Bartholomew.

'The steps broke,' explained Heltisle, pointing to where the wheeled stairs lay on their side. 'We heard the crash, and came racing in here to find him . . . But he cannot be dead, Bartholomew! He is just knocked out of his wits. Look again.'

'His neck is broken,' said Bartholomew gently. 'I am sorry, but there is nothing I can do. If it is any consolation, death would have been instant. He felt nothing.'

'It is no consolation at all!' shouted Heltisle. 'He owes me ten shillings.'

To mask his bemusement at the remark, Bartholomew went to inspect the ladder. One of the legs had split, causing the whole thing to topple sideways when Rolee reached the top. It was not much of a drop from the mezzanine, and he had been acutely unlucky to land so awkwardly.

'Will there be an investigation?' asked Heltisle in an uncharacteristically small voice. He hated situations that involved the Senior Proctor, because bad publicity affected benefactions.

Bartholomew shrugged. 'Michael will need to examine the steps, and he will want you to tell him exactly what happened. Beyond that, I cannot say.'

'Very well,' sniffed Heltisle. 'Although it is a waste of time. He can do more good by looking into those four corpses at the Common Library. The grace to found such an institution should never have been passed, you know. It is a wicked scheme, and will end in tears.'

There was a chorus of agreement from his Fellows. Bartholomew said nothing, knowing the remarks were aimed at him for having had the audacity to support it.

'We are not paying you for this visit, by the way,' said Heltisle. 'We called you to help Rolee, but instead you only pronounced him dead. You did not use your skills to save him.'

A fee had been the last thing on Bartholomew's mind – he frequently forgot to charge for his services anyway – and he waved away Heltisle's comment as of no consequence.

'So you may have this instead,' Heltisle went on, pressing a book into his hands.

'No!' Bartholomew tried to hand it back. 'This is far too valuable for—'

'I have never heard a physician try to negotiate his fee downwards before,' said Heltisle with a grim smile. 'Perhaps the tales about your honesty are true after all.'

'Oh, he is honest,' muttered Teversham. 'That has never been in question. It is his pact with the Devil that I am worried about.'

Bartholomew sighed wearily. 'I have no pact with the Devil. Why will no one believe me?'

'Because no *medicus* should enjoy as much success as you do,' explained Teversham shortly. 'It is not natural.'

'You condemn me for saving people?' asked Bartholomew archly.

'If Satan does not help you, then how do you explain your victories?' demanded Teversham.

'Hot water mostly,' flashed Bartholomew, and then wished he had not.

Evesham's eyebrows shot up. 'Water that has been cooked in the fires of Hell?'

'Water from the town well,' snapped Bartholomew,

angry with himself for not guessing how Bene't would respond to his remarks, especially after his recent conversation with Gyseburne about boiled bandages. 'Which has been heated in our kitchen.'

'We do not want to know, thank you,' said Heltisle, cutting across Teversham's response. 'However, to return to the book, we decided before you arrived that we would give it to the *medicus* who tended Rolee. Not only is it a bestiary – and we do not have room for such foolery in our library – but he cut his hand last week, and managed to smear blood all over it.'

Bartholomew peered at the ominous stain in the gloom. 'I am sure it will wash off. But I cannot take a book, even so. It is far too—'

'It is yours now, whether you like it or not,' added Teversham. 'Put it in your Common Library if you decline to keep it yourself. God knows, that foundation is tainted enough, so Rolee's nasty volume should feel perfectly at home there.'

Bartholomew objected to being bullied into accepting a gift he did not want, but he was too tired for further confrontation. He nodded cool thanks, and left Bene't without another word. He began to walk home again, craving the gentler company of Michaelhouse, but running footsteps made him spin around in alarm. He braced himself for trouble, but it was only Cynric.

'Come quick,' the book-bearer gasped. 'Coslaye was not in when I arrived, so the students went to look for him. They found him in his garden, and his head has been stove in by a book.'

'Again?' asked Bartholomew in dismay.

'Yes,' panted Cynric. 'And your surgery will not save him this time. He is utterly dead.'

CHAPTER 8

It was not far from Bene't College to Cholles Lane, and it took only a few moments for Bartholomew to run the distance, Cynric at his heels. It was now pitch black, and the streets smelled of warm dust and horse manure, overlain with the dank, rich odour of the river.

The door to Batayl was open, and Bartholomew walked inside to find the hostel deserted. Raised voices told him that everyone was in the tiny garden, which was accessed through a second door at the back of the house. Batayl's eight students, Browne, Michael and two beadles were crammed into it, all clustered around Coslaye, who lay on the ground.

'Perhaps you should take your lads inside, Browne,' Michael was saying. 'There is no need for them to witness this sad sight.'

'There is every need,' Browne snapped. 'Their Principal has been most wickedly slain by Carmelites, and they *should* see this vile handiwork.'

'Enough,' said Michael warningly. 'We must assess the evidence before—'

'Evidence be damned!' shouted Browne. 'We all know who did this terrible thing.'

The students howled their support, and it was not easy for Bartholomew to dodge through their waving fists to reach Coslaye. He managed, finally, shoving his new bestiary at Cynric, and inspecting the fallen Principal in the feeble light shed from a lamp held by Pepin.

Coslaye lay on his front, arms thrown out to the sides. He had been dealt a substantial blow from behind, heavy enough to smash his skull. An examination revealed no other suspicious marks, except a bad bruise on his left foot.

'How did he come by this?' he asked.

'It probably happened in Newe Inn, which is always littered with dangerous bits of wood and tools,' said Browne, his sullen expression making it clear that he considered the injury of far less importance than the one to Coslaye's head, which had killed him. 'Walkelate is always inviting us in there, probably in the hope that we will be maimed – in revenge for us opposing his stupid library.'

Bartholomew inspected the foot more closely, and deduced that something sharp had struck it, such as might have happened if a dagger had been lobbed. He stared at the mark. Had Coslaye been among the men who had ambushed him, injured by one of Pelagia's knives? But why would he want a formula for wildfire? Or had Coslaye been hurt attacking the castle, and Robin *had* seen him among the raiders? But Coslaye claimed to have been quarrelling with the Carmelites at the time, and so could not have been wielding a sword.

Michael nodded to his beadles, who began to usher the Batayl men back into their hostel. They objected, particularly Browne, but the beadles were used to recalcitrant academics, and soon had them where they wanted them to be.

'What can you tell me, Matt?' asked Michael, once they had gone.

'That Coslaye was hit from behind with something heavy. And that the damage to his foot is several days older.'

'Did he know his killer? Or is this the work of a stranger?'

Bartholomew regarded him askance. 'How am I supposed to deduce that?'

'By the way the body landed?' suggested Michael. 'Or the position of the wound? You have drawn such conclusions before, so do not look at me as though I am short of wits.'

'He is on his front, so he may have been running from a stranger when he was struck. Of course, he could equally well have been trying to escape from a murderous friend. Alternatively, his body could have been moved after he died, to make us think he was fleeing from someone.'

'That is hardly helpful,' said Michael reproachfully. 'Let us discuss his foot, then. What do you make of that?'

'It looks as though the damage was caused by a pointed implement that struck it with some force, but that was prevented from breaking the skin by his hard-leather shoe.'

'Did you ever notice Coslaye limping? If we can ascertain when he came by this injury, we may be able to work out how it happened.'

Bartholomew thought hard. 'I was attacked on Wednesday night, and we met Coslaye the next day when he was quarrelling with the Carmelites, but I do not recall whether he hobbled or not. The next time I saw him, he was lying down – he was ill from bad food. And the time after that he was sitting, reading to his students.'

It told them nothing, and Michael's expression was unhappy as he led the way inside the hostel, where he asked the Batayl men again what they thought had happened.

'And do not accuse the Carmelites unless you have solid evidence to prove it,' he warned.

Browne glowered and folded his arms, petulantly declining to speak unless he could reiterate his firmly held convictions.

'Perhaps it was suicide,' suggested Pepin with a Gallic shrug. 'Coslaye has not been himself since Dunning gave Newe Inn away.'

'It was not suicide,' said Bartholomew, trying to gauge the Frenchman's expression in the flickering light. Had he dispatched his Principal for being a Francophobe? 'Killing yourself with a blow to the back of the head is virtually impossible.'

'*Virtually* impossible,' pounced Pepin. 'That means there is a chance that I am right. Yes?'

'A very small one.' Bartholomew gave up trying to read Pepin, and turned to Browne. 'Did you and Coslaye come straight home after visiting Newe Inn earlier this evening?'

'Coslaye did, but I had business elsewhere.' Browne scowled when Michael indicated that this was not enough of an answer. 'All right, I went to watch the Carmelite Priory. But so what? It is not illegal to stare at friaries. I only wish I had stayed longer, because then they could not have sneaked into our home and murdered our Principal!'

There was a growl of agreement from the students, while Bartholomew thought that Browne's reply did Pepin no favours – if Coslaye had arrived home without Browne, and all the others had been at a sermon in St Mary the Great, it meant that Coslaye and Pepin had been alone together.

'The Carmelites hate us,' said Browne, eagerly seizing the opportunity to put his case. 'And it is obvious what happened: when Coslaye did not immediately agree to Etone's offer of a truce, one of them came here and murdered him, just as they tried to murder him when they threw that book at the Convocation.'

'*Mon Dieu!*' cried Pepin suddenly, raising the lamp to illuminate what Cynric held. 'Maybe you are wrong to accuse the White Friars, because here is a big book – one with blood all over it!'

'It is Bartholomew's,' said Browne. 'I saw him bring it. Is he Coslaye's murderer, then?'

'Do not be ridiculous,' said Michael, raising his hand when several students moved threateningly towards the physician. 'He is not in the habit of dispatching patients, especially after expending so much effort on making them well.'

'Surgery!' spat Browne. 'Such techniques are contrary to God's will. Doubtless Satan wanted the soul he should have had at the Convocation, and ordered Bartholomew to put matters right.'

'If Coslaye's surgery was against the will of God, then it cannot have been the Devil demanding his death now,' said Michael scathingly. 'If you must make slanderous accusations, at least ensure they are logical. However, I think we had better inspect your own books before we go any further.'

Without waiting for Browne's response, he stalked towards the shelf where Batayl kept its small collection of reading material. When all eyes were on the monk, Cynric promptly shoved the bestiary back at Bartholomew with a moue of distaste.

'Here is our murder weapon,' said Michael, withdrawing the tome at the very bottom of the pile. He held it aloft, so the Batayl men could see the dark mess along its spine. 'The blood is still wet, and you can see hair adhering to it. Coslaye's.'

'It is Acton's *Questio Disputata*,' breathed Pepin. 'The book that almost killed him last time.'

Browne's face was white with horror. 'The fact that Coslaye was dispatched with one of our books does not mean that we did it. Anyone could have come in, grabbed the tome and hit him.'

'Perhaps,' said Michael flatly. 'Now answer some questions. Who found him out here?'

'Browne did,' replied Pepin, rather quickly. 'When everyone came back from the sermon, we had something to eat, then sat inside together , waiting for Cynric to come and talk to us about Poitiers. Browne—'

'Poitiers!' spat Browne angrily. 'I am sick of hearing about Poitiers! We won – France is demoralised, she is crippled by debt, her peasants are on the verge of revolt, and our own army continues to ravage her farms and villages. Is this not enough? Must we continue to gloat over the bloody slaughter of her boys, too?'

'Coslaye was not here,' Pepin went on, after a brief pause in which everyone looked startled by the outburst. 'And after a while we became worried, because we all knew how eager he was to hear Cynric. We went to look for him. Browne came out here to check the latrines and there he was . . .'

'How long had he been missing?' Michael demanded.

'When he returned from Newe Inn, he sent me out to buy some ale to drink while we listened to Cynric,' replied Pepin. 'He was not here when I got back, and none of us saw him again until Browne found his corpse.'

'You have three choices for suspects, Brother,' said Browne tightly. 'Namely Bartholomew, a Carmelite or the Devil. It is a pity you did not bother to catch the villain who tried to kill poor Coslaye the first time, because if you had, we might not be mourning him now.'

The next day was cloudy, and the dry heat of the past few days had turned humid. Bartholomew was called before dawn to tend one of the men in the castle, and then was summoned to the hovels on the towpath, where the riverfolk lived. As usual, they were uncommunicative, and it took some time to ascertain exactly what they wanted him to do. Eventually, he managed to evince that several were suffering from stomach pains.

'Carp,' said Torvin tersely.

Bartholomew was not surprised. The river was an open sewer, and waste was discharged into it by several friaries, Colleges and hostels, not to mention private houses and two mills. The fish in it were far from healthy, but the riverfolk devoured them anyway, despite his repeated urging to set their nets farther upstream.

'When did they eat it?' he asked.

The riverfolk exchanged glances, and he had the feeling that a silent conversation was taking place, one from which he was excluded.

'Friday,' replied Torvin eventually.

'Three days,' mused Bartholomew. Pangs from tainted food usually eased sooner. He examined all five patients, then sat back perplexed. They looked unwell, with ashen complexions and dark smudges under their eyes, but did not seem to be in unbearable discomfort. He wrote out the remedy he usually dispensed for upset stomachs, then sent a child to the apothecary, remembering to include threepence with the note, because the riverfolk had no money of their own.

'Perhaps you should avoid fish from the river until after it rains,' he suggested. 'Then the rubbish will be washed away, and the water will be cleaner.'

'They were not from the river,' said Torvin. 'They came from Newe Inn's pond.'

Bartholomew remembered how ill *he* had felt after swallowing water from the pool. Then he frowned as something occurred to him: Batayl had also suffered from roiling innards, and Browne had admitted to poaching from the library's grounds – fish that Pepin had added to his stew.

Had the stolen carp been responsible for the sickness that had claimed an entire hostel, rather than the dangerously old meat that he had assumed was the culprit?

'It is not stealing,' said Torvin, misunderstanding his silence. 'No one else wants it.'

'It is University property now,' said Bartholomew. 'You do not want to be caught there, so it might be wise to stay away. Besides, I think there is something wrong with the water.'

'It did stink,' conceded Torvin.

'Stink of what?'

'Corpses,' replied Torvin darkly. 'But we were too hungry to care. Will this mean you lose five marks to Surgeon Holm? Because we are caught taking carp?'

'Not unless you tell him. I certainly will not.'

Amused and conspiratorial smirks flew between the riverfolk, and they all nodded. When the child returned with the remedy, Bartholomew fed it to his patients, then walked home. He had missed church, and the procession was making its way down St Michael's Lane. Ayera was talking to Langelee at the front of the column, and Bartholomew experienced a twinge of unease when he remembered that he would have to tackle the geometrician that day about Gyseburne's accusation. With a lurch of alarm, he saw Ayera was limping.

'Not now,' said Ayera, when Bartholomew indicated he wanted to talk. 'I have an appointment, and I am late already. Suttone's masses are much longer than William's.'

'An appointment?' asked Thelnetham, overhearing. 'Surely, it is too early for business?'

'Not when horses are being discussed,' said Ayera, although his smile was distinctly strained.

'This is important,' pressed Bartholomew.

'So is the horse. I have been negotiating to buy it for weeks now, and would hate to lose it after all my efforts.'

'Buy it with what?' asked Bartholomew sceptically. 'I thought your uncle had left you with nothing.'

Ayera's smile froze. 'I hardly think my finances are your affair, and it is ungentlemanly in you to raise such matters. Now, if you will excuse me, I have people to meet.'

He strode away, leaving Bartholomew staring helplessly after him. Now what? Should he follow, to see where Ayera was really going at such a peculiar hour? He took a step up the lane, but someone grabbed his arm and stopped him.

'No.' Clippesby's face was pale, and his eyes had the curiously wild expression that said something was upsetting him. 'He will prove to be too dangerous an adversary.'

'What do you mean?' Bartholomew relented when the Dominican flinched at the agitation in his voice, and spoke more gently. 'What have you seen, John?'

'The owls in Bridge Street . . .' Clippesby saw Bartholomew's exasperation and began again. '*I* happened to be in the castle when that raid took place, hiding with two frightened cows. And I saw Ayera. He was mud-splattered, fully armoured, and he was talking to that scribe.'

'What scribe?'

'The Carmelite Willelmus, whom Doctor Rougham later spirited away for personal nursing. I did not catch much of the discussion, because they kept their voices low, but I did hear Ayera say that the attack had failed because the raiders had retreated too soon.'

'So?' asked Bartholomew, although his stomach churned. 'He was a soldier once, and is more than qualified to make that sort of assessment.'

'But what was he doing at the castle at such an hour? Especially wearing armour.'

Bartholomew shrugged, loath to accept the conclusions to which Clippesby's claims were driving him. 'Perhaps he has taken a lover outside the town, and he stopped at the castle on his way home when he saw there was trouble.'

'His lady lives in the Jewry, and he tends to dress nicely for her – his best tabard, not a grubby cloak with a hood that conceals his face. He does not don full battle gear for her, either.'

'What are you saying?' demanded Bartholomew, hating what the rational part of his mind was telling him; he still did not want to believe it. 'That Ayera joined the attack on the castle?'

'The bats assure me that he will have an excuse that exonerates him completely,' said Clippesby, taking refuge in his eccentricity with considerable relief. But the guileless smile he tried to force would not come. 'Unfortunately, the cows do not agree.'

'We must catch Coslaye's killer before Thursday, Matt, or Batayl is certain to make trouble at the ceremony,' said Michael worriedly after breakfast. 'They will blame the Carmelites, whose feisty novices will react with violence. Or worse, Batayl may accuse one of the library's supporters – such as you – of the crime. They already know you own a bloodstained book.'

'I have an alibi for Coslaye's death,' objected Bartholomew. 'I was at Bene't College.'

'You think Heltisle will rally to your defence, do you? He has never liked you, and I imagine he will be delighted to see you in trouble.'

'It would please him,' acknowledged Bartholomew. 'However, he will not stand by and see me accused of murder when he knows I am innocent. Besides, he gave me a book, so perhaps he—'

'A book he wanted out of his College. He was not being generous – he just saw it as a convenient way to avoid giving you cash. But never mind this. We are going to be busy today, not just with Coslaye's murder, but with the other deaths, too.'

'And the castle raid,' said Bartholomew. He took a deep breath and forged on when Michael regarded him questioningly. 'Because Ayera may be involved. Two witnesses saw him there.'

'What witnesses?' asked Michael sceptically.

'Clippesby and Gyseburne,' supplied Bartholomew reluctantly. 'But Gyseburne will deny it if you question him, because he says Ayera frightens him.'

Michael shook his head firmly. 'Their claims are a nonsense. Langelee told me only last night that Gyseburne had a reputation for secret drinking in York, which led him to all manner of lunatic imaginings, while Clippesby has been odder than usual of late. He announced before church this morning that his rat would be enrolling as a Regent in the Faculty of Canon Law.'

Bartholomew should have been relieved that the accusations against Ayera had been explained away – and he knew for a fact that Gyseburne did enjoy a drink, while Clippesby was currently in one of his more fey phases – but there remained an unpleasantly niggling doubt at the back of his mind, and he knew it would only ease when he had heard Ayera deny the charges himself. He decided to speak to the geometrician as soon as he could corner him alone.

'How will you move forward on your investigations?' he asked of Michael, forcing his mind back to the present. 'You have no new leads to follow.'

'No,' agreed Michael. 'So we must go out and find some. Please note that I am including you in my plans. I cannot manage alone, not without a Junior Proctor. Besides, you did mention a desire to see justice for Northwood, a man you liked and who was your friend.'

Bartholomew said nothing, loath to admit that what he had learned about Northwood since had made him wonder whether he had really known the man at all: his bullying of novices, his inexplicable dealings with exemplars, the possibility that he had blackmailed Vale, and the fact that he had probably been experimenting with lamp fuel on the sly. Of course, to counter all that was his patient tutoring of Julitta and the fact that he had refused to help Tulyet build a weapon. In all, Bartholomew was not sure what to make of Northwood.

Their first stop was the Carmelite Priory, where they learned that everyone had an alibi for Coslaye's death, because they had all been at a meeting to discuss arrangements for Corpus Christi. Etone had even conducted a roll call, as he had wanted to ensure that every friar, novice and lay-brother was briefed on his responsibilities for the forthcoming festivities. It would have been impossible for anyone to slip out and go a-murdering.

'Thank God!' sighed Michael as they left. 'We had better inform Batayl immediately, to ensure they do not stage a revenge killing.'

'Yes, but exonerating the Carmelites means you have no good suspects. Personally, I thought Riborowe or Jorz might be responsible. For friars, they are vindictive men.'

'They are,' agreed Michael. Then he stopped walking and closed his eyes. 'Blast! I neglected to ask them to confirm Coslaye's claim that he was arguing with them over soot when the castle was raided, and now it is too late – they will be at their prayers. I must be losing my touch.'

Bartholomew studied him closely. 'You seem distracted. Is anything specific worrying you?'

Michael's smile was wan. 'Other than the prospect of a riot when the library opens, and the unsolved murders of Vale, Northwood, the Londons, Coslaye and possibly Sawtre and Rolee, too? Well, there is the rumour my beadles reported this morning – that something terrible will happen on Corpus Christi. Several of them have heard it, and the tale seems to have taken root among scholars and townsmen alike.'

'What sort of "something terrible"?'

'They were unable to say. Regardless, I am extremely concerned.'

While Michael went to inform Batayl that the Carmelites did not kill Coslaye, Bartholomew returned to College, where he put his students through their paces until the bell sounded for the noonday meal. They escaped with relief when Clippesby approached to report that Langelee had asked William to preside over dinner that day because he was busy elsewhere; the meal would be delayed for a few moments while the Franciscan tried to learn the appropriate grace. Puzzled, as the Master rarely delegated mealtime duties, Bartholomew used the spare time to hunt down Ayera, but the geometrician had not been seen in the College since church.

Uneasy in his mind – he and Michael were the only ones with permission to leave Michaelhouse during teaching hours, so Ayera should have been home – Bartholomew took his place at the high table. As usual, Michael sat on one side of him, while Clippesby was on the other, although the Dominican did not stay there for long: his rat escaped during William's muddled and largely improvised prayers, and he was asked to leave.

Dinner was a paltry affair of stale bread and a watery stew that tasted powerfully of old fish. It reminded

Bartholomew of the concoction that had poisoned Batayl, which then made him think of the riverfolk and his own illness. Had Newe Inn's water killed Northwood and the others? Cynric was adamant that the pond was evil, and while Bartholomew did not believe such notions, he did know that superstitions sometimes held a grain of truth. Perhaps there *was* something wrong with the pool, and Cynric was right to be wary of it.

'I think I was overly ambitious earlier, when I suggested we just go out and unearth a few clues,' said Michael, dispiritedly. 'It is easier said than done.'

'Do you have no new information at all?' asked Bartholomew. 'Or no good suspects?'

'I have hundreds of suspects – that is the problem. Northwood, the London brothers and Vale supported the library, which means half the University bore them malice. Literally. And their sly experiments with lamp fuel mean we must include the *medici* on the list, too.'

'Holm is the only one you should seriously consider.'

Michael gazed at him. 'It is unlike you to take against someone so. What has he done wrong?'

Bartholomew did not want to admit that his antipathy stemmed from the fact that he hated the thought of Holm hurting Julitta. 'He is an abysmal surgeon,' he hedged. 'He was on the side of the French at Poitiers, and he can barely open his mouth without lying. He told Dunning that he was at the castle all Saturday night, but he was not – he slunk off at dusk. And Clippesby says he has a lover.'

'Really?' asked Michael keenly. 'Who is she?'

'I did not let him say.' Bartholomew shrugged defensively when Michael rolled his eyes. 'It was gossip, Brother, and I am no Weasenham.'

'I suppose Holm is unappealing, but no more so than the rest of your colleagues.'

264

'Gyseburne is a decent man,' objected Bartholomew. 'He—'

'He is abnormally fascinated with urine, which you now tell me can be used to make things explode. Coupled with his secret drinking, it means he is a man to watch very carefully.'

'It does not,' argued Bartholomew. 'My colleagues – with the exception of Holm – are only interested in healing.'

'And in making their fortunes with lamp fuel,' added Michael dryly. 'There is no group of men better qualified to kill by stealth, as I have said before.'

'But that assumes Northwood and the others were experimenting with lamp fuel, and we have no evidence to prove they were. They may have been trying to make ink or paper. There will be money in those commodities, too.'

'I suppose so,' conceded Michael reluctantly. 'And Northwood was a Carmelite, so was in a position to monitor what Riborowe and Jorz were doing.'

'I cannot see Northwood spying,' said Bartholomew. 'And I am not sure what to make of the tales we have been told about him, either. He never gave me the slightest indication that he was eager to amass riches. He was just a man keen to stretch his mind and learn new things.'

'That is not necessarily a virtue.' Michael grimaced. 'I know I sound like William, but we must set some limits on scholarship, or who knows where it might lead? Look at Tynkell, Riborowe, Langelee and Walkelate, who helped to build a ribauldequin for the French wars. Is that any way to use the wits God gave them?'

'Restrictions will not prevent that sort of activity, Brother. It will only hinder those who are trying to make discoveries for the common good. It is—'

The debate was interrupted by the sudden appearance of Cynric.

'Come quickly,' the book-bearer said. 'Someone has knocked Master Langelee over the head.'

Langelee was sitting disconsolately in Michaelhouse's kitchen with Agatha hovering protectively behind him. Ayera was there, too, telling her how he had found the Master staggering around dazedly in Cholles Lane. Bartholomew inspected the bump on the back of Langelee's head, but although it was no doubt uncomfortable, there did not seem to be any serious damage.

'What were you doing in Cholles Lane?' asked Michael, watching Langelee wince as Bartholomew applied a cool compress. 'Visiting a tavern?'

'I do not frequent taverns during the daylight hours,' replied Langelee haughtily. 'I was in Newe Inn's garden, if you must know. I was curious to see the place where those four scholars died.'

'Why?' asked Bartholomew suspiciously.

'Because it was a peculiar business, and it involved my University,' replied Langelee tartly. 'You two do not seem to be making any progress, so I decided to poke about myself.'

'And did you learn anything?' asked Michael, ignoring the slight.

Langelee grimaced. 'No.'

Michael turned to Ayera. 'And what were you doing in the vicinity? You do not have licence to wander about the town during teaching hours.'

Ayera's expression was difficult to read. 'I do not answer to you, Brother.'

'I gave him permission to be out today,' explained Langelee. 'His family have offered to lend him the money

266

to purchase that horse – the one that will benefit the College if we put it to stud – so he went to inspect it. And thank God he happened by! I can well imagine the rumours that would have started if the Master of Michaelhouse had been discovered lying insensible in Newe Inn's garden.'

'But Ayera claimed he found you in Cholles Lane,' said Bartholomew. 'Not in—'

'I was stunned, so my memory is foggy,' interrupted Langelee curtly, while Ayera's face remained curiously blank. 'Do not nit-pick, Bartholomew.'

'Newe Inn's pond is haunted,' declared Agatha matter-of-factly, before the physician could press the matter further. 'Everyone in the town knows it. And on certain very dark nights, strange smells seep out. It is the reek of Hell escaping.'

'I did not notice any smells,' said Langelee. 'But someone came along and hit me very hard. It is fortunate I have a thick skull, because I am sure he meant to kill.'

'Do you have any idea who the rogue might have been?' asked Ayera.

'None at all, but when I find out, I am going to hit him back!'

'Please do not,' begged Michael. 'I do not want another murder to investigate, and there may be an innocent explanation for what happened – one of the workmen may have seen you, and mistook you for a thief. But I shall visit Newe Inn as soon as I have set my students some work. No one strikes the Master of my College and gets away with it.'

Agatha and Langelee followed him out, leaving Bartholomew alone with Ayera. The geometrician went to pour himself a cup of wine, at which point Bartholomew noticed two things: that Ayera's hands were unsteady and that he was still favouring his left leg. He decided there would not be a better time to ascertain the truth.

'There has been a report that you were among the men who attacked the castle,' he said baldly.

Ayera gaped at him. 'Me? Why would I be involved in such a thing?'

'I cannot imagine,' replied Bartholomew. 'But perhaps it explains why you are wearing half-armour under your academic tabard now, and possibly why you are limping, too.'

Ayera continued to stare. 'I often wear armour under my tabard. This is a dangerous town, in case you had not noticed. And I hurt my knee just now, helping Langelee back to the College.'

'May I see it?' Bartholomew was more than capable of distinguishing between sprains and injuries sustained in armed skirmishes.

'No, you may not.' Ayera's expression was impossible to read. 'Or are you calling me a liar?'

'I will apologise if you show me a wrenched knee.'

'What is going on?' came a voice from the door. It was Langelee, and Bartholomew wondered how long the Master had been listening. For a large man, he could move with considerable stealth, a skill learned when he had performed dubious deeds for the Archbishop of York.

'Bartholomew is accusing me of attacking the castle,' replied Ayera, with a short laugh to tell the Master what he thought of such a ridiculous assertion.

'Then he will stop it at once,' said Langelee angrily. 'There is discord enough in the College with William and Thelnetham sparring all the time. I will not have you two at it, too.'

'Where lies the problem?' asked Bartholomew, spreading

268

his hands. 'I am a physician, and I do not like to see my colleagues suffer. I may be able to ease this painful joint.'

'I said stop,' snapped Langelee. 'And if you persist with these absurd claims, I shall do what other Masters would have done years ago – withdraw permission for you to put patients before your academic duties. That will make you think twice about causing friction in the Fellowship.'

The accusation was wholly unfair, because Bartholomew had never shirked his teaching responsibilities and Langelee knew it. 'But—'

'No buts. You enjoy considerable freedom at the moment. Do not make me curtail it.'

Bartholomew watched unhappily as the Master stalked from the kitchen. He half expected Ayera to shoot him a gloating smile as he followed, but the geometrician's face was oddly impassive. When they had gone, Bartholomew flopped on to a bench and rubbed a hand through his hair. Perhaps he should have been more subtle, and attempted to solicit information without Ayera realising what he was trying to do. But Ayera was not stupid, and would certainly have seen through such tactics. He looked up tiredly when Cynric came to find him.

'There has been another death, boy,' Cynric said quietly. 'In Gonville Hall's library this time.'

Bartholomew's stomach lurched. 'Who?'

'The messenger did not say, but you had better hurry. The dead do not like to be kept waiting. There are too many angry souls floating around the town already, without adding another.'

It was not far to Gonville and Bartholomew, with Michael puffing at his heels, arrived there in moments. He was relieved when he saw Rougham waiting.

'This is terribly embarrassing,' Rougham said, wringing

his hands. 'I hope we can rely on your discretion. We do not want trouble with Bene't College – they have the ear of the Guild of Corpus Christi, and we cannot afford to lose benefactions over this matter.'

'What matter?' gasped Michael. 'What are you talking about?'

Rougham did not answer, and instead led them to the library. It contained mostly books on law, so Bartholomew had visited it only rarely. Like the libraries in King's Hall and Bene't, it was an elegantly appointed chamber, with a profusion of dark polished wood. The books sat in neat lines, each one attached to the wall by a chain to prevent theft. The room was usually busy with students, but it was quiet that day, and empty. Except for one man.

The feisty little scholar called Teversham was lying at a very peculiar angle by one of the lecterns, almost as if his upper half was suspended in thin air. At first, Bartholomew did not understand what he was seeing, but when he crouched next to the Bene't Fellow, he saw a book-chain wrapped around his neck. He examined the body quickly, noting that there was a triangular indentation in Teversham's forehead, which matched perfectly the corner of the lectern.

'The floor is dreadfully uneven,' said Rougham. 'We will fix it one day, but at the moment, all our spare cash is going towards the chapel. Teversham must have tripped and struck his head.'

'And landed on the book-chain?' asked Michael sceptically. 'Which strangled him?'

'It is technically possible,' said Bartholomew. 'His head certainly came into contact with the lectern at some point, and he may well have fallen·forward and become entangled.'

'Where, unable to breathe but too dazed to do anything

about it, he died,' finished Rougham. 'Thank you, Bartholomew. 'Perhaps you are not such a bad Corpse Examiner after all.'

'Of course, he might equally well have been shoved into the lectern deliberately, and the chain wrapped around his throat when he was too befuddled to resist,' added Bartholomew.

Rougham glared. 'I take it back.'

'Teversham is not a member of Gonville – he is a Fellow of Bene't,' said Michael. 'So what was he doing here? I surmise he was alone, because otherwise someone would have rescued him.'

'He came to consult Leycestria's *Qui Bene Praesunt*,' explained Rougham. 'And he *was* alone, because I was lecturing on Plato, and ordered all the Gonville scholars to listen to me. Teversham was an old friend, and I thought he could be trusted not to do anything silly. Clearly I was wrong.'

'Clearly,' agreed Michael dryly. 'Have you had any other visitors today? Or seen anyone loitering who should not have been here?'

'No,' said Rougham. 'Yet your questions imply foul play, but this was an accident. Of course it was! We cannot have Bene't scholars murdered in Gonville! It would cause trouble for certain.'

'It would,' acknowledged Michael. 'However, I do not see how this can be a mishap. It is too . . . contrived. It is surely a case of unlawful killing.'

'Not necessarily,' said Bartholomew. 'There is no sign of a struggle, and the floor really is uneven. In other words, there is nothing to say one way or the other what really happened.'

Michael rubbed his eyes tiredly. 'Yet another death with a curious paucity of clues. Either we are dealing with a very sly killer, or we are both losing our touch.'

'Or there is nothing to find,' countered Rougham. 'Not every death in the University is suspicious, Brother, and if you think so, it is time to follow Tynkell's example, and retire.'

There was no more to be done, so Michael went to break the news to Bene't. Bartholomew was ordered to wait outside, lest Heltisle took exception to his presence. The physician sat on the edge of a horse trough and pondered Teversham's curious end. He had not been doing it for long before a shadow fell across him, and he looked up to see his sister.

'What is happening in your wretched University now, Matt?' she asked, perching next to him.

'In what respect?' asked Bartholomew anxiously.

'All these deaths. Browne from Batayl has just told me that not only did four men die in the Common Library garden, but that Sawtre and Rolee died in libraries, too. He is braying to everyone that such places are dangerous.'

'They seem to be, at the moment,' said Bartholomew, supposing the rumours would really fly when word seeped out about Teversham's demise.

'Then please stay out of them,' begged Edith. 'I could not bear to lose you.'

When she had gone, Bonabes and Ruth strolled past. Every so often, one would bump against the other, and their hands would touch. They obviously thought they were being discreet, but a number of people noticed and grinned behind their backs. Michael appeared after what felt like an age.

'They took it badly,' he said, his plump face pale. Breaking such news was never pleasant. 'But that is not surprising after Rolee. Two Fellows is a lot to lose in as many days.'

'If Teversham *was* murdered, his death raises a whole

272

new set of questions,' remarked Bartholomew. 'Because he, unlike the other victims, opposed the Common Library. Violently.'

'True,' said Michael. 'And it means that I am now extremely confused and can no longer see even a glimmer of sense in all that has happened.'

'Perhaps there is none to see,' suggested Bartholomew. 'And they are just a series of random and unconnected events.'

'You do not really believe that,' said Michael grimly. 'And neither do I.'

Bartholomew groaned when Michael said they needed to visit Newe Inn to investigate the assault on Langelee – he was rapidly becoming sick of the place. When they arrived, it was to find Walkelate dealing with parcels of books donated by people who wanted to be recorded as the foundation's first benefactors. The door to the *libri concatenati* was closed, and the chamber holding the *libri distribuendi* was frantically busy. Sawdust was everywhere, and Bartholomew wondered how Walkelate could possibly think it would be ready in three days.

'Langelee was assaulted?' Walkelate whispered in horror, when Michael explained why they were there. 'Here?'

'In the garden,' replied Michael. 'By the pond, apparently, shortly before sext.'

'Then his assailant chose his time well, because everyone was out then except Kente. The labourers and their apprentices went to a meeting in the Guild Hall about the pageant, while Frevill and I went to the Carmelite scriptorium, to commission labels for our shelves.'

'But Kente was here?'

'Yes. He is out at the moment, purchasing gilt, but he will not be long. Will you wait?'

Michael nodded. 'The attack on our Master is a serious matter, and—'

He turned at the sound of feet on the stairs. It was Dunning, come to inspect progress again. His daughters were with him, with Bonabes behind. Walkelate promptly abandoned Michael, and scurried to greet them, assuring them that the work was much further forward than the untrained eye might think. Dunning did not look convinced.

'It must be perfect,' he said, worriedly, 'or my Guild will think me a fool for wasting my money.'

'It will be perfect,' promised Walkelate. 'But Aristotle is finished at last, and we will mount him on his shelf later today. Have you ever seen more exquisite craftsmanship?'

'It is fine,' acknowledged Dunning, running appreciative fingers across the bust. 'Especially now you have given him less of a nose. I was right to ask you to remodel it, because he looked foreign with the great beak he had originally.'

'Yet I think you will find he *was* foreign,' Michael pointed out, amused. 'Greek, I believe.'

'Nonsense,' declared Dunning dismissively. 'Aristotle was an Englishman.'

'The opening ceremony is important to him,' said Julitta, coming to talk to Bartholomew while Michael regaled her sceptical father with an account of the philosopher's antecedents. 'He is beginning to be nervous, lest all does not go according to plan.'

'Why should it not?' asked Bartholomew.

'Well, not every scholar likes the place,' Julitta pointed out wryly. 'Brother Michael told me only yesterday that he spends half his life quelling arguments about it.'

'There was one between Essex Hostel and Bene't College

274

in our shop this morning,' added Ruth, who was listening. Bartholomew was not surprised to see Bonabes close behind her. 'I thought they were going to start hitting each other, but Bonabes managed to evict them first. They slunk away once they were outside, because several beadles were watching.'

'Father is afraid there will be a spat during the ceremony,' elaborated Julitta. 'But I imagine that is less likely if Brother Michael arrests the villain responsible for whatever happened to poor Northwood and the others.'

'Michael will find the culprit,' Bartholomew heard himself promise. 'And I shall help.'

'Thank you.' Julitta smiled as she laid a hand on his arm. It felt warm through the material of his shirt, and made his skin tingle. She lowered her voice. 'I am looking forward to you teaching me how to read once our patients no longer need such time-consuming care. I cannot wait to see my husband's face! As I said the other night, it will be the most wonderful gift for him.'

'He will hate it,' predicted Bonabes, when Julitta had gone to stand with Dunning. 'Because it means she will be able to monitor his spending of her father's money.'

Ruth winced, and turned the subject back to the University's troubles. 'Did you know that Browne is telling everybody that the London brothers died because God does not approve of libraries? I doubt trouble will be averted if Michael produces God as his villain!'

'Browne is talking rubbish,' said Bartholomew. 'There is a human hand at work here.'

'I agree,' said Ruth. 'And I have learned something that might help you find the culprit. It is about Northwood. Apparently, he used the money from selling the novices' exemplars to buy materials for his experiments. The apothecary told me.'

'What kind of materials?' asked Bartholomew.

'Red lead and myrrh. Both in very large quantities. And I think I know why, too. Rougham and Holm refused to let him help you invent lamp fuel, and my husband declined his offer to be part of our paper-making trials. So he must have decided to branch out on his own. He was inspired by those scholars from Oxford and their clever inventions, and he wanted to do something similar.'

'I wish we had included him,' said Bartholomew ruefully. 'We might have solved the problem by now, because he had a sharp mind.'

'Lots of scholars have sharp minds, yet their work proceeds at a snail's pace,' said Bonabes disapprovingly. 'Surely, it cannot be that difficult to make lamp fuel and ink? Perhaps I shall turn *my* hand to these questions when we have mastered paper. There is a lot of money to be made from them, and I could do with some extra pennies.'

He glanced at Ruth, and Bartholomew was under the distinct impression that any additional income would be used to buy something for her. And her returning smile told him that whatever was purchased would be treasured far more than anything from her husband. When they saw him watching, they flew apart abruptly, Bonabes to inspect Aristotle with exaggerated interest and Ruth to look out of the window.

'This garden is a sad, forlorn place,' she said. 'I have never liked it, and I hate to think of anyone breathing his last here. There is an odd smell, too. Do you think the tales are true, and the pond is home to demons?'

'Of course not,' called Bonabes, indicating his ears were still attuned to her voice, even across the room. 'It is just marsh air, which has a reputation for foul stenches. Some are even poisonous.'

Bartholomew stared at him. Could Northwood and the others have inhaled toxic gases released by the peaty mud at the bottom of the pond? He recalled the beadles claiming they had felt sick when they had disturbed the water, so it was certainly possible. He bowed a brief farewell, and hurried into the garden, aware of Michael puffing behind him, demanding to know where he was going. He did not stop until he reached the pool.

Beadle Meadowman was there, coated with slime as he continued the messy business of dredging through the deeper layers of sediment. He looked hot, tired and cross.

'I have not found anything, Brother,' he said. 'This is a waste of time.'

'Were you here when Langelee was attacked?' asked Michael, watching in bafflement as Bartholomew knelt at the water's edge and leaned down to sniff it.

Meadowman pursed his lips. 'No – or I would have stopped it.'

'Then did you see anyone loitering?' asked Michael, as Bartholomew abandoned the pond and turned his attention to the excavated silt, taking handfuls of the stuff and smelling it carefully.

Meadowman nodded bitterly. 'Oh, yes. Half the town likes to gawp at the spot where four men died, and opinions are divided as to whether the Devil or God is responsible.' At last, he could contain himself no longer. 'What are you doing, Doctor Bartholomew?'

'I thought the pond or its sediment might contain toxic fumes,' explained Bartholomew. He saw Michael's hopeful expression, and shrugged apologetically. 'But they do not.'

'Pity,' muttered Michael, disappointed. 'That would have been the best solution: death by misadventure and no murder at all.'

* * *

While Michael waited for Kente to return, Bartholomew went back to his teaching, hoping it would take his mind off the worries that clamoured at him. His students did not appreciate his zealous attentions, however, and when Cynric arrived with an invitation from Meryfeld, asking him to visit that evening for a resumption of their experiments, they used his momentary distraction to flee.

As there were no pupils to divert him, and the atmosphere in the conclave was icy – Langelee snapped at him when he tried to speak to Ayera – he went to check the wounded soldiers at the castle. Julitta was there, and he lingered far longer than necessary, just to be in her company. When he finally tore himself away, he found Cynric waiting to say that Isnard was unwell. He arrived at the bargeman's house to find him hunched miserably over a bucket.

'Have you been eating fish? Perhaps poached from Newe Inn and sold by the riverfolk?'

'No,' said Isnard weakly. 'My malady is much more serious. Holm is trying to poison me.'

Bartholomew regarded him askance. 'Why would he do that?'

'For your five marks,' replied Isnard dolefully. 'He knows I am innocent, but is unwilling to pay you, so he is trying to kill me instead. He bought me an ale at the King's Head, and I should have known better than to accept it.'

'How many other ales did you have?' asked Bartholomew pointedly.

Isnard waved an airy hand. 'Not many. Do you think he has done for me, Doctor?'

Bartholomew gave him the remedy he always dispensed for over-indulgence, and watched the colour seep back into the bargeman's cheeks. When Isnard began to feel better, he started to chat.

'That armed raid was nasty. It is said by some that the

278

villains are local men, like Ayce of Girton, who bear a grudge against the town and will do anything to harm it. However, there is another rumour that the raiders are strangers – specifically a remnant of the French army, determined to avenge themselves for Poitiers. What do you think?'

'I doubt the French would pick on Cambridge.'

Isnard sniffed. 'If you say so. What do you make of the four bodies in Newe Inn? I suspect they are connected to the attack – the victims heard or saw something, and were murdered for their silence. Like Adam, the soldier and the riverman.'

'I wondered the same. But those three had their throats cut, and there was no obvious cause of death for Northwood and his companions.'

'So what? There were lots of raiders, and each probably has his own preferred way of killing.'

It was a valid point. 'Have you learned any more about them? Or have the riverfolk?'

'Only that they have been slinking into our town regularly after dark – as you found out when we had to rescue you the other night. Obviously, they come to look around.'

'To look around for what?'

Isnard shrugged. 'Sheriff Tulyet believes they are smugglers, but I have been thinking about that, and I am sure he is wrong.'

'Why?'

'Because I would have seen their boats. No, the raiders are not smugglers, Doctor, and you can tell the Sheriff that I said so.'

By the time Bartholomew arrived at Meryfeld's house, his medical colleagues had been at the wine. They were not as drunk as they had been when they had thrown together the lethal combination of ingredients to create wildfire, but they were certainly frivolous. Meryfeld laughed a lot anyway, but Gyseburne and Rougham were serious men, and it was disconcerting to see them in boisterously silly spirits. Bartholomew's heart sank.

'It is all right,' said Meryfeld, misinterpreting his concern. 'We saved you some claret.'

'Where have you been, Matthew?' asked Gyseburne conversationally. 'With a patient?'

'Isnard,' replied Bartholomew. 'He drank too much last night, and has been sick all day.'

Holm sniggered. 'The man is a terrible sot.'

'He told me you bought him the offending ale,' said Bartholomew, rather accusingly.

'I *was* in the King's Head,' acknowledged Holm. 'A patient invited me there, and it would have been churlish to refuse, but I did not buy Isnard ale. As everyone in Cambridge knows – except you, it would seem – he is a criminal, and I do not associate with those.'

'You do if you imbibe at the King's Head,' retorted Rougham, holding out his goblet for more wine. 'No one who frequents that place is innocent in any sense of the word. Except Agatha the laundress. She drinks there, but I would not dare say anything rude about her – she would make garters of my innards.'

'A lady drinks in a tavern?' asked Gyseburne disapprovingly. 'Surely, that is irregular? Or is she a whore?'

Rougham crossed himself. 'Have a care, Gyseburne! That woman does as she pleases, and she is extremely dangerous.' He tossed off the contents of his goblet, and indicated he wanted more.

'She is not that bad,' said Bartholomew, sipping the wine. It was very good, and when he had finished one cup and was on the second, he, too, felt his anxieties recede. 'But she cannot cook.'

'I am an extremely good cook,' said Holm. 'My father taught me, and he baked for the King.'

'The King hires surgeons to prepare his food?' asked Meryfeld, bemused.

Holm coloured. 'My father had many talents,' he hedged.

'How fare your patients at the castle?' asked Rougham of Bartholomew. 'Will any more die?'

'No, they will all live,' replied Holm, before Bartholomew could speak. 'I healed the lot.'

'So you tell everyone, but it was Matthew who did all the work,' said Gyseburne, rather acidly.

'Yes, but he laboured under my direction,' declared Holm. 'I am a surgeon, and he is a physician, so how can he have performed these delicate techniques alone? He does not have the skill. Only I do.'

'You might deceive your fiancée with your bragging lies, but *we* are not stupid,' said Gyseburne, coolly. 'We know the truth.'

'We do, but it is better for Bartholomew if folk believe that it was Holm who undertook the surgery,' said Rougham. 'I say we let him have the credit.'

He had a point, and Bartholomew was certainly prepared to overlook Holm's conceit in exchange for a quiet life. He nodded his appreciation of Rougham's suggestion.

'I can cure stones in the kidneys, too,' announced Holm, aware that he had lost his colleagues' approbation and aiming to remedy the matter. 'I am sure the rest of you cannot.'

'I have had some success with potions that break them up,' said Gyseburne. 'I have detected their remnants in urine after treatment, and patients have claimed a lessening of pain.'

'I direct a hard punch to a specific area,' Holm went

281

on, ignoring him. 'Which smashes the stones into pieces and allows them to pass harmlessly through the urethra.'

Bartholomew cringed. 'I cannot imagine such a technique would work. It is—'

'It does – every time. Indeed, I am thinking of going to London when I am married, to punch the stones of the wealthy. I shall make a fortune.'

'You and Julitta will leave us?' asked Bartholomew, trying to mask his dismay.

Holm regarded him oddly. 'We might. I have not decided yet.'

'Let us go to the garden and begin our experiments,' said Meryfeld, tiring of the discussion. 'Time is passing, and I would rather not work in the dark, if it can be avoided.'

His apprentices had already set out a table and various ingredients, along with the large cauldron they used to mix their potions. It bore ominous stains, while parts of the rim had been blown away when trials had not gone according to plan. As usual, Holm, Rougham and Meryfeld sighed impatiently when Bartholomew insisted on measuring each ingredient and recording it in the ledger they had kept since the winter.

'This is why it is taking so long,' grumbled Holm. 'We should just toss in whatever we like.'

'But then if we do discover a good mixture we will not know what went in it,' argued Bartholomew, just as he did every time they experimented together.

'Honey,' said Meryfeld, approaching with a jar and a wooden spoon. 'Let us add honey. And if we do not produce decent fuel, I can decant the stuff and sell it as cough syrup.'

'You cannot let anyone drink this!' cried Bartholomew, shocked. 'There is brimstone in it!'

'Brimstone is not poisonous in small quantities,' declared Meryfeld. He dipped his spoon in the mixture and took a sip before anyone could stop him. 'See?'

The others watched him intently, but although he pulled a face to indicate the mixture did not taste pleasant, there was no other reaction.

'Here is some lye,' said Rougham, hurling a substantial dose into the basin. Bartholomew threw down the pen and folded his arms in disgust. Rougham had not allowed him to measure it, so the test was over as far as he was concerned. 'Now you cannot give it to your patients, Meryfeld, because lye is definitely not good for people.'

The calculating expression on Meryfeld's face suggested he might overlook that fact, and Bartholomew found himself wondering whether the man always declined to reveal what he included in his medicines because half of it was unsuitable for human consumption.

'And here is some urine,' said Gyseburne, producing a jar and adding a generous glug. Immediately, something began to fizz, and there was a terrible smell.

'You have spoiled it!' cried Meryfeld, hand over his nose. He scowled, and Bartholomew had the distinct impression that Gyseburne had just spared Meryfeld's clients from being sold a very dangerous "cure".

There was no more to be done once the mixture was ruined, so the *medici* left to go home. It was dark, and the streets were unusually deserted; neither townsfolk nor scholars wanted to be out when armed invaders were at large. Gyseburne went north, and Bartholomew found himself walking down Bridge Street with Rougham and Holm. The surgeon was holding forth about his skill with broken limbs, and Rougham was talking about his designs for Gonville's chapel windows, neither listening to the other, when Bartholomew heard a sound.

'What was that?' He cocked his head to listen.

'The raiders?' asked Rougham, fearfully. He increased his pace to what was almost a run. 'We should not linger. It feels dangerous tonight, and we still have some way to go.'

He stopped abruptly when several figures materialised in the darkness ahead of them. He swallowed hard, and Holm whimpered.

'You may have our purses,' Rougham called unsteadily. 'But you must leave us unharmed. We are physicians, on an errand of mercy.'

'These two are physicians,' bleated Holm. 'But I am a surgeon. I heal people, whereas they only dispense expensive remedies and calculate horoscopes.'

'God's blood, Holm!' breathed Rougham, shocked. 'That was not comradely.'

'You can go,' said one of the figures to Holm. 'We are not interested in you.'

Holm scuttled away without a backward glance, and Bartholomew hoped he would have the sense to summon help. The shadows approached, but he could not tell whether they were the same men who had waylaid him before. He slipped his hand inside his medical bag, fingers curling around the comforting bulk of the childbirth forceps.

'Tell us the formula for wildfire,' said one man softly, following a brief scuffle after which Bartholomew and Rougham were pinned against a wall with swords at their throats and the forceps lay on the ground. 'Refuse, and you die. And do not expect rescue a second time, because it will not be coming.'

'But we do not know it,' squawked Rougham. 'We hurled random ingredients into a—'

'Then think. We know it involved brimstone, pitch and

284

quicklime, along with a lot of other substances that are irrelevant. But there was one other vital element. What was it?'

'Rock oil,' blurted Rougham, desperation in his voice.

'No!' cried Bartholomew, horrified. 'It was not—'

The spokesman hit him with the hilt of his sword, hard enough to knock him to his knees. The next few words were a meaningless buzz as his senses swam.

'Rock oil was the secret ingredient,' Rougham went on weakly. 'It was a gift from a patient, but I could not find a medical application for it, so I tossed it in the pot. That is why we will never recreate wildfire in our quest for lamp fuel. We have no more rock oil.'

'What is rock oil?'

'A black, jelly-like substance,' replied Rougham. 'It can be—'

'Rougham, stop!' gasped Bartholomew, appalled. He had honestly believed that he was the only one who had remembered the rock oil, and was shocked to learn he had been wrong.

'Wait!' cried Rougham, when the leader raised his sword to hit Bartholomew again. 'I can tell you more. It is not found in England – you will have to order it from the Holy Land.'

'If you are lying—' began one of the others, taller and heftier than his companions.

'He is not,' said the first man. He turned to his cronies. 'Now kill them.'

'What?' shrieked Rougham, shocked. 'But I told you what you wanted to know!'

'Yes, and we are grateful. But not grateful enough to spare you.'

Staggering to his feet, Bartholomew fumbled in his bag for one of his surgical knives, determined not to go without a fight. He lashed out at the big man, causing him to howl in pain, but the others moved in quickly and the 'weapon' was dashed from his hand. He was groping desperately for another when there was a shout from farther down the street. Tulyet's soldiers were coming.

The attackers promptly turned and shot down a nearby alley, pausing just long enough to roll a cart across its mouth. By the time Tulyet's guards had scrambled across it, the ambushers had vanished into the night.

'You told them about the rock oil, Rougham,' breathed Bartholomew, making no effort to disguise his dismay. 'How could you?'

'Because I did not want to die.' Rougham's voice was unsteady, and he leaned heavily against the wall. 'I was trying to save both our lives.'

'Dying would have been preferable to revealing such a deadly secret to men like them!'

Rougham rubbed a hand across his eyes. 'Do not rail at me, Bartholomew. I am not proud of what I did, but I was frightened. And all is not lost, anyway. As you no doubt know, rock oil comes from a wilderness far east of the Mediterranean, not the Holy Land. I misled them rather cleverly.'

'It will not deter them for long. What have we unleashed on the world? What evil have we done?'

Rougham was silent, and Bartholomew knew there was no point in berating him further. He walked away, to stand alone and bring his temper under control. As he bent to retrieve his forceps and knife, he glimpsed the merest of movements in the shadows. Hands raised, he approached.

'They have the secret,' he told Dame Pelagia. 'You alerted Tulyet's men too late.'

'Damn!' she whispered. 'I should have known you physicians were too dangerous to leave alive. Did I hear you mention rock oil to Rougham just now? Is that the secret ingredient?'

Bartholomew started to deny it, but faltered into silence as her beady eyes bored into his – he was not good at lying at the best of times, but it was a lost cause with Pelagia.

'What are we going to do?' he asked numbly. 'We cannot let them escape with this knowledge.'

'No,' agreed Pelagia. 'But you have done more than enough tonight. Go home.'

And with that enigmatic remark, she slipped away into the darkness.

CHAPTER 9

Breakfast that Tuesday was a dismal affair, and Bartholomew's stomach churned with anxiety. He was appalled that Rougham had capitulated so easily, and was in an agony of worry over what Dame Pelagia might do with the information – not only that she might arrange for the attackers to die in order to prevent them from using the formula, but that she would pass what she had learned to the King, who might well order experiments of his own. And what of Rougham and Bartholomew himself? Would she take steps to ensure that *they* never revealed the secret again?

He was also concerned about Ayera, who had not appeared for church. A furtive glance into his colleague's room showed that the bed had not been slept in, and Ayera's students said they had not seen him since the previous night. Normally, Bartholomew would have reported his worries to Langelee, but the Master was also absent, and no one knew where he was, either.

Julitta troubled his thoughts, too, because she was about to bind herself to a man who was both a brash, conceited fortune-hunter and a coward, too – it had quickly become apparent that Holm had run straight home and barricaded himself in, making no effort to tell the soldiers and beadles he had passed en route that his colleagues were in danger.

'Lord!' breathed William, wiping pottage-spotted hands on his habit as they stood to leave the hall. Some of the lumps were large, and Bartholomew felt queasy when he saw them mashed into the already-filthy fabric. 'That was an unpleasant repast. I shall have to visit my brethren at the priory for victuals again. Would you like to come, Matthew? They have eggs on Tuesdays.'

Bartholomew shook his head. 'I should see what my students—'

'They are more than ready for their disputations,' interrupted William. 'There is no need to persecute them.'

'Yes, let them be,' added Michael, overhearing. 'They will not disgrace you in the debating chamber, and I have need of you today, anyway.'

'They speak the truth,' said Thelnetham, the most academically gifted of the Fellows, and so someone whose opinion Bartholomew was willing to trust more than Michael, who just wanted his help, or William, who was not really qualified to say. 'You have prepared them well.'

'Set them some reading, and then we shall leave,' ordered Michael.

Bartholomew's anxieties were such that he hastened to comply, but Valence, who had accompanied him to see a patient before dawn that morning, waylaid him with a question.

'You applied an ointment of elder leaves for that bruised hand earlier,' the student said. 'But Meryfeld's apprentices told me that he uses a poultice of red lead.'

'Then he will be angry with them – he likes to keep the contents of his concoctions to himself.'

Valence waved a dismissive hand. 'There is nothing special about any of his potions – they are either the same as yours, or they contain inert elements that will neither harm nor benefit the taker. Except for the red lead that he adds to his remedy for contusions. It is because red lead is cold and dry in the second degree?'

Bartholomew did not want to denigrate his colleague by saying that Meryfeld probably had no idea what red lead would do, other than perhaps provide a particular colour or smell.

'You must ask him,' he replied. Then he relented; it was not a helpful answer, and Valence was trying to learn. 'I performed a series of tests on rats once, and concluded that any benefits accruing from red lead are outweighed by its toxicity. So I never use it in any of my medicines.'

'I see,' said Valence. 'How did you determine that it is toxic?'

'Because the rats suffered convulsions. When I looked inside them, their digestive tracts were inflamed, their brains were swollen and their livers . . .' Bartholomew trailed off, suddenly realising that admitting to conducting dissections, even on rodents, was unwise.

Valence smiled. 'Your secret is safe with me, sir. And now I shall go to read to the others.'

Bartholomew climbed the stairs to Michael's room, hoping Valence could be trusted, because he did not like to imagine what would be made of the fact that he chopped up dead animals with a view to assessing the impact of poisons. He would be expelled from the University for certain!

The monk had been briefing his own students. They were by far Michaelhouse's most diligent pupils, quite happy to work alone, which was fortunate, because his duties as Senior Proctor often called him away. He sighed when they left to read the texts he had recommended.

'I had a busy night,' he said, flopping on to his bed in a way that made it creak ominously, and Bartholomew fear it might crash through the ceiling into his own room below. 'After the attack on you, Tulyet ordered every soldier and available beadle out on patrol.'

'But nothing happened?' Bartholomew leaned against the wall and folded his arms.

'The town was as quiet as a tomb – except for a fight between Essex Hostel and Bene't.'

'Again?' asked Bartholomew.

'Yes, again. In case you had not noticed, your wretched library is still causing considerable discord among our scholars – discord that is intensifying as its opening draws nearer. If only I had a Junior Proctor to help me keep the peace . . . But never mind this. I have reached some conclusions about the raiders. It is obvious now what is happening.'

'It is?'

'They have been sneaking into the town for weeks to reconnoitre. Adam and the others must have seen them, and they were murdered to prevent them from telling the Sheriff that trouble was afoot. And Saturday's raid was the culmination of all their spying.'

'But it was unsuccessful,' said Bartholomew. 'They were driven off empty-handed.'

'Quite, which means they will try again – they will not let all their efforts go unrewarded. My grandmother heard a rumour, one she believes, that says they will strike during the Corpus Christi pageant, when all our soldiers and beadles will be busy policing the crowds.'

'Then cancel it.'

'We cannot cancel Corpus Christi!' exclaimed Michael, shocked. 'It is one of the most important celebrations of the year – religious *and* secular.'

'Then call off the launch of the library. That will free the beadles to—'

'If we do, we will never have a benefaction from a townsman again, because Dunning's disappointment will know no bounds. We shall just have to be vigilant.'

'Vigilant for attacks by robbers who have already stormed the castle and killed experienced soldiers, *and* for mischief by the disaffected half of the University that does not want a Common Library?' asked Bartholomew archly. 'That should be easy enough!'

Michael shot him a nasty look. 'If we solve these murders by the day after tomorrow, perhaps our rebellious scholars will stop saying that repositories for books are dangerous.'

'I think it is time that we reviewed what we know,' said Bartholomew. 'To see if there are clues we have overlooked.'

Michael brightened. 'Very well. We shall do it in the Brazen George, then, where a small repast might stimulate our minds into some constructive thinking.'

The streets were busy as Bartholomew and Michael walked to the High Street. Soldiers were everywhere, and Bartholomew could only suppose that Tulyet had drafted reinforcements from other towns. People continued their Corpus Christi preparations, but uneasily, much of the pleasure of the occasion stripped away by the fear of invasion.

'I am going to close on Thursday,' confided Landlord Lister, as he served them bread and a selection of cold meats. 'I do not want to attract the attention of mercenaries by selling ale.'

'They will not come if everyone is expecting them,' said Bartholomew. 'The element of surprise is an important factor in raids like these. And they have lost it.'

'Perhaps,' said Lister. 'But the burgesses are taking no chances. Most of the wealthier ones have already left town, taking their families and valuables with them. Your sister and brother-in-law are among them, as a matter of fact, Doctor. They left this morning with their apprentices. Still, if these villains do attack, at least they will not get the taxes. Those are no longer in the castle.'

'No?' asked Michael. 'Are they dispatched to London, then?'

'There is no need to be sly with me, Brother,' said Lester, tapping the side of his nose. 'Everyone knows the University has agreed to hide them for us.'

Michael stared at him. 'That is untrue. We have done nothing of the kind!'

Lister winked knowingly. 'Of course not.'

Michael rubbed his eyes when the landlord had gone. 'This tale is false, but I doubt anyone will believe me. So you had better start analysing clues before I jump on a horse and follow your family to some peaceful village, because I am beginning to feel unpleasantly overwhelmed.'

Bartholomew was not sure how to begin, as they had scant evidence to analyse. He ate some bread, and tried to concentrate, but his mind kept straying back to what Rougham had done.

'I did not think anyone else had remembered,' he said unhappily. 'The others recalled the pitch, brimstone and quicklime, but not the rock oil. How could Rougham have been so weak?'

'Not everyone possesses your courage, Matt, especially when confronted by sword-wielding criminals. Incidentally, my grandmother knows a great deal about experiments to produce wildfire, but admitted that rock oil did not feature in any of the ones she is aware of.'

'Lord!' muttered Bartholomew, appalled. 'If she intends to make some herself, she will be taking a serious risk. Rock oil needs to be distilled first, which is an extremely hazardous process. Then it must be dissolved in brimstone or resin, which is not easy, either.'

'I will warn her,' said Michael. 'Although I cannot see her looming over a cauldron, preparing wicked substances to be used in battles.' Bartholomew could, rather easily.

'She thinks the men who attacked you are from the same band that has been spying . . .'

'Probably. I noticed last night that the armour they wore was identical to that of the fellows who chased me along the river last week.'

'You were a victim of your own predictability,' chided Michael. 'Everyone knows that the *medici* meet of an evening to meddle with lamp fuel, and that you walk home afterwards in the dark. All these villains had to do was wait until you happened by.'

Michael was right, and Bartholomew was disgusted with himself. He did not think he would ever sleep easy again, knowing that he bore at least some of the responsibility for the disaster.

'Eight deaths,' said Michael, after a while. 'Four men in a library garden, Sawtre crushed by a bookcase, Rolee toppled from his library's steps, Teversham strangled by a book chain, and Coslaye brained with a tome – twice. This cannot be coincidence, so tell me what it means.'

With an effort, Bartholomew dragged his thoughts away from wildfire. 'Five of these victims supported the Common Library, two opposed it, and Rolee voted against it, but later decided to give it one of his books. It seems unlikely that they all died by the same hand.'

Michael frowned. 'Northwood, Vale and the Londons were seen loitering in Cholles Lane before entering Newe Inn's garden; Coslaye and the apprentice thought they heard a bell ringing; and we have reason to believe that they were trying to invent lamp fuel.'

Bartholomew's stomach lurched as a terrible thought occurred to him. 'Do you think *they* were experimenting with wildfire? I liked Northwood, but he did allow his intellect to lead him – he might have overlooked the ethics of the situation for the thrill of solving a mystery.

Meanwhile, Vale wanted to be rich, and the secret for such a weapon will be worth a great deal of money . . .'

'And the London brothers seemed decent, but were quiet and private and no one knew them very well. It would certainly explain why my grandmother searched their home.'

They were both silent, thinking hard.

'I am sure Newe Inn's pond holds a clue,' said Michael after a while. 'There is definitely something sinister about it – it is unusually deep for a start.' He sighed. 'We shall need our wits about us if we are to crack this case, for I sense a very devious mind behind it.'

'Ayera,' said Bartholomew softly. He held up his hand when Michael started to object. 'I know you had good reasons to dismiss what Gyseburne and Clippesby said about him being involved in the castle raid, but I tackled him about it anyway, and—'

'You did what?' Michael was shocked.

'I asked why he was wearing armour under his tabard,' said Bartholomew. 'And why he was limping. He had no convincing explanation for either. Moreover, he was to hand when Langelee was attacked, and he has taken to going out at peculiar hours.'

Michael was pale. 'I hope to God you are wrong.'

'So do I.' Bartholomew hesitated, but then forged on. 'I am anxious about Langelee, too. He has also been leaving Michaelhouse at odd times and was strangely defensive of Ayera.'

'They are friends – of course he was defensive. And there will be a good reason for his disappearances. The College is in debt, so perhaps he is working to raise new funds.'

'Yes,' said Bartholomew unhappily. 'That is what worries me.'

* * *

Beadle Meadowman came with urgent documents for Michael to sign, and while he waited for the monk to finish, Bartholomew returned to Michaelhouse and took his new bestiary to Deynman. The Librarian was sitting in the corner of the hall, making an inventory of his books, although as he rarely let anyone, not even Fellows, remove them for personal study, it was hardly necessary.

'I am never lending anything to anyone again,' Deynman declared angrily. 'No one knows how to treat books.' He pointed accusingly at the volume Bartholomew held. 'And to prove my point, look at that one. It is drenched in blood.'

'Hardly drenched,' said Bartholomew, handing it over. 'Just a smear or two. If you do not want it for Michaelhouse, you can take it to Newe Inn.'

'I do want it,' said Deynman, clutching it possessively. 'I shall clean it off and keep it safe.'

'You do not know what it is yet,' said Bartholomew, amused.

'I do not care. It has pages and a cover, so it is a book. And books belong with me, because *I* am Librarian.' Deynman pronounced the last word grandly, still delighted with the way it sounded. 'No one is going to write "arse" in this little beauty.'

Bartholomew regarded him in bafflement. 'Has someone—'

'Yes, someone has!' snapped Deynman. 'In Apollodorus's *Poliorcetica*.'

'Do you know who?'

'I do.' Suddenly, Deynman's indignation evaporated, and he reverted to the likeable but dim-witted lad Bartholomew knew and loved. 'My remit is to care for these books, but when a senior member desecrates one, what am I supposed to do?'

'A Fellow?' asked Bartholomew, trying to think of who might have done such a thing.

'Langelee,' confided Deynman in an agonised whisper. 'He asked to borrow it last week, and I let him, because he is the Master. But when it came back . . . look!'

He opened the offending tome, and there was the word scrawled in the margin, definitely in Langelee's untidy hand. The fact that it was in the vernacular, not Latin or Greek, spoke volumes, too. Langelee's grasp of classical languages was not the best.

'Why did he want such a book?' asked Bartholomew. 'He teaches philosophy, and he, unlike the rest of us, tends not to venture into other disciplines.'

'He is not clever enough,' said Deynman, blithely oblivious of the fact that he was in no position to criticise anyone's intellect. 'The rest of us like to hone our minds, but he would rather play camp-ball. He has never asked to borrow a book before, and I should have thought of an excuse not to let him have it.'

'You cannot prevent the Master from using his own library.'

'I can and I will,' vowed Deynman. 'I saw him reading it with Ayera later. Now *he* would never deface a book. He cares too deeply about them.'

Bartholomew was puzzled and worried. Langelee was not a man for academic chitchat, especially with someone who possessed an intellect as formidable as Ayera's, so what had they really been doing? He patted the Librarian's shoulder, and bent to read what had prompted Langelee to do such a terrible thing. It was the chapter on devices that could be used to attack a castle. A wash of cold dread flooded over him as he scanned descriptions of siege engines, weapons for undermining rocks, and recipes for making things that exploded.

'Langelee borrowed this last week?' he asked.

Deynman nodded. 'Yes, why? What is the matter? You look as though you have seen a ghost.'

Bartholomew gripped Deynman's arm urgently. 'Forget about this. Do not mention it to the Master or to anyone else.'

'Why?' pressed Deynman. 'I do not understand.'

'Neither do I,' admitted Bartholomew. 'But I do know we need to be careful.'

When Bartholomew found Michael, the monk was just finishing a discussion with Clippesby. The Dominican was agitated, and shot towards the stables when Bartholomew approached, muttering something about needing a sensible conversation with a horse to calm his nerves. Michael's expression was one of exasperation and bemusement in equal measure.

'What did he tell you?' asked Bartholomew.

'That the rat declines to visit libraries any more, because they are too dangerous; the Carmelite Friary's blackbirds have a low opinion of Riborowe; and the College cat reports that Langelee and Ayera have taken to going out at strange times, sometimes together but usually alone.'

Bartholomew watched Clippesby disappear into the stable, and wondered what to do about the cat's intelligence in particular.

'There will be a grain of truth in it all,' sighed Michael. 'There usually is, although it is difficult to extract fact from fiction where he is concerned. The man is a lunatic, and I often wonder why we do not dismiss him and appoint someone sane.'

'Because he is gentle and good, and that is worth a great deal.'

'I suppose so. But I can tell from the expression on

your face that something else is wrong now. Did Deynman refuse you access to some text?'

'Ayera and Langelee have been reading up on warfare. And things that explode.'

Michael swallowed hard. 'What you said earlier has jogged my memory – *I* noticed Ayera's limp, too. Could he have been one of the trio my grandmother drove away from you on Wednesday? She told me later that she thought she had injured two of them enough to slow them down.'

'She hit one in the foot and the other in the thigh. Coslaye had a damaged foot . . .'

'And Ayera walked as though his injury was higher up. Yet I cannot see him joining forces with the likes of the Principal of Batayl. But having said that, Ayera has always been something of an enigma. I hope to God he has not led Langelee astray.'

'No one "leads" the Master anywhere he does not want to go.'

Michael was sombre. 'True. And we must not forget that he was the chief henchman for a powerful churchman with a lot of enemies. He must have been very good at it – those sorts of occupations tend to have a short life expectancy, and he did it for years.'

'Not as long as your grandmother, though,' remarked Bartholomew.

'She is a remarkable woman, is she not?' said Michael fondly. 'There cannot be many elderly ladies who played a role at the Battle of Poitiers.'

'No,' agreed Bartholomew. The victory had been attributed to the skill of English and Welsh archers, the lie of the land, and the reckless over-confidence of the French commanders, but now he wondered whether the Prince of Wales had had a secret weapon – not ribauldequins or wildfire, but Dame Pelagia. He frowned. 'Weapons and warfare.'

'What about them?' asked Michael, bemused.

'Langelee and Ayera have been reading about them; Northwood and the others may have been experimenting with them; Riborowe and Coslaye drew them; Chancellor Tynkell professes to know about them; while any number of scholars were at Poitiers – Northwood, Holm, Walkelate and Riborowe . . .'

'And Pepin of Batayl says he was not there, although you caught him out in inconsistencies about the area. Moreover, he is a Frenchman in a hostel that is named for the English victory, which must be uncomfortable to say the least.'

'I am sure this is important,' said Bartholomew. 'But I have no idea why.'

'Then we had better find you some answers.'

They decided to speak to Riborowe first, and arrived at the Carmelite Priory to find the friars spring-cleaning ready for Corpus Christi. Their bedding had been put to air, and clerics and lay-brothers alike were busy with mops and brushes. Etone was in the scriptorium.

'Out, out!' he was crying, driving his querulous scribes before him like a flock of geese. 'It reeks in here, and the floor is in desperate need of a scrub.'

'But we cannot afford the time, Father Prior,' objected Riborowe, clasping his skeletal hands in dismay. 'Dunning wants this Book of Hours by Thursday, because he is going present it to the Common Library. At its opening.'

'It will not be ready then, will it,' said Etone sweetly. 'What a pity!'

'He will take his custom to Ely,' warned Jorz, hopping from foot to foot in distress.

'So what?' demanded Etone. 'What can he do to us now? Decline to give us Newe Inn? He is an untrustworthy man, and I would sooner not treat with him again anyway.'

'We have company,' said Riborowe, whipping around suddenly when he sensed they were being observed. 'What do *you* want, Bartholomew? To inspect Jorz's pictures, and tell him whether his portrayal of Satan is accurate?'

'Stop!' ordered Etone sharply. 'What have I told you about being rude to Matthew?'

'That he may refuse to tend your chilblains if I insult him,' replied Riborowe sullenly. He glowered at Bartholomew, and ignored his Prior's pained wince at the lack of tact.

'How can we help you, Matthew?' asked Etone with an ingratiating smile that did not sit well on his naturally austere features.

'For a start, you can tell us whether Coslaye visited you early on Saturday morning,' replied Michael. 'To accuse you of spoiling his mural with soot.'

'Yes, he did,' replied Etone uncomfortably. 'And I have disciplined the novice responsible. However, I can see the lad's point. Coslaye's painting is a glorification of war, and while I am as patriotic as the next man, I do not condone slaughter.'

'What time did Coslaye arrive?'

'Just before nocturns. I remember, because his ranting distressed us, and we found it difficult to concentrate on our prayers afterwards.'

Bartholomew and Michael exchanged a glance. So Coslaye had no alibi for the raid after all, because nocturns was in the middle of the night, a long time before dawn.

'How long was he here?' asked Bartholomew.

'A few moments,' replied Etone. 'He howled at me, I howled back, then he stormed out.'

'I do not suppose you noticed whether he was limping, did you?'

Etone frowned. 'It is odd that you should ask, because I saw him hobbling quite painfully, but that was much later in the day. I did not observe any obvious limp when we raged at each other over his horrible painting.'

'Did he explain what had happened to him?'

'He said a book had fallen on his foot. I quipped that perhaps a Common Library was not such a bad idea after all, because it would save the heads of impecunious hostels from being injured by tomes stored on cheap shelving. He did not find my remark amusing.'

'We also need to speak to Willelmus,' said Bartholomew, intending to ask whether Ayera had spoken to the scribe during the raid, as Clippesby had claimed; and if so, what about.

Riborowe scowled. 'Tulyet still has him. How are we expected to manage when we have no one to draw chickens? What are my ribauldequins supposed to shoot at?'

'Or my demons to eat?' added Jorz.

'Ribauldequins,' mused Michael. 'How familiar *are* you with those, Riborowe?'

The thin friar was delighted to be asked. 'I have never seen one in action, because I was too far away at Poitiers, but I have read a good deal about them and . . .'

He trailed off when he saw his Prior regarding him coldly, disapproving of his obvious pleasure in devices designed to take human life. He flushed, and slunk away to the chamber at the rear, where he stirred something red that was bubbling in a pot.

'I shall speak to him later,' said Etone, watching Riborowe with troubled eyes. 'It is time this unseemly fascination with artillery ended.'

He returned to the business of driving the reluctant scriveners from their desks in his quest for a dust-free environment, leaving Bartholomew and Michael to make their own way out.

'Coslaye would have had plenty of time after this altercation to join the attack on the castle,' said Bartholomew, as they walked across the yard. 'So perhaps Robin did see him, and he injured his foot in the fracas. Etone's testimony certainly points that way.'

'Lord!' breathed Michael. 'I sincerely hope they are wrong!'

Outside the friary, the roads were quieter than they had been, and several families had given up decorating their homes, leaving them oddly lopsided. Michael and Bartholomew had reached the High Street when they saw Tulyet arguing with the head of the Frevill clan. The debate was cut short when Frevill stalked into his house and slammed the door.

'I was trying to persuade him to cancel the pageant,' explained Tulyet. 'He refuses, although he has spirited his family and valuables to the country. Hypocrite! What about those who do not have a refuge, and who may lose everything if the raiders strike during his damned festivities?'

'I thought he was to lead the procession,' said Michael. 'If he flees the town, then—'

'Oh, he will lead it,' said Tulyet bitterly. 'It will take more than the prospect of a raid to deprive *him* of an opportunity to flaunt his finery. He will enjoy himself, safe in the knowledge that all he holds dear is beyond the raiders' reach, and that a fast horse will be waiting to whisk him away at the first sign of trouble.'

'Then perhaps you should not have arranged for his cope to be repaired,' said Michael. 'He might have been less eager to strut if his ceremonial regalia was full of lye-holes.'

'I wish I had let it dissolve,' said Tulyet viciously. 'His actions are the worst combination imaginable. Either he should have cancelled the pageant and left the town to organise a proper defence, or he should have proved that there is nothing to worry about by keeping his family and jewels here. As matters stand, folk are confused and frightened by his example.'

'The rumours of an attack do seem to be growing stronger,' said Michael. 'Several Colleges and a number of hostels have declared an end to their programmes of beautification, on the grounds that we shall all be in flames soon anyway. And my grandmother is afraid they may be right.'

Tulyet sighed tiredly. 'I shall ask the other burgesses to cancel the festivities, but I doubt they will oppose Frevill: the Guild of Corpus Christi is powerful, and money has been invested in the arrangements. Dunning would be furious, too – he wants the whole town to witness his largesse in funding your Common Library.'

'Can you not order them to do it?' asked Bartholomew.

'Not on the basis of rumours. Still, at least I know who murdered Adam, the beggar and my guard. It was definitely the robbers. I have witnesses now, along with a distinctive piece of armour that was gripped in my soldier's dead hand.'

'When did they claim their first victim?' asked Bartholomew. 'In other words, how long have they been spying on the town?'

'The beggar was murdered on Easter Day – more than two months ago.'

'Holm arrived here to live on Easter Day,' said Bartholomew.

'Ignore him,' said Michael, when Tulyet's eyebrows rose. 'He has taken a dislike to Holm.'

'He is not the only one,' said Tulyet grimly. 'Holm was useless when my men were injured. Incidentally, were you aware that he keeps a lover? Clippesby knows, so I imagine he told you. He stumbled across them when he was debating some lofty theological tract with a goat. Or was it a pig? I cannot recall now.'

'Did Clippesby give you a name?' asked Michael. 'Prudishly, Matt stopped him from revealing it when they discussed the matter, and I keep forgetting to ask.'

'Browne of Batayl Hostel.'

'Browne?' asked Michael, startled. 'I was not expecting that! Still, I suppose it explains why Holm seems immune to Julitta's very considerable beauty, and why Clippesby is so certain their union will be unhappy. You will have to prevent her from marrying him now, Matt. Make her fall in love with you instead. It would be a kindness.'

'How will you catch the individual who killed Adam, Dick?' Bartholomew asked, before the monk could embarrass him further.

'I have every available soldier out scouring the Fens. Unfortunately, these raiders are elusive and extremely well organised, and I am not hopeful of nabbing them before they next attack.'

'Speaking of their next attack, there is a tale that the tax money has been moved from the castle and hidden in the University,' said Michael. 'Do you have any idea who invented such a lie?'

'No, but the story is all over the town. There is gossip about Gyseburne, too – namely that his interest in urine stems from the fact that it can be made to explode. Is it true?'

'Urine does contain combustible—' began Bartholomew, but then stopped abruptly.

'He is still horrified by Rougham's capitulation,' explained Michael to the Sheriff. 'And he is loath to discuss substances that blow up with anyone now. Even you.'

'Good,' said Tulyet sourly. 'It was a secret that should have been carried to the grave, and he had no right dabbling in such matters in the first place. If that vile concoction is ever used against my men, I shall . . . well, let us hope it does not happen.'

'Christ!' groaned Bartholomew when Tulyet had gone. 'What if it is? What if the raiders manage to create some?'

'They cannot, not when you say rock oil is difficult to obtain and dangerous to distil. But perhaps we are taking too bleak a view of the situation. There may be no raid – the robbers may have given up after their rout on Saturday.'

'That is not what everyone else seems to think,' said Bartholomew, aware that several High Street houses had boards over their windows. 'Including your grandmother.'

'But they may be wrong. There is nothing except rumour to suggest there will be an attack. I am sure this tale did not come from the culprits, and they are the only ones who really know.'

'Perhaps,' said Bartholomew, although he was far from convinced.

The interview with Willelmus was delayed yet again when Michael was intercepted by a beadle saying that Walkelate needed some requisitions to be signed as a matter of urgency. Bartholomew went with him to Newe Inn, still worrying that wildfire might play a role in the looming trouble.

The clouds had lifted and it was hot by the time they reached Cholles Lane. The streets were clogged with dust, and Bartholomew wished it would rain, to dampen it down. People were already complaining about the heat, worried that the crops might fail again. The town's children were happy, though, and frolicked in the river's shallows, squealing their delight amid fountains of brown spray. Bartholomew hoped it would not make them ill, because they had chosen to play not far from where the Carmelites discharged their sewage.

Bartholomew and Michael entered Newe Inn, where they met Dunning in the basement, just leaving. He was whistling cheerfully to himself, and smiled when he saw Michael.

'You are prompt,' he said approvingly. 'Walkelate has the documents ready, and I appreciate you coming so quickly. Time is of the essence now that Corpus Christi is only two days away.'

'Yes,' said Michael gloomily.

Then Dunning's face darkened. 'I wish I did not have to waste so much of it quashing these ridiculous tales about a raid, though. Of course there will not be an attack! These villains are still Christians, and know better than to risk the wrath of God by interrupting religious ceremonies.'

'Opening a library is hardly a religious—' began Bartholomew.

'Nonsense!' interrupted Dunning. 'Prayers will be said, will they not? And monks and friars will be in attendance? I want it to be a day to remember – and I do not mean because everyone skulks at home, too frightened to come out and admire what we have achieved here.'

He bustled away before they could argue, leaving them to climb the stairs to the upper rooms. When they arrived, they could not help but notice that the reek of oil was just as powerful as it had been the last time they had visited, and Holm's 'remedy' sat ineffectually in a bowl on the windowsill. Aristotle, now affixed in his permanent position atop the first bookshelf, seemed to be grimacing his disapproval at the stench.

Walkelate and Frevill were at the *cista*, anxiously studying the plans that were spread across it, but the architect's face broke into a smile when he saw Michael and Bartholomew.

'We are almost ready,' he said, eyes dancing with delight as he handed the monk the documents that needed his approval. 'There is no question at all now that we will make the Corpus Christi deadline. We shall present the University a building that every scholar can be proud of.'

'Yes,' agreed Bartholomew, looking around appreciatively. 'But where is Kente? Have the fumes made him ill again?'

'He has not arrived yet. He must be mixing more wood-grease in his workshop at home. He likes to employ it liberally, which is why there is something of an aroma.'

'Or perhaps he is with the *libri concatenati*,' suggested Michael.

'No, that room has been locked up since yesterday.' The eager gleam was back in Walkelate's eyes. 'Would you like to see it? It is completely finished, and—'

'No,' said Michael, before Bartholomew could say he would.

'We have been discussing that nasty attack on Langelee,' said Frevill, both hands to the small of his back. 'But we have come up with nothing useful. We were not here when it happened, more is the pity – he may have been assaulted by the same villain who did away with Northwood

308

and the others, and it would have been good to catch the rogue.'

'It would,' agreed Walkelate fervently. 'Unpleasant incidents on the eve of our opening are not good news. Are you sure you two would not like to see the finished chamber?'

'I would,' said Bartholomew, before Michael could decline a second time.

Michael heaved an impatient sigh as, with a happy grin, Walkelate took a key from a chain around his neck. He inserted it in the door, but it did not turn, and he frowned his puzzlement.

'It is unlocked,' he said, rattling it impatiently. 'Yet it will not open. What is wrong?'

Bartholomew pointed to a small wedge at the bottom of the door. He kicked it out of the way, and the door opened easily.

'We must have forgotten to secure it last night,' said Frevill anxiously. 'That is not good! I would not like one of our enemies to get in and damage something.'

'You believe someone would be so petty?' asked Bartholomew, yet as soon as the question was out, he knew it was a foolish one. He could name at least a dozen scholars who would think nothing of despoiling the place. Walkelate could, too, and began to do so.

'Some of the Carmelites, Browne and that Batayl rabble, the Master and Fellows of Bene't College, the Fellows of King's Hall, Doctor Rougham of Gonville—'

'Quite a lot, then,' interrupted Bartholomew, suspecting the list was likely to continue for some time. He stepped into the room and looked around in awe. 'It is splendid! I cannot imagine anywhere I would rather read.'

'That is the best compliment you could have paid us,' said Walkelate sincerely.

'Master Walkelate designed this place to last,' said Frevill, resting a callused hand on one of the shelves. 'It is strange to think that scholars will be sitting here in a hundred years' time.'

'A thousand years,' corrected Walkelate. 'Our names will be read out at Corpus Christi masses long after our souls have been released from Purgatory.'

He and Michael went back to their documents, leaving Bartholomew to explore alone. The physician walked slowly, running his fingers along the polished wood as he admired the intricacy of the carvings. He smirked when he saw a dragon with Etone's dour features, while Adam and Eve bore an uncanny likeness to Bonabes and Ruth. The only negative was the powerful aroma of oil and the somewhat earthy scent of the bale of hay that had been set in the middle of the room.

He was just walking past it, eyes fixed on the handsome sconces on the wall, when he tripped over something that had been left in the way. It was Kente, face-down on the floor. Quickly, he rested a hand on the carpenter's neck, but Kente was cold and had clearly been dead for hours. Bartholomew could only suppose that he had lain there all night.

'Brother!' he called urgently. 'It seems libraries really are dangerous places.'

Walkelate was distraught when he saw his artisan. He dropped to his knees, and began imploring Kente to sit up and announce that it was all a terrible joke. Bartholomew needed Frevill's help to pull him away and seat him at the *cista* in the adjoining room with his back to the corpse. Michael fetched him a cup of wine, and urged him to sip.

'How did it happen?' demanded Walkelate, after several gulps had given him back some of his colour. 'He was perfectly well when we parted last night. He said he just wanted to check that all was well before going home, and I left him to lock the door.'

'What time was this?' asked Michael.

'Dusk,' replied Walkelate shakily. 'He was nearing the end of his endurance, so I suppose our gruelling schedule must have given him a seizure. He is not as strong as the rest of us.'

'Or do you think he was murdered by one of the many scholars who hates what we have done here?' asked Frevill with a scowl. 'If so, it will not stop us from finishing. Indeed, I shall do all in my power to ensure it *does* open as planned, because the bonus Dunning promised . . . well, Kente's family will need it now he has gone.'

'Will you inspect him for us, Matthew?' asked Walkelate brokenly. 'His wife and children will want to know how he died.'

Bartholomew went to oblige, Michael at his heels. Walkelate began to weep, and Frevill tried to comfort him, gruff and awkward. The other workmen gathered around them, all shocked.

Bartholomew stared at the body, sensing something amiss. He knelt next to it, stretched out his hand, then jerked it away as something moved under Kente's tunic. He leapt backwards when the sinuous body of a snake appeared.

It was the biggest viper he had ever seen, as long as his arm and unsettlingly thick. Michael shrieked his horror, and shot out of the room, displaying remarkable speed for someone so large. He slammed closed the door, then opened it a crack.

'Matt, come out!' he whispered, as if he imagined that the snake might hear and try to stop him. 'Quickly.'

'It must have been in the hay,' said Bartholomew,

311

standing with his hands on his hips. 'I suppose it crawled out, and bit Kente when he inadvertently trod on it.'

'Then come over here,' hissed Michael urgently. 'Before it bites you, too.'

When the monk turned to explain what was happening to the craftsmen, Bartholomew took Kente's shoulders and moved him carefully. The adder slithered further into the carpenter's clothes; it was cold, and wanted somewhere warm to hide.

There were two wounds in Kente's ankle, ringed faintly with blood, and his leg was swollen and purple to the knee. His gums were inflamed, too – another symptom of snake poisoning. Bartholomew glanced at the door, recalling the wedge that had been jammed in it, but then saw that the floor of the adjoining chamber was littered with identical fragments.

'Enough,' shouted Michael, when he saw his friend still pondering over Kente's body. 'Come out immediately. That is an order!'

'There is no danger, Brother. Snakes only attack when they are threatened.'

'I doubt Kente would agree. And you are not Clippesby, who enjoys a peculiar rapport with wild beasts. Walk towards me now, before it is too late.'

Ignoring him, Bartholomew upended his medical bag, then took his forceps and gently placed them around the snake's head. It did not struggle, so it was not difficult to pick it up and drop it into an empty sack. Michael screeched his horror at every stage, but Bartholomew ignored him. He closed the bag carefully and carried it towards the door.

'Put it down,' ordered Michael. 'I shall stamp on it.'

'I am going to release it in the garden.'

'No, you are not!' declared Michael, appalled. 'Meadowman is there, dredging.'

312

'Fling it over the wall towards Batayl,' suggested Frevill, quite seriously.

'Or even better, put it in the Carmelite Friary,' added one of his workmates.

Bartholomew paid no attention to any of them. It was not far to the river, where there was plenty of long grass. When he arrived, he looked carefully both ways. Torvin the riverman was approaching from one direction, and Jorz from the other. Neither was close enough to be a problem. He opened the bag and watched the snake slither out.

'I saw that,' said Jorz, eyes wide as he backed away and crossed himself. 'I saw you release your familiar – the Devil in serpent form.'

He dashed away before Bartholomew could respond to the charge. The physician sighed, realising he should have waited until Jorz had gone.

'Ignore him.' Bartholomew jumped; he had forgotten Torvin was there. 'You were right to let it go. They are peaceful creatures, and want only to be left alone. Just like us riverfolk, in fact.'

By the time Bartholomew returned to Newe Inn, Michael had summoned beadles to carry Kente's body to the nearest church. The physician was obliged to remove some of the artisan's clothes first, though, to show the nervous pall-bearers that there were no more vipers hidden within. Meanwhile, the hay was wrapped in sacking, and Walkelate gave the order for it to be burned in the garden. Walkelate, Frevill and their colleagues watched the blaze for a while, but soon sought comfort in the familiarity of their work.

'So what happened?' asked Michael, when he and Bartholomew were alone. 'I have known others bitten by snakes, and although they were ill afterwards, none died.'

313

'Kente was suffering from exhaustion,' explained Bartholomew. 'Had he been fit and sought immediate help, the bite might not have been fatal.'

Michael shuddered. 'So what stopped him from summoning assistance? The door was unlocked, and that piece of wood was not wedged in especially tightly. I saw it.'

'It was easy to dislodge from this side, but it would have been much harder from the other. However, one of the windows was ajar. I suspect he did call for help, but no one heard.'

'An accident, then?' asked Michael. 'Yet another one connected to books?'

'I suppose so.'

'Meaning you are not sure?'

'The snake may have emerged from the bale to bite Kente when he inadvertently stepped on it, but it may equally well have been placed there deliberately. There is no way to know. Similarly, there is no way to know whether the wood blocked the door by chance, or whether someone put it there.'

Michael regarded him uneasily, then led the way away from the smouldering hay, along the overgrown path that led to the pond. 'Who would do such a terrible thing?'

'Anyone who wants to see the Common Library fail, I suppose. Or wants to fuel the rumour that repositories for books are perilous places.'

As if to prove his words, Bartholomew overheard Cynric saying this to Meadowman when they approached the pool. The beadle was nodding sagely, agreeing with every word.

'Meadowman,' called Michael curtly. 'Have you finished dredging yet?'

'Yes, but it was a waste of time, Brother. The pool is

314

extraordinarily deep, as you know – deeper than the height of three men. I did my best, but there was nothing to find.'

'Nothing?' asked Michael, disappointed. 'You mean it was empty of everything except fish?'

'I put those back,' said Meadowman. 'I wanted to take one home for supper, but Cynric said that Satan might join me at the dinner table if I did, because they belong to him.'

'They made the riverfolk sick,' said Bartholomew. 'And the Batayl scholars.'

'I told you,' said Cynric, gratified. 'There are evil faeries in that water, and they harm anyone who steals their produce.' He crossed himself, and muttered an incantation to some heathen god.

'I pulled out plenty of rubbish, of course,' Meadowman went on. 'But nothing that will help you understand what happened to the scholars who died here.'

Michael sighed. 'We had better inspect what you have recovered anyway.'

The beadle pointed to a substantial mound of refuse, reeking and stained with brown mud; flies swarmed hungrily. There were rusted knives, broken pots, half-rotted baskets, countless oyster shells, what appeared to be part of a wooden chest, an ancient helmet, and a large number of animal bones. Michael regarded it all in distaste.

'So what did that fellow expect to find when we almost laid hold of him here the other night?'

Meadowman shrugged. 'Treasure? People hid their riches in all sorts of funny places during the Death, and I kept hoping we would discover a hoard.'

'Unlikely,' said Michael. 'The Dunning family has rented Newe Inn to impecunious taverners for years. None had fortunes to conceal.'

'Personally, I suspect those four scholars were trying to harness the power of demons,' began Cynric. 'And—'

'No,' interrupted Bartholomew sharply, wondering whether his own reputation as a warlock owed anything to his association with Cynric. He pointed. 'When did you haul that large metal pot out?'

'The witches' cauldron?' asked Cynric brightly. 'Would you like it for your experiments? I can take it back to Michaelhouse and clean it off for you. I am sure it will scrub up beautifully.'

'I do not want it,' said Bartholomew quickly, aware of Meadowman's knowing smirk. 'But did you find it relatively quickly or later on? In other words, was it near the top of the items you uncovered, or buried deep?'

'It was almost the first thing I hauled up,' said Meadowman. 'Why?'

Bartholomew tapped it with his forceps. It rang melodiously.

'So Coslaye and the apprentice were right when they said they heard bells,' said Michael thoughtfully. 'Can we assume that Northwood and his friends were doing something with this cauldron when they died, then, and it went in the pond at or near the same time that they did?'

Bartholomew nodded. 'We have suspected all along that they were conducting alchemical experiments. Moreover, here are jars that almost certainly contained pitch and brimstone – two ingredients used to make lamp fuel.' Or wildfire, he thought, but did not say. 'But why here?'

'That is easy to answer,' replied Cynric. 'Because the London brothers lived next door to Weasenham, the town's biggest gossip; Vale lived in Gonville Hall, but they could not work there, because Rougham would have demanded an explanation—'

'And Northwood would face similar problems at King's

316

Hall,' finished Bartholomew. He glanced around him. 'Yet it would be easy to work here undisturbed. Of course, it does not explain *how* they died.'

'Perhaps they accidentally set themselves alight,' suggested Meadowman. 'And flung themselves in the pond to extinguish the flames.'

'There was no evidence of burning,' said Bartholomew. 'Not on their clothes or their bodies.'

'Then I was right all along,' said Cynric with immense satisfaction. 'They entered a place that belonged to the Devil, and he claimed them for his own.'

The day had turned hot and sultry, and there was not so much as a breath of wind. Michael grumbled bitterly as they walked along the High Street, aiming for the castle and Willelmus.

'I was not designed for all this racing around,' he said, wiping the sweat from his eyes. 'And we have missed the midday meal. Of course, that is no great tragedy, given the quality of food at Michaelhouse these days. Even dinner on Trinity Sunday was dismal.'

Mention of College meals reminded Bartholomew of his concerns about his colleagues.

'Do you think Ayera threw in his lot with the robbers because he wants to save us from debt?' he asked worriedly. 'The man who was caught – Ayce – said he and his fellow mercenaries had been very well paid.'

Michael nodded. 'It is possible. Ayera was deeply disappointed when nothing came from his uncle's benefaction. Embarrassed, too, after raising our hopes. His family lent him the money to buy the horse he wants, but the loan will have to be repaid – not easy on a Fellow's salary.'

'Then do you think that Langelee learned what Ayera

was doing, and agreed to look the other way for a share of his earnings?'

'Or for a chance to enrol with the robbers himself,' said Michael soberly. 'He was a warrior once, and we know from our recent journey to York that he has forgotten none of his brutish skills. Moreover, he takes his duties as Master seriously, and might see this as an opportunity to raise some quick and much-needed cash.'

Bartholomew agreed unhappily. 'It would certainly explain why he prevented me from asking Ayera any more questions, and why Clippesby has seen them leaving the College at odd hours.'

'Lord, Matt!' breathed Michael, his face pale. 'If Dick Tulyet ever finds out . . .'

He did not need to finish, because Bartholomew knew exactly the damage it would do. Langelee and Ayera would be obliged to resign – or worse; Tulyet might demand reparation from Michaelhouse that would plunge it even deeper into debt; and the King would be furious to learn that scholars had set greedy eyes on his taxes. The harm caused by such an incident would be vast, and although Bartholomew was generally opposed to concealing unsavoury secrets, this was one he would be more than happy to suppress.

As they approached the Jewry, they saw Weasenham sitting outside his shop. Ruth and Bonabes were just inside the door, she polishing some inkwells and he sharpening quills. Weasenham was watching passers-by with calculating eyes. He turned his head occasionally, to regale his wife and Exemplarius with his observations, but neither were paying him much attention.

'I hear there have been nine deaths connected with libraries now,' he called to Bartholomew and Michael as they passed. 'It seems they are deadly places.'

'They are nothing of the kind,' said Michael tiredly. 'So please do not spread silly tales.'

'How can you deny it?' demanded Weasenham. 'I heard Walkelate telling Chancellor Tynkell about the snake that killed Kente, and the whole affair sounded downright sinister!'

'You should not have eavesdropped,' murmured Ruth. 'It was not decent, especially given that Walkelate was obviously distressed. It was distasteful.'

'The discussion took place in my shop,' said Weasenham indignantly. 'I have a right to listen to what is said in my own business premises.'

'It was a private conversation,' said Bonabes quietly. 'Not intended for our ears.'

Weasenham turned away impatiently. 'It seems to me, Brother, that some fiend is at large, dispatching scholars in libraries. You had better catch him, and fast.'

Michael was about to take issue with him when Riborowe and Jorz arrived with a list of supplies needed for their scriptorium. Weasenham leapt to his feet to see to them personally – the Carmelites were valued customers – although it was obvious that the stationer intended to ply them with his theories at the same time.

'Jorz told me about your snake, Bartholomew,' whispered Riborowe as he passed. 'It proves what I have always suspected: that you are a warlock in the pay of Satan.'

Bartholomew groaned, knowing he would tell Weasenham what had happened by the river, and the tale would be all over the town by nightfall. Bonabes and Ruth emerged from the shop as the scribes entered, 'accidentally' brushing each other's fingers. It was clear they were in love, and Bartholomew was sorry that Weasenham's disagreeable presence meant they would never be together.

'My husband has decided not to open the shop on

Thursday,' Ruth told the scholars. 'And I shall bury all our valuables in the garden tomorrow. These horrible raiders are not going to get rich on our hard-earned money.'

'They will not come,' said Bonabes. He sounded exasperated, as if it was a subject they had discussed before, but could not agree upon. 'Why would they? They have been repelled once. Besides, the tales that say they plan to attack derive from a baseless story started by Weasenham.'

'I am going to hide the more expensive ingredients we use in our paper-making experiments, too,' Ruth went on, ignoring him. 'It is unlikely that thieves will want to tote heavy pots when they leave, but you cannot be too careful, and I should not like to think of some of those compounds in such hands. They can be dangerous.'

'You do not have any rock oil, do you?' asked Bartholomew.

'We did,' replied Bonabes. 'But when I went to fetch it this morning, it had gone.'

'I suspect the London brothers had it,' said Ruth. 'Probably to use when they were with Northwood. If you happen across it during your enquiries, we would not mind it back. It is costly and difficult to obtain.'

'Why did you want it this morning?' asked Bartholomew, alarmed.

'I was going to give some to Riborowe,' explained Bonabes. 'He read somewhere that it has drying properties, and asked if he might have a bit for his ink.'

'But it had gone?' pressed Bartholomew. 'All of it?'

Bonabes nodded. 'Although I suppose it does not really matter. We discovered early on that it is no good for manufacturing paper.'

'I have a terrible feeling that none of this will matter

after Thursday,' said Ruth, like a dog with a bone. 'The invaders will have razed our town to the ground by then.'

'You seem very sure this attack will happen,' said Bartholomew, dragging his thoughts from wildfire to robbers.

'She is,' said Bonabes. He smiled fondly at her, to take the sting from his words. 'But she is wrong. They will not strike again, because they have lost the element of surprise.'

'I hope you are right,' said Bartholomew.

He nodded a farewell to them, and fell into step at Michael's side as they resumed their walk to the castle. Michael was troubled.

'So now we learn that the London brothers stole expensive materials for their experiments and . . . Blast! Here comes Cynric. Now what? Will we never get to speak to Willelmus?'

'Batayl has just sent word,' Cynric said. 'Apparently, Browne is missing. He has been gone since last night, but as he has taken none of his belongings with him, his students fear the worst.'

CHAPTER 10

Batayl Hostel had altered dramatically since Bartholomew and Michael had last visited. The vivid mural had been obliterated with a smart wash of white, and the sour smell of feet and burnt fat was overlain by the sweeter scent of rose petals. Bartholomew could only suppose that Holm had supplied his lover Browne with them, as he had supplied Walkelate with a remedy for Newe Inn's reeking oil.

'Browne made some changes when he declared himself Principal,' explained Pepin, assuming the role of spokesman in the absence of his seniors. 'I, for one, was glad to see the painting go.'

'I am sure you were,' said Michael, looking hard at him. 'It cannot have been pleasant for you, seeing your countrymen depicted as demons wading through oceans of blood.'

'No, and I often felt like punching Coslaye.' Pepin flushed when he realised the remark was somewhat incriminating. 'But I did not kill him. That was someone else – someone who is eager for the Common Library to open, and who was afraid Coslaye might have interfered.'

'Would he have interfered?' asked Michael.

'Oh, yes,' replied Pepin. 'He planned to smear dung and mortar over Newe Inn's windows – a combination of materials that will set hard and that would have been difficult to scour off. I tried to talk him out of it, but he was not a man to listen to reason.'

'No,' agreed Michael. 'Not about the library. And not about the French, either.'

'He hates us,' said Pepin quietly. 'Yet there is no need. Poitiers did us irreparable damage, and we are no threat to England now. It shattered our army, dealt our pride a mortal blow, killed the flower of our nobility, and took our King prisoner. We are in chaos, unable to pay the ransoms you have demanded, and our peasants are set to rise up against their masters.'

'Yes,' said Michael, a little impatiently. He had not come to debate France's problems. 'But let us discuss Browne. I understand he and Holm are . . . close.'

'Lovers,' nodded Pepin. 'We do not mind that – ladies are hard to come by in Cambridge, so a man must take comfort where he can – but we disapprove of Holm. He is devious and conceited, and only made friends with Browne because his cousin knows the King. We hate him.'

'When did you last see Browne?' asked Michael.

'Last night.' Pepin gnawed his lip uneasily. 'And we have a bad feeling about him going missing. All his belongings are here, including Apollodorus's *Poliorcetica*, which was his pride and joy. He would not have gone anywhere without taking that with him.'

'A book on sieges and war?' asked Bartholomew, recalling Deynman's distress over what had been done to Michaelhouse's copy.

'It was a gift from Holm,' explained Pepin. 'I cannot imagine what would have happened when he got married, and thus became unavailable. Perhaps it is better this way.'

'You speak as though you think Browne is dead,' observed Bartholomew.

Pepin nodded, and so did his fellow students. 'We believe Holm killed him, because he was afraid that Julitta would find out about their friendship and cancel the wedding. Holm is desperate to have her money, you see, and will not let anything – not even Browne – stand in his way.'

'I shall instruct my beadles to look for Browne,' said Michael. 'And we shall pay a visit to Holm now. Meanwhile, your disputations will be soon, so I recommend that you concentrate on your exemplars today. Stay here, and leave the hunt to me.'

Pepin nodded acquiescence. 'As you wish.'

Michael started to leave, but then paused. 'My grandmother claims that Angoulême – your birthplace – has a large paper-making industry, but I think she is mistaken. Am I right, or is she?'

Pepin gave a tight smile. 'You are, Brother. Angoulême has never produced paper.'

'Just as I thought,' said Michael with a small bow. 'Thank you.'

Bartholomew followed him outside, but there was no time to enquire why he had asked Pepin such an odd question, because the monk was already knocking on Holm's door.

'What do you want?' the surgeon demanded, answering it himself. 'I am busy.'

The fact that his clothes were rumpled, and he was stifling a yawn, suggested his business involved sleeping, even though it was the middle of the day.

'Browne is missing, and his students are worried,' said Michael without preamble. 'They think you and he might have had a lovers' tiff.'

Holm scowled, then indicated with an irritable flap of his hand that Michael and Bartholomew were to step into his house. Glancing furtively up and down the lane to assess whether anyone else had heard the monk's remark, he then closed the door.

Once inside, Bartholomew saw Julitta's hand everywhere, from the tasteful rugs on the floor, to the cushions on the benches and the way the silver goblets had been arranged on the table. There was even a small library, which he supposed she had assembled for their married life together.

'Browne and I are not lovers,' the surgeon said, walking to the table and pouring himself some wine. He did not offer any to his guests. 'The Batayl lads have never liked me, and they fabricated that vile accusation to show me in a bad light.'

'It is not just Batayl,' said Michael. 'We have heard it from others, too. Indeed, half the town seems to know you prefer Browne to your hapless fiancée.'

Holm's expression hardened. 'Well, perhaps I do, although I shall take legal action against anyone who tells her so before we are married.'

'When did you last see Browne?' asked Bartholomew, struggling to mask his distaste.

'Yesterday evening,' replied Holm icily. 'However, the louts of Batayl were with him long after I had made my farewells, so do not look to me as the last man who saw him alive.'

'Now *you* seem convinced he is dead,' said Michael.

Holm shrugged. 'He was not popular with his students, so it stands to reason. They are a vicious horde, and I imagine they are responsible for braining Coslaye, too.'

'Do you have any evidence to say that?' asked Michael.

'Yes – the evidence of common sense.'

'Browne was your lover, yet you do not seem upset by his disappearance,' mused Michael. 'Why not? Because you know he is alive, so grieving is unnecessary? Or because you have experienced a cooling of affection for each other?'

'Neither. I am devastated, actually, but my father taught me never to show needless emotions. He said it is unbecoming in a medical man.'

Bartholomew was thoughtful as they left the surgeon's cottage. 'Do you think he *has* dispatched Browne, perhaps because Browne learned some of his sinister secrets?'

'What sinister secrets?' asked Michael. 'And do not say his preference for men, because I doubt Browne sees that as a crime, given that he is like-minded.'

'What about his greedy determination to have Julitta's dowry?' suggested Bartholomew. 'Or the fact that he sided with the French at Poitiers? Or his lies, hollow boasts and cowardice?'

Michael laughed. 'They are not secrets! Besides, there is nothing to say Browne is dead. Or that Holm killed him. And anyway, if I had to choose a suspect, it would be Pepin.'

'Pepin might have murdered Coslaye, but he has no reason to harm Browne. Browne shared his distaste for Coslaye's fascination with Poitiers.'

'And what if Pepin did kill Coslaye, and Browne found out?' asked Michael. 'That is a motive for murder. Moreover, Pepin's determination to have Holm implicated in Browne's disappearance is suspicious. Then there is the fact that I tripped him up with my question about Angoulême, which *does* produce paper, and has done for years; my grandmother waxed lyrical about it the other night. If he does not know this simple fact, then he is lying about his origins.'

'I suspect that is because he actually hails from Poitiers,' said Bartholomew. He shrugged when the monk regarded him in surprise. 'I might lie, too, were I a Poitevin living in England, and I imagine he did turn out for the battle.

He looks more like a warrior than a scholar.'

'He does,' agreed Michael. 'But how do you know he comes from Poitiers?'

'Because of the name he gave the stew that made everyone ill: *tout marron*. It is called *tout brun* everywhere but Poitiers. I cannot imagine why he did not abandon Batayl and enrol with a Principal who is less rabidly anti-French.'

'That is easier said than done,' explained Michael. 'Students pay fees, and no hostel wants to lose those, so moving between foundations is strongly discouraged. Of course, Pepin is not the only candidate for dispatching Browne. Julitta has a powerful reason to dislike the fellow, too: no wife wants a manly lover waiting in the wings.'

Bartholomew gazed at him in shock. 'That is a terrible thing to say!'

'And people do terrible things, as we have learned in the past. Especially, it would seem, ones with angelic faces and kindly dispositions.'

'But Julitta is—'

'Julitta is about to marry a man she adores, but she is no fool, and may well know about his preferences. Browne's demise can only benefit her, and if your be-fuddled emotions would let you view the situation objectively, you would agree with me.'

'Killing Browne will not resolve anything – Holm will still be attracted to men. She is not stupid, Brother; she will understand that.'

Michael regarded him critically. 'It seems to me that love blinds even the sanest of people to reason.'

'I do not love her,' Bartholomew snapped. 'There is still Matilde . . .'

'Is there? When was the last time you thought about her?'

Bartholomew was chagrined to feel colour rise into his

327

cheeks. 'I have not had time to think of anything except my teaching and your investigation for days,' he replied stiffly.

Prudently, Michael changed the subject to their students' upcoming disputations, for which Bartholomew was grateful. He did not want anyone to know the full extent of the affection he was beginning to feel for a woman who was shortly to become another man's wife.

Tulyet's hopeful smile quickly faded when he heard that Bartholomew and Michael had not come to the castle because they had something useful to report about the raiders.

'Only more of the same,' said Michael apologetically. 'That they will come at Corpus Christi.'

'I called a meeting in the Guild Hall earlier,' said Tulyet gloomily. 'To urge the burgesses to cancel the pageant. But a lot of money has been invested in it, so they voted to ignore me.'

'Money for what?' asked Bartholomew, puzzled.

'For the cakes that have been baked, the ale that has been brewed, the performers who have been hired. Calling it off now will mean heavy financial losses. But perhaps my fears are unfounded. The raiders may not come when they learn the taxes are no longer in the Great Tower, and so will not be easy to find.'

Michael grimaced. 'Unfortunately, there is a tale that they are now hidden in the University. The castle may be safe, but we must expect to be ravaged.'

'You will not be,' said Tulyet confidently. 'Not even the most determined thief could consider searching eight Colleges, forty hostels and half a dozen convents.'

Bartholomew gazed at him horror as understanding dawned. 'It was you! You started this rumour, to dissuade the robbers from coming!'

'Steady on, Matt!' breathed Michael, shocked. 'That is a nasty accusation.'

But Tulyet's expression was sheepish. 'I may have mentioned something to Weasenham . . .'

Michael gaped at him. 'You did *what*?'

'Who seized your idle musings and turned them into rumour,' finished Bartholomew.

Michael continued to gape. 'No, Dick! I cannot believe you would do something so recklessly irresponsible!'

'What is irresponsible about using all the means at my disposal to avert trouble?' asked Tulyet defensively, although he would not meet Michael's eyes.

'Well, for a start, there is the very strong possibility that your ruse will work, and that the University will bear the brunt of these marauders' attentions,' snapped Michael, anger taking the place of disbelief. 'How could you? It is not—'

'Is the money still here, in the castle?' asked Bartholomew, speaking quickly to prevent a spat. Having the Sheriff and Senior Proctor at loggerheads would be disastrous at such a time.

'Locked in the Great Tower.' Then Tulyet's defiant glare faded. 'But with hindsight, I see that I should not have acted without consulting you, Brother. I am sorry.'

'We came to speak to Willelmus,' said Bartholomew, seeing Michael gird himself up to reject the apology. But while Tulyet was certainly in the wrong, nothing would be gained from remonstrating with him further. 'Is he here?'

'May I ask why?' asked Tulyet.

'Just an avenue of enquiry,' replied Michael coldly. 'If it leads anywhere, you will be the first to know. I shall not exclude *you* from anything important.'

Tulyet inclined his head rather stiffly, and pointed to

the Great Tower. Michael fumed as he and Bartholomew crossed the bailey towards it.

'How dare he put us at risk! What was he thinking?'

'That it was a way to avert trouble,' said Bartholomew calmly. 'Do not quarrel—'

'I understand the importance of good relations in a time of crisis, even if he does not,' hissed Michael. 'But what he has done is unforgivable. How can I ever trust him again?'

'He has barely slept since the attack, and the deaths of his men hit him very hard. He made an error of judgement, which he had the grace to acknowledge. I doubt it will happen again.'

Michael scowled. 'It had better not!'

Willelmus was working on a document when Bartholomew and Michael arrived, leaning close to the text as he strained to see. He glanced up when the visitors were shown in, his milky eyes squinting in an effort to identify them. Still angry with the Sheriff and eager to vent his spleen, Michael homed in on him like a hawk after a rabbit.

'You were seen talking to one of the raiders during the attack,' he began curtly. 'Why?'

'He approached me,' replied Willelmus, alarmed by the monk's belligerence. 'And I was so frightened that it caused a seizure. Surgeon Holm and Doctor Rougham say I am lucky to survive.'

'You seem well enough now,' said Bartholomew, knowing it took rather longer to recover from genuine seizures. Holm and Rougham had exaggerated its seriousness to their patient, probably so they could charge a higher fee for their services.

'I am mending,' acknowledged Willelmus. 'But I am not as fit as I was before it happened.'

'What did you discuss with this terrifying individual?' demanded Michael.

'He asked where the tax money was kept,' gulped Willelmus. 'I am afraid I told him, because I feared he would kill me otherwise.'

'That makes no sense.' Bartholomew regarded him doubtfully. 'Every other witness says the robbers aimed straight for the Great Tower – they already knew where to go. So why did this one man stop to question you, especially once the raid was under way?'

'I cannot be expected to know what is in the minds of criminals,' said Willelmus, swallowing hard. 'They probably think differently from normal men. All I can say is that he must have picked on me because I do not look brave and I was unarmed. He thought I would crack easily.'

'No,' said Bartholomew, regarding the friar intently. 'You are lying. Our witnesses implied it was more conversation than interrogation, which suggests to me that you had spoken before. Do you not think it is time to tell us what is going on, so we can prevent another attack?'

'No!' squeaked Willelmus. 'Your witnesses are wrong! I never—'

'Tell us the truth,' snapped Michael. 'Or you will never see your scriptorium again.'

Willelmus was close to tears. 'All right! I did know him, but they will kill me if I talk. They said so, and I have no reason to doubt them. They will crush me like a snail.'

'You talked to Ayera,' said Michael harshly. 'From Michaelhouse.'

Willelmus closed his eyes. 'Yes,' he replied in a whisper.

Bartholomew narrowed his eyes at the easy capitulation. 'No! Ayera is not the one you really fear. Who else threatened you?'

But Willelmus was silent, rocking back and forth in

331

distress. Fortunately, small threads of evidence began to come together in Bartholomew's mind.

'It has been suggested that the invaders aimed straight for the Great Tower because they are local, so they know where the Sheriff stores his valuables. But they have been reconnoitring the town for weeks, killing anyone who sees them. However, perhaps they let some folk live in exchange for information.'

'I see,' said Michael, his eyes steely. 'They knew to assault the Great Tower not because they had a local's knowledge, or because it was an obvious conclusion to draw, but because someone told them all they needed to know.'

Willelmus's face was a mask of anguish. 'What will happen to me?' he breathed.

'That is for the Sheriff to decide,' said Michael harshly. 'However, I imagine it will involve a spell in his gaol, next to the villain he has already caught.'

'That man will kill me, too,' said Willelmus miserably. 'I have been doomed from the start.'

He tried to dart away, but it was not difficult for Bartholomew to intercept him. Moreover, his pathetic attempt at flight revealed a significant limp.

'Was this miserable specimen one of those who attacked you the other night, Matt?' asked Michael. 'I thought you were more of a warrior than that.'

'I have not attacked anyone in years,' sobbed Willelmus pitifully. 'Not after . . .'

'Not after the disaster that occurred when you tackled someone else,' said Bartholomew, understanding coming in a blinding flash. 'Willelmus is the Latin form of William. You are William Hildersham!'

'Hildersham,' mused Michael. 'Where have I heard that name before?'

'It is the name of the scrivener who killed Ayce's son all those years ago.'

'How in God's name did you reason that?' asked Michael, when Willelmus slumped to the floor and began to sob. 'An ancient murder was the last thing on my mind today.'

'Because Willelmus could have warned the Sheriff, and remained safely hidden in the castle until the raiders were caught and the danger was over. But he let the attack take place without a word. *Ergo*, they have some other hold over him.'

'I accept that,' said Michael. 'But what made you think of John Ayce? I know he was stabbed by a scribe, but there have been hundreds of them in Cambridge over the years.'

'The clues are obvious with hindsight. What are the two letters Willelmus specialises in illustrating at the scriptorium?'

'J and A,' said Michael, round eyed. 'John Ayce!'

'He also draws chickens. And how did Ayce earn his living? By supplying the castle with eggs!'

'It was an accident,' wept Willelmus. 'A secular jury declared me guilty, but they would have found against me no matter what the evidence, because my trial took place at a time when relations between town and University were strained. But it was an accident!'

'Yes, probably,' agreed Michael. 'The University thought it was a case of self-defence, and was willing to look the other way when you escaped into the Fens. Why did you come back?'

'I fled to London, where I joined the Carmelites to atone for my crime,' replied Willelmus miserably. 'But they transferred me to Cambridge five years ago, to help in the scriptorium here. Fortunately, no one recognised me, and I took care to stay inside the friary as much as possible. But then Sheriff Tulyet demanded a scribe for the taxes . . .'

'Which necessitated coming to the castle,' surmised Bartholomew. 'Where someone *did* recognise you. No wonder you have been driving Dick so hard! You itch to be safe back inside your sanctuary again.'

'I was accosted as I walked home one night,' said Willelmus, wiping his eyes with the back of his hand. 'By a fellow who had been on the jury. He said he would tell Prior Etone my real name unless I did as I was ordered. Yet I have tried to make amends for John Ayce's death! People will see the letters I drew, and will admire the chickens. They are my way of honouring the man I . . .'

'I want the juror's name,' said Michael. He sighed irritably when Willelmus looked frightened again. 'Your secret is out now, and you have confessed to it. The worst has already happened, so what more do you have to lose?'

'I did not know what the raiders intended,' bleated Willelmus. 'I swear it! They just asked questions, and I answered. Besides, this is a big fortress – I assumed it could defend itself.'

'The juror's name,' repeated Michael between gritted teeth.

'Ayera terrifies me,' replied Willelmus, more tears sprouting.

'I am sure he does, but *he* was not on the jury. Now tell me the truth.'

'You are right,' said Willelmus with sudden resolve. 'I have no more to lose, and it is time I faced up to my past. I will tell you the name, but I want to speak to Ayce first, to explain . . .'

'He will not listen,' warned Bartholomew. 'He believes his son was brutally murdered, and you are unlikely to

334

convince him otherwise. Moreover, he is a warrior who is eager to die. It will be dangerous for you.'

'I will be dead when I tell you what I know anyway,' said Willelmus with quiet dignity. 'But I want to make my peace with Ayce first.'

Bartholomew thought it was a bad idea to bring Ayce face to face with his son's killer, but Willelmus was adamant, and Michael was eager to have the information he held. So was Tulyet, when the situation was explained to him.

'It is irregular, but I suppose we can oblige,' he said. 'But answer me one thing first, Willelmus: how did you come by your limp? You claimed you fell down the stairs in the dark. Is it true, or did you grab a sword and fight for these damned marauders?'

That notion coaxed a reluctant smile to Willelmus's pale face, and he pulled up his robe to reveal a badly swollen ankle. 'I *did* fall down the stairs, but not in the dark. My eyesight . . .'

'He is going blind,' said Bartholomew to Tulyet. 'Etone intends to make him Girton's parish priest soon, so that he will have to give up scribing in the hope of saving what little vision he has left.'

'And I would have been miserable,' said Willelmus softly. 'Perhaps it is better this way.'

Tulyet led the way to the dungeon, Willelmus walking between Michael and Sergeant Helbye, dwarfed by both. Bartholomew brought up the rear, convinced they were making a mistake. Ayce was unstable, and he could not see him or Willelmus benefiting from the confrontation.

Ayce stood when the door to his cell was opened, mystified by the arrival of visitors, none of whom spoke as they parted to let Willelmus through. He stared in confusion at the scribe, but then recognition dawned, and his face registered a gamut of emotions – shock, horror and finally rage.

'You mean to torment me by bringing my son's killer here?' he snarled. Bartholomew braced himself to intervene, but Tulyet grabbed his arm and held him back.

'He wants to talk to you,' explained Michael. 'To tell you what happened.'

'I already know what happened,' shouted Ayce, fists clenched at his sides. 'Take him away. I do not want to look at him.'

'I have been living in terror of recognition every day for the past five years,' whispered Willelmus. 'I rarely leave my priory . . .'

'I do not care,' yelled Ayce. 'You may be a friar now, but you are still a killer.'

'Wait, Matt!' hissed Tulyet, when the physician tried a second time to reach for the scribe. 'The sooner Willelmus says his piece, the sooner we can have the information he—'

'John deserved to die!' screamed Willelmus suddenly, lunging forward. 'He was a mindless, bullying, self-serving brute. I could have lived happily here, were it not for *your* bitter ramblings. The pair of you destroyed my life.'

Bartholomew fought free of Tulyet's restraining grip, but it was too late. Willelmus had a knife, and had thrust it into Ayce's chest before the astonished onlookers could stop him. Helbye reacted instinctively. His sword flashed and Willelmus dropped to the ground, even as Tulyet yelled for him to stop. Bartholomew shoved past the sergeant, and went to kneel next to Ayce – he did not need to examine Willelmus to know that he was beyond help.

'You see?' Ayce whispered weakly. 'Hildersham was a killer, and felt no remorse. He would have claimed benefit of clergy a second time, had your soldier not acted.'

'He spent his life drawing your son's initials in books,' said Bartholomew, confused and uncertain. 'And chickens. He said it was to honour John's memory.'

'I doubt his motives were pure,' breathed Ayce. 'Still, at least fear of exposure seems to have tainted the freedom he should never have had. Some justice was served, at least.'

'This should not have happened.' Bartholomew tried to stem the gush of blood from the wound in Ayce's chest, but it was hopeless.

'You were kind to me, so I shall tell you something,' whispered Ayce, almost inaudible. 'You should look to your own house if you want to identify the raiders. Ayera was with us.'

It was not long before his laboured breathing faltered into silence. Bartholomew stood, sickened and angry by what had been allowed to happen.

'I am sorry, Matt,' said Tulyet helplessly. 'I thought the danger would come from Ayce, and it never occurred to me to search Willelmus for weapons. But why did he do it? Surely, only a fool or a madman would commit murder in front of the Sheriff?'

'Because he had nothing to lose,' explained Bartholomew tiredly. 'His days at the scriptorium were numbered because of his failing eyesight, and Prior Etone intended to send him to Girton. But who lives in Girton? The Ayce family.'

'I feel as though I have been used,' said Tulyet in distaste. 'By Willelmus *and* by Ayce – two men who would rather their blood was on my hands than face what their own futures held.'

'Willelmus pretended to be meek, but he was anything but,' said Helbye in the silence that followed. 'Some of the lads were fooling about the other day, teasing him, and he grabbed a sword and drove them back like a lion. It is why I did not hesitate when I saw he had a dagger.'

'You did the right thing,' said Tulyet tiredly. 'He might have turned on us after dispatching Ayce. Unfortunately, we are now deprived of two men who had valuable information.'

'You can find the name of the juror from court records,' said Bartholomew. He was thoughtful. 'However, I suspect the man who really terrified him into a swoon was Ayce. In other words, he fainted from shock when he saw his victim's father.'

'What did Ayce tell you as he breathed his last?' asked Tulyet. 'I tried to listen, but his voice was too low.'

'It was not . . . he was difficult to hear,' mumbled Bartholomew. He was not good at lying.

'Tell me,' ordered Tulyet sharply. 'It is no time for games.'

'He claimed Ayera was among the raiders,' replied Bartholomew unhappily, supposing Tulyet had a right to know, although his stomach twisted with guilt and shame as the words came out.

'Ayera?' echoed Tulyet. 'He must be mistaken!'

'Of course he was,' agreed Michael smoothly. 'And in the interests of harmony between town and University, I recommend that Matt and I look into the matter, Dick. Not you.'

'Very well,' said Tulyet, after a brief moment of reflection. 'But will you send Cynric with news of what you discover? Whatever it may be? The moment you know it?'

'As fast as he can run,' agreed Michael.

'I am sorry, Brother,' said Bartholomew, as he and Michael hurried back to the College to confront Ayera. 'I tried to dissemble, but Dick saw straight through me.'

'It is not you who should be apologising,' said Michael

338

grimly. 'It is Ayera. Thank God we have a Sheriff who appreciates the importance of good relations. Any other secular official would have raced to directly Michaelhouse and made an arrest. I am still furious with him over the rumour he started, but his prudence has gone some way to mollifying me.'

'Our task will not be easy or pleasant,' said Bartholomew. 'And Gyseburne . . .'

'Gyseburne what?' demanded Michael, when Bartholomew trailed off.

'Gyseburne mentioned several men poisoned in Langelee's house in York – by Ayera's cook. They died from eating lily of the valley, which is one of Ayera's favourite flowers.'

'Ayera likes flowers?' asked Michael doubtfully.

Bartholomew nodded. 'Toxic ones. And they grow in Newe Inn's garden, by the pond.'

Michael stared at him. 'What are you saying now? That Ayera killed those four scholars? And that Langelee may have helped him, because they have poisoned people together in the past?'

'We now have three witnesses – Gyseburne, Willelmus and Ayce – who claim that Ayera is involved with the raiders, and Langelee was attacked in Newe Inn, which is where a lot of those particular flowers are growing.'

Michael's eyes were enormous saucers in his plump face. 'Lord, Matt!'

'But Gyseburne does not like Ayera,' said Bartholomew, trying to think of ways to exonerate his colleagues despite the evidence that was beginning to build against them. 'He says he has been afraid of him ever since the incident in York, and I imagine he will be delighted if Ayera is forced to leave the town. Thus he has good reason to twist the truth.'

339

'Perhaps,' nodded Michael. 'Gyseburne is a sly, selfish fellow with a penchant for the wine barrel. He might well lie to incriminate a man who unsettles him.'

Bartholomew was not sure whether it was worse to believe ill of Ayera or Gyseburne, and uncomfortably, it occurred to him that both could not emerge well from the affair.

'No one else knows our suspicion that Northwood and the others were poisoned,' he went on. 'Well, I mentioned it to Julitta, but everyone else seems convinced that the Devil is responsible.'

'Or God,' agreed Michael. 'But what is your point? That Ayera suggested lily of the valley as the culprit, and so incriminated himself by knowing the real cause of death?'

'It crossed my mind,' said Bartholomew unhappily.

'Then we had better hurry,' said Michael grimly, when Bartholomew began to drag his feet.

But Ayera was not home when they arrived, and none of the other Fellows knew where he had gone. Langelee was missing, too, and although it was not unusual for the Master to disappear of an evening – he had many friends, and often went out when work was finished for the day – his absence that night was worrying.

'We need to find them,' said Bartholomew, standing in the conclave and looking around helplessly. Suttone and William were sharing a plate of cakes, and Clippesby was playing with the College cat – back in favour now the rat had deemed places with libraries too dangerous.

'I know, but they might be anywhere,' said Michael, exasperated.

There was a flurry of Gilbertine habit and perfumed accessories as Thelnetham arrived. He flopped into a chair, and waved an imperious hand to say that Clippesby should bring him some wine. It was on the tip of Bartholomew's tongue to tell him to fetch it himself, but Clippesby shot him a warning glance. The Dominican hated discord, and the look said that pandering to Thelnetham's supercilious manners was a small price to pay for peace.

'Have you seen Ayera or Langelee?' Michael demanded.

'Yes,' replied Thelnetham, fanning himself with a beringed hand. 'I passed them when I—'

'Where were they going?' interrupted Michael urgently.

Thelnetham frowned. 'Why? What has Langelee done now? I have always said that he is not the kind of man who should be Master of a College, so it does not surprise me that—'

'Where were they going?' repeated Michael angrily.

'To visit the White Friars,' replied Thelnetham. He made a moue of distaste. 'That particular priory is not a place I would set foot in, because Riborowe and Jorz are hardly conducive company. Of course, our Master is not very particular about—'

'There is nothing wrong with Riborowe and Jorz,' declared Suttone, rallying to the defence of his Carmelite brethren. Then he frowned. 'But Langelee never ventures into our friary. He says we are too religious for his taste.'

'He wanted some ink from its scriptorium,' elaborated Thelnetham. 'Apparently, they have invented a new kind, which is said to dry faster than the stuff Weasenham sells.'

'It is red, too,' put in Clippesby. 'And Master Langelee likes red.'

'Probably because it looks like blood,' said Thelnetham with haughty contempt. 'Once a soldier, always a soldier.'

'He *does* like red pigments,' agreed Suttone. 'Agatha complained to me not an hour ago that he had just handed her a tabard that was drenched in the stuff.'

He and Thelnetham began a discussion about annoying stains, but Bartholomew did not wait to hear it. He strode quickly through the hall and clattered down the stairs to the yard, aware of Michael behind him, especially once he started along Milne Street and the monk began to pant.

'I still do not believe it,' he said, his mind a whirl of confusion. 'I cannot see Ayera or Langelee stealing the King's taxes. Men died in that raid.'

'"Only soldiers".' Michael echoed the geometrician's chillingly callous words and Bartholomew recalled that he had been so shocked to hear them from the lips of a scholar that he had reported it to the monk. 'Men who are expendable in battle.'

Bartholomew began to move faster, leaving Michael behind. When he arrived at the Carmelite Priory, he rapped hard on the gate. The doorman took his time answering, and Michael had caught up by the time the grille slid open.

'God save us!' the doorman muttered, crossing himself. 'How did you know you were needed? We only discovered what happened a few moments ago. Perhaps the Corpse Examiner *does* have diabolical powers, and can detect the scent of cadavers.'

Bartholomew was too fraught to ask what he meant. 'Are Langelee and Ayera here?'

The doorman grunted as he removed the heavy bar that secured the convent after sunset. He yanked open the gate and indicated they were to enter. 'No, why?'

'Have they left?' asked Bartholomew.

'I have not seen them. Of course, they could have come in when I was doing my rounds.'

There was a shout, and Etone trotted towards them, all agitated hand gestures and swirling habit. 'How did you know? We have only just discovered it ourselves.'

'That is just what I said,' muttered the doorman, crossing himself again.

'How did we know about what?' demanded Michael.

'Come with me, Brother,' said Etone grimly. 'You, too, Matthew.'

They followed him to the scriptorium. The light had begun to fade, so work was finished for the day: lids were on inkpots, pens were laid in neat rows ready for the morning, and half-finished books and scrolls were locked in a chest for safekeeping. At the far end of the room was the little chamber where Jorz and Riborowe experimented. Etone beckoned them towards it.

Jorz was lying face-down in a bowl of ink. He had been sitting at a table, and there was a spoon in his right hand: he had evidently been stirring his potion when he had pitched forward. Red pigment was splattered everywhere.

Carefully, Bartholomew pulled Jorz upright. He was cool to the touch, and there was a stiffness around the jaws that suggested death had occurred some time before. The scribe's face was stained bright scarlet, and the sight was so disturbing that Bartholomew covered it with a cloth.

'We finished work early today, to decorate the chapel for Corpus Christi,' Riborowe sobbed. 'But Jorz stayed behind, because we had an experiment running.'

'He was keen to perfect his invention,' said Etone sadly. 'He told me he was going to work for as long as the light allowed. I wish I had refused, then he would not have died alone.'

'I came to see how he was getting on the moment we had finished the chapel,' wept Riborowe. 'But he must have had a seizure, and dropped face-down into his ink.'

'Is that possible, Matt?' asked Michael uncertainly.

Bartholomew nodded. 'The cause of death does appear

to be drowning, and the bowl is deep enough to submerge his nose and mouth.'

'It could happen to any of us, at any time,' said Etone. He whispered a brief prayer.

'Did you make any attempt to pull him out, perhaps to see whether he was still breathing?' asked Bartholomew, studying the explosion of droplets and smears around the bowl.

'We could see he was dead, so we did not try,' said Etone. 'I thought it would be more helpful if you saw him just as he was discovered.'

'It *is* helpful; thank you,' said Bartholomew, homing in on a clue that would have been lost if the body had been moved. 'Jorz said he preferred to draw with his left hand, and was clumsy with his right. Yet he is holding the spoon in his right hand.'

'That means nothing.' Riborowe wiped his eyes with his sleeve. 'He often poured with one hand, while stirring with the other. Like most of us, he was adept with both.'

'But there is nothing on the table for him to pour,' said Bartholomew. 'He was stirring only. And even if he was two-handed, it is natural to perform such a task with the dominant one.'

'Why are you asking these questions?' Etone was beginning to look alarmed. 'Surely, you do not think someone did this to him? That he was murdered?'

'Batayl!' cried Riborowe immediately. 'They do not believe we are innocent of killing Coslaye, and now Browne is missing. They think we dispatched him, too, and they killed Jorz in revenge!'

'Batayl did not do this,' said Michael quickly, although Bartholomew recalled that Browne had crept into the scriptorium on a previous occasion and made Jorz jump violently enough to burn himself. It was entirely possible

344

that he had done it again, this time with fatal consequences – assuming he was still alive himself, of course.

'I agree,' said Etone quietly. 'The Batayl men are unpleasant, but they are not killers.'

'Regardless,' said Riborowe, suddenly fearful, 'Jorz's death is another connected to libraries.'

'What do you mean?' demanded Michael, narrowing his eyes.

'I refer to the rumour that libraries are dangerous places,' began Riborowe. 'And—'

'This is a scriptorium, not a library,' interrupted Michael.

'It is a place associated with books,' countered Riborowe.

Etone crossed himself. 'Perhaps God *is* trying to tell us something with all these accidents.'

'Accidents?' hissed Michael in Bartholomew's ear. 'I detect a human hand at work in this – and not one directed by the Almighty, either.'

'Have you seen Langelee this evening?' asked Bartholomew. 'Or Ayera?'

'I think I saw Langelee cross our yard earlier,' said Etone, clearly taken aback by the question out of the blue. 'But I may have been mistaken. Why?'

'Because we need to speak to him,' replied Michael when Bartholomew hesitated, not sure what to say. 'In fact, we were looking for him when your doorman dragged us in to inspect Jorz.'

'Well, if he appears, we shall pass the word that you want him,' offered Etone agreeably.

Bartholomew helped two lay-brothers load Jorz on to a bier, to be carried to the chapel. Then, while Riborowe organised vigils and prayers for his dead friend's soul, Etone accompanied the Michaelhouse men to the gate.

'I suspect Jorz's seizure was induced by the noxious substances he put in his ink,' the Prior confided as they

345

walked. 'Some of them reeked, but he always resisted my efforts to encourage him into the fresh air. Northwood used to say the same, but Jorz never listened.'

'Well, Matt?' demanded Michael, once he and Bartholomew were outside and alone again. It was almost dark. 'What do you really think?'

'That Etone may be right: Jorz was using red lead in his ink, and that is very toxic. Perhaps he did faint from lack of clean air and toppled forward to drown. Or perhaps someone crept up behind him, and held his head in the basin until he stopped breathing. If the latter is true, whoever it was will be splattered with red ink – you saw the mess on the table.'

Michael was worried. 'Suttone said that Langelee gave Agatha some ink-stained clothes to wash this evening. And Etone thought he saw him in the friary earlier. We *must* find him, and demand to know what is going on.'

'Find him where?' asked Bartholomew, equally anxious. 'He might be anywhere. I will set Cynric to track him down, but he may not even be in the town.'

'You mean he might have gone with Ayera to meet the raiders in the Fens?'

'It is possible. Regardless, I have a terrible feeling that he is in danger – that Ayera has enmeshed him in something he does not fully understand and that may prove fatal to him. Perhaps Ayera killed Jorz, and Langelee tried to stop him. That would explain the inky clothes.'

'Yes, it would.' But Michael did not look convinced.

'We are out of our depth here, Brother. Where is Dame Pelagia? We need her help.'

Michael winced. 'Unfortunately, Browne, Langelee and Ayera are not the only ones who have disappeared. I cannot find my grandmother, either.'

*   *   *

Knowing it would be impossible to locate Langelee and Ayera on their own, Michael reluctantly enlisted the help of the other Fellows. He silenced their objections by furnishing a terse account of what Gyseburne, Willelmus and Ayce had claimed, adding that Ayera had not been the only Michaelhouse man to roam the town at odd hours, because the Master had been doing it, too.

'I knew it!' hissed Thelnetham, when the monk had finished. 'I knew the villain in that pair would not lie dormant for long. And now they harm the rest of us by association.'

'Let us not jump to conclusions,' said Father William warningly. 'Nothing has been proven.'

'Quite,' agreed Clippesby. 'Ayera has been meeting dangerous men in dark places for the last two months or so, because the rat told me, but there will be an innocent explanation.'

Michael rounded on him. 'What have you seen, exactly.'

Clippesby looked more lunatic than ever that evening, with spiky hair and wild eyes. 'The rat saw robbers prowling, and Ayera was with them. But when I told the Sheriff, he said she was mistaken, because his patrols would have seen them, too. However, it was easy for the raiders to avoid his officers, because they knew which routes they would take. I heard them say so.'

'Willelmus,' said Bartholomew to Michael. 'He overheard Dick's plans and passed them on.'

'I wish I was in a normal College,' muttered Thelnetham. 'But no, I am at Michaelhouse, whose Fellows chat to vermin and consort with thieves. What did I do to deserve this?'

'Well, you dress like a woman, for a start,' replied William, who did not understand the concept of a rhetorical question. 'And God does not like it. However, you had better be discreet with what you have learned about the Master and Ayera tonight. If their antics become public, it will signal the end of our College.'

'Oh, I shall be discreet,' said Thelnetham bitterly. 'I have my own reputation to think of. Where do you want us to look for these rogues, Brother? And what shall we do if we find them?'

'Bring them home,' replied Michael. 'I shall be waiting.'

'What if they decline to come?' asked Suttone anxiously. 'I shall point out that the game is up, and that their only recourse is to return to Michaelhouse, but what if they refuse? We can hardly remove them by force. They are warriors!'

'Fetch me, so I can do the explaining.' Michael began to assign tasks. 'William will look in the taverns, Suttone will explore the brothels—'

'Really?' asked Suttone, brightening. 'Perhaps this will not be such a terrible night after all.'

'Matt can visit those hostels where Langelee has friends, Thelnetham will make enquiries in the Colleges, and Clippesby will take the convents. Now go – and remember that no one must know why we are looking, or we shall be ruined for certain.'

It was a long and unrewarding night. Langelee was a friendly soul, with many acquaintances, and Bartholomew trudged from hostel to hostel, knocking on doors if lamps burned within, and listening outside when the buildings were in darkness. He persisted for hours, ignoring the rational voice at the back of his mind that told him he was wasting his time.

Tulyet's soldiers and Michael's beadles were out in force, and it was not easy to convince them that he was visiting patients every time they met. Eventually, he hid in doorways or crouched behind rubbish heaps when he heard them coming, and was alarmed when he discovered how easy it was to elude them. No wonder the raiders had been able to reconnoitre so efficiently!

It was during the darkest part of the short summer night that he ran into trouble. He had just endured a fruitless foray to Maud's Hostel, an establishment favoured by wealthy men of low intelligence – Langelee had always felt at home there – when he saw shadows moving at the end of the street. They were clad in short cloaks, and all wore hoods to conceal their faces. He froze, then eased forward, trying to remember Cynric's lessons about stealth as he aimed to get close enough to eavesdrop. They were speaking French.

'. . . for tonight,' one was saying. 'And then she will tell us all we need to know.'

'I doubt it,' another replied with conviction. His voice was familiar, but Bartholomew could not place it. 'Do you not know who she is?'

'Just some crone who will have her throat cut once we have drained her of information,' said the first. 'But it is your fault she overheard us talking. I told you that someone was watching, and you should have heeded me.'

'It was—' The second man broke off suddenly. 'She is escaping! Stop her!'

A small shape scuttled from the base of a wall, and Bartholomew thought he could make out a pile of discarded ropes. However, while Dame Pelagia was remarkably spry for a woman of her age, she was no match for men in their prime. He saw they were going to catch her again, and reacted instinctively, hauling a knife from his bag and racing forward. Too late, it occurred to him that *he* was no match for so many villains, either.

349

'Here they are!' he yelled over his shoulder to non-existent help. 'We can take them now!'

He did not know whether he was more relieved or surprised when the invaders promptly melted away. He continued shouting, and it was not long before the racket drew Tulyet's guards. Shakily, he jabbed a finger in the direction the robbers had taken, although he doubted they would be caught now. He leaned against a wall, his legs like jelly once the danger was over.

'That was brave,' said Pelagia, materialising at his side and making him jump. 'They would have caught me again, which would not have been pleasant.'

'Were you spying on them?' he asked, trying to control the unsteadiness in his voice.

'Of course. Unfortunately, they said nothing of value, and I still do not know their identities, their plans or the whereabouts of their camp. I was careless in my eagerness to learn, and I tripped over some rubbish. I must be getting old.'

'What will you do now?' asked Bartholomew.

'Go to bed.' Despite her efforts to conceal it, he could hear the exhaustion in her voice. 'They will have left the town by now, so there is no point in my staying out any longer.'

'Michael was worried when he could not find you earlier.'

'He is a dear boy, but he need not concern himself. Will you give him a message? Tell him that I am sure there will be another raid during Corpus Christi, and that the tales claiming that their previous failure means they are too frightened to try again are a nonsense.'

'I do not suppose you have seen Langelee this evening, have you?' asked Bartholomew.

Pelagia shook her head. 'But I imagine he is tucked up in bed with someone else's wife.'

350

Bartholomew escorted her to the inn where she was staying, then turned towards Michaelhouse. He had done all he could that night.

The other Fellows had also decided that the hunt for Langelee and Ayera was a waste of time, and most had retired to their rooms by the time Bartholomew arrived home. Michael was in the hall, the bestiary from Bene't College open in front of him. Rolee's blood had been meticulously scoured off it.

'I shall stay here, just in case Ayera and Langelee decide to return,' he said tiredly. 'But you should rest. One of us should be alert tomorrow, because it is the day before Corpus Christi, and if we do not have answers then, we shall have trouble for certain.'

'I think we shall have it anyway,' said Bartholomew worriedly. 'Solving the murders will make no difference one way or the other now.'

'I disagree. The armed raiders may still attack, but presenting our scholars with a culprit for these suspicious deaths will soothe troubled waters. *Ergo*, it is imperative that we succeed. But I cannot stop thinking about Jorz. Etone may be right: perhaps he did have a seizure.'

'Perhaps, but he was a healthy man with no history of them. Moreover, it is suspicious that he should die now, after what happened to Rolee, Teversham, Sawtre and Kente. All look like mishaps, but there are too many of them to be innocent.'

'Yes,' agreed Michael sombrely. 'But rest now, Matt, or you will be no good to me tomorrow.'

Bartholomew fell into a restless sleep, and was awake long before the bell chimed for mass the following morning, staring at the ceiling and trying to make sense of the jumble of facts he had accumulated. He kept coming

351

back to Holm, whom he had caught out in several lies and who was certainly ruthless enough to kill to suit himself. He tried to be objective, analysing the information from different angles, but the surgeon seemed to be the guilty party whichever way he viewed it.

Langelee and Ayera were still missing when the scholars assembled to process to the church, and so was Clippesby. The Dominican had not been seen since he had given up his trawl of the convents the previous night, when he had told William that he was going to visit some bats.

'You know what he is like,' said William apologetically. 'I tried to tell him it would be safer to come home, but he would not listen. And I was too weary to reason with him.'

They attended their daily devotions, which went on longer than usual because Suttone was officiating and he was inclined to be wordy – and there was no Langelee to hurry him along with impatient sighs and meaningful glares. When the ceremony was finally over, Cynric was waiting to tell Bartholomew that Holm had visited the wounded men in the castle, and had meddled with their dressings. Several were now in pain.

Bartholomew strode there quickly, aware that the streets were busier than they had been the previous day. The atmosphere was curious – a mixture of fear and unease from those who had possessions to lose if the raid did occur; and happy expectancy from those with nothing, who were looking forward to the celebrations that had been so long in the planning.

Determined to have the pennies folk had been hoarding for the occasion before anything went wrong, the Guild of Corpus Christi had decided to start the festivities early. Bakers' ovens were going full blast, ale was being sold in the churchyards, portable stalls were open to sell trinkets, and entertainers were ready with their miracle plays. The taverns were open, too, and there was a maypole near the Round Church where a band of musicians filled the air with a lively jig.

'It was not his fault,' said a pale Julitta, when Bartholomew arrived at the castle and regarded Holm's handiwork with dismay. 'He was trying to help.'

'She is an angel,' murmured Tulyet in Bartholomew's ear. 'She visits my men every day, and they rally when they see her. It is a pity her fiancé is rather less adept with the sick.'

Bartholomew unbound the dressings, appalled by the amount of 'healing balm' Holm had slathered on the wounds. It smelled rank, and took him some time to rinse off. Julitta helped, but said little, and he saw she was distressed by the patients' suffering. He recalled Michael saying she would be a suspect if Browne transpired to be dead, and wondered how the monk could think ill of such a dignified, compassionate woman.

'He did it last night,' she said, after a while.

Bartholomew had been enjoying her proximity and the soft touch of her hands when their fingers met. Idly, it occurred to him that he had not visited his widow since meeting Julitta, and was surprised to discover that he had not thought of her once. The realisation made him ashamed, and he supposed he would have to go to her and explain his recent neglect, although he did not know what he could say: he could hardly inform her that his mind had been full of another man's bride.

'Who did what last night?' he asked, wondering whether his reverie meant that he had missed part of a discussion.

'My fiancé – he came to minister to the wounded. I was worried when some of the men said their wounds were throbbing afterwards, so I came early this morning, to see how they were. I sent for him when two seemed feverish, but he was out. So I summoned you instead.'

'You did the right thing,' Bartholomew assured her.

'Holm will not touch them again,' vowed Tulyet, when she had gone to fetch clean water. 'He is banned from now on. Julitta is a fool for him – he does not deserve her.'

'No,' agreed Bartholomew, watching her stop to exchange words with Robin. Agatha's nephew was in pain, but her approach made him smile, which said a good deal about the place she had claimed in his heart. In fact, Bartholomew was sure her nursing had made a difference between life and death for some of the wounded, and he was grateful to her for it.

'My wife thinks I should tell her what she is marrying,' Tulyet went on. 'But I doubt she would listen to me. Even her sister cannot make her open her eyes.'

'It is worth a try,' said Bartholomew. '*She* is worth a try.'

'Yes,' agreed Tulyet. 'Although you must remember that her father is a very powerful and decisive man, yet Julitta can wind him around her little finger. She is not a submissive nonentity, but an extremely intelligent, capable and determined young woman.'

'Even more reason for her not to wed Holm, then,' said Bartholomew.

CHAPTER 11

It was evening by the time Bartholomew had finished at the castle, and he left to find Cynric waiting with a message that Isnard needed to see him. The bargeman had taken full advantage of the Guild of Corpus Christi's decision to celebrate early, and had managed to knock himself senseless as he had tottered drunkenly along the towpath.

'The riverfolk found me and brought me home,' he explained feebly.

Bartholomew frowned when he saw the painful-looking lump on the back of Isnard's skull. 'How did you say this happened?'

'I tripped,' explained Isnard. 'One moment I was walking along, thinking about Holm's five-mark bet with you, and the next thing I knew was Torvin looming over me.'

'It is hard to bang the back of your head when walking forward. I suspect you were struck from behind.'

'The bastard!' exclaimed Isnard in sudden indignation. 'He smiled and simpered at me so prettily, too, the Judas!'

'Who did?' asked Bartholomew, applying a poultice to the bump and indicating that Isnard should lie back. He decided to fetch Valence to sit with him, because the blow had been vicious.

'Frevill,' replied Isnard. 'The one who is the carpenter, working at Newe Inn.'

'Why would he hit you?'

Isnard frowned. 'I cannot recall now. Perhaps

355

accusations were made . . . but no, it will not come. The clout he gave me must have knocked it clean out of my head.'

Or the copious quantities of ale he had consumed had addled his wits, Bartholomew thought uncharitably. He left the bargeman and walked back to Michaelhouse, where his students had finished reading the texts he had set them, and were about to escape.

'When was the last time you heard Nicholas's *Antidotarium*?' he asked, raising his hand to stop them. One or two regarded him with expressions that verged on the murderous, although the bulk merely sighed and looked resigned.

Valence brightened, though, seeing an avenue of escape. 'We consulted it this week, when you mentioned poisoning by lily of the valley.'

'Consulting is not the same as reading,' said Bartholomew, and set them a section that he could manage easily in an hour, blithely unaware that it would take them considerably longer.

They slouched back to the hall with faces like thunder, while Valence danced towards the gate, delighted to be granted a reprieve in the guise of monitoring Isnard. Then Michael approached, grey with fatigue and scowling.

'Where have you been all day? I have been racing all over the town like a bluebottle, trying to investigate murder and find our errant colleagues. It would have been good to have had your help.'

'Shall we resume our hunt for Ayera and Langelee tonight, Brother?' asked William, coming to join them before Bartholomew could reply. The other Fellows – except Clippesby – were at his heels. 'Thelnetham has offered to stay here and supervise our students, if you think we should.'

'Our lads should not be allowed out this evening,' explained Thelnetham. 'Far too much ale has been swallowed by the town's rowdier elements, and the streets do not feel safe.'

'I agree,' said Suttone. 'So I shall stay in, too, while the rest of you find Langelee and Ayera. I am not very good at fighting, and I am exhausted anyway, from exploring brothels all last night.'

William sniggered, and Bartholomew supposed the Carmelite did look rather the worse for wear, although a gleam in his eye said the experience had not been altogether unpleasant. Despite his habit, Suttone liked the company of ladies.

'I do not want anyone out tonight,' said Michael. 'Servants, students or Fellows. Langelee and Ayera will just have to fend for themselves.'

'We shall keep everyone in,' promised William. 'How long will it be for, do you think? Until after Corpus Christi? Or shall we wait until the next raid is finished before venturing out?'

'The robbers may not come again,' said Suttone, although with scant conviction.

'They will,' countered William. 'The only question is when. Personally, I think it will be tomorrow night, when everyone has had too much to drink – for then we will struggle to mount any form of defence.'

'No,' countered Thelnetham, unwilling to let anything uttered by the Franciscan pass unchallenged. 'It will be during the pageant or the opening of the library.'

'In daylight?' scoffed William. 'I do not think so!'

'These men are professional and ruthless,' argued Thelnetham. 'They have taken care to hide their faces thus far, but they may decide that anonymity will not matter once they have fired the town and slaughtered all its inhabitants. They will launch their assault during the ceremonies, because that is when they are least expected – and when they will have the element of surprise.'

'But they have already lost it,' objected William. 'We all know they are coming.'

'Yes, but we do not know exactly when,' persisted Thelnetham. 'And during the festivities, all the soldiers and beadles will be struggling to monitor the crowds, so they will be too busy to notice anything else. The robbers will use this as a diversion to launch their assault.'

'Our beadles will certainly be distracted if the Common Library's opponents use these murders as an excuse to disrupt the opening ceremony,' said Suttone soberly. 'Its supporters will retaliate, and the resulting fracas will involve every member of the University.'

Michael groaned and put his head in his hands. 'That means I have one night to find our killer, because Suttone is right: a brawl will provide exactly the "diversion" these villains want.'

'Cancel the opening,' said William. 'Indeed, cancel the library. It never was a sensible idea.'

'I wish I could,' sighed Michael. 'But Chancellor Tynkell has made promises that are difficult to break, and wealthy townsmen will never give us anything again if we spoil Dunning's day.'

'That may not matter,' warned William, 'if we have no University left to receive gifts.'

Michael groaned again. 'Thank God Tynkell is retiring soon, because I cannot work with a Chancellor who meddles. Shame on him and his desire to make a name for himself!'

'The name he makes will not be a good one if his library opens in a welter of blood,' said William ghoulishly. 'But do not worry about Michaelhouse, Brother. We Fellows will keep it safe.'

'And do not look so glum,' added Suttone kindly. 'You will catch your villain. No sly killer will best our intrepid Senior Proctor.'

'I am not so sure,' said Michael unhappily. 'I have a very bad feeling about this whole affair.'

Because Michael was silent as they left the College, Bartholomew confided his suspicions about Holm, thinking it would do no harm to review the evidence against the surgeon.

'You want Holm to be guilty, because you have taken a fancy to Julitta,' said Michael acidly. 'And you do not want him to wed her.'

'You are right: I do not want her life spoiled by a man who only wants to inherit her father's money,' Bartholomew snapped back. 'However, it has nothing to do with my—'

'Do not dissemble with me. However, while I appreciate that Holm as the villain will please you – especially as you will save five marks if he is hanged – the fact is that there is no proof.'

'Of course there is proof,' said Bartholomew impatiently. 'He is not a real surgeon for a start, yet he still wanders the town at night on the pretext of seeing patients. It must be because he is spying for the invaders. Moreover, he arrived on Easter Day, which is when the raiders claimed their first victim. And he lies about his whereabouts.'

'Explain,' ordered Michael.

'Dunning wanted help with reorganising the pageant after the attack on the castle, but Holm excused himself on the grounds that he would be with the injured. At the time, I assumed it was simple indolence, but now I wonder if he had another motive.'

'Not necessarily. He *is* lazy – he was napping yesterday when we visited in the middle of the day, so he probably lied to secure himself a good night's sleep. Or a frolic with Browne.'

'Then what about the fact that Browne is missing? Perhaps Browne discovered Holm's guilt, and was killed to ensure the secret was shared with no one else.'

'That is not proof, Matt. It is rank supposition without a shred of evidence.'

'He pestered me and the other physicians for the wild-fire formula,' Bartholomew went on, determined to make Michael see his point of view. 'He started the moment he found out what we had done, and was talking about it just before I was first ambushed. Perhaps he was among the three who threatened to—'

'Again, there is no proof.'

'The singers,' persisted Bartholomew. 'He hired singers to entertain Walkelate and his people on the night that Northwood, the Londons and Vale died. Obviously, he did it to mask any noise he might make while he poisoned them.'

Michael shot him a sidelong glance. 'Julitta must really have captured your heart! It is unlike you to draw wild conclusions from such scant evidence.'

Bartholomew did not respond, reluctantly conceding that perhaps his dislike of Holm *did* stem from his admiration for Julitta, and it was jealousy speaking. Yet he knew, with every fibre of his being, that there was something amiss with the surgeon, something dark and unpleasant.

'We had better go to Cholles Lane again,' said Michael. 'The more I think about it, the more I feel that place holds the key to unravelling our mysteries.'

'Yes – it is where Holm lives,' pounced Bartholomew.

This time it was Michael's turn not to reply. They met Clippesby as they turned the corner. The Dominican looked fretful, and his habit was stained with wet mud.

360

'Frevill,' he said without preamble. 'As we could not find Langelee or Ayera, I decided to watch for reconnoitring raiders instead. The water voles invited me to hide near their homes.'

'They should not have done,' said Bartholomew, worried for him. 'These robbers are dangerous men.'

'Very,' agreed Clippesby soberly. 'They even bested Dame Pelagia, although you helped her escape. I was glad, because the voles and I could not have done it.'

'What is this?' asked Michael, alarmed.

Bartholomew waved him quiet. 'What did you hear? What is this about Frevill?'

'He is one of the raiders,' replied Clippesby. 'The voles saw his face quite clearly. He was talking to several other armed men here, in Cholles Lane, and he was issuing them with orders.'

'Which Frevill?' asked Michael. 'The Master of the Guild of Corpus Christi, who has been spiriting his family and valuables out of harm's way these past two days? Perhaps because he knows for a fact what is about to befall his town?'

'No, his carpenter kinsman, who works at the Common Library,' replied Clippesby.

'I imagine he would be too weary for such antics,' said Michael dismissively, beginning to walk away. 'Walkelate has been driving his artisans very hard.'

'Wait!' said Bartholomew urgently. 'Isnard claimed Frevill hit him earlier, and knocked him out of his wits.'

'Why would Frevill do that?' asked Michael, bemused.

Bartholomew thought fast. 'Isnard must have seen or heard something he should not have done. Unfortunately, he was too drunk to make sense of it. The blow was a vicious one, and I think Frevill meant to kill him – which means he must have wanted Isnard silenced very badly.'

'Quite,' said Clippesby softly. 'Isnard is lucky his throat was not cut, too, like poor Adam, the beggar and the night-watchman.'

Michael was silent for a moment, thinking, then he turned to Clippesby. 'Tell the Sheriff what you saw. But please do it properly: say what *you* witnessed, and leave the water voles out of it.'

'Yes, Brother.' Clippesby sped away.

Michael looked down Cholles Lane. 'I was right about this place, Matt. There is something untoward unfolding here.'

As the evening shadows lengthened, Bartholomew and Michael walked up the library stairs to find Walkelate sitting by the *cista*. He was alone, and the place felt oddly abandoned without craftsmen and apprentices bustling about. Even Aristotle, gazing down from his lofty perch, seemed forlorn.

'The work is finished at last,' Walkelate said softly. 'Although Kente's death has cast a pall over it, and I shall not enjoy the opening ceremony without him at my side.'

'I am afraid I have more bad news for you,' said Michael. 'We have just learned that Frevill has been consorting with the raiders.'

Walkelate gave a pained smile. 'I appreciate your efforts at humour, Brother, but I am not in the mood. And that is not a particularly amusing joke, anyway. Frevill is—'

'It is no joke,' said Michael. 'We have a reliable . . . we have a witness. Where is Frevill?'

Walkelate's kindly face crumpled into a mask of dismay. 'But he cannot be involved with the robbers! He has been toiling with me these last six weeks, and has had no time to—'

'You do not work at night.' Michael interrupted a

362

second time. 'Which is when this gang meets local trai-tors, who guide them around the town, pointing out our weaknesses.'

'No! I will not believe this!' Walkelate turned at the sound of feet on the stairs. 'Dunning! Thank God! Brother Michael is saying some terrible things about Frevill. Please stop him.'

'What nonsense!' exclaimed Dunning, when Michael had repeated his accusations. 'You have been working too hard, Brother, and it has addled your wits.'

'He is right,' said Walkelate kindly. 'Perhaps a rest will—'

'We cannot rest,' said Michael shortly. 'Our scholars are still bitterly divided over this wretched library, and there will be trouble unless we can pre-empt it.'

'There will be no trouble,' stated Dunning impatiently. 'When your scholars see this fine building, even its most fervent detractors will change their minds. It will be a fabulous success, and Walkelate and I will be hailed as visionaries for seeing it through.'

'Do you think so?' asked Walkelate dubiously. 'Because I am extremely nervous. Suppose people say there is too much beech? Or that the shelves are too low . . .'

'When did you last see Frevill?' demanded Michael, not interested in the architect's insecurities. 'And please think carefully, because the safety of our town may depend on it.'

Walkelate gulped. 'Last night. I told him he need not come today, as we have finished.'

'I have not seen him, either,' said Dunning. 'But he has lived in Cambridge all his life, and would never harm it. His family is powerful and respected here.'

'Look for Frevill in the stationer's shop,' said Walkelate suddenly. 'The Carmelites promised labels for our shelves, but Jorz's death has thrown them into confusion. Frevill mentioned last night that he might ask Weasenham to provide us with an alternative set.'

'He may have gone to order them, I suppose,' said Dunning. 'He *was* worried that the Carmelites would not fulfil their obligations in time.'

Walkelate stood. 'I shall come with you to find out.'

Bartholomew and Michael set off at a trot towards the High Street, the architect at their heels. Neither Michaelhouse man spoke. Michael was too breathless from what was a very rapid pace, while Bartholomew's mind was teeming with questions and worries. Their silence allowed Walkelate to indulge in an agitated monologue about the height of his shelves.

It was dusk, and the holiday atmosphere had intensified since morning: people were determined to enjoy themselves no matter what. Most were armed, though, and Bartholomew was alarmed to see that many scholars were, too, despite the fact that they could be fined for carrying knives, swords and sticks. All were heading home, however, and it would not be long before the streets were deserted.

They reached Weasenham's shop to find its windows shuttered, and the stationer escorting out the last of his customers. It was Riborowe, laden down with several heavy packages.

'Someone has started a rumour that the Devil haunts our priory,' Riborowe said angrily. Weasenham's face went suspiciously bland. 'But Jorz and Northwood were *not* killed by Satan.'

'Well, they did not die because libraries are dangerous, either,' said Walkelate firmly. 'Whoever started that stupid story is a wicked villain who deserves to rot in Hell for his lies. I only hope the tale does not prevent people from using Newe Inn.'

'I wish I owned a ribauldequin,' muttered Riborowe, regarding the architect with naked hatred. 'I would set it on our highest wall, and blast anyone who entered that accursed place.'

'You would be just as likely to blast yourself,' Walkelate flashed back. 'You know as well as I do that those machines are extremely unreliable and a danger to their operators.'

'Yet you still helped Sheriff Tulyet to build one,' said Bartholomew, a little sharply.

'Because I could see that he would make dangerous mistakes without me,' explained Walkelate. 'What would you have done? Let him produce a device that would definitely maim its crew? Or help him devise one that would at least give them a fighting chance?'

'Bartholomew would have produced one that kills soldiers on both sides,' said Riborowe unpleasantly, before the physician could think of a suitable reply. 'Because that would please Satan.'

The Carmelite put his head in the air and sailed away while Bartholomew winced. Weasenham was listening, and would almost certainly repeat the remark to his other customers.

Unwilling to ask his questions in the street, Michael barrelled past the stationer and entered the shop. There was a brief scuffle within, and Bonabes and Ruth shot away from each other. Surreptitiously, Ruth straightened her clothing.

'Have you seen Frevill?' demanded Michael, ignoring their mortification. 'The carpenter?'

'Yes – he came to commission some shelf labels not long ago,' replied Weasenham. His eyes narrowed when he saw the information was important. 'Why?'

'Did he say where he was going next?' asked Bartholomew urgently.

'He did,' said Weasenham, looking from monk, to physician and then to architect with a face full of open curiosity. 'But I will not tell you unless you explain why you want to know.'

'Then I shall answer,' said Ruth, shooting her husband an admonishing look. 'He said he was going for a nice ride in the Fens, as Master Walkelate had given him a free day.'

Walkelate smiled at Michael. 'You see? Frevill is innocent of your horrible suspicions after all. He is just enjoying a little peace after the fever of finishing our work.'

But Bartholomew disagreed. 'No one rides into the Fens when the sun is about to set. He is almost certainly going to meet the raiders.'

'Raiders?' pounced Weasenham. 'Frevill is one of them? I heard Coslaye had joined—'

'You are mistaken, Doctor,' cried Bonabes, horrified. 'Frevill is a good man – kind and hard-working. He is not the sort of fellow to join assaults on the King's taxes.'

'I agree,' said Ruth. Then she frowned. 'Although he said one strange thing . . . He was talking to another customer in the shop, and I heard him say that the University was about to learn its lesson. I thought it was an odd remark, but perhaps with hindsight . . .'

'He must have meant learn them in the library,' explained Walkelate patiently. 'It is a place of education, after all.'

'No,' said Ruth. 'There was something in his voice that was rather more . . . more menacing.'

'Damn Tulyet and his ruse!' muttered Michael. 'It has worked – the raiders have decided to attack the University now that they believe that the King's taxes are no longer in the castle!'

'But that would be impossible,' said Walkelate

dismissively. 'The University is a scattered entity, with no identifiable centre. And the greater part of it comprises poverty-stricken hostels.'

'What about the library?' suggested Bartholomew. 'That might be seen as a secure building in which to hide large chests of coins. It has thick walls and a sturdy door, after all.'

Walkelate shook his head. 'You are panicking over nothing. There will be no raid.'

'I beg to differ,' said Michael. 'And I intend to warn every College, convent and hostel in our *studium generale* to be on their guard.'

It was dark when they left Weasenham's shop, and even in the short time that they had been inside, the streets had emptied considerably. Bartholomew detected an uneasiness among those who were still out, and the town felt dangerous and uninviting.

'Where are you going?' demanded Michael, when he set off towards the Great Bridge. 'We need to ensure that every scholar in the University knows what might happen tomorrow.'

'To tell Dick Tulyet what Ruth just said about Frevill.'

'Very well.' Michael sketched a quick benediction, then began to hurry in the direction of St Mary the Great, calling over his shoulder, 'But watch out for ambushers.'

Bartholomew kept to the shadows. It was an unsettling journey. He jumped every time there was an odd sound – and the night was full of them: whimpering dogs, the creak of the sign above the Griffin tavern, the squawk of a startled bird, a slithering sound made by a fox among some rubbish. He was relieved when he reached the castle, although as he approached it he felt he was being watched by dozens of hidden eyes. It was not a comfortable feeling.

'You should not be wandering about alone,' Tulyet admonished Bartholomew, who had stated his purpose to at least four guards before being allowed inside. The Sheriff wore full armour, and his broadsword was strapped to his waist. He appeared calm and confident, although Bartholomew detected the tension within him. 'It is asking to be attacked again.'

'Frevill the carpenter is one of the raiders,' explained Bartholomew tersely. 'And there is reason to believe that they will attack the University next. Your trick worked well, it seems.'

Tulyet winced. 'Then Michael will have his hands full tomorrow. There will be trouble at the library ceremony anyway, and if the raiders attack while your scholars are skirmishing . . .'

'Will you help him?'

'I shall do what I can, but I must bear in mind that this intelligence may be a canard, to draw me out of the castle, thus leaving it vulnerable. And the King's taxes are still in the Great Tower.'

Bartholomew's stomach churned; he was sure that the beadles and academics would be all but powerless against the professional warriors who had so efficiently stormed the bailey.

'Have you learned any more about the raiders?' he asked.

Tulyet shook his head. 'But they have picked a good time to invade. Normally, we could repel them by putting rein-forcements on the town gates, but the dry weather of the last few days means that the river and the King's Ditch are low – shallow enough to wade across without recourse to—'

He was interrupted by an echoing boom, and there was a flicker of red over the eastern wall. For a moment, nothing happened, then there was a curious whooshing sound, and something plummeted into the bailey, flinging up a great spray of earth that made both him and Bartholomew dive for cover. Pebbles and soil pattered all around them. When it stopped, they scrambled to their feet to see a small lump of rock, half buried in the hole it had made.

'What in God's name . . .' began Tulyet.

'Artillery!' exclaimed Bartholomew. 'I saw it used at Poitiers. I imagine that missile came from a bombard.'

'God's tears!' exclaimed Tulyet, appalled. 'Who *are* these men?'

Tulyet began to yell orders to his guards, who were gazing in open-mouthed shock at the spectacle. Then there was a second boom, and a stone hit the wall outside with an almighty crack. The sound jolted the garrison into action and they raced to carry out Tulyet's commands. Within moments, the castle was alive with activity. Some soldiers were detailed to draw buckets of water to douse fires, others were moving horses to a safer place, while others still were breaking out weapons from the armoury. Bartholomew felt a sword thrust into his hand.

'No!' he exclaimed in alarm, trying to pass it back.

'You do not want to be unarmed tonight, believe me,' said Sergeant Helbye tartly. 'You may need to defend yourself.'

After a while, another projectile slammed into the eastern wall. It made a terrible noise, but Tulyet's engineers peered over the parapet and shouted that there was no appreciable harm.

'What are they trying to do, Matt?' demanded Tulyet. 'You have seen these infernal machines in action. Do they intend to shatter my walls, then pour through the breach?'

'Not unless they plan to be here a while. Bombards do

369

not have the power of trebuchets, or the ability to cause widespread injuries like ribauldequins.'

'Then why bother?' asked Tulyet, white-faced.

'To unsettle you, probably. You have not seen artillery deployed before, and they anticipate that you will not know how to react.'

Tulyet scowled. 'Then they will discover that I am not as easily dismayed as the French.'

'Unless . . .' Bartholomew regarded Tulyet in alarm. 'Do you think this is a ruse, to keep you inside while the real attack is elsewhere? It does not take many men to handle one of those devices, leaving the bulk of the robbers free to do as they please.'

Tulyet stared back. 'In other words, I shall later be accused of cowering inside my stronghold, while the town and its University is razed to the ground.'

He whipped around to issue more orders, and Bartholomew found himself included in the party that was to venture outside. He was grateful, no more keen to skulk in the castle than the Sheriff. He followed Tulyet through the Gatehouse, and was certain his suspicions were right when they met no resistance. Sergeant Helbye led a small group east, to work their way behind where they thought the bombard was set. The rest followed Tulyet down the hill, towards the Great Bridge.

'The watchman!' cried Bartholomew, hurrying over to a dark shape on the ground. The fellow was dead, and his companions were in their shelter, too frightened to come out.

'There was a whole army of them, sir!' cried one, when he looked through the window and recognised Tulyet. 'They were on us before we could react, so we decided to stay here . . .' He hung his head, aware that he had not behaved honourably.

370

Tulyet did not waste time berating him, and merely gestured that the rest of his unit was to advance. The streets were oddly deserted, and somewhere a dog barked frantically. Bartholomew saw a shadow in front of them, and tensed, but it was only Cynric.

'Some are on the High Street,' the Welshman whispered. 'Thirty or so, all armed to the teeth.'

Tulyet broke into a trot, his warriors at his heels, so Bartholomew and Cynric followed. As they turned into the High Street, they saw shadows outside King's Hall. They were fiddling with something below the gate, and it did not take a genius to see that they planned to set it alight.

Tulyet ducked out of sight, and issued a series of low-voiced instructions. Immediately, several of his men lit lanterns. The instant they were ready, he released a resounding whoop and tore towards the enemy, his men baying behind him. Bartholomew saw the robbers' shock as they whipped around: clearly, they had not expected trouble from the castle. Several took flight, panicked by the shouting and sudden profusion of lights. Bartholomew grabbed Cynric's arm.

'Go to All Saints and ring the bell,' he ordered urgently. 'Quickly!'

Cynric hesitated, preferring to fight, but then ran to do as he was told. Bartholomew looked back to the affray, and saw Tulyet down on one knee while a raider prepared to make an end of him with a mace. He raced forward, and knocked the fellow off his feet with a punch that hurt his hand.

'Use your sword,' advised Tulyet, scrambling upright. 'Fists have no place here.'

Bartholomew heard a sound behind him, and only just managed to parry the blow that was intended to decapitate him. His assailant was tall and bulky, and he could not help but wonder whether it might be Ayera or Langelee. The man advanced with deadly purpose, and Bartholomew saw he meant to kill. Panic made him inventive, and in a somewhat unorthodox move he lashed out with his left hand and caught his opponent a sharp jab on the chin. It sent the fellow's helmet flying from his head and made the hood fall from his face.

'Frevill!'

Furious at being recognised, the carpenter stabbed viciously. Bartholomew twisted away, but tripped over a dead skirmisher who was sprawled behind him. Frevill leapt forward to stand over him, raising his weapon above his head to deal the killing blow. The sword began to descend.

At that moment, the bell began to clang. It made Frevill start and spoiled his aim. Snarling in fury, he lifted the blade again, but suddenly pitched forward, a dagger protruding from his back. Bartholomew looked around wildly, and saw a shadow in a doorway. His first thought was that it was Dame Pelagia, but it was too large. Then another raider attacked, and all his attention was taken with trying to prevent himself from being skewered.

But Cynric's alarm bell turned the tide of the skirmish, and the raiders retreated as townsmen and scholars poured from their homes to see what was happening. The withdrawal became a rout when arrows began to rain down from the walls of King's Hall. Tulyet quickly regrouped his men, and set off in pursuit. Then Warden Shropham appeared, his Fellows at his heels. Those who were armed ran to help Tulyet, leaving those who were priests to tend to the dead and dying.

'Were any of the raiders captured alive?' Bartholomew

asked of Cynric, as he struggled to save the life of a man with a severed arm. 'Dick will want to question them.'

'No,' replied the book-bearer. 'The fighting was violent and bitter – the invaders could not afford to be taken prisoner, while the castle wanted to redress the humiliation of last time. But the robbers lost seven men, and we lost only two. We conducted ourselves more respectably this time.'

Cynric's bell had filled the streets with indignant townsmen and scholars, all of whom had armed themselves with sticks, cudgels and even garden tools. They helped Tulyet hunt for the raiders in the dark lanes, and so did Michael's beadles, although it was not long before the Sheriff returned to King's Hall, his face dark with anger and disappointment as he reported that they had all managed to escape. Cynric offered to track the villains back to the marshes, but although Tulyet dispatched a unit of soldiers to accompany him, he did not look hopeful.

Dame Pelagia was among those who came to inspect the aftermath of the skirmish.

'Have you seen Langelee?' Bartholomew asked her. He was looking at the raiders' bodies, relieved beyond measure when none were familiar. 'Or Ayera?'

Pelagia shook her head, her expression unfathomable as always. 'Why?'

'Damn these villains!' cried Tulyet, sparing Bartholomew the need to answer. 'Who are they? And what did they want at King's Hall?'

'It is the best fortified of the Colleges,' explained Shropham in his quiet, understated manner. 'And there is a rumour that the taxes are hidden in the University. King's Hall is certainly where I would look first, were I a thief intent on acquiring crates of money.'

'Well, yes,' mumbled Tulyet, not looking at Bartholomew. 'There is a tale to that effect.'

'You did well, Sheriff,' said Pelagia with a sinister grin. 'You saw through their sly plot to divert you, and taught them that Cambridge is a force to be reckoned with.'

'Thank you,' said Tulyet, although he was looking at his dead guards and did not smile back. He glanced up when someone hurried towards him.

'We found the bombard, but it was abandoned,' gasped Helbye. 'They must have heard us coming and took flight. We tried to follow, but it was too dark.'

'Christ!' muttered Tulyet. Then resolve filled his face. 'We shall gather every able man in the town and hunt them down the moment it is light enough to see.'

'That would not be wise,' said Pelagia softly. 'You will not catch them, and your absence will leave the town vulnerable. They will launch another raid tomorrow, and you must be here to meet them.'

'You seem to know a lot about them, madam,' said Tulyet suspiciously.

'I have been listening to rumours and questioning travellers. Stay here, and help my grandson defend the University when they strike again.'

'Are you sure they will come?' asked Shropham. 'You do not think they have learned that we are no easy pickings? That they will leave us alone now?'

'I do not,' stated Pelagia firmly. 'They will appear again tomorrow – during the celebrations, almost certainly, when everyone is distracted.'

'Then we shall cancel the pageant,' said Tulyet grimly. 'The Guild of Corpus Christi will have to listen to me now. And if they refuse, I shall declare a state of military law, one that will last until all these villains are safely inside in my gaol.'

'These brigands are nothing if not patient,' said Shropham, thinking like the soldier he had once been. 'Look how long they have spent reconnoitring and planning. *Ergo*, I suspect that if you do cancel the festivities, they will simply wait for another occasion. And we cannot remain in a state of high alert indefinitely.'

'Then what do you suggest?' demanded Tulyet angrily. 'That we carry on as normal, and let them saunter in to take whatever they please?'

'That we carry on as normal as a way to lure them here,' replied Shropham. 'And then launch an attack of our own, to ensure they do not "saunter" out again.'

'It might work,' said Pelagia. 'But then again, it might not.'

While Pelagia, Shropham, Tulyet and Michael argued over tactics, Bartholomew set about carrying the dead to All Saints' Church. There were too many of them, and even though most were raiders, he deplored the carnage.

'I need a drink,' said Michael, when Bartholomew had finished. 'I know it is the middle of the night, but Landlord Lister will accommodate me, and we should discuss what has happened.'

If Lister was surprised to receive guests at such an hour, he hid it well. He brought wine and a plate of pastries, then left them alone to talk.

'Lord!' said Michael, scrubbing his face with his hands. 'What a terrible night!'

'Tomorrow will be worse,' came a soft voice from the door. Both scholars leapt in alarm as Dame Pelagia glided into the room and casually took a seat.

'How did you get in?' Bartholomew's nerves were raw. 'I saw Lister lock the door behind us.'

Pelagia merely smiled. 'Is there a spare cup of wine? It has been a long evening, and I am not as young as I was.'

She looked perfectly sprightly to Bartholomew.

'Why are you here?' asked Michael. 'I thought you were discussing battle tactics with Tulyet.'

'He can manage without me,' replied Pelagia, nodding appreciatively at the quality of the claret. 'And I wanted to talk to you, because it is time to use your clever wits – you have more than enough information to identify the villain who has been murdering scholars in libraries. And you are right: if we present a culprit it may avert trouble.'

'We have nothing of the kind!' exclaimed Michael, stunned by the claim. 'Or I would have made an arrest already.'

'You have failed to analyse the facts with your usual acuity,' countered Pelagia. 'And it is time to rectify the matter. So think!'

Bartholomew struggled to push his disgust at the recent slaughter to the back of his mind, and do as she ordered. 'The first murders were the four men who died in Newe Inn's pond,' he began.

'No,' said Pelagia. 'You are allowing a coincidence of location to mislead you, and I do not believe they are all the same case. Whose was the first death connected to a *library*?'

'Sawtre's,' replied Bartholomew. 'He was crushed under a bookshelf.'

'Good,' said Pelagia, sipping more wine. 'Continue.'

'It was an accident. It cannot have been murder, because that would have entailed Sawtre waiting patiently while the rack was hauled on top of him, but people talked about it as though it were retribution for him supporting the Common Library.' Bartholomew glanced at Pelagia, encouraged to see her nodding. 'So it gave someone an idea?'

Pelagia clapped her hands. 'There! You have it at last!'

'The next to die was Rolee,' Bartholomew went on. 'Dead of a broken neck. This looked like a mishap, but it would not have been difficult to tamper with the steps.'

'Not difficult at all,' agreed Pelagia.

'The third victim was Coslaye, brained with Acton's *Questio Disputata*. He was followed by Teversham, who choked to death when he became entangled in a book-chain. Teversham's demise might have been bad luck – but it is more likely that a killer was on hand to ensure his victim fell in such a way as to strangle himself.'

'Next was Kente, dead of a snake bite,' said Michael, joining in. 'The snake was in the bale of hay that Walkelate had bought to eliminate bad odours.'

'Was it?' asked Pelagia. 'And was Kente the intended victim, or did the killer hope to bag another scholar? Walkelate himself, for example?'

'And last was Jorz, drowned in ink,' finished Bartholomew. 'Probably not after a seizure.'

Michael rubbed his eyes. 'Just tell us the killer's name. I am too tired for games.'

But Pelagia declined to make it easy for him. 'Your choices are limited. It must be a scholar, because no townsman could have gained access to King's Hall, Bene't, Gonville, the Common Library, the Carmelite Priory and Batayl, where all these deaths occurred.'

'Three victims supported the Common Library,' said Michael tentatively, 'while two were—'

Pelagia slapped her hand on the table irritably. 'No! The killer could not have predicted it would be Rolee who would break his neck when the stair broke, or that it would be Kente who was bitten by the snake. The point was to make scholars think that libraries are dangerous. The victims' identities are irrelevant to him.'

'So the culprit is a library detractor,' surmised Michael. 'But the knowledge does not help us.'

'Of course, it does,' coaxed Pelagia. 'Consider the death that does not seem to fit with the others. That is the one that will give you the key to the killer. Which death was different from the rest – more brutal, less subtle and perhaps more personal?'

'Coslaye's?' suggested Bartholomew tentatively. 'He was brazenly murdered, whereas the others could ostensibly be accidents.'

'Yes,' said Pelagia encouragingly. 'Go on.'

'Is the culprit Pepin, then?' asked Michael uncertainly. 'Because Coslaye painted a rather grim mural of a battle in which he doubtless lost friends and family, and rage led him to batter out his Principal's brains? He did not plan it carefully like the others, but attacked in a blind fury?'

Pelagia rolled her eyes. 'How could a mere student gain access to Colleges and the Carmelite Priory? However, your analysis of the crime and the killer's motivation is probably correct.'

'Browne!' exclaimed Bartholomew. 'The man who has been spreading the tale that libraries are dangerous! He and Coslaye quarrelled constantly, and Coslaye was a violent man himself. An altercation may well have led to a murder committed on the spur of the moment. And Browne became Principal of Batayl once Coslaye was dead.'

'At last!' muttered Pelagia. 'I thought we would never get there. Now go and arrest him.'

'We cannot,' said Michael tiredly. 'He is missing.'

Pelagia looked exasperated. 'It is summer and the nights are mild. Sleeping outside is no hardship, especially to a man who is wont to frequent a certain garden, poaching fish . . .'

*   *   *

As Bartholomew and Michael hurried to Cholles Lane, they were astonished to see that dawn was not far off – at which point Corpus Christi would be upon them with all its attendant problems. The gate that led to Newe Inn's garden was locked, but Michael had a key.

'These grounds are extensive,' he said, fumbling in his haste to insert it. 'Do you think we should summon my beadles? It would not do to let Browne slip through our fingers.'

Bartholomew held up his hand. He had heard a noise.

'There cannot be anyone here,' whispered Michael. 'The work is finished. It should be empty.'

'Well, it is not,' Bartholomew whispered back. 'I can hear hammering inside the library.'

They crept forward, and saw a light gleaming in one of the upper windows. The front door was ajar, so they stepped inside and made for the stairs. Bartholomew's boots made far too much noise on the wooden steps, but he was as silent as a mouse compared to Michael. Fortunately, the trespasser was more intent on his own work than creaks from the stairwell, and when they reached the room holding the *libri distribuendi*, they saw him busily defacing one of the carvings with a mallet. He had lit a candle to see what he was doing, and it illuminated a face filled with malicious savagery.

'Browne!' exclaimed Michael.

Browne spun around, drawing a knife and holding it in a way that showed he was ready to lob it. 'You should not be here,' he snarled.

'Neither should you,' retorted Michael. 'We know what you have done – and I do not refer to your despoiling of Walkelate's artwork. I mean murder.'

Bartholomew winced. It was no way to address an armed man. He fumbled in his medical bag for the childbirth forceps, but they were tangled in a bandage, and would not come free.

'Drop your sack on the floor,' ordered Browne immediately. 'And put your hands in the air. Both of you. I am good with knives, and I have two of them. I will kill you if you disobey me.'

The fierce determination in his face told Bartholomew that he would be wise to do as he was told. The bag fell with a thud, although he managed to palm a pot of salve first.

'My beadles are waiting outside,' lied Michael. 'This is over, Browne. Put down the weapon before more blood is spilled – including your own.'

'I cannot stop now,' said Browne, glancing out of the window. 'I have won! Scholars are frightened of what might happen to them in libraries, and this vile place will founder from lack of support – especially when it cannot open today because it is damaged. Of course, that will pale into insignificance compared to what else will happen this morning.'

'And what is that?' asked Michael uneasily.

'I have been sleeping in the garden here – to go about my business without nosy students clamouring questions at me – and I overheard the robbers talking in the lane outside.'

'I suppose it was you that I almost caught poking about by the pond on Saturday night,' surmised Michael. Browne nodded, and started to answer, but the monk overrode him. 'Never mind that. What did these villains say?'

'They were discussing their plan for today,' Browne gloated. 'The one that will go down in the annals of history as the most cataclysmic event ever to befall this town.'

'Then you must help us stop it,' ordered Michael, alarmed. 'This is your home, too, and—'

'I shall *use* it,' declared Browne viciously. 'I shall ensure that all these suspicious deaths *and* the raid are blamed on the Common Library. That God smote Cambridge for founding one.'

'That is lunacy!' whispered Bartholomew, appalled. 'It is—'

There was a sudden clatter of footsteps on the stairs, and before Bartholomew or Michael could shout a warning, Walkelate had bustled in. The architect's eyebrows shot up in surprise when he saw he had visitors.

'Have you come to help me prepare for—' Then he saw the destruction Browne's mallet had wrought, and his face crumpled in horror and dismay. 'No! Oh, no! What have you done?'

'Shut up,' snapped Browne. There was a wild light in his eyes: he had not expected to be caught, and fear and agitation were turning him dangerous.

Walkelate's jaw dropped in shock when he saw the knife. 'I do not understand! What—'

'I said shut up!' snarled Browne. 'Now stand against the wall, and put your hands on your heads. The first man to make a hostile move is dead. And so is the second.'

With no alternative, Bartholomew and Michael did as they were told. Walkelate, stunned and bewildered, opened his mouth to argue, but the monk hauled him to where Browne had indicated.

'Give up, Browne,' he urged softly. 'You cannot win now. Too many people know—'

'What do they know?' sneered Browne. 'No one knows anything.'

'We know it was you who threw the book at Coslaye during the Convocation,' said Bartholomew. He was aware of Michael's surprise at the claim. 'We thought it was an accident – an act of frustration rather than an attempt to kill. But we were wrong: you did intend murder.'

Browne blanched. 'What nonsense is this?'

'It was a perfect opportunity,' Bartholomew went on. 'A lot of scholars were angry with him for speaking out against this library, and you knew that they – not you – would be suspects. Unfortunately for you, Coslaye had an unusually thick skull.'

'Why would I kill my Principal?' demanded Browne. 'You are out of your wits, just like he was! Poitiers addled you!'

'For two reasons,' replied Bartholomew with a calm he did not feel. 'First, because you disapproved of his obsession with the French wars. Batayl was originally called St Remegius—'

'Batayl is a ridiculous name,' spat Browne. 'I shall change it now I am Principal.'

'And second, because you wanted Coslaye's post,' pounced Bartholomew. 'But you will never have it. You have murdered too many people.'

'Who else's life has he taken?' asked Walkelate in a small, frightened voice.

'Sawtre's fate gave you the idea,' said Bartholomew, continuing to address Browne. 'And then you went out and killed Rolee, Teversham, Kente and Jorz in sly ways that were intended to make people think that libraries were dangerous places to be. But you left clues.'

'I never did! I was supremely careful.' Browne grimaced his annoyance when he realised the remark was an admission of guilt. 'They were all accidents – Rolee was not meant to break his neck; the adder was never meant to kill Kente; and I would not have had to strangle Teversham if he had stayed down after I knocked him into the lectern. However, I did *not* kill Jorz.'

'God help us!' breathed Walkelate, white-faced. 'How could you have done such dreadful things?'

'Because this damned library should never have come into existence!' Browne rounded on him with fury. 'It was born out of the Chancellor's selfish desire to be remembered, and my fellow Regents should have voted against it. Newe Inn should have come to Batayl.'

'But Coslaye was—' began Walkelate.

'He was a liability,' Browne went on, cutting across him in his eagerness to spill the vitriol he had suppressed for so long. 'Did you know he was helping the raiders? I know times are hard, but there are other ways to raise capital. And his savage temper made Batayl a laughing stock. *I* should have been Principal – I would have been, if Bartholomew had not saved Coslaye with his stupid surgery. You cannot begin to imagine how much I hate him for that.'

'How did you choose your victims?' asked Michael quickly, when Browne's arm started to go back, all his pent-up rage and frustration focused on the physician.

'I did not choose them,' snarled Browne. 'I just laid traps, and Rolee, Kente and Teversham were the ones who happened to walk into them.'

'Did you kill Northwood, the London brothers and Vale, too?' asked Walkelate unsteadily.

'No!' Browne's livid glare went from Bartholomew to the architect. 'I was as shocked as anyone to discover bodies in the pond where I go fishing.'

'Please give up, Browne,' begged Michael, glancing towards the window, where the sky was already pale blue. 'Time is of the essence, and there has already been too much bloodshed.'

But Browne's reply was to take aim again, his eyes blazing with hatred and rage. All Bartholomew could do to stop him was to lob the salve he had palmed, which he did with all his might. It missed by a considerable margin, but it was enough to spoil Browne's aim. Michael cringed as the blade thudded into the panelling by his shoulder.

The resulting damage to the fine woodwork was more than Walkelate could bear. With a bellow of outrage he charged, fists flailing wildly. Browne flung up his hands to defend himself, and Walkelate's momentum carried them both into the nearest bookcase. It teetered as they fell to the floor, depositing several heavy volumes and the bust of Aristotle on top of them.

'You scoundrel!' Walkelate sobbed as he pounded the culprit. 'My beautiful library! What would poor Kente say if he could see what you have done?'

Bartholomew hauled him away and shoved him into Michael's arms, although he could already tell that something was badly amiss with Browne.

'His skull is cracked,' he said after a brief examination. 'He is dead.'

Walkelate stopped struggling, and what little colour remained in his face drained away. 'You mean I have killed him?' he whispered, wrath turning quickly to horror. 'But I did not hit him that hard – not nearly as hard as he deserved!'

'No,' agreed Bartholomew. 'The fatal wound came from Aristotle. His Principal was blessed with an unusually thick skull, but it seems Browne has an unusually thin one.'

There was nothing to be done for Browne, except to wrap him in his cloak ready to be taken to St Botolph's Church. Bartholomew and Michael worked in silence, the only sound being Walkelate's shocked whimpers, as his eyes went from the body to the damage that had been inflicted on his exquisite carvings. He did not seem to know which was worse.

'Will presenting Browne as the villain be enough to avert trouble today, Brother?' Bartholomew asked.

Michael rubbed his eyes with fingers that shook. 'I do not know. It would have been better to present a living suspect – a corpse looks contrived. And Batayl will deny the charges, of course.'

'Browne was lying,' said Walkelate, regarding the body with a mixture of anger and distress. 'He denied killing Northwood and the others, but I wager you anything you like that he *did* poison them as they experimented.'

Bartholomew looked at him sharply. 'What makes you say they were poisoned? We have not mentioned that theory to anyone else.'

'Other than Julitta, apparently,' muttered Michael. 'And possibly Ayera.'

Walkelate shrugged. 'Four men do not die of natural causes all at once, and Dunning told me that you found no signs of violence on their bodies. What else is left but poison?'

'Everyone else seems to believe that God or the Devil is responsible.' Bartholomew narrowed his eyes. 'Yet Clippesby and Riborowe said those four dead men met here on a regular basis, and it is unlikely that they could have done it every time without you noticing. You spend all your time here, after all. And the answer is that *you* were experimenting with them!'

'Steady on, Matt,' murmured Michael. 'You cannot accuse everyone of—'

'But I was not with them the night they died,' cried Walkelate. 'How could I have been? I would have been poisoned, too. I was in here with my artisans, listening to the singers that Holm hired as we polished the shelves.'

Michael's jaw dropped. 'But that answer implies you joined them on other occasions! Why did you not mention it sooner? We have been desperate for clues about their deaths, and your testimony might have helped.'

Walkelate hung his head. 'I did not dare, Brother. I was afraid you would stop me working on the library if I admitted to sharing their passion for invention. But I was going to confess tonight, when this place is open and nothing else will matter.'

'So tell me now,' said Michael angrily. 'What were you doing? Making lamp fuel?'

'Yes,' admitted Walkelate. 'I am sorry, Bartholomew, I know you are working to that end, too, but I did it to raise money for the library. Vale said that whoever discovers clean-burning fuel will be rich, and Northwood invited me to join their team when I caught them in the garden one night.'

'Why did he invite you?' demanded Michael suspiciously.

'Because I was able to make several useful suggestions,' explained Walkelate. 'Such as adding rock oil and red lead. He said my extensive knowledge of alchemy was invaluable.'

Michael scrubbed tiredly at his face. 'We shall discuss this later, when you do not have bookcases to repair, and I do not have a "cataclysmic" raid and rebellious scholars to worry about.'

'Thank you, Brother,' said Walkelate gratefully. 'I shall go to round up my artisans at once, and see what can be done to disguise Browne's handiwork.'

While the architect disappeared about his business, Michael and Bartholomew carried Browne to the street, where the monk ordered three passing beadles to take the body to St Boltoph's. The physician half listened to Michael telling his men what Browne had overheard, and let his mind wander to an image of Northwood, the London brothers and Vale conducting their experiments in the overgrown garden, and of Walkelate helping with new ideas. Then he thought about the substances Walkelate had recommended, and tendrils of unease began to writhe in his stomach.

'Oh, no!' he breathed, as understanding came crashing into his mind. 'They were not making lamp fuel – you do not need red lead and rock oil for that. They were concocting something else.'

'What are you talking about?' demanded Michael irritably. 'I am too tired and fraught for—'

'Wildfire! Rock oil is what makes *wildfire* sticky and unquenchable.'

'I sincerely doubt Walkelate and the others were making that! They—'

But Bartholomew's mind was racing. 'Northwood would have been interested only from an alchemical standpoint, but Vale liked money. And now we have Walkelate, eager to raise funds for his library. Of course, there are other clues that prove they were dabbling with weapons . . .'

'There are?' asked Michael warily.

'Warden Shropham told us that Walkelate is the son of the King's sergeant-at-arms, and such men will certainly receive military training in their youth.'

'So did I, but it does not make me a candidate for inventing incendiary devices.'

'The ingredients for lamp fuel must not be expensive,' Bartholomew forged on. 'If they are, the invention will be useless, because no one will be able to afford to buy any. But military commanders rarely baulk at the cost of materials for weapons.'

'So? I do not understand your point.'

'The compounds Northwood was using *were* expensive, because he was stealing exemplar money to pay for them – Ruth told us.'

'We did not find money in his cell,' conceded Michael. 'So it clearly was spent. But Walkelate just said Browne was lying – that our villainous Batayl man poisoned Northwood and his cronies. Why would Walkelate—'

'To prevent you from seeing the truth, of course! And maybe it was he, not the raiders, who demanded the formula from Rougham and me. He probably recruited others to help him waylay us. Such as Holm – he is greedy and ruthless.'

'Matt!' cried Michael. 'You are allowing dislike to interfere with your reason. Calm down and—'

'I am perfectly calm! And if we dither over this, blood will be spilled.'

'It will be spilled if we go adrift with erroneous assumptions,' Michael shot back. 'But if you are right, and Walkelate and his cronies *were* striving to invent something sinister, they would not have chosen Holm to assist them. They would have picked Gyseburne – a man fascinated with urine, which is combustible.'

'No, it is Holm. He is Walkelate's friend, who provides him with remedies to rid the library of unwanted smells.' More solutions cracked clear in Bartholomew's mind. 'And if they were making wildfire, they will have used some very dangerous materials as well as expensive ones – such as red lead. They *were* poisoned, but they did it to themselves!'

Michael regarded him dubiously. 'Then why did Vale have an arrow in his back?'

Bartholomew thought quickly. 'Because when Walkelate tried to conceal the bodies by dumping them in the pond,

Vale got caught on that platform. The others would have surfaced eventually, because of gases, but Walkelate probably does not know that. He must have shot the arrow in an effort to haul Vale free, and—'

'That seems excessive,' said Michael in distaste. 'Why not just wade in and grab him?'

'Impossible – the water is too deep. And perhaps he was in a hurry, because he was short of time – Browne often went fishing in the mornings. Or more likely, he did not want to immerse himself in toxic water.'

'How would he know it was toxic?'

'I think they dumped their failed experiments in it. It would certainly explain why I was ill after falling in, why your beadles felt unwell after dredging for bodies, and why the riverfolk and Batayl were sick after eating its fish. There is Agatha's testimony, too.'

'What testimony?'

'She said the pond emits bad smells on certain nights – doubtless when Northwood and his helpmeets worked, producing stenches that people noticed. Cynric remarked on it, too. Red lead releases toxic fumes when it is heated. And the bowl that Meadowman dredged up – the one that rang like a bell – suggests the experimenters were boiling their concoctions . . .'

'Could red lead in a basin that size produce enough fumes to kill four men?'

'Yes. It is a pity anatomy is forbidden, because had I looked inside the bodies, we would have had answers days ago.'

'No,' said Michael, after reflecting for a moment. 'Walkelate would not have tried to conceal what was essentially an accident. He would have reported it.'

'And risked trouble for his beloved library? I think not!'

'Very well,' said Michael. 'As we have no better way

forward, we shall explore your theory. The first step is to find Walkelate. I seriously doubt he would create wildfire to secure future funding for his library, but I will never sleep easy again if I am wrong and he sells it to the robbers.'

'I hope we are not too late,' said Bartholomew soberly. 'Because I have an awful feeling it might feature in Browne's "cataclysmic" event.'

CHAPTER 12

The residents of Cambridge were already up and about, many dressed in their best clothes. There was an atmosphere of excited anticipation, for the previous night's rout had been hailed a success, and people were confident that the raiders would never dare return. Edith waved cheerfully to Bartholomew as she and her husband removed the boards that had covered their windows, while the head of the Frevill clan was ushering his family back into their home.

'We received word during the night that the town had bloodied the robbers' noses,' said Edith, as Bartholomew skidded to a standstill. 'So we decided to return.'

He was dismayed. 'But one of our scholars heard the raiders talking, and they plan to strike again today. The danger is far from over!'

Stanmore waved a dismissive hand, and nodded that his wife should begin decorating the windowsills while he dealt with her agitated brother.

'He probably heard that before we taught them a lesson in the High Street,' he said with quiet reason. 'They will not try a third time. They are not stupid, and will know when they are defeated.'

'But they have not stolen the tax money yet,' argued Bartholomew. 'They will not give up so easily when they have invested so much. Moreover, I think they intend to unleash a—'

'Enough!' said Stanmore sharply. He lowered his voice,

so Edith would not hear. 'It has been a dismal winter, and this is the first opportunity we have had to enjoy ourselves in months. Do not spoil it with your alarmist notions. There will be no raid today.'

There was no point arguing with such firmly held convictions. With one last, agonised glance at his sister, Bartholomew ran after Michael, who was aiming for King's Hall in the hope that Walkelate's colleagues would know where the architect was.

'Walkelate is not here,' said Shropham, when they were shown into his office. 'He has been out all night, but we expected that – he is determined to have his library perfect for today.'

'Where else might he be?' demanded Michael.

'There is nowhere else. The library has been his consuming passion these past few weeks. Of course, there is also his other obsession . . .'

'What other obsession?'

'He is fascinated with artillery and siege warfare, an interest that began at more or less the same time as that beggar was murdered – the one whose throat was cut.'

'You think he is connected to the invaders?' asked Michael, struggling to understand what he was being told.

'Of course not.' But the Warden's eyes were uneasy. 'Yet he has strong opinions . . .'

'Shropham!' shouted Michael in exasperation. 'Please! We have told you why we need to find him, so do not make this more difficult. Or do you want King's Hall blamed for whatever happens?'

'No!' Shropham was in an agony of conflicting loyalties. 'Yet I fear Walkelate has done something terrible. About two months ago, he performed a lot of experiments that involved explosions and I had to order him to desist, because he was disturbing our students. I was relieved when the library began to take up more of his time, as I thought it would distract him . . .'

'Did he work alone, or with others?' asked Michael.

'With Northwood and the Londons,' replied Shropham. 'And Vale the physician, too, I believe. They were also interested in alchemy.'

'Walkelate lied,' said Bartholomew to Michael, although the monk did not need to be told. 'He did not stumble across Northwood and the others in Newe Inn – he took them there when King's Hall became unavailable. Clippesby and Riborowe said they could not identify everyone who assembled in Cholles Lane before slipping into the garden. One of them must have been Walkelate.'

'Hovering there with a key to let them in,' finished Michael.

'I think he has designed a new weapon,' blurted Shropham. His face was ashen. 'There were diagrams in his room . . . I was a soldier myself once, and his pictures look like modified ribauldequins to me. He spent hours discussing such devices with Holm and Riborowe, who were at Poitiers.'

Something dreadful occurred to Bartholomew. 'Do you think he might have conceived one that can discharge wildfire? As matters stand, the stuff is not very easy to deploy, but if he has devised a contraption that can propel it into the ranks of the enemy . . .'

Shropham would not meet his eyes. 'That is exactly what it looked like to me. But I am not too concerned, because no one knows the recipe for wildfire any more. It has been lost, thank God.'

'The discharge of wildfire from a ribauldequin would certainly be cataclysmic,' said Michael, exchanging an appalled glance with Bartholomew.

'There is one more thing.' Shropham's expression was

one of inner torment: it pained him to tell tales on a colleague. 'I happened to glance in his room this morning. The drawings have gone.'

'Why did you not tell us this immediately?' demanded Michael, horrified.

'Why would I? Sketching weapons is not illegal, and he has not actually done anything wrong.'

But Shropham did not look convinced by his own argument, and neither were Bartholomew and Michael. Without further ado, they left King's Hall and hurried into the High Street, feeling that time was slipping inexorably away.

'Walkelate has not gone to muster his artisans,' said Bartholomew in despair. 'He has gone to consort with the robbers – to give them what he has invented. Assuming he has not done so already.'

'No,' said Michael, albeit uncertainly. 'There is nothing to connect him to them.'

'Yes, there is. Browne heard the raiders talking in Cholles Lane – the place where Walkelate's helpmeets assembled before they went to experiment. That cannot be a coincidence. Besides, why else would he have taken his diagrams?'

'Even if you are right, drawings are not the same as an actual device,' Michael pointed out. 'He can sell his theory, but he cannot sell the weapon itself.'

'Dick Tulyet has a ribauldequin,' said Bartholomew wretchedly. 'I saw it at the castle. Walkelate was one of several scholars who helped him design it.'

'Then we need not worry,' said Michael in relief. 'If it is in the castle, then the invaders do not have it. And if a ribauldequin is the only way wildfire can be deployed, then they are foiled.'

'It is stored in the chapel now, but it *was* in the Great

Tower.' Bartholomew's thoughts were racing. 'I suggested that the robbers might have wanted it, but Dick said no.'

'He may be right, Matt – such a device would not be easy to whisk away in a lightning raid. But forget it for now: we need to concentrate on Walkelate. I doubt he has gone to the Fens, because if he *is* involved with the robbers, he will know that they are coming here. He will have gone to one of his surviving accomplices. And *not* Holm, before you say it.'

'Riborowe has an unhealthy interest in artillery.' Bartholomew jabbed a finger. 'And there he is now, slinking along in a manner that is distinctly furtive!'

Riborowe broke into a run when he saw Bartholomew and Michael bearing down on him, his skeletal legs pumping furiously as he tore towards his friary. He moved fast, and had reached St Mary the Great before Bartholomew managed to bring him down with a flying tackle. He struggled, spat and scratched furiously until Michael arrived to help secure him.

'Walkelate,' growled the monk, seizing him by the scruff of his neck. 'Where is he?'

'I have no idea,' snapped Riborowe. 'But if you think to accuse me of helping Northwood cheat the friary over those exemplars, then you have the wrong man. It was Jorz. *He* was the one who told Northwood how many to expect, and which ones could be declared inferior. He confessed it to me the night he died. He, Northwood and Walkelate were experimenting together.'

'Then why did you not tell me immediately?' demanded Michael angrily.

'Because I am frightened of *him*,' shouted Riborowe, jabbing a bony finger at Bartholomew. 'It was unnerving when he appeared so soon after we discovered Jorz's corpse, especially given that Jorz had seen him releasing Satan's familiar by the river.'

Michael grimaced his exasperation. 'Tell me about Walkelate and his love of weapons.'

'Why do you—' Riborowe saw the dangerous expression on the monk's face and began to gabble. 'He is especially interested in ribauldequins, and we worked together on the one the Sheriff built for the King. He imposed some peculiar modifications, although he declined to tell me why. He made a second one, too, but I do not know where he keeps it.'

'A second one?' cried Bartholomew in dismay. He turned to Michael. 'Supposing the raiders already have it?'

Michael regarded the Carmelite in distaste. 'And you accuse Matt of dealing with the Devil! He cures people, while you devise ways to kill them.'

'I am not the only one,' bleated Riborowe. 'Northwood was interested in artillery, too. He pretended to find it shocking, and refused to help the Sheriff, but in reality he was fascinated by it.'

'Tell me about the second ribauldequin,' ordered Michael. 'How is it different from Tulyet's?'

'I do not know. Walkelate and Northwood never let me see the final result.' Riborowe freed himself from the monk's grasp and backed away. 'I am going to leave Cambridge today. It is too full of men with alarming ideas. I shall join a convent in another town – one without mad experimenters and Corpse Examiners running riot.'

'Hypocrite!' spat Michael, watching him scuttle away. 'He knows he has contributed to something terrible, but is not man enough to admit it.'

'Why are you letting him go?' asked Bartholomew, agitated and unhappy. 'He is our only lead to Walkelate.'

'He does not know where Walkelate is, or what his plans

are. Walkelate has been using him, pumping him for technical information while telling him nothing in return. And I suspect Walkelate did the same with Jorz, Northwood, Vale and the London brothers.'

Bartholomew was not so sure, but there was no time to discuss it. 'How do we find Walkelate now?'

'By interrogating another of his accomplices,' said Michael grimly. 'Gyseburne will be—'

'Holm,' countered Bartholomew. 'We should check Holm first because . . . because he lives nearer, and you are tired.'

Michael shot him a rueful glance for his transparency, but turned towards Cholles Lane anyway. All along the High Street, houses were being bedecked with red blossoms, and the churches had their doors open. The flowers smelled strong, and Bartholomew was uncomfortably reminded of Ayera and his penchant for poisonous blooms. Everywhere, people were greeting each other cheerfully, and scholars and townsfolk alike were girding themselves up for fun.

'You *must* postpone the library's opening – at least, until we find Walkelate,' said Bartholomew.

Michael nodded. 'Yes. Although Dunning will never forgive us . . .'

'Tell Dick to cancel the pageant, too. Every dignitary and cleric in Cambridge plans to take part in it, while virtually every man, woman and child will be watching. We cannot let it go ahead when we fear an atrocity in the making. It would be immoral.'

'What about the plan to lure the raiders here, so we can engage them in battle?' panted Michael. 'They will not come if the ceremonies are called off, and Shropham was right – we cannot endure weeks of uncertainty while we wait for their next assault.'

'Dick thought Shropham's plan reckless, and so did Dame Pelagia. The Guild of Corpus Christi has supported it, but only because cancelling the event will lose them money. Dick should do as he suggested last night – declare a state of military law until the robbers have been caught.'

Michael was silent for a moment, then burst out with, 'But wildfire, Matt! I do not think that Walkelate would unleash such a terrible substance on us.'

'He took two of the most wicked weapons ever to be invented, and combined them. How can you even think that such a man has a conscience?'

Michael waylaid two passing beadles, and sent one to the castle with the recommendation that the Sheriff postpone the pageant, and the other to Dunning, to explain why he was going to be deprived of his moment of glory. Then he and Bartholomew ran the short distance to Holm's house, which they found with all its windows shuttered and its door closed. They exchanged a glance: was the fact that the surgeon had declined to lower his guard evidence that he knew what was about to befall the town?

'I will wait a few moments, then knock,' said Michael. 'You go around the back, to make sure he does not escape. Here is a dagger.'

Bartholomew had not known Michael was armed, and was unsettled that the monk should think such draconian measures necessary. Without a word, he took the weapon, and eased down a smelly alley until he reached a gate. It was unlocked, so he opened it and stepped into Holm's yard.

He was startled to see the surgeon slumped over a garden table. There was no sign of Walkelate. He approached cautiously, and saw a lump on the back of Holm's head; ropes secured his hands and feet. He felt for a life-beat, and at his touch, Holm's eyelids flickered open. The surgeon moaned and cursed his way back to wakefulness, while Bartholomew struggled to unravel the knots.

'Who did this to you?' asked Bartholomew urgently. 'Quickly, man! Speak!'

'Walkelate,' groaned Holm. 'It happened last night, and I have been stuck out here ever since. Thank God you came to save me.'

'Why did he hit you?' demanded Bartholomew, agitation and concern making him rougher with the ropes and his questions than he might otherwise have been.

'You are unsympathetic, because of Isnard,' said Holm sullenly. 'He claims I tried to poison him, because it transpires that he is innocent of wrongdoing and I owe you five marks.'

'Never mind that,' said Bartholomew. 'Do you know—'

'But I only used a mild dose of henbane,' Holm went on. 'I would not have given him any, but he was gloating about me having to pay you, and I could not help myself.'

Bartholomew gaped at him. 'Isnard was right? You did try to dispatch him?'

'Not dispatch,' corrected Holm, rubbing his abused wrists. 'Teach him a lesson. And I shall give you your five marks as soon as I am married.'

'You will pay me from Julitta's dowry? I hardly think that is right.'

'No?' pounced Holm. 'I am glad you think so. I shall keep it for myself, then.'

It was no time to discuss money. 'Did you know that your lover is a murderer? He has just confessed to killing several scholars in order to frighten them out of libraries.'

Holm squinted up at him, and Bartholomew felt uncharitably disappointed when he saw the astonishment in his eyes. He could tell it was genuine. The surgeon blew out his cheeks as he assimilated the information.

399

'Well,' he said at last. 'Who would have thought it? I know he was always saying that times are hard, but to kill to make them better . . . Oh, well. I was beginning to tire of him, anyway, and I can do a lot better for myself, even if his cousin does know the King.'

Bartholomew did not care about the surgeon's ambitions. 'Where is Walkelate now?'

'I have no idea. And I cannot imagine why he hit me, either. All I did was offer to spruce up his library – I decided it would do my reputation no harm to be associated with the finished product, you see. Besides, it was an excuse to be away from the annoying Julitta.'

With difficulty, Bartholomew ignored the last remark. 'He hit you for wanting to help him?'

At that moment, Michael appeared. 'The door was unlocked, so I—' He gaped in confusion when he saw Holm holding his head and the ropes on the ground. 'What happened?'

'I suppose I was rather insistent,' admitted Holm, continuing to address Bartholomew. 'However, he did not have to resort to violence. I would have desisted eventually.'

'He could not take the risk that you would foist yourself on him anyway.' Bartholomew spoke more to himself than the surgeon. 'I suspect he had a lot to do last night. Tell us what you recall.'

'Me begging to accompany him, and him saying that he was too busy. I told him I did not require entertaining, and I suppose we quarrelled. The next thing I knew was him coming at me with the hilt of a dagger. I am lucky he did not skewer me.'

'You hired singers to entertain the craftsmen at Newe Inn the night Northwood and the others died,' began Michael. 'Why did you choose that particular night to be generous?'

'Because Walkelate said it would be a kindness, and I was keen to stay on his good side. He is an important member of King's Hall, as I have said before.'

Again, Bartholomew knew Holm was telling the truth; the open selfishness had the ring of honesty about it. 'Clearly, Walkelate wanted to drown out any sounds his accomplices might have made doing God knows what in the garden,' he said to Michael.

'Yes,' agreed the monk. 'And now we had better look for him in Gyseburne's home, where we should have gone in the first place.'

'He will not be there,' said Holm. He shrugged rather sheepishly. 'Ayera told me a tale that Gyseburne's mother is a witch, and I repeated it to Walkelate, thinking he would find it amusing, but he was appalled, and has avoided the fellow ever since. But why are you so eager to find him?'

'Because it transpires that he has an unsavoury interest in artillery,' explained Michael tersely. 'And because we fear that he may be in league with men who want to use some on our town.'

Holm considered the accusation, then nodded slowly. 'He might. He is interested in armaments, and he has been meeting villainous men for weeks. French-speaking men. I overheard him arranging to sell them something a fortnight or so ago. He told me that they were visiting scholars from Paris, but I did not believe him. They were warriors without a doubt.'

'We have not had visiting scholars from Paris for months,' said Michael immediately, who as Senior Proctor was in a position to know.

'Are you saying that the raiders are French?' asked Bartholomew, bewildered. But then he recalled that the ones he had encountered had spoken that language.

'Well they are rather more than common brigands,' said Holm curtly. 'Or they would not be so damned persistent.'

Bartholomew struggled to understand what he was hearing. 'We think Walkelate has invented a wildfire-spitting ribauldequin, and we are at war with France. Selling Frenchmen weapons – or even plans and formulae – amounts to treason!'

'Only if he is caught,' said Holm. 'And he told me himself that he is cleverer than you.'

'I thought he was your friend,' said Michael, before Bartholomew could point out that siding with the French at Poitiers had hardly been an act of patriotism. suspicious of the surgeon's disloyal revelations. 'How can you betray his confidences so readily?'

'He forfeited my friendship when he hit me on the head,' said Holm with a pout. 'Besides, I have my reputation to consider. I do not want to be associated with treason.'

'Think very carefully,' instructed Michael, before Bartholomew could point out that siding with the French at Poitiers had hardly been an act of patriotism. 'Can you suggest anywhere he might be? He is not at King's Hall or his library.'

Holm frowned, still rubbing his wrists, while Bartholomew struggled with the urge to grab him by the throat in an effort to speed up his ponderings.

'Try the Carmelites' scriptorium,' he said eventually. 'He mentioned buying some labels there.'

'Go to the castle and tell the Sheriff everything we have just reasoned,' ordered Michael, turning to leave. 'Even the parts you do not understand. It is a matter of life and death, so do it immediately – as quickly as you can run.'

'He will not oblige,' said Bartholomew, regarding the surgeon with loathing. 'Just as he did not bother to raise the alarm when Rougham and I were accosted. He ran straight home and shut himself safely inside. If he had been braver, we might have been rescued before Rougham revealed the secret of wildfire to what we now suspect were French spies!'

'That was different,' objected Holm indignantly. 'It was dark then, and I was frightened.'

'You will do as I ask,' said Michael sharply. 'Or you may find your wealthy bride-to-be hears certain nasty truths about her beloved fiancé.'

Holm's face was a mask of furious resentment as Michael turned on his heel and stalked out. Bartholomew stared at him for a moment, then followed.

'We cannot trust him, Brother,' he warned. 'He is more likely to run straight to Julitta, and start spinning yarns as to why your accusations are untrue.'

'He would not dare.' Michael broke into the waddle that passed as a run for him. 'He knew my threat was in earnest. Besides, what else can we do? We do not have time to explain everything to another messenger. Holm will come through, Matt. He has too much to lose by failing.'

Bartholomew was unconvinced, but they had reached the Carmelite Priory, and he was obliged to turn his thoughts back to Walkelate. The convent was deserted; the friars and their servants were in the chapel, singing gustily as they performed the first of many offices that would take place that day. He and Michael tore across the yard to the scriptorium. It, too, was empty, except for one man who was busily rifling through some ledgers, his hands stained red with ink.

'Langelee!' they exclaimed in unison.

Bartholomew and Michael were so astonished at seeing the Master that neither spotted the figure that had been loitering in the shadows until it emerged with a sword at the ready. It was Ayera, unshaven, dishevelled and tense.

'Damn,' he murmured softly. 'Now what?'

'Now they help us,' said Langelee, beckoning Bartholomew and Michael forward. 'Because we cannot do this alone.'

'Help you do what?' asked Michael warily, declining to move.

'Foil the men who are determined to betray our country,' replied Langelee, turning back to the ledgers. 'Ayera and I have been racing about blindly for days now, and we are at our wits' end.'

'I know the feeling,' said Michael icily, still not moving. 'What is going on?'

'Walkelate has invented a ribauldequin that can eject wildfire,' explained Langelee tightly. 'And we believe he has gone some way to producing wildfire itself. He and his cronies have been experimenting with the stuff in Newe Inn's garden.'

'Who are his cronies?' asked Bartholomew, acutely aware that Ayera had not sheathed his sword, and that it hovered unnervingly close to his back.

'Enough questions,' said the geometrician sharply. 'I do not like this.'

'Northwood, the London brothers, Vale, Jorz and possibly others,' replied Langelee, ignoring him. 'Although I doubt any of them knew what they were doing, or what Walkelate intended to do with the formula once he had it. They have been mercilessly used. And all are dead, of course.'

'Jorz drowned in a bowl of red ink.' Michael looked pointedly at Langelee's scarlet hands.

'Knocked on the head first, though,' said Langelee. 'Otherwise there would have been too much splashing. Knocking people on the head is becoming quite a habit with Walkelate. I now know that it was he who attacked me in Newe Inn's garden. Ayera found out.'

'I overheard him telling Frevill about it,' explained Ayera, although he spoke reluctantly.

'How do you know Jorz was knocked on the head first?' asked Bartholomew of Langelee.

'Because I was spying here, and I saw it happen. I raced to help him the moment Walkelate had left, but it was too late. And I splattered ink all over myself into the bargain.'

'Are you saying you delayed before going to Jorz's assistance?' asked Bartholomew uneasily. 'You stood in the shadows watching while murder was committed, and only emerged when the killer had gone?'

Langelee waved a dismissive hand. 'I could not afford to let Walkelate see that he was discovered lest he went to ground. And then we would never have answers. Still, at least one thing is clear: I now know why Northwood quizzed me so relentlessly about my battlefield experiences – he wanted information to share with those damned raiders.'

Michael turned suddenly to Ayera, who took an involuntary step backwards when he saw the dark expression on the monk's face. 'We have it on good authority that you were among the raiders, too. Walkelate might be betraying his country, but you have betrayed our town.'

Ayera regarded Langelee with weary resignation. 'Did you tell them?'

Langelee looked indignant. 'Of course not. However, I did say that you would be unlikely to deceive Michael, and that you should take him into your confidence. You should have listened.'

'What is going on?' snapped Michael. 'And you can put down that blade, Ayera, because we all know you will not use it on us.'

Bartholomew knew no such thing, and waited, taut as a bowstring, while Ayera stared at the monk. Then the geometrician sighed, and the sword dipped towards the floor.

'I did join ranks with the robbers, but I had my reasons.'

'I suppose you wanted money because your uncle failed to bequeath you any,' surmised Bartholomew coldly. 'And you were eager to buy that horse.'

'It is a little more complex than that,' said Ayera shortly.

Michael folded his arms. 'Then explain.'

'Perhaps one day,' said Ayera. 'But not now.'

Michael took an angry step towards him. 'That is not good enough.'

'Leave him be,' came a voice from the door. 'He cannot tell you what you want to know, because he is under orders to keep his silence. You see, he is in *my* employ, as is Master Langelee.'

Bartholomew spun around, Michael's dagger in his hand, but lowered it quickly when he recognised the speaker. It was Dame Pelagia.

'At last!' cried Langelee in relief. 'Where have you been, madam? We need more directions, because Ayera and I are hopelessly out of our depth here.'

Michael gaped at his grandmother, still struggling to understand. 'They are working for *you*?'

Pelagia inclined her head. 'Ayera has been with me for a while now, ever since the King decided it was time I had an assistant to perform some of my more physically demanding duties.'

'Ayera is your *apprentice*?' Michael looked as astonished as Bartholomew felt.

Pelagia nodded again. 'And he recruited Langelee when we needed more help.'

'Why Langelee?' demanded Michael indignant and hurt. 'Why not me?'

'Because Langelee is a warrior,' explained Ayera. 'We fought together at the Battle of Neville's Cross, and we were friends in York. You are a brave and intelligent man, Brother, but I needed a soldier.'

'Ayera joined the raiders on my orders,' said Pelagia, when Michael was silent. 'He told them he needed the pay because he feared his uncle's bequest would prove to be a disappointment.'

'It did prove to be a disappointment,' said Ayera ruefully. 'My family lending me money for that horse is not the same at all.' He turned to Bartholomew. 'I am afraid I did not handle your questions very well, Matt. You caught me off guard, and I suspect my answers did nothing to alleviate your concerns.'

'And I am sorry I threatened to restrict your access to patients,' added Langelee. 'But it was the only way I could think of to bring an end to the discussion. You kept catching us in inconsistencies – such as whether Ayera found me wandering dazed in Cholles Lane or in Newe Inn's garden – and I had to end it before it went any further.'

'It was Ayera who saved my life last night!' exclaimed Bartholomew in sudden understanding. 'Frevill was about to kill me in the scuffle outside King's Hall, but Ayera threw a knife. The shadow was too large to be Dame Pelagia.'

'Now you know why I am so certain that there will be an attack today,' said Pelagia, as Ayera shot the physician a brief smile of acknowledgement. 'Ayera heard it from the raiders' own lips. We must do all we can to prevent it, so—'

'Yes, but I still have questions,' interrupted Michael. 'Clippesby saw Ayera talking with the villainous Willelmus during the attack on the castle—'

'Of course I spoke to him,' said Ayera impatiently. 'I needed to know what intelligence he had passed to the robbers. I did my best to win their confidence, but they never did trust me fully – especially after the first raid, when my premature battle cry gave the defenders time to grab their bows.'

'You should have told me all this,' said Michael accusingly to Pelagia. 'Here is a terrible plot unfolding in my town, and you chose to keep me in the dark.'

Pelagia laid a conciliatory hand on his arm. 'I did not know until a few hours ago that the four scholars in the library pond were connected with my mission here – or that Walkelate was the arch-villain. Meanwhile, you had several suspicious deaths to unravel, and two factions of querulous academics to hold apart. I admire your skills greatly, but you are only one man.'

'You do?' asked Michael, the wind taken out of his sails. Praise from Pelagia was not dispensed very often.

She smiled briefly, then became businesslike. 'It seems that all our cases have converged – my French spy, the lunatic scholar-inventors whom Ayera has been monitoring, and Michael's Newe Inn deaths – so it makes sense to join forces.'

'What French spy?' asked Bartholomew, puzzled.

A frown of impatience crossed Pelagia's face. 'The one I have been tracking for the past few months, and who I now know is commanding these raiders. There is no time for more detailed explanations. Now tell me what *you* have learned.'

Michael obliged, painting a succinct but detailed account of Walkelate's dealings.

'His Majesty has known for weeks that a few Cambridge scholars have turned their talents to designing weapons,' said Pelagia, when he had finished.

Michael gaped at her yet again. 'How? I did not!'

'Because he had heard that a group of Oxford men had come here and bragged about their achievements, and he guessed that Cambridge would aim to outdo them. He asked me to monitor the situation, but an elderly woman is not the best person to infiltrate a community of male scholars, so I sent my trusty assistant to do it for me.'

'Langelee enrolled me as a Fellow in January.' Ayera took up the tale. 'The cover has worked brilliantly, because no one suspects that a University geometrician – one of their own Regents – is a government spy. Then, about two months ago, I heard whispers that some scholars were devising a new and deadly weapon . . .'

'He also heard tales that strangers were gathering in the marshes, recruiting men who were willing to risk their lives for quick gold,' added Pelagia. 'Ayce, Coslaye . . .'

'I sent for Dame Pelagia at that point,' said Ayera. 'And I warned the King. But she was busy with her French spy, and it took some time for my message to reach her. She only arrived here a few days ago.'

'We had better discuss this later,' said Bartholomew, more interested in averting a catastrophe than satisfying his curiosity. 'Something terrible is going to happen – and soon.'

'You are quite right,' agreed Pelagia. 'Ayera learned last night that the robbers plan to make another assault on the taxes. This will achieve two things: first, provide a diversion so that Walkelate can hand over his ribauldequin and wildfire; and second, allow them to recoup their losses – this whole operation has been very expensive.'

'Do they still believe the taxes are in the castle?' asked Michael urgently. 'Or will they assault King's Hall again?'

Ayera grimaced. 'Unfortunately, Walkelate was party to a conversation in the stationers' shop, during which the

Senior Proctor denounced the rumour about the taxes being moved as a ruse. The robbers now know that they are in the castle, which is a pity. It was better when they thought they might have to search eight Colleges, forty hostels and half a dozen convents.'

'We must warn Tulyet,' said Bartholomew, as Michael winced. 'He needs to prepare.'

'He is as ready as he ever will be, and the town can be taxed again should he fail to repel these rogues,' said Pelagia, coldly professional. 'It is far more important to ensure that Walkelate's invention does not fall into French hands. Forget the castle, and concentrate on him.'

'But the taxes include a ribauldequin,' argued Bartholomew, 'which is in the castle chapel.'

'It is true,' Ayera told her. 'I was told not an hour ago that we mercenaries will be given a hefty bonus if we acquire it in addition to Tulyet's chests of money.'

'Yes, but Walkelate made two ribauldequins, not one,' said Pelagia. 'And it is the hidden one that can deploy wildfire – Tulyet's is just like any other.' She nodded to the ledgers that Langelee was still rifling through. 'Have you discovered anything in those to tell us where it might be?'

'It is not in King's Hall,' said Ayera, when Langelee shook his head. 'I searched it thoroughly.'

'It must be in the Common Library,' said Bartholomew suddenly. 'Walkelate spends every waking moment there, so it stands to reason that he has been doing more than overseeing the construction of shelves. We should go there now and search for it. All of us, together.'

'It is as sensible a notion as any,' said Pelagia, indicating that he should lead the way.

Pelagia lagged behind as they ran to Newe Inn, reminding Bartholomew that while she seemed an unstoppable force, she was actually an elderly lady who could hardly be expected to keep pace with men less than half her age. Ayera fell back to walk with her, but she waved him on with an impatient flick of her hand. When he ran to catch up with the others, Bartholomew noticed that he was limping.

'Yes,' the geometrician said, seeing what he was thinking. 'I was injured during the raid on the castle. I had to fight Tulyet's men, or my cover would have been lost.'

'Speaking of Tulyet, Holm and my beadle will have reached him by now,' said Michael. 'After he has cancelled the pageant, he will almost certainly aim straight for Cholles Lane, because he will want more detailed answers from us. We shall soon have help in confounding these villains.'

'If he does, he leaves the castle vulnerable,' said Bartholomew worriedly. 'And Dame Pelagia just said that grabbing the taxes is the diversion Walkelate needs to pass his weapon to the French.'

'He has not cancelled the pageant,' said Ayera, gesturing around him at the empty streets, and cocking his head at a distant cheer. 'The warning must have arrived too late.'

With despair, Bartholomew saw he was right. The town was virtually deserted: everyone had gone to the Guild Hall to watch the start of the ceremonies. A few drunkards lounged outside an alehouse, and two dirty boys slunk along carrying a trussed goat between them, but there was no other sign of life.

'Lord!' he muttered. 'It is a perfect opportunity for a hostile force to wade across the river or the King's Ditch – both are low, because of the recent dry weather. And Dick said the ditch is so full of silt that it is possible to walk—'

'Hurry!' interrupted Langelee urgently. 'We must find

and destroy this infernal machine, no matter what the cost to ourselves.'

He and Ayera drew their swords when they reached the library, and he indicated that Bartholomew and Michael should arm themselves, too. A heavy stick appeared in the monk's beefy paw, while Bartholomew had his childbirth forceps in one hand and Michael's dagger in the other. Treading with silent grace, Ayera led the way up the spiral staircase, turning to glare when Michael trod on a creaking floorboard.

They arrived upstairs and peered around the door to see Walkelate in the larger of the two rooms. A number of men were there with him. All wore armour, and they were unquestionably the raiders. One was limping from what appeared to be a wound in his thigh. They were cloaked and hooded, and Bartholomew knew, without the shadow of a doubt, that they were the men who had ambushed him. Mentally, he cursed Rougham again for caving in to their threats, but then supposed it was irrelevant if Walkelate had discovered the formula independently, anyway.

'There is no need to incinerate the castle, Rougé,' Walkelate was saying. 'The pageant will provide a perfectly adequate diversion for you to leave Cambridge with the weapon.'

'Unfortunately, the tales of our imminent arrival have made the Sheriff overly vigilant,' replied Rougé. His French was flawless, indicating that he was a native speaker. Bartholomew gaped when the man turned, and he saw his face. 'So bombarding the castle with fire-arrows is necessary to keep him busy. We cannot let him foil us – too much is at stake. Besides, I want the tax money.'

'We cannot tackle all these soldiers alone,' whispered Michael, drawing back a little to speak. 'I am no coward, but I see no point in suicide.'

412

'But you just said that Tulyet will be on his way,' Langelee whispered back. 'I am sure we can keep these paltry villains busy until he arrives. Eh, Ayera?'

'He will not come if he is being barraged with burning arrows,' hissed Michael, although Ayera raised his sword in a salute and grinned rather diabolically. 'Come away. We cannot achieve anything by staying here.'

'We will listen, then,' hedged Langelee. 'But if I say we must attack, you had better be ready. You, too, Bartholomew. The experience you gained fighting at Poitiers will be vital today.'

Bartholomew was horrified, knowing his meagre abilities would not match up to the Master's expectations, but Langelee waved him to silence when he started to object, and eased forward again.

'No one believes you will strike today, Rougé,' Walkelate was saying. 'I enlisted Weasenham's unwitting help – I got him to tell everyone that you are licking your wounds and will not be back. Even Oswald Stanmore believes it, and he is less gullible than most. My ploy worked.'

'Why does he call him Rougé?' whispered Michael. 'That is Bonabes the Exemplarius.'

'Bonabes is French,' said Ayera in a low, disgusted voice. 'And I can tell by the way he carries himself that he is a skilled warrior. Moreover, his weapons are of excellent quality, and well honed.'

Even Bartholomew could see that. He recalled the incident at the castle, when Bonabes had claimed to be out of practice when Holm had insisted that he wore an ancient sword to protect them. The Exemplarius was an accomplished liar, because he had been convincing.

'The merchants might believe you,' Bonabes was saying. His amiable demeanour had been replaced by something hard and ruthless. 'But Tulyet does not.'

413

'It does not matter what Tulyet thinks,' said Walkelate impatiently. 'My carpenter Frevill has used his family connections to ensure that the Guild of Corpus Christi has ignored Tulyet's worries, leaving him effectively isolated. Besides, he is hopelessly confused. I was rather clever to start the rumour that your little army hails from inside the town, because he does not know where to look for his enemies and—'

'Rumours!' spat Bonabes in distaste. 'There have been so many of them that even I have wondered which were truth and which were lies. But never mind this. Is the weapon ready?'

'It is in the *cista*,' replied Walkelate. He smirked. 'All manner of folk have used it as a table and workbench, but no one has thought to look inside. What a shock they would have had if they did! I always say that the best hiding places are those in plain sight.'

'Yet it is an obvious feature, and people will ask where it has gone once we take it. How will you explain its disappearance without incriminating yourself?'

Walkelate's smile was smug. 'I shall set a small fire in the corner of this room – not enough to cause serious harm but enough to mask the departure of the *cista*. I shall say it was started by a stray fire-arrow. After all, we had better sustain some damage in this raid, or folk will be suspicious.'

'A fire?' asked Bonabes, startled. 'With all this wood? Is that wise?'

'I can control a small blaze,' said Walkelate haughtily. 'I am a skilled experimenter.'

'Show me the weapon again,' said Bonabes, shrugging to show he did not care what happened to the library. 'I want to see it one more time.'

Walkelate opened the *cista*, and by craning forward,

414

Bartholomew could just make out a compact machine with several barrels. It looked like the Poitiers ribauldequins, but Walkelate's had bulbous mouths, presumably to allow the wildfire to splatter in a wider arc. There was a waft of something unpleasant, too.

'This pot contains a sample of my other creation,' said the architect, handing it to Bonabes. 'I told you there was no need to bother with the physicians. Not only have I reinvented wildfire, but my recipe is far superior.'

'And you did it alone?' asked Bonabes. 'We cannot afford witnesses.'

'I had to enlist associates, but none are alive to tell the tale.'

Bonabes regarded him narrowly, and his voice turned soft and a little dangerous. 'Do these dead associates include the London brothers and Northwood? I was fond of them.'

'They were talented alchemists, and I needed their expertise,' said Walkelate sharply. His expression became sly. 'Their deaths were not my fault, anyway – any more than Adam was yours.'

Bonabes flinched, indicating that his affection for the boy-scribe he claimed to have loved like a son had been genuine. He turned his attention to the pot. 'It took you long enough. Weeks. And even then, you only succeeded after I forced Rougham to name rock oil as the missing ingredient, and procured you some from Weasenham.'

Walkelate regarded him coolly. 'You told me it was important not to arouse anyone's suspicions, so of course I took longer than if I had been granted a free hand. Besides, I did better than you – you have come nowhere near a solution for making paper. And anyway, I was not aware that you were in a hurry.'

'Of course I am in a hurry,' snapped Bonabes. 'Not only is France desperate for a miracle, but working for

Weasenham has been torture. It was agony, pretending to be subservient to such a man. The only saving grace is Ruth, and I am coming back for her when this is over.'

'I still do not understand why you hired all those mercenaries,' said Walkelate after a moment. 'Our business could have been managed much better without them.'

'It could not. Pelagia's spies would have discovered us in an instant without the confusion they provided. They were an absolute necessity. Moreover, I have enjoyed myself, doing to your town what Englishmen have been doing to France for the past three decades. Now *your* people know what it is like to live in constant fear.'

Bartholomew grabbed Langelee's arm. The Master, patriotic soul that he was, was finding the discussion hard to stomach. Meanwhile, Bonabes nodded to his men, who sealed the *cista*, then lifted it, straining under its weight.

'France owes you a debt of gratitude, Walkelate,' he said with a smile that was neither friendly nor sincere. Bartholomew suspected the architect would not live long to enjoy the fruits of his labours. 'This may turn the tide of the war.'

'I do not want your gratitude,' said Walkelate. 'I want your money. I spent funds I do not have perfecting my library, and I cannot allow it to be tainted with the reek of debt.'

At that point, Langelee wrenched away from Bartholomew and exploded into the room, sword at the ready. Ayera rolled his eyes, but went to stand next to him, shoulder to shoulder.

'This diabolical weapon is not going to France,' Langelee snarled. 'Your game is over.'

The men holding the *cista* dropped it in alarm, and fumbled for their weapons as Langelee tore towards them with a battle cry that hurt the ears. Ayera dropped into a defensive stance as several mercenaries advanced on him, while Michael waved the cudgel around his head. Bartholomew gripped his childbirth forceps more tightly, although he did not hold much hope of besting trained warriors, and as far as he was concerned, Langelee had just signed their death warrants.

But it was no time to apportion blame, because Walkelate's fine library was full of the sounds of a frantic skirmish. Langelee was yelling furiously, and the clash of his sword against his opponents' was ear-splitting as he laid about him with wild abandon. Ayera fought more steadily and rationally, and two raiders quickly fell under his scientific blade.

Bartholomew and Michael were less adept, although the physician managed to knock one man senseless, and break the fingers of another. But the odds were too heavily stacked against them, and it was not long before both were pinned against the wall with knives at their throats.

His stomach lurched when he saw blood spurting from a wound in Ayera's neck. Horrified, he tried go to his colleague's aid, but his captor dealt him a stinging blow that made him see stars. By the time his vision cleared, Ayera was dead and Langelee was a prisoner, too, breathing hard and glowering furiously at the three soldiers who kept him in place with the tips of their swords.

'You will not get away with this,' the Master snarled. 'Dame Pelagia knows all about you and your plans.'

'You should have killed her when she fell into your hands, Rougé,' said Walkelate angrily. 'As I recommended. But no, you insisted on taking her to the marshes. And what happened? She escaped, and will continue to be a danger to us.'

417

Bonabes only indicated that his men were to lift the *cista*, but one of its handles had been broken in the scuffle, and he fretted impatiently while they fashioned a replacement with a belt.

'Why does he call you Rougé?' asked Michael. He sounded calm, although Bartholomew was in an agony of tension, appalled by what had happened to Ayera – and by what might befall their country now the ill-advised attack had failed.

'I am Bonabes, Sire de Rougé et de Derval,' replied Bonabes haughtily. 'Vicomte de la Guerche and Châtelain de Pontcallec. And a loyal subject of His Majesty King Jean of France.'

'But the Sire de Rougé was taken prisoner after the Battle of Poitiers,' said Langelee in confusion. 'And is locked in the Tower of London until a ransom can be paid.'

'I escaped,' said Bonabes coolly. 'But I was still on Poitiers field when I determined to acquire a ribauldequin and learn the secret of wildfire. And God is with me, for it cannot have been by chance that I heard about your University and its scholars' inventions.'

'Northwood,' said Bartholomew in disgust. 'He was at Poitiers: *he* told you about us.'

Bonabes inclined his head. 'He came to the Tower a few months ago, to ask after my welfare – we had become acquainted on the journey there, you see. He was a chaplain, and had been given the care of the French captives' souls. We became friends.'

'He helped you escape,' surmised Bartholomew. 'But why would he do such a thing?'

'Academic glory,' replied Bonabes. 'I promised to finance certain alchemical projects.'

'Do not waste time in idle chatter,' hissed Walkelate. 'They would not have burst in here if beadles and soldiers

418

were not far behind. Kill them, and take your weapon before it is too late.'

'How will you explain the presence of corpses in your library?' asked Bonabes, gritting his teeth in frustration when his soldiers grabbed the *cista* and the new handle snapped. 'It is due to open soon.'

'I shall dump them in the pond. I intend to live here and enjoy the adulation of grateful scholars, so you can trust me to do it properly. Not like last time, when I slipped up with Vale.'

'Yes, kill them,' came another voice from the door. 'We cannot afford loose ends.'

'You?' gasped Langelee, while Bartholomew sagged in despair. How much deeper did the rot of treachery run in Cambridge?

'We should have known that Dunning was involved,' he said tiredly. 'Developing weapons is expensive, and Walkelate has just said that he needs Bonabes's blood-money to prevent the library starting its life in debt. Dunning funded the experiments. It explains why he was always here – not assessing the progress of the library, but the progress of the weapon.'

Dunning shrugged. 'I never liked this building, and Walkelate needed somewhere to work. It was a convenient arrangement for all, and the University will benefit, so do not complain.'

'Julitta,' said Bartholomew wretchedly. 'It was her idea to give us Newe Inn.'

'She knows nothing of this,' said Dunning sharply. 'She would disapprove. She believes my generosity will leave me poor, but the money I shall make from selling Walkelate's weapon today will make me fabulously rich. And then *I* shall head the Guild of Corpus Christi.'

'So that is why you have insisted on a grand opening

419

ceremony today,' said Langelee in utter disgust. 'And why you have spent so much time planning the pageant. You have been preparing the ground for your election as Guild Master.'

'Yes and no,' replied Dunning. 'I do want the pageant and the opening ceremony to be a success – and the beadles you sent to order them cancelled have been dealt with, by the way, Brother – but I also need them to serve as a diversion for our other business today.'

'At least we know now why everyone here was always so tired,' muttered Michael. 'Working on the library all day, and labouring over weapons all night . . .'

'Iron filings,' said Bartholomew suddenly. 'Kente thought they were from metal brackets to fit bookcases to the walls, but they were from the ribauldequin.'

'Tulyet's blacksmith unwittingly provided me with a basic set of barrels.' Walkelate was unable to resist a brag. 'But it was still necessary to make one or two fine adjustments—'

'Why did you not kill Michael and Bartholomew when they came here asking after Frevill yesterday?' interrupted Bonabes, turning on Dunning. 'You must have seen it was too risky to leave them alive.'

'I did not have a sword with me,' snapped Dunning. 'Why do you think Walkelate sent them to the stationer's shop? So you could do the honours. But you did not oblige, either.'

'Ruth was there,' said Bonabes angrily. 'How could I?'

'You are going to be disappointed, Dunning,' said Langelee, making no effort to conceal his contempt. 'Because any funds Bonabes has will be used to pay his mercenaries and to transport the weapon to France. Betraying your country will not make you wealthy.'

'The King's taxes are more than enough to cover all

our needs,' said Dunning comfortably. 'The rest of Bonabes's men are securing them for us as we speak.'

'If they can find them,' goaded Langelee. 'Tulyet has hidden them, and not even his most trusted warriors know where. You will never have them. He has concealed his ribauldequin, too.'

Bonabes regarded Dunning in alarm, and there was consternation among the mercenaries, too. 'Is this true? Our arrangement stipulates that I am to have both weapons.'

'Langelee is lying,' said Dunning coldly. 'And I want to hear no more of his tales. Kill them.'

There was nothing Bartholomew, Michael or Langelee could do as they were forced to kneel in a line. One mercenary stood behind them, executioner style, and drew his sword. His cool proficiency indicated it was a task he had performed before.

'Wait!' shouted Michael. 'You have not killed anyone, Walkelate. It is not too late to turn back.'

'But I do not want to turn back,' said Walkelate, grabbing a handful of kindling from the hearth. 'I have learned a lot from my experiments, and I can make a significant contribution to the alchemical sciences now. And what is more important than the advancement of knowledge?'

'What are you doing?' asked Dunning, watching the architect in bemusement.

'He *has* killed, Michael,' said Bartholomew in disgust. 'He poisoned his helpmeets. You just heard him admit that he hid their bodies in the pond.'

'It was an accident,' objected Walkelate, casting an uneasy glance at Bonabes, whose eyes had narrowed. 'How was I to know that red lead is toxic when heated?'

'Of course you did,' said Bartholomew scornfully. 'It is basic alchemy. You knew exactly what would happen, and you even persuaded Holm to hire singers to drown the sounds of their final agonies. You condemned them to horrible deaths with calculated and ruthless efficiency. And Northwood and the London brothers were men Bonabes was fond of.'

But his effort to cause friction failed: Bonabes was too determined to have his weapons to allow himself to be distracted by the mere murder of friends.

'For God's sake,' he snapped to the executioner. 'What are you waiting for?'

'Jorz was no accident, though,' said Bartholomew, twisting to one side, and thus spoiling the man's aim. Impatiently, he was tugged upright again.

'He grew suspicious of me,' explained Walkelate. 'So I had no choice. But I did it in such a way that everyone assumed he had a seizure. No one will ever know what I did.'

'You will never clean our blood away in time for your grand opening,' said Michael quickly, watching the executioner grab Bartholomew's hair. 'It will stain your beautiful floorboards.'

'He has a point,' said Dunning worriedly. 'Nothing can be allowed to spoil my ceremony.'

'I will borrow some rugs from King's Hall,' replied Walkelate, his attention on the kindling.

'Setting the castle alight will ruin the library's grand opening,' shouted Michael, desperation in his voice as the mercenary prepared to deliver the fatal blow. 'All eyes will be on that, and no one will care about your generous donation.'

But Dunning was not listening: he was looking at Walkelate. 'What are you doing?'

'He plans to set a fire,' yelled Michael, toppling sideways and knocking Bartholomew out of the executioner's grasp with his bulk. 'Your foundation will be reduced to ashes.'

'What?' demanded Dunning. 'There will be no fires here!'

'Just a small one,' said Walkelate calmly. 'To eliminate evidence of our activities. We cannot have Dame Pelagia poking around and discovering clues we have overlooked. Bartholomew has drawn conclusions from stray metal filings, and it might prove fatal if she does the same.'

'No!' cried Dunning. 'I forbid it!'

But Walkelate had already touched a flame to his sticks, and there was a low roar as they ignited. The resulting blaze was evidently fiercer than he had antici-pated, as he flinched away in alarm. Dunning's jaw dropped in horror.

'It is the wood oil,' gasped Bartholomew, fighting back as the executioner tried to manoeuvre him into position again. 'Kente used buckets of the stuff, and it is highly combustible. Your library will burn to the ground.'

'No!' howled Dunning, hauling off his cloak and begin-ning to beat at the flames. It served to make them burn more ferociously. 'Bonabes! Help me!'

The heat was so intense that the executioner raised his hand to protect his face. His momentary distraction allowed Bartholomew to lurch forward and punch the pot from Bonabes's hand. It fell into the fire. With a screech of fury, Bonabes tried to grab it back, but the flames were too powerful.

'Oh, God!' shrieked Walkelate, when he saw what had happened. 'Run!'

'No one is going anywhere!' Dunning blocked the door. 'You will stay here and put out this blaze. The library is my path to immortality, and I am not prepared to lose it.'

But the executioner had had enough, and so had his cronies. They began to advance on the door, swords at the ready, and it was clear that they were not going to let

Dunning stop them. Immediately, Langelee surged to his feet and snatched up the blade Ayera had dropped. At the same time, thick, black smoke began to pour from the wildfire pot, and everyone near it started to cough.

'Damn you!' cried Bonabes, racing towards Bartholomew with murder in his eyes. 'You do not know what you have done!'

Langelee leapt forward to deflect the brutal thrust, and the two blades slid down each other with a tearing scream that drew sparks.

'On the contrary,' said Dame Pelagia. She was standing behind Dunning, who whipped around in alarm. 'He knows exactly what he has done.'

Bartholomew slumped in relief as Tulyet and his soldiers poured into the room. There were several brief skirmishes, but the mercenaries knew when they were outmatched, and soon threw down their weapons, claiming they were only hired hands and knew nothing of importance. Then he saw that the pot containing the wildfire was glowing, and his blood ran cold.

'It is going to explode!' he shouted urgently. 'Get away from it! Now!'

But his warning came too late. There was a dull thump, and suddenly burning wildfire was everywhere. It landed mostly on the mercenaries, who had happened to be closest. Then all was confusion, noise and choking smoke. Bartholomew saw Michael's habit smouldering, and hurried to slash off the smoking material with a knife. He flung it to the far side of the room, where it burst into flames. Michael looked from his ravaged habit to the little inferno in horror.

Bartholomew ran to Ayera, and tried to drag his body to the door, loath to leave him to be incinerated, but the

424

geometrician was heavy and the room was filling with dark, acrid fumes.

'Leave him,' gasped Michael, sleeve over his mouth. 'Outside! Quickly!'

Bartholomew staggered after him, stopping only to haul Langelee away from a skirmish with a defiant mercenary. Tulyet yelled the order for his own men to retreat, and they joined a tight pack who pushed and jostled in their desperation to escape. Coughing hard, his eyes stinging so badly he could barely see, Bartholomew reeled gratefully into the fresh air.

It was a chaotic scene. Several of Tulyet's soldiers had been injured in the fracas, while the Sheriff himself was hastily divesting himself of armour that smoked ominously. Michael reached out to grab Bartholomew's arm when the physician turned back towards the door.

'What are you doing? You cannot go back in there!'

'Dunning and Walkelate,' gasped Bartholomew, appalled by the speed with which the fire had taken hold. We cannot leave them in there.'

'Dunning is dead,' said Langelee, wiping his dagger on some grass.

'But Walkelate and the mercenaries!' Bartholomew tried to struggle free.

'Most were sprayed with wildfire,' said Dame Pelagia. 'Even if you do manage to pull them to safety, all you will do is sentence them to a lingering death. It was on their skin, not their clothes.'

'But Walkelate is—'

At that moment, a window was flung open, and the architect appeared. He was alight, and his mouth opened in a scream that Bartholomew could not hear over the roaring of the flames.

'It is too late,' said Langelee, looking away. 'The fire

425

will never be extinguished now. Walkelate was a fool to think he could control a blaze with all that oily wood around. And he dared call himself an alchemist!'

'The castle,' said Bartholomew urgently. 'The mercenaries intend to attack it—'

'I guessed they might try,' said Tulyet, 'so I counterattacked at dawn. The leaders are in my dungeons, and Helbye is rounding up the rest as we speak.'

'Did Holm tell you to come here?' asked Bartholomew, sagging in relief.

The Sheriff frowned his bemusement at the question. 'No. Dame Pelagia chose a better place to eavesdrop than you – one where she would not be taken prisoner by the men she was trying to thwart. She sent word with a fleet-footed beadle.'

'There will be no fire-arrows now,' she said, patting Bartholomew's arm kindly. 'The good people of Cambridge can enjoy their pageant and never know how close they came to losing their castle.'

'Thank God!' breathed Michael. 'Although our scholars are going to be disappointed when they see what has happened to their library.'

'Only half of them,' said Langelee. 'The rest of us will be glad to see it gone.'

Bartholomew stood for a long time after the others had left, watching the flames consume the building that should have been one of the University's finest achievements. He wondered whether anyone would ever be brave enough to found another.

EPILOGUE

It rained when Julitta married Holm in St Mary the Great.
For the first time in more than two weeks, the sky was heavy
with clouds, and the scent of dampness was in the air. It
was cold too, and a chill breeze sliced in from the east.

'I suppose that is summer over,' said Michael, as he and
Bartholomew waited for the ceremony to begin. 'Two
weeks of sunshine followed by three months of wind and
drizzle.'

The gloomy weather suited Bartholomew's mood. Julitta
was beautiful in her wedding gown, and his heart sank
when he thought of how unhappy her new husband was
going to make her.

'Holm failed to tell Dick about Walkelate, you know,'
he said, watching the surgeon with bitter dislike. 'It was
your grandmother's message that brought him to our
rescue. So why did you not make good on your threat,
and regale Julitta with the truth about him?'

'Because it was not Holm's fault that he failed,' replied
Michael. 'He really did run straight to the castle, but Dick's
low opinion of him meant the guards refused to let him in.'

'Did Holm tell you this tale?' Bartholomew was disinclined to believe it.

'No, Dick did.' The monk shrugged. 'So, as Holm did
not renege on our agreement, I had no just cause to tattle
to Julitta.'

'I see,' said Bartholomew flatly.

'Still, at least you are five marks richer,' said Michael, to cheer him up. 'Dick gave a written statement saying that Isnard and the rivermen are model citizens. Julitta will ensure you have your money.'

'I do not want it. As it turns out, Isnard and his friends *have* been smuggling. They were lying when they said they had not, and Holm was right to call them criminals.'

'Take the five marks and spend it on medicine for the poor,' advised Michael. 'If you do not, Holm will use it to buy yet more new clothes for himself.'

Bartholomew glanced at the surgeon at the altar. Holm was wearing a fabulously embroidered gipon that must have cost a fortune, while his boots and gloves were the finest money could buy. He had adopted a casually arrogant posture, one hand on his hip, specifically to show off the silken lining of his cloak.

'Your grandmother was clever, not racing into a situation she could not handle,' Bartholomew said, turning away and taking refuge in discussing what had happened in Newe Inn. 'I thought she was falling behind us because she was old, but she was just exercising caution.'

'Well, she has had many years of experience at that sort of thing,' said Michael. 'The King was right to ask her to foil Bonabes, Sire de Rougé et de Derval, or whatever he called himself.'

'I cannot imagine how he escaped from the inferno. Still, I suppose if anyone can track him down and return him to the Tower of London, it is her. I am sorry she will have to do it without Ayera. He was a decent man.'

'He made an error of judgement when he recruited Langelee to help, though,' said Michael, still hurt that he had not been taken into Pelagia's confidence. 'He would have done better with you and me. We would not have let the plot go as far as it did.'

'I assumed Pelagia was lying when she said she was here to hunt a French spy, but it was true – she was tracking Bonabes, escaped from prison. I thought she would never tell us her real agenda, because . . .' Bartholomew waved his hand, not sure how to say that he had never met a more artful woman than Michael's grandam.

'It has been difficult to separate truth from lies,' sighed Michael. 'A number of people used false rumours to achieve their objectives, and they muddied the waters. Walkelate and Dunning spread tales that the raiders would not attack at Corpus Christi; Browne said libraries were dangerous places; Tulyet said the King's taxes were hidden in the University—'

'He is sorry for that,' said Bartholomew. 'How much longer will you hold it against him?'

'Until I need a favour,' said Michael comfortably. He continued with his list. 'And my grandmother circulated tales that an attack *would* take place at Corpus Christi, as she hoped the festivities would be cancelled, and everyone would concentrate on laying hold of the invaders.'

'Prior Etone was telling the truth when he said Dunning had promised him Newe Inn, though,' said Bartholomew. 'Julitta found documents to say so. She has taken to reading like a duck to water, and is already skilled enough to trawl through her father's affairs.'

Michael saw Bartholomew's expression darken when his eyes were drawn back to the couple at the altar, and changed the subject.

'We might have solved these mysteries much sooner had we realised that there were two completely separate conspiracies. First, Browne killing Rolee, Teversham and Kente to put scholars off libraries, and murdering Coslaye because he had failed to dispatch him at the Convocation. And second, Bonabes arriving in Cambridge and recruiting

429

scholars to build him a weapon – Walkelate, Northwood, Vale, the London brothers and Jorz.'

'And recruiting mercenaries to raid the town,' added Bartholomew. 'Aided by Dunning and Frevill. And by Coslaye, too – Agatha's nephew did see him, as he claimed.'

'Dick said yesterday that he has caught the last of the mercenaries. Several told him that it was Frevill who murdered Adam, so justice was served when Ayera killed him outside King's Hall.'

They were silent for a while, Bartholomew watching the priest talking to Julitta and Holm, and Michael thinking about the plots they had exposed. Julitta was listening intently, but Holm looked bored, as if he wished the rite were over so that he could do something more interesting instead. Then the priest began to chant the sacred words that would bind the couple together for the rest of their lives, and Bartholomew wondered what it was about love that made people so blind. He turned away, directing his mind back to their mysteries so as to block it out.

'Browne must have been insane to think that a few peculiar deaths would keep us from books,' he said. 'This is a University, and we are scholars. Deaths in libraries will not stop us from reading.'

Michael laughed softly. 'Some of us are scholars. Langelee is not, or he would have refrained from writing obscenities in Apollodorus's *Poliorcetica*. Apparently, he was trying to research wildfire for Ayera, and grew frustrated when his reading did not tell him what he wanted to know. But let us think of happier things. Your students' disputations, for example.'

Bartholomew smiled. 'They did better than I expected.'

'They performed magnificently, thanks to your tyranny in the classroom. However, you might consider being a little more gentle on the next batch. And if you have any affection for Julitta, incidentally, you will stop this farce of a marriage. The priest has not reached the vows yet.'

'How am I to do that?' asked Bartholomew, tiredly.

'By telling her the truth about Holm. It would be a kindness. She deserves better.'

'She will never forgive me if I make a scene on her wedding day. And he is the town's only surgeon – I am obliged to work with him.'

'Clippesby is so sure she will be miserable that he tried to persuade the priest not to conduct the ceremony. Unfortunately, he took the rat to support his case, so the man declined to listen.'

Bartholomew looked at Julitta, and for a moment considered doing what Michael suggested, but then she turned to Holm and gave a smile of such blazing happiness that his resolve crumbled.

'I cannot. And even if I did, she would spend the rest of her life wondering what she has lost. As I do with Matilde.'

'Very well, but you will come to regret your faint-heartedness. Bitterly, I think. Still, one good thing came out of all this unpleasantness.'

'A new Junior Proctor?' A volunteer, inspired by the service Michael had performed for the country, had stepped forward as the beadles were helping Tulyet to round up the last few mercenaries.

'Well, yes,' said Michael. 'But I was thinking of something else.'

'You were?' Bartholomew could not think of anything.

'The Common Library is a pile of smoking rubble,' said Michael with a wicked grin. 'Julitta offered to fund another, but I persuaded her against it.'

'But a central repository for books is a *good* idea.'

'Rubbish,' said Michael. 'Incidentally, Holm told me

yesterday that he will be so wealthy after his marriage today that he need never pick up a surgical blade again. You will have to return to your old ways of sawing and stitching.'

'Really?' Bartholomew smiled suddenly. 'Then perhaps you are right: something good *has* come out of this affair!'

Two months later, Rouen

It had been a scorching hot day, and the evening air smelled of burnt earth and parched vegetation. Two men stood together in a quiet grove, within sight of the mighty cathedral. Bonabes, his burned face still swathed in bandages, felt a surge of excitement.

All had not been lost that terrible day in Cambridge, when the ridiculous Walkelate had lit his fire. The specially adapted ribauldequin had been destroyed, of course, its metal barrels melted unrecognisably in the heat, and Walkelate's wildfire had also gone. But Bonabes had managed to snag two items before he had crawled to safety. One was Walkelate's design for the weapon, and the other was the scrap of parchment containing the physicians' formula for wildfire. Walkelate had taken his own recipe to the grave, of course, but Bonabes had the feeling that the compound contrived by the *medici* was better anyway.

After his escape, Bonabes had lain low for a while. He had expected Ruth to nurse him back to health, but she had turned her back on him when she had learned his real identity. So much for love! But she did not matter any more, because something far more important was about to take place. Bonabes had commissioned a French blacksmith to reconstruct Walkelate's ribauldequin, and he had undertaken to mix the wildfire himself. Well, he had required a little help.

'Are you sure we added enough rock oil?' he asked of Gyseburne, who stood beside him.

432

'Quite sure,' replied the physician. 'Your mixture looks identical to the stuff we created in Meryfeld's garden all those months ago, although this is superior, because I added urine, which is highly combustible under the right circumstances.'

'But you told me you could not remember a thing about that particular night,' said Bonabes, rather accusingly. 'If you had, I would not have had to waylay Bartholomew and Rougham.'

'It all came back to me once we put the ingredients together,' replied Gyseburne coolly.

'Well, let us hope your memory is reliable.' Bonabes pointed into the trees, where a shadowy figure was emerging. 'Because the general is here, and I have promised him a miracle.'

'And he shall have it. Are you sure he has enough money to pay me? If not, there are plenty of other commanders who will not baulk at the sum I have requested.'

'Quite sure. How did you explain your absence from Cambridge, by the way?'

'My mother needs me,' said Gyseburne gravely. 'And when I told him I was unsure how I would finance the journey, Matthew gave me the five marks he had won from Holm. It was guilt-money, of course, to apologise for the fact that a Michaelhouse scholar, namely Ayera, started a rumour that my mother is a witch.'

'Weasenham told me.' Bonabes glanced cautiously at the physician. 'And is she?'

'She likes to cast the occasional spell.'

'I thought Bartholomew and the monk would guess that you were among the men who helped Walkelate,' said Bonabes wonderingly. 'I heard Michael had you high on his list of suspects.'

Gyseburne shrugged. 'I think they were so appalled to

learn that Walkelate, Northwood, the London brothers, Vale and Jorz had been dabbling with wildfire that they could not bring themselves to think ill of any more colleagues. They never once asked me about it.'

'Ayera was suspicious of you, though,' said Bonabes. 'I saw him watching you several times. Of course, I did not know he was Pelagia's spy at the time, or I would have killed him.'

Gyseburne grimaced. 'He unnerved me, so I told Bartholomew the tale about Langelee's poisoned guests in York, placing the blame firmly on Ayera. I also told him that Ayera was one of your raiders.'

'That was reckless! I was too wary of anyone to confide my plans, so he knew little to harm us, but it was a risk that should not have been taken.'

'I had to protect myself,' said Gyseburne sharply. 'Besides, I have long been afraid that Ayera might know that it was *I* who exchanged garlic for lily of the valley all those years ago at Langelee's house in York, and I felt the need to take precautions.'

'I heard you gave up Willelmus, too.'

Gyseburne shrugged. 'He was a low worm, and I distrusted him intensely. I could not kill him – he was a friar, and I have scruples about dispatching men of God – so I decided to let Tulyet do it for me. I was afraid that he might tell someone it was I who persuaded him to turn traitor, and not some fictitious juror.'

'You almost died, too,' observed Bonabes, watching the general approach and then glancing around again to ensure that all was ready. 'Walkelate.'

Gyseburne nodded. 'Yes, he certainly would have killed me, as he did his other helpmeets. It was fortunate that an excursion to see a patient in Girton put me out of harm's reach that night. I—'

'Is it ready?' asked the newcomer, breaking brusquely into their conversation. As one of France's highest-ranking military men, the general considered himself far too important to waste time with polite greetings.

'The wildfire is loaded, and all we need do is touch a flame to this fuse,' said Bonabes. His heart thudded with excitement. This was the culmination of all he had worked for since that terrible day at Poitiers. It was his revenge on the English for the humiliation his country had suffered, and for the continued marauding of the Prince of Wales and his greedy rabble.

'Then do it,' said the general. Prudently, he took up station some distance away.

Bonabes's hands were shaking as he took a taper and lowered the dancing flame to the ribauldequin. Beside him, he heard Gyseburne take a deep breath and hold it.

At first, nothing happened. Then there was a bright flash and a resounding boom. The general saw Gyseburne and Bonabes flung backwards like bundles of rags, and when the smoke cleared, the weapon was nothing but a mess of smoking, twisted barrels. The general approached cautiously, stepping carefully over the places where the grass burned. One of his men tried to stamp the flames out, but something sticky adhered to his boot, and then that too was blazing.

Incredibly, Bonabes was still alive – he had taken the precaution of wearing armour, which had protected him to a certain extent. Gyseburne had been killed instantly.

'The recipe for wildfire,' the general said urgently. 'Where is it?'

It was clear that Bonabes did not understand what had happened. His hand moved weakly towards a sheaf of parchments. The general made a grab for them, but they were spotted with wildfire, and he jerked away. Aghast, he watched flames consume them, teasing him with a tantalising glimpse of diagrams and formulae.

'Tell me,' he ordered urgently, grabbing Bonabes by the front of his tunic. 'Quickly, before it is too late.'

But there was wildfire on Bonabes's clothes, and he was far too dangerous to hold. The general let him drop back to the ground, assuming from the dazed expression in Bonabes's eyes that the explosion had knocked him out of his wits. Disgusted, he walked back the way he had come, ignoring the screaming plight of the soldier who had been foolish enough to step on the wildfire. Perhaps it was just as well the secret was lost, he thought. Such weapons were hardly ethical.

Another shadow emerged from the trees when he had gone. She smiled her satisfaction: the dabs of molten lead she had put in the ribauldequin's barrels had taken care of all her problems. The weapon was unrecognisable, and would rust into the ground eventually, while the formula for wildfire was safe from the French.

Bonabes was able to turn his head and look at her.

'You followed me!' he said softly, shocked but not surprised.

'All the way from Cambridge,' replied Dame Pelagia. 'I admire your tenacity and courage, but I could not let you hand such a weapon to your masters. And there was Ayera to avenge.'

'But you have not won everything,' said Bonabes, forcing a note of triumph into his feeble voice. 'You do not have the secret, either.'

'No?' asked Dame Pelagia softly, removing a scrap of parchment from her sleeve.

HISTORICAL NOTE

Although Oxford had a University library in the 1300s, Cambridge does not seem to have had one until the following century. There are references to an earlier central collection of books, perhaps stored in chests in Great St Mary's (the University Church), or in one of the convents, but there appears to have been no specific building. The first purpose-built library (raised in the 1400s) was located in the complex still called the Old Schools, and there it remained until the twentieth century, when plans were laid to move it west of the river. In May 1934, the first books were carried to a new building designed by Sir Giles Gilbert Scott, which is still in use today.

The University Library is one of Britain's copyright libraries, and a magnificent resource for research and learning. Its atmospheric jumble of tightly packed shelves, spacious reading rooms and echoing staircases are remembered affectionately by generations of students and Fellows, and as it is constantly expanding, will continue to be for generations to come.

Many people in *Murder by the Book* were real. The Dunning family was a powerful clan in Cambridge in the thirteenth and fourteenth centuries, and several members were mayors and burgesses. They owned a pretty stone-built house, later named Merton Hall, which has survived the ages, and still forms part of St John's College. The Tulyet family, including several Richards, was another town family of note, as were the Frevills.

The office of University Stationer was an important one, because this was the man charged with producing exemplars for students to hire. John de Weasenham held the office in 1361. He was born in 1328, and records show he was married. He would have hired scribes to produce his exemplars; they were known as *exemplarii*.

A scribe named Willelmus de Hildersham murdered one John Ayce of Girton in Cambridge on 7 February 1334; Ayce's father was named Robert. Hildersham was arrested, but pleaded benefit of clergy, and was released into the care of the Church after the secular jury had found him guilty.

The head of the Carmelite Priory in the mid-fourteenth century was William Etone. He held the post until about 1381. Thomas de Riborowe and John Jorz were two of his friars.

In terms of the medical men, John Gyseburne was a Cambridge physician in the mid-fourteenth century, and John Meryfeld later went to work in St Bartholomew's Priory in London. William Holm was a royal surgeon in 1361; records show him being awarded a fur-lined robe for his services to Princess Isabella. William Rougham was one of Gonville Hall's foundation Fellows, and became its Master in 1360. He paid for the completion of the College chapel.

Michaelhouse's Master in 1357 was Ralph de Langelee, and College Fellows included Michael de Causton, William de Gotham, Thomas Suttone, John Clippesby, William Thelnetham, Thomas Ayera and John Valence. Michaelhouse, along with neighbouring King's Hall and several hostels, became Trinity College in 1546. Michaelhouse's name survives in St Michael's Church, which has been lovingly restored, and is now a community centre, art gallery and a popular coffee shop called Michaelhouse.

Other real characters include John Rolee, who was associated with Corpus Christi College (often called Bene't) in 1357; Robert de Sawtre, a Fellow of Peterhouse from 1339 until his death in 1352; Philip and John de London, who were King's School scholars in 1319 and 1327 respectively; and Thomas Northwood, who died in 1354. William Walkelate was admitted to King's Hall in about 1350; he was the son of another William Walkelate, who was the King's sergeant-at-arms, and he was 'removed' from the College in 1358. William de Tynkell was Chancellor of the University in the 1350s, and died in 1370.

The Battle of Poitiers in 1356 was a significant event in French history. Many noble families lost heirs in the slaughter, and the defeat rocked the nation's confidence and pride. A large number of prisoners were taken, most of whom negotiated ransoms within a few days, although others, like King Jean, the Archbishop of Sens, the Count of Eu and Bonabes IV de Rougé de Derval were taken to England first. Bonabes was kept in the Tower of London until his ransom (£1886) could be paid. The money was handed over, although he managed to escape from the Tower in the interim.

The ransoms were crippling to a country in economic and political turmoil, which was probably exactly what Edward III intended. The burden of providing the money fell on the peasantry, who resented it deeply: the nobles had failed to keep their end of the bargain by protecting them from invasion, so why should they buy their overlords' release? It was one of the factors leading to the Jacquerie Revolt in the summer of 1358 – a popular uprising that was quelled with vicious brutality by the nobles.

By the time Poitiers was fought, rudimentary artillery had been in use for several years. One such device was the ribauldequin. It was capable of discharging several missiles simultaneously, and for this reason it has (probably erroneously) been hailed as the precursor of the modern machine gun. It was not noted for its accuracy, and was often more dangerous to the men operating it than to the enemy. Its power was probably psychological, along with the fact that its noise and smoke frightened warhorses.

Wildfire was known in ancient times, although historians disagree as to what it contained, and in what ratios. Sulphur (brimstone), pitch and charcoal were likely ingredients, while distilled rock oil was thought to provide the sticky, jelly-like quality that made it adhere to whatever it touched. In essence, it was a primitive form of napalm, and would have instilled horror in those who thought it might be deployed against them.

There is no evidence that wildfire was used in the Hundred Years War, and it had been banned by the popes as 'too murderous', anyway, but spies would have been alert for any weapon that might confer an advantage on their respective countries.